Stuart Johnson Reid

A Sketch of the Life and Times of the Rev. Sydney Smith

based on family documents and the recollections of personal friends. Second

Edition

Stuart Johnson Reid

A Sketch of the Life and Times of the Rev. Sydney Smith
based on family documents and the recollections of personal friends. Second Edition

ISBN/EAN: 9783337093631

Printed in Europe, USA, Canada, Australia, Japan

Cover: Foto ©Raphael Reischuk / pixelio.de

More available books at **www.hansebooks.com**

Sydney Smith

Engraved by permission from a miniature on ivory
in the possession of Miss Holland.

A SKETCH

OF THE

LIFE AND TIMES

OF THE REV.

SYDNEY SMITH

RECTOR OF COMBE-FLOREY, AND CANON RESIDENTIARY OF
ST. PAUL'S.

*BASED ON FAMILY DOCUMENTS AND THE RECOLLECTIONS
OF PERSONAL FRIENDS.*

BY

STUART J. REID.

SECOND EDITION.

London:
SAMPSON LOW, MARSTON, SEARLE, AND RIVINGTON,
CROWN BUILDINGS, 188, FLEET STREET.
1884.

LONDON:
PRINTED BY GILBERT AND RIVINGTON, LIMITED,
ST. JOHN'S SQUARE.

PREFACE.

THE chief sources from which this book has been drawn are indicated on its title-page, though, in a lesser degree, information has also been derived from a number of other channels. To the relatives of Sydney Smith, and particularly to his granddaughter, Miss Holland, I feel greatly indebted, alike for the confidence with which they have honoured me, and for their generosity in placing, without restriction, documents of the most valuable nature at my disposal. This attempt, indeed, to set the many-sided character of Sydney Smith in a somewhat different light from that in which it has hitherto been commonly regarded could never have been made but for the manuscripts, letters, and reminiscences which were thus rendered accessible. At the same time, it is only right to add that I am entirely responsible for the selection of letters and papers contained in these pages, as well as for the interpretation placed upon them ; and the same remark, of course, applies to the inferences which are drawn from every incident recorded in the book.

Many old friends of Sydney Smith have rendered assistance of various kinds, and have added to the interest and value of these memorials by personal reminiscences, and by information which they alone could impart. Space will not permit me to mention all the help thus generously afforded ; nor am I sure that some who have rendered it—and they belong to every grade of society—would care to be directly named in this expression of my thanks. To Mrs. Malcolm, who, as the daughter of Archbishop Harcourt, can recall many delightful episodes in Sydney Smith's career, and still cherishes vivid recollections of his visits to Bishopthorpe and Nuneham, I am indebted for some interesting facts, and several characteristic notes dashed off in the intimacy of a life-long friendship ; and to Mr. R. A. Kinglake, J.P., of Taunton, I am scarcely less indebted for many minute details concerning the closing years at Combe-Florey, as well as for the constant encouragement which he has given me at every stage of the work.

I desire gratefully to acknowledge the obligations I am under to the Marquis of Lansdowne, the Earl of Durham, the Earl of Morley, Lord Edmond Fitzmaurice, M.P., Sir Michael Hicks-Beach, Bart., M.P., Sir Wm. Vernon Harcourt, M.P., Mr. George Howard, M.P., Mr. George Fortescue Wilbraham, J.P., and the late Mr. W. Bromley Davenport, M.P., for the cordial manner in which they have given me permission to insert family letters and papers in their possession.

My thanks are also due, though in differing degrees, to the Countess of Camperdown, the Lady Elizabeth Grey, the Honourable Mrs. J. Stuart Wortley, Mrs. Bond, of the British Museum, and Miss Laura Leycester, formerly of Toft, for the kind way in which they have enriched the pages of this book by facts which came under their own observation, and by suggestions and hints which have thrown fresh light on a number of obscure but important incidents in the full and varied life of their distinguished friend.

I am likewise indebted to the clergy for the willing co-operation they have invariably afforded me in matters of local research, as well as for the information which they have given me concerning Sydney Smith's relations towards his parishioners in different places, and at different periods of his life. My thanks are especially due to the Rev. Canon Girdlestone, of Bristol; the Rev. Canon Tinling, of Gloucester (curate to Sydney Smith at Halberton); the Rev. Dr. Sewell, Warden of New College, Oxford; the Rev. Dr. Cazenove, of Edinburgh; and the Revs. John Still, of Nether Avon; C. H. Rice, M.A., of Cheam; Albert Hughes, B.A., of Woodford, Essex; Francis Simpson, M.A., of Foston; W. L. Palmes, M.A., of Naburn, York; Richard Wilton, M.A., of Londesborough; Edward A. Sanford, M.A., of Combe-Florey; E. J. Gregory, M.A., of Halberton; and W. R. Milman, M.A., Librarian of Sion College, and Minor Canon of St. Paul's, for their unfailing courtesy in doing all in their power to obtain accurate and reliable facts concerning both the man and his ministry.

To Mr. Henry Johnson, of Richmond, Surrey, I am also indebted for voluntary investigations pursued with patience and skill at the British Museum, by means of which several complicated points have been elucidated. I desire also to place on record the obligations I am under to my father, the Rev. Alexander Reid, formerly of Newcastle-on-Tyne, but now resident under my roof—himself a close student of political and ecclesiastical movements for nearly fifty years—for information concerning far-off public events and half-forgotten controversies, which, but for such constant and kindly assistance, must otherwise have been overlooked.

My acknowledgments are also due to Mr. Walter Tomlinson for the artistic pilgrimage which he undertook to the chief places associated with the public and private life of Sydney Smith, in order to obtain the illustrations which embellish these pages; and I am also greatly obliged to Messrs. Longman and Co., for their immediate permission to avail myself of the invaluable information contained in what must ever remain a great and authoritative work on the subject, the charming " Memoir of the Rev. Sydney Smith," by his daughter, Lady Holland. Reference is made throughout these pages to the obligations thus incurred ; and it is therefore, perhaps, sufficient to add that extracts from the Letters of Sydney Smith, edited by Mrs. Austin, and appended to Lady Holland's work, are referred to under the general title of " Published Correspondence."

Most of the materials in the shape of note-books, documents, and letters which Lady Holland had at her disposal have been open to my inspection and use through the kindness of her daughter, Miss Holland, and I have therefore been able to weave into the present narrative letters and facts which it seemed premature to disclose twenty years ago.

Two or three words are enough to state the chief object of this book, which is intended to supplement, and not to rival, the biography which is already before the world. I have ventured to paint the figure of Sydney Smith against the background of his times, and to describe the men with whom he mingled, and the movements in which he took part. I have sought to point out the fidelity to duty in small things as well as in great, which marked every stage of his brave and busy career, and which, indeed, created the bracing

atmosphere in which his entire life was spent.   I have
done what lies in my power, by an appeal to indisput-
able facts, to dispel some lingering errors concerning
the character of a man whose conduct and motives
have been occasionally maligned, and frequently misunderstood.

And I have also attempted—with what success
others must judge—to show how substantial are the
claims of Sydney Smith on the gratitude of the English
people for his persistent and courageous endeavours to
promote by his peculiar but powerful advocacy all
kinds of social improvement and political reform.

WILMSLOW, CHESHIRE,
   8th July, 1884.

PREFACE TO THE SECOND EDITION.

Two or three minor corrections as to matters of fact,
and the alteration of a few expressions, exhaust the
changes which have been made in this volume.

The author is grateful for the immediate and cordial
recognition which his work has won from the reviewers,
and—whilst conscious that the portraiture he has
endeavoured to present is still incomplete—his pleasure
is enhanced by the knowledge that the public have
endorsed the literary verdict pronounced upon the
book, by calling for the present edition within a month
of its first appearance.

WILMSLOW, CHESHIRE,
   5th November, 1884.

CONTENTS.

CHAPTER I.

1771—1793.

PARENTAGE—CHILDHOOD—YOUTH.

PAGE

Born at Woodford, Essex, June 3rd, 1771—Recklessness and eccentricity of his father—Maria Olier, his mother, of French extraction—Her influence over her children—Sydney Smith's brothers and sisters—Scholar of Winchester, 1782—Rapid progress there—Youthful adventures of Sydney and Bobus—"Gregory Griffin"—Subsequent career of Bobus Smith—Sydney proceeds to New College, Oxford, 1789, and obtains a Fellowship at the age of twenty—His self-reliance and poverty—Generosity to Courtenay—Quits Oxford in 1794, and with some misgivings prepares to enter the Church   1

CHAPTER II.

1794—1800.

CURATE AT NETHER AVON—TUTOR TO MICHAEL BEACH—MARRIAGE.

Loneliness as Curate in remote Wiltshire village—Establishes Day and Sunday Schools with the help of Mr. and Mrs. Beach—The Beach family and Nether Avon—Mr. Verrey's list of Nether Avon poor, 1793—Characteristic comments by Sydney Smith—Correspondence with the Squire on the wants of the parish—Mr. Hicks-Beach proposes that the Curate should accompany his son on his travels in the two-fold capacity of tutor and friend—Weimar scheme abandoned on account of the war—Arrival in Edinburgh as tutor to young Beach in June, 1798—The literary and

social condition of the Scottish capital—Sydney Smith's first
impressions of the Scotch—Preaches at Charlotte Chapel,
and publishes his first book—Marriage to Miss Catherine
Pybus, of Cheam, June, 1800—Lines on Mrs. Pybus's dog
—Returns to Edinburgh with his bride—Generosity of
Mr. Hicks-Beach   22

CHAPTER III.

1802.

PROJECTION OF THE "EDINBURGH REVIEW"—JEFFREY, HORNER, AND BROUGHAM.

Sydney Smith's account of the origin of the *Review*—Lord
Jeffrey's reminiscences of its early days—Lord Brougham's
statement concerning the memorable enterprise—Comparison of the three accounts—Appearance of the *Review*,
October, 1802, and immediate success—Jeffrey's hesitation in accepting the Editorship—His services as Editor,
and ability as Critic—Francis Horner—His brilliant career
and early death—His contributions to the *Review*—Henry
Brougham—His rapidity as a writer—His energy and versatility—The impression which he made upon friends and
foes—The lights and shadows of his character .   .   .   55

CHAPTER IV.

1798—1803.

LIFE IN EDINBURGH AS TUTOR, PREACHER, AND REVIEWER.

The *Edinburgh Review* and the growth of public opinion—
Sydney Smith's contributions—Characteristics of his style
—His courage and candour as a literary man—His injustice
to Missions—His wit, the vehicle for his wisdom—An unpublished essay—His letters from Edinburgh concerning
his pupil—Birth of Saba—Death of his mother—Attends
the Lectures of Dugald Stewart on Moral Philosophy—
Studies Medicine and Anatomy—The Friday Club and its
members—Generosity towards John Leyden—A note to
Jeffrey   76

CHAPTER V.

1803, 1804.

ARRIVAL IN LONDON, AND EARLY STRUGGLES THERE.

PAGE

Resolves to settle in London—Reasons for the step—The Squire of Nether Avon's reluctance to part with him—His prospects in the Church—Regret at severing his Edinburgh ties—His home at 8, Doughty Street—An act of self-sacrifice on the part of his wife—His difficulties in obtaining clerical recognition—"The Cultivation and Improvement of the Animal Spirits:" an unpublished essay —His remedy for nervousness—Attitude of his ecclesiastical superiors—The fascination of his character for all sorts and conditions of ordinary men   100

CHAPTER VI.

1805—1807.

HOLLAND HOUSE—PREACHER AT THE FOUNDLING HOSPITAL—LECTURER AT THE ROYAL INSTITUTION—"PETER PLYMLEY" —GIFT OF FOSTON BY LORD ERSKINE.

The historical and literary associations of Holland House—Lord Holland and his guests—Dr. John Allen and his position at Holland House—Sydney Smith's introduction to society there—Home life in Doughty Street—Sydney Smith as a preacher—Sir Thomas Bernard and the Foundling Hospital —Berkeley Chapel—Appointed to lecture at the Royal Institution—His success as a lecturer—His criticism of Aristotle—Birth of Douglas—Removal to 18, Orchard Street—Death of Pitt and Fox—The Ministry of "All the Talents," and Horner's vindication of its policy—Sydney Smith appointed to the living of Foston by Lord Erskine— Appearance of the "Peter Plymley" letters—Their effect upon the public mind   117

CHAPTER VII.

1807—1814.

REMOVAL TO YORKSHIRE—LIFE AT HESLINGTON—BUILDS
FOSTON RECTORY.

PAGE

The Clergy Residence Bill—Sydney Smith's dilemma—His first
glimpse of Foston—Sydney Smith's avowed motives for
writing reviews—The cost of removal, and how it was met
—Settles at Heslington—His friendship with the local
Squire—Lord Grey and Howick—Sydney Smith at his
own fireside—His intimacy with Archbishop Harcourt—
Sydney Smith's treatment of scientific and clerical bores at
Bishopthorpe—Sydney Smith as a diner-out—Decision to
build at Foston—Birth of Wyndham—Mrs. Sydney Smith's
account of the building of Foston Rectory—On the threshold
of a new life 150

CHAPTER VIII.

1814—1817.

LIFE AT FOSTON—THE CHURCH, THE RECTORY, AND THE PEOPLE
—KINDNESS TO THE POOR AS "VILLAGE PARSON AND DOCTOR"
—FONDNESS FOR CHILDREN—POPULARITY WITH SERVANTS.

A comfortable house—Castle Howard opens its gates to the new
Rector—Foston to-day—Description of the Church—The
Rectory and its grounds—Personal recollections of Sydney
Smith at Foston—The Rector's medical skill—"Sydney's
orchards"—He turns farmer—The village children—His
quarrel with the tailor over the alteration in the "Immortal"—Establishes a Bible-class—The reverence of his old
servants for the memory of their master—Bunch and her
successor—Robinson, the joiner; Kilvington, the coachman
—Friendship with Sir George Philips, of Manchester—
Charity Sermon at Prestwich Church, Manchester, 1817,
and Miss Leycester's recollections of it—His wit and
humour 172

CHAPTER IX.

1818—1824.

FAMILY CHANGES—ATTITUDE ON PUBLIC QUESTIONS—THE TREAT-
MENT OF PRISONERS—THE GAME LAWS—AN ACCESSION OF
FORTUNE—BUSY LIFE AT FOSTON.

PAGE

Isolation of his position—Love of Reading—His own statement
concerning his expenses at Foston—The living of Ampthill
offered him by Lord Holland—Illness of Douglas—Visits
Earl Grey and Mr. Lambton—Correspondence with Lord
Lansdowne on Prison Reform—His opinion on the " heirs
apparent" at Castle Howard and Holland House—Lady
Georgina Morpeth—Scotch sheep and their vagaries—
Spring-guns and man-traps, and his denunciation of them—
His clemency as a magistrate—Popular discontent in 1819
—His views on Lord Fitzwilliam's dismissal—An unexpected windfall—Death of his father—Advice concerning
low spirits—A comical episode on the Malton Road—Re-
visits Edinburgh—Lambton Castle—The introduction of
gas—A frank criticism—Appointed High Sheriff's Chaplain,
and preaches in York Minster—Lady Camperdown's account
of Sydney Smith's visits to Weston House   .   .   . 199

CHAPTER X.

1825—1829.

SYDNEY SMITH AND THE CATHOLIC CLAIMS—APPOINTED CANON
OF BRISTOL BY LORD LYNDHURST—FAREWELL TO FOSTON.

O'Connell and the Catholic Association—Death of Canning—
Condition of Public Affairs—Sydney Smith's last contribution to the *Edinburgh Review*—His connection with Londesborough, and traditions of him there—Friendship with
Lord and Lady Wenlock—Statement on the subject, and
personal reminiscences by the Hon. Mrs. J. Stuart Wortley
—Marriage of youngest daughter to Mr. Hibbert—Canon
of Bristol—Preaches on Religious Toleration before the
Mayor and Corporation of Bristol, and gives great offence—

PAGE

Catholic Emancipation—Death of Douglas—Obtains the
living of Halberton with his prebendal stall—Exchanges
Foston for Combe-Florey, to the grief of his Yorkshire
parishioners   239

CHAPTER XI.
1829—1832.

FIRST IMPRESSIONS OF COMBE-FLOREY—HIS MANNER OF LIFE
THERE—APPOINTED CANON RESIDENTIARY OF ST. PAUL'S BY
EARL GREY—TAKES PART IN THE STRUGGLE FOR REFORM—
DAME PARTINGTON'S COMBAT WITH THE ATLANTIC.

The scenery around Combe-Florey—Letter to Lord Lansdowne—
Lord Jeffrey in Somerset—Sydney Smith's practical bene-
volence towards the suffering and the poor—His foreign
deer—His encouragement of thrift—His connection with
Halberton—Canon Tinling's reminiscences—Earl Grey and
Reform—*Gazette Extraordinary, Glorious Victory!*—Reads
himself in at St. Paul's—Sydney Smith and the Episco-
pate—Mrs. Partington's Battle with the Atlantic—Mr.
Arthur Kinglake's recollections of the famous speech—The
Reform Bill becomes law   271

CHAPTER XII.
1832—1839.

COMBE-FLOREY AND LONDON—OLD FRIENDS AND NEW—LETTERS
TO ARCHDEACON SINGLETON—REPUBLISHES HIS CONTRIBU-
TIONS TO THE "EDINBURGH REVIEW."

A graceful old age—Death of Sir James Mackintosh—Lord and
Lady Morley—Marriage of eldest daughter to Dr. Holland
--Letter to Lady Grey—His appearance in the pulpit of
St. Paul's—Luttrell and Sharp—Difficulties in the way of
Trial by Jury in Australia—In France with Mrs. Smith—
His neighbours at Combe-Florey—The poetical Medicine
Chest—His controversy with the Ecclesiastical Commis-
sion—His services in the pages of the *Edinburgh Review*
to the cause of Political and Social Reform—His way of
putting things   304

CHAPTER XIII.

1839—1843.

POLITICS—SOCIETY—WEALTH—FAME.

PAGE

His opinions on the Ballot—Death of Courtenay—Unexpected wealth—Dickens, Macaulay, and Carlyle—Mrs. Grote—The Athenæum Club—Growing love of London—Some characteristic sayings—"The brilliant reptile's venomed fang"—Social changes—In church at Combe-Florey—Sermon at St. Paul's on the Vestments Question—Antipathy to the Puseyites—Letter from Bobus—Correspondence with Miss Martineau—"What is a Puseyite?"   337

CHAPTER XIV

1843—1845.

OLD AGE—"HONOUR, LOVE, OBEDIENCE, TROOPS OF FRIENDS"—ILLNESS AND DEATH—HIS PLACE IN ENGLISH LITERATURE, AND LIFE.

Sydney Smith as a member of the Chapter of St. Paul's—His ability as a man of business—The railroad, one of the consolations of his old age—Mr. Gladstone's recollections of a conversation with him—Professor Owen and Sydney Smith—His friendship with Lord Granville—Lord Houghton—The alleged irreverence of Sydney Smith—Letter from Mrs. Malcolm, the most intimate of his surviving friends, on the subject—Testimony of others—Sydney Smith and John Ruskin—His failing strength, but unfailing mirth—A letter to Lady Holland—Sydney Smith's petition to Congress on the subject of Pennsylvanian Bonds—His American friends—Final words at the Cathedral—The beginning of the end—Last letter to Mrs. Malcolm—His illness and death—Inscription on his grave at Kensal Green Cemetery—A conspicuous omission among the monuments in St. Paul's—His claims on national gratitude.   364

LIST OF ILLUSTRATIONS.

PAGE

Engraved Portrait . . . . *Frontispiece*
Gateway of Winchester College 21
Yew-tree Walk, Nether Avon 26
Nether Avon House and Church 30
38, South Hanover Street, Edinburgh 43
The House to which Sydney Smith took his Bride . . . 45
Charlotte Chapel, Rose Street, Edinburgh . . . 48
Nether Avon Church 54
Jeffrey's house, Buccleuch Place, Edinburgh 59
Craig's Close, Edinburgh 75
Facsimile of Autograph Letter . . . . *To face page* 88
The Canongate Tolbooth, Edinburgh 99
Edinburgh Castle 116
Holland House 120
Early London Home—18, Orchard Street, Portman Square . 139
The Foundling Hospital 149
Sydney Smith's House at Heslington, near York . . . 158
Porch of Foston Church 171
Interior of Foston Church 177
Foston Rectory 179
Chair from Foston Rectory 198
Foston Church 230
York Minster 238
Bristol Cathedral 270
A Glimpse of Combe-Florey Rectory 274
The Castle Hall, Taunton 303
Combe-Florey Church 336
Mrs. Grote's Sketch of Combe-Florey Rectory . . . 345
Interior of Combe-Florey Church 355
St. Paul's Cathedral 263
Last London Home—56, Green Street, Grosvenor Square . 389
The Grave of Sydney Smith 394

A

SKETCH OF

THE LIFE AND TIMES

OF THE

REV. SYDNEY SMITH.

CHAPTER I.

1771—1793.

Parentage, childhood, and youth.

SYDNEY SMITH was born at Woodford, in Essex, on the
3rd of June, 1771. Beyond the official record at the
parish church of his baptism, on the 1st of July in the
same year—which contains no information except the
names of his parents—nothing is now known concerning the family in Woodford, and local tradition is
even unable to point out the house in which the great
wit was born. This, whilst a matter of regret, need
occasion but little surprise, for the birth of a lowly
child, like the death of a lowly man, is an event which
the busy world has no time to notice; they pass un-
heeded, except in the narrow circle in which the child
thenceforth figures, or from which the man is missed
Sydney Smith belonged, as indeed his ubiquitous
surname itself suggests, to a race which is more
numerous than select, and from the outset of his career

B

he was proudly conscious that his claims to honour must of necessity rest on a more substantial basis than that which inherited distinction affords. "The Smiths," said he to an heraldic compiler, who was anxious to include the armorial bearings of the renowned Canon of St. Paul's in his work,—"the Smiths never had any arms, and have invariably sealed their letters with their thumbs."[1] He relates with roguish glee that on another occasion when questioned —apparently somewhat narrowly—by a lady of title, concerning his grandfather, he gravely informed her that "he disappeared about the time of the assizes, and —we asked no questions."

In spite of such merry fabrications, his descent, without being noble, was respectable on the side of each parent. His father, Robert Smith, was the eldest son of a wholesale Whitney merchant in Eastcheap, who came from his native Devonshire to London in the early years of last century, and eventually amassed a moderate fortune in trade. Left whilst still a youth to his own guidance, Robert Smith abandoned the business in Eastcheap to his brother John, who—unlike himself—was of a plodding and methodical nature, and, on the strength of a small competency, set out to see the world. There was a dash both of restlessness and eccentricity about Robert Smith, and he certainly transmitted the latter, if not the former characteristic, to the most distinguished of his sons. Few better illustrations of the saying that truth is stranger than fiction can easily be found than that which the career of Sydney Smith's father presents. He was a man of

[1] "Memoir of Sydney Smith," by his daughter, Lady Holland, chap. ix. p. 163. Longmans, Green, and Co.

considerable ability, endowed with great force of character, and a keen sense of humour; but his disposition
was selfish, and his temper capricious; and there is no
doubt whatever that he was impulsive in his movements and arrogant in manner. He seems to have had
a mania for doing rash and unaccountable things, and
—in his more vigorous years at least—he was fickle in
purpose and uncertain in action.

His marriage is a case in point, and his conduct
then was eccentric in the extreme; and, considering the entire circumstances of the case, he was
guilty of an almost unpardonable freak. Having
won the affections of a beautiful girl, he duly led
her to the altar; but no sooner was the ceremony
concluded than he left his bride at the door of St.
George's, Bloomsbury, in the care of her mother,
and abruptly departed for America—a formidable
undertaking, especially to the imagination of a young
girl, in the middle of last century. After spending
some of the best years of his life in half-random
excursions up and down the world, Robert Smith
eventually returned to England and his patient wife, to
diminish still further his patrimony by a series of
speculations in houses and land. At length, having
worked off some of his superfluous and ill-directed
energy in buying, selling, and not getting gain, he
settled down, when quite an old man, at Bishop's
Lydiard, Somerset, where he died in 1827, at the age
of eighty-eight. His last years were probably his
happiest, for he grew more gentle and considerate with
time; and Sydney was accustomed to declare that his
father was one of the few people he had ever seen
improved by age.

The beautiful girl—who assuredly was worthy of more handsome treatment—was Maria Olier, the youngest daughter of a Languedoc emigrant exiled from France for conscience' sake at the Revocation of the Edict of Nantes. In appearance Miss Olier is said to have resembled Mrs. Siddons, and all who knew her seem to have been attracted towards her by the charm of her manners and the goodness of her heart. Maria Olier, indeed, both before and after her marriage, was distinguished amongst her friends by the strength of her principles, the kindliness of her nature, and the sparkling vivacity of thought and expression which lit up her lively speech. Without an effort she won golden opinions from all who knew her, and retained—amid the general admiration which her goodness and beauty evoked—to the close of a life that was all too short, the gentle and modest spirit with which she began it. Much of that peculiar fascination which Sydney Smith exerted over so many of his contemporaries can be distinctly traced to the rare qualities of mind and heart which met in the refined and sensitive nature of his mother.

Five children were born in rapid succession to Robert and Maria Smith. Robert Percy—better known to the world by the familiar household name, which clung to him through life, of "Bobus"—was born in 1770; Sydney, as we have already seen, a year later; Cecil in 1772; Courtenay in 1773; and Maria in 1774. As this is not a history of the Smith family, but only of the most brilliant member of it, it may not be out of place if some reference is here made to those who, in the same home, began together the battle of life, ere we pass on to pay undivided attention to the character and career of the man whose genius has awakened wide-spread interest in that household group. After the death of Mrs. Smith, which occurred in 1802, Maria devoted herself entirely to her father. In many respects she resembled her mother, especially in the gentleness and unselfishness which marked her character, and though always more or less of an invalid, that fact did not check her sympathy with others or hinder those services which it was her delight to render. She died under her father's roof at Bath in the year 1816, and next to the old man himself no one mourned her loss more keenly than Sydney, though all her brothers were warmly attached to her.

The four sons, born in such a home, were uncommonly well equipped with mental and moral endowments for the course which lay before them. From their father they gained courage, self-reliance, determination, and impetuous energy of spirit; from their mother, quickness of perception, delicacy of feeling, and brilliancy of expression. All the lads soon gave evidence of considerable talent, and three of them were industrious and eager to excel; Cecil, however, at this period of his life was frolicsome, idle, and careless. They were precocious lads, and read and wrangled like grown-up men, and forsook boyish romps in order to devour books or to discuss questions which were far beyond their years. The consequence was that many boys of their age grew shy of them, and slunk away abashed, unable to hold their own against these fierce young reasoners. The usual result followed; the young Smiths, one and all, grew very conceited and overbearing until the summer of 1782, when their erratic father—with more than his usual wisdom—

suddenly pounced down upon them, and packed them off to learn their limit and to find their level on the crowded forms of a great public school.

As there was only a year between Bobus and Sydney, Mr. Smith determined to send them to different schools, and to entrust each of them with the care of a younger brother. Under this arrangement Bobus and Cecil went to Eton, and Sydney and Courtenay to Winchester. Sydney had previously spent some time at an excellent preparatory school at Southampton, conducted by a clergyman of the name of Marsh. His father at that time was living at the village of South Stoneham, near Southampton, and Sydney, at the age of six, was sent to Mr. Marsh's school in that town. It is perhaps worthy of passing note that old Mr. Smith, who evidently believed that variety is the spice of life, was "settled" at no less than eighteen different places in England before he found a final resting-place at Bishop's Lydiard. The register of Winchester School shows that Sydney Smith was admitted as a scholar on the 19th of July, 1782, and when he began his career within its walls—a quick-witted, ambitious boy of eleven—there is evidence enough that he was already a lad of promise, and not deficient in either pluck or persistency.

Winchester College, when Sydney Smith entered it, a little more than a hundred years ago, was under the control of Dr. Joseph Warton, the friend of Johnson, Goldsmith, and Burke, and himself a conspicuous, rather than a brilliant member of the little group of men of letters, who moved like satellites around the burly "Sultan of English literature" in the closing years of his reign. Warton, who probably owed his position at Win-

chester to his well-known translation of Virgil, though
a finished classical scholar, was a very indifferent
schoolmaster. It is one thing to be learned and
accomplished, but quite another matter to be able to
instil, not only knowledge, but an enthusiasm for it,
into the minds of listless and reluctant boys. Dr.
Warton greatly preferred London to Winchester, and
the society of the literary circles of the metropolis to
that of the sixth form of the school, and as the master
himself did not throw much ardour into his work, the
majority of his pupils were quite content to follow his
example. William Howley, afterwards Archbishop of
Canterbury, was one of the head boys at Winchester
when Sydney Smith entered the school; and when the
latter proceeded to Oxford, in 1789, he found his former
associate in high repute at New College, and already
well advanced on the road to preferment. When they
were both old men, Sydney Smith, in his first Letter to
Archdeacon Singleton, alluded, in a sly reminiscence,
to his acquaintance in their Winchester days with
the Primate: "I was at school and college with the
Archbishop of Canterbury. Fifty-three years ago he
knocked me down with the chessboard for checkmating
him, and now he is attempting to take away my patronage. I believe these are the only two acts of violence
he ever committed in his life." The subject of the
Ecclesiastical Commission was not the first or the most
important question on which the Archbishop of Canterbury and the Canon of St. Paul's had found themselves
in hostile camps; for Dr. Howley stoutly opposed the
Catholic Emancipation Bill in 1829 as inimical to the
interests of the Church, and the Reform Bill two years
later as fraught with peril to the Constitution; as for

Sydney Smith, there was no more ardent friend than he to both measures in the ranks of the clerical profession.

The Winchester lads of that period seem to have been half-starved, and the young and timid amongst them found themselves in an evil case. The remembrance of what he had endured there made an indelible impression on the mind of Sydney Smith, and even in old age he was accustomed to kindle into indignant eloquence whenever he was led to recount his schoolboy experiences of hunger, hardship, and abuse. The cane was skilfully and powerfully handled in the Winchester of those days, and was regarded as a stimulus to mental exertion, and a spur to learning. Neglected, browbeaten, and half-fed, the buoyant spirits of even the young Smiths proved unequal to the strain, and poor little Courtenay—a lad of more mettle than the friendless child who, two centuries earlier, carved "Dulce domum" on a tree and then died broken-hearted—twice ran away, unable any longer to endure the sorrows of his lot. A chance incident, which Lady Holland relates, supplied Sydney with a more worthy incentive to learning than that which was afforded by his preceptor's angry frown or lifted rod. One day a visitor to the school, who found him during play-hours absorbed in the study of Virgil, gave the lad a shilling, and with it a few kind words of sympathy and praise. "Clever boy, clever boy," exclaimed the stranger, "that is the way to conquer the world!" Such unlooked-for encouragement broke like a gleam of sunshine across the dreary and troubled life of the neglected boy, and roused within a capable heart the laudable ambition for distinction. Sydney Smith never forgot that man, and to the end of his life he maintained that it was not only just but wise to "hold such in reputation." The stranger quickly finished his survey of the playground, and went his way, little dreaming of the good which his pleasant words had accomplished; whilst the lad he had cheered soon afterwards rose to the proud position of a prefect of the school. Even Courtenay plucked up heart, and began to appear at the top of the class lists, until at length the Smiths were so victorious in the school that the other lads declared in a round-robin, which they had the audacity to send to Dr. Warton, that they would try no longer for the prizes if Sydney and Courtenay were allowed to compete, as "they always gained them." That this assertion was at least founded on fact is clearly proved by the statement that Courtenay four years in succession carried off one of the two gold medals annually awarded by the Crown for the best compositions in Latin verse and prose.

Among the eighteen prefects of Winchester the prefect of the Hall stands first; he is the governor of the school among the boys, and all their communications with the head master pass through him. It was this position—the most responsible and honourable which a Winchester scholar can gain—that Sydney Smith held in the closing year of his stay there. Foremost in work, the young Smiths were also foremost in play, and an amusing incident in the latter direction has fortunately escaped oblivion. Dr. Warton, whilst pacing solemnly round one night, surprised the "clever boy" of the school in the act of making a catapult in the flickering lamplight. The

great man in blissful ignorance of the motive which
had prompted such labours, graciously stopped and
condescended to praise his pupil's ingenuity. Sydney
felt not a little guilty under the doctor's commenda-
tions, for the truth was that the weapon of aggressive
warfare, which his skilful fingers were constructing,
was designed to bring about the swift destruction
of a certain well-fed turkey belonging to the master,
whose plump appearance had at length tempted the
ravenous youths beyond the point of further resistance.

Whilst Sydney and Courtenay were thus distin-
guishing themselves in various ways at Winchester,
Bobus and Cecil were pursuing an almost identical
course at Eton. More especially was this the case
with Bobus, who was renowned at school for his
classical attainments, and for the ability he displayed
in the composition of Latin verse. Amongst his class-
mates at Eton were John Hookham Frere and George
Canning, and the youths who afterwards became Lord
Holland, Lord Carlisle, and Lord Liverpool. Though
only a matter of conjecture, it seems more than likely
that Sydney Smith's introduction at Holland House in
the early period of his London life, and the welcome
which met him at Castle Howard, when circumstances
placed him at its gates a few years later, sprang in the
first instance out of his brother's acquaintance at Eton
with Lord Holland and Lord Carlisle. With Frere and
Canning, Bobus was on terms of close friendship, and
as they were all three full of life and literary ambition,
they started a magazine, in the autumn of 1786, called
the *Microcosm*. Frere was seventeen, Bobus and Canning a year younger when they launched their venture

upon the world. The *Microcosm* had a brief, but on the whole a brilliant career; the summer vacation of 1787 was, however, too great a trial for its strength to survive, and it slipped out of existence somewhere in the dog-days of that year, amid the regrets of many youthful admirers. Years afterwards, curious to relate, the light which Canning's fame cast upon it led Charles Knight to republish the schoolboy essays of the great statesman and his friends, and the *Microcosm* thus produced in book form ran swiftly through no less than five editions, the last of which was published in 1825.

The *Microcosm*, by "Gregory Griffin, Student of the College of Eton," began to appear in the autumn of 1786, and after going on prosperously week by week until the following summer, symptoms that a decline had set in began to reveal themselves. At length the thirty-ninth number contained a melancholy statement concerning the alarming illness of the once vivacious Gregory, and a week later the climax was reached when, not only was there an account of his last moments given, but also a copy of his last will and testament. This document was signed "B and C," the first letter being that under which George Canning wrote, and the second that under which the effusions of Bobus Smith appeared. Four lads were responsible for "Gregory Griffin," and each of them contributed something characteristic to his vigorous personality; "B" and "C" just named, who were the chief sources of his inspiration, and "A" and "D," or in other words, John Smith and Hookham Frere. It is not difficult to trace the influence of the *Rambler* in this unusually clever and ambitious school magazine.

The little magazine was not allowed to disappear without receiving a word of praise from an unexpected and exalted quarter. Its readers were not all Eton lads, for the *Microcosm* had found its way to the library-table in the neighbouring Castle of Windsor, and Queen Charlotte had read number after number with growing approbation. The fact that their magazine had won the royal favour came to the knowledge of the young editors under the following circumstances. In the early summer of 1787, Sydney was spending a few days at Eton on a visit to his brother Bobus, and one Sunday evening the two lads went on the terrace at Windsor and mingled with a great concourse of people who were patiently waiting there in the hope of catching a passing glimpse of the King and Queen. Boylike, the brothers had pushed their way to the front of the crowd, and when the royal party appeared, her Majesty, who seems to have made previous inquiry concerning the youthful authors, despatched an attendant to ask if the boyish spectator was the lad who wrote in the *Microcosm* under the *nom de plume* of " Gregory Griffin." The Queen had seen a notice in the last number of the magazine announcing the fact that the publication was about to cease, and hence when the veritable " Gregory Griffin " approached in the person of Bobus Smith, she said to the delighted young scribe, who could only bow his acknowledgments, " I am sorry, Mr. Smith, to hear of the approaching death of ' Gregory Griffin.' His papers have been to me a great pleasure, and I am grieved to lose so agreeable a companion." Sydney— who from childhood to old age was devotedly attached to Bobus—was proud to be able to relate to excited groups of Eton and Winchester lads the story of the Queen's recognition of his brother's ability.

On leaving Eton, Bobus went to King's College, Cambridge, where he distinguished himself by his remarkable proficiency as a classic. He took his degree of Master of Arts in 1797, and on the 4th of July in the same year was called to the Bar by the Honourable Society of Lincoln's Inn, and joined the Western Circuit. A few months later he married Miss Caroline Vernon, daughter of R. Vernon, Esq., M.P. for Tavistock, and Evelyn, Countess Dowager of Upper Ossory, and daughter of Earl Gower. Miss Vernon was half-sister to his friend Lord Henry Petty (afterwards third Marquis of Lansdowne), and they were married in the library at Bowood on the 9th of December, 1797, by Sydney, who had entered the Church a year or two previously. Through the influence of Lord Lansdowne and Sir Francis Baring, Bobus obtained the lucrative appointment of Advocate-General at Calcutta. He left England in 1803, and after a residence in India of seven years returned home with a fortune, whilst still on the right side of forty. A sentence from Sir James Mackintosh's journal is enough to show how highly he was esteemed in the East:—" I hear frequently of Bobus ; his fame amongst the natives is greater than that of any pundit since the days of Menu." Sir James, who was in India at the same time as Bobus, declared that he found him always merry and always kind. Upon his return from India Mr. Smith settled at Saville Row, London, and his house there continued to be his home until the day of his death, and Sydney was very frequently his guest during the years when the pleasures of society in

London were enhanced by contrast with the background of solitude at Foston.

At the General Election of 1812, Mr. Robert Smith entered Parliament as member for Grantham, but he never excelled as a public speaker, although his language, according to Canning, was the "essence of English." The fact seems to have been that he was too sensitive as a public man, and too fastidious as a Parliamentary debater to make a reputation in the House of Commons. At the General Election of 1818, he contested Lincoln, but was defeated; but two years later he was returned as member for that city, and sat as its representative until he finally retired from Parliament at the Dissolution of 1826. Bobus Smith retained to the close of his life the reputation which he won in India of being "merry and kind," and few men were more popular in London society sixty years ago than the member for Lincoln. His wit was proverbial, and his conversational powers excited the admiration of the brilliant Madame de Staël. Sydney Smith is responsible for the statement that his brother Robert in George III.'s time translated the family motto of Viscount Sidmouth—"*Libertas sub rege pio*," in the following manner—"The pious king has got liberty under."[2] When Bobus saw Vansittart (Lord Bexley) enter the House of Commons in the company of the great economist, Joseph Hume, he exclaimed, according to Sydney, "Here comes penny wise and pound foolish."[3] Another anecdote, which has not always been correctly told, is taken in the present

---

[2] Life of R. H. Barham, vol. i. p. 254.
[3] Ibid. vol. i. p. 291.

instance from an unpublished manuscript, preserved in the library at Munden, in the handwriting of the younger daughter of Sydney Smith, the late Mrs. Nathaniel Hibbert. Bobus Smith and Sir Henry Holland were talking of the comparative merits of the learned professions in affording agreeable members of society. " Your profession " (the law) " certainly does not make angels of men," said Sir Henry. " No," quietly answered Bobus, as he glanced with an inno- cent air at the physician,—" no —but yours does ! " Bobus was born a year before Sydney, and died exactly a fortnight after him, March 10, 1845; " pleasant in their lives, in their deaths they were not divided." His son, the Right Hon. Robert Vernon Smith, M.P. for Northampton, a Lord of the Treasury under Mel- bourne, was raised to the peerage as Baron Lyveden, and the present Lord Lyveden is the grandson of Bobus Smith.

Sydney Smith's three brothers were all, at one time or another, settled in India. The Chairman of the East India Company, at the beginning of the century, was a Mr. Roberts, with whom the father of the lads was on terms of intimate friendship, and under his auspices both Cecil and Courtenay followed their eldest brother's example and went to India. Cecil obtained a writership at Madras, and eventually rose to be Accountant-General of the Province. He died at the Cape of Good Hope in 1814, whilst on his journey home. Courtenay, who left Winchester a mere lad, with the reputation of great linguistic ability, obtained through Mr. Roberts' influence a writership at Calcutta. He carried the studious habits acquired at Winchester to the East, and in a comparatively

short time became known as one of the best Oriental
scholars in India. He rose to the rank of a Supreme
Judge, and was appointed to a district nearly three
times as large as that of all England, where he was
exceedingly popular with the natives. He amassed
considerable wealth, and, after an honourable career
in the East, returned to England. At his death, which
occurred suddenly in 1839, Sydney, who inherited a
third of his fortune, found himself, to his own great
surprise, in affluent circumstances.

Sydney Smith, like most brilliant Wykehamists,
proceeded to New College, Oxford. He stood third
on the roll for admission as a scholar at the election
held in the autumn of 1788, and on the occurrence of
a vacancy was admitted on the 5th of February,
1789. At the end of his second year of residence
he obtained a fellowship, which he held for nine
years, and which he relinquished upon his marriage in
1800.

Dr. Sewell, the present Warden of New, who has
kindly furnished the above facts from the archives of
the college, states that he is not aware of any records,
or even traditions, respecting the years spent by
Sydney Smith in Oxford, and adds that he was pre-
cluded from obtaining any university honours in the
schools by the so-called privilege enjoyed by the Fellows of New at that time, of being examined in their
own college for degrees, without being required to
pass the University Examination. Even by the members of his own family surprisingly little is known of
this period of Sydney Smith's career, and at this late
hour of the day it is not at all probable that any fresh
information on the subject will ever come to light.

He seldom referred in after-days to his experience at the University, and there is a significant dearth of allusion in his published works to this phase of his life. The five years he spent at Oxford was a time of difficulty, anxiety, and suspense; a period when the responsibilities of life were first distinctly seen, and the privations of a straitened lot first keenly felt. At the age of twenty he obtained a fellowship of 100*l*. a year, and from that time forward ceased to make any demand on his father for pecuniary aid. To a student at Oxford, 100*l*. a year was a most inadequate pittance, but from 1791 until he entered the Church, three years later, it was all that Sydney Smith had to rely on. His father's resources were, at that time, considerably taxed by the claims made upon him by his other children. Robert was studying for the Bar, and Cecil and Courtenay, both of whom inherited the roving propensities of their sire, were already restlessly eager to try their fortune in the East. Mrs. Smith, moreover, was gradually slipping into a delicate state of health; the long suspense and anxiety which she had endured at the outset of her married life, and the uncertainty and fear which her husband's impulsive and ill-balanced temperament had thrown into its entire course, had evoked tendencies which she was no longer able to withstand. It seems more than likely, therefore, that Sydney, who could never do enough for his mother, undertook, with that self-reliance and generosity which afterwards became so conspicuous in his character, to free the harassed family exchequer of all further claims immediately after gaining the modest emoluments attached to his fellowship. But whatever the reason may have been, it is at least certain that from 1791 he ceased, directly or indirectly, to tax his father's purse.

Strictly conscientious in money-matters, the poor student resolutely reduced his expenditure within the narrow limits of his scanty income, and doubtless he found the endeavour very hard at times to make, as he expressed it, "sixpence assume the importance and do the work of a shilling." Like Samuel Johnson, however, half a century earlier, and scores of sturdy students before and since, Sydney Smith preferred "short commons and a rusty coat" to the galling burden of debt, or the bitter bread of dependence. New College, ninety or a hundred years ago, had not the most distinguished reputation for learning; but if the Fellows did not yield that "attention to reading" which their lettered seclusion suggests, they at least fulfilled another Apostolic injunction, for they certainly were "given to hospitality." Sydney, however, was too proud to accept invitations which it was not in his power to return, and he seems therefore to have held aloof—from pride as much as from necessity, to an extent that must have been very trying to a man of his instincts—from the social side of university life. There is one golden deed associated with the straitened, anxious years spent at Oxford, which reveals the goodness of his heart, and shines with heightened beauty because of the dreary setting which surrounds it. Courtenay, the little scamp, less careful than his elder brother, ran up a bill at school for 30*l.*, and was too timid to confess the fact to his father, who by this time had enough in hand in fitting out his younger sons for India. Sydney, unable to bear the sight of the lad's distress, generously came to his rescue, and sent him

off to seek and find his fortune in the East, with the
reassuring promise that he would pay his Winchester bills; and little by little, in trivial yet costly
instalments, the kind brother bravely kept his word.
How costly those instalments were, let his own words,
now first published, reveal:—" I did it with my heart's
blood; it was the third of my whole income, for, though
I never in my life owed a farthing which I was unable
to pay, yet my 100*l.* a year was very difficult to spread
over the wants of a college life."

Curiously enough, Francis Jeffrey was at Queen's
College, Oxford, during part of the time that Sydney
Smith was studying at New; but the future colla-
borateurs appear never to have met until they were
thrown together a few years later in Edinburgh. The
moral tone of the University, as indeed of society
in general, was extremely low at the close of last
century. " It is possible to acquire nothing in this
place," wrote Jeffrey, with grim Scotch humour, to a
friend, " except praying and drinking." Nor was
Sydney Smith's testimony less emphatic. In a short
article, entitled " Modern Changes," which he wrote
when a gray-haired Canon of St. Paul's, he declares
that when he started in life, one-third at least of the
gentlemen of England, even in the best society, were
always drunk.

Quitting Oxford in 1794, he was called to face the
first serious question of life—the choice of a profession. His personal predilections at this stage of his
career would have led him to follow Bobus to the
Bar, but he was compelled, through the insufficiency of
the means at his disposal, to abandon his dreams of
forensic distinction. There can be no question that

his brilliant gifts would have soon won reputation and reward for their possessor, had he devoted himself to the difficult tasks of a public pleader. His silvery voice, his dignified appearance, his unfailing self-command, his masculine common sense, his occasional eloquence, his ever-present humour, formed a union of strength and beauty which would under any circumstances have been appreciated by an English jury.

Old Mr. Smith, however, evidently thought that one lawyer in the family was enough, and therefore brushed aside the first hint of Sydney's proposition with the somewhat harsh exclamation, " You may be a college tutor or a parson !" Sydney told his father that whilst he would have preferred the law above all other professions, he was very sensible that he was making a great sacrifice to maintain Bobus at the Bar, and that he should deem it both selfish and unfair to tax him in the same way himself. He accordingly announced his intention of entering the Church. " The law," Sydney Smith was accustomed to say, " is decidedly the best profession for a young man if he has anything in him. In the Church a man is thrown into life with his hands tied, and bid to swim ; he does well if he keeps his head above water." That remark, true perhaps in the main, required, even when it was first uttered, some qualification ; and in these days at least few men, if any, enter the Church with their hands tied, unless indeed they themselves have fastened the knot. At the same time it must be admitted that if Sydney Smith entered the Church with little enthusiasm, and not a few misgivings, he gallantly addressed himself, to the best of his ability, to its

noble and self-denying work, and evinced greater
patience and cheerfulness in the midst of the cares
and trials to which his new position inevitably exposed
him, than many a man displays who has deliberately
chosen the sacred vocation.

GATEWAY OF WINCHESTER COLLEGE.

CHAPTER II.

1794—1800.

Curate at Nether Avon—Tutor to Michael Beach—Marriage.

It was in the spring of 1794 that Sydney Smith was
ordained on his appointment to the curacy of Nether
Avon, a small village six miles distant from the
ancient but sleepy town of Amesbury, in Wiltshire.
He was three-and-twenty when he accepted this position, and settled at Nether Avon as curate in sole
charge.   The change from university life at Oxford to
a curate's lowly round of labour in a remote Wiltshire
village, peopled with farm-labourers, was not a little
trying; and it would be difficult to imagine a more
uncongenial lot for a young man of Sydney Smith's
spirit, culture, and tastes than that which Nether
Avon afforded.   The village was not on any of the
coaching-roads; and nothing, except the arrival of a
market-cart from Salisbury once a week, broke the
dull monotony which reigned over the place.   No
meat was to be obtained except when this butcher's
shop on wheels rumbled with noisy importance into
the half-deserted village street.   The arrival of unexpected visitors on any other day than that on which
the cart from Salisbury drew up would have driven
the perplexed curate to the verge of despair; and even

under ordinary circumstances, he sometimes narrowly escaped compulsory and most unwelcome vegetarianism. Neither books nor attractive scenery were within his reach; and, with the exception of three months which the squire spent annually at the Hall, there was scarcely any society above the rank of the parish clerk.

Nether Avon is only a few miles from Stonehenge; and the dreary and uncultivated downs of Salisbury Plain, with their vacant and oppressive spaces, shut the young curate out from a world with which he had so much in common. Happily, even at this distance of time, there is evidence enough to prove that if Sydney Smith was occasionally disheartened by his new surroundings, he never allowed the sense of loneliness or lack of sympathy to stand in the way of the manful discharge of his duties. He spent between two and three years in Nether Avon, and finally quitted the spot in March, 1797. There are not many parishes in England where curates are remembered after nearly ninety years have rolled away, and exceedingly few men in a similar position contrive to leave a favourable impression behind them for so long a period, even when their personal influence has been exerted in a neighbourhood for twenty instead of two years. Sydney Smith, however, furnished an exception to the general rule; and a tradition, which still lingers in the cottages of Nether Avon, is responsible for the statement that he was fond of the children and young people, and took pains to teach them.

The schools which he was instrumental in establishing on weekdays and Sundays attest the truth of this kindly tradition, and form an enduring memorial of his interest in the young of his parish. The condition

of the poor in all parts of the country at the close of
last century was in many respects most deplorable,
and the existing means of education, especially in rural
districts, were not only very defective, but also inadequate in the extreme. Commerce was crippled with
unjust and tyrannical laws, and taxation was increased
by long and costly campaigns. The labouring classes
—ignorant, depressed, and in many cases, debased—
had few opportunities of improving their own condition, or even of shielding the children who followed in
their steps from a repetition of the same hard and
dismal experiences of life. Theophilus Lindsay, Robert
Raikes, Hannah More, and other benevolent people
had already done something by precept and example,
in their different spheres, to awaken in the public
mind an intelligent and tender concern for the thousands of neglected and destitute children scattered
over the land. One of the earliest and most enthusiastic friends which the new movement found amongst
the clergy of the Established Church was Dr. Shute,
Bishop of Salisbury, who, in 1789, brought the subject
before his diocese, and did all in his power to advance
the noble and large-hearted scheme which will ever be
associated in the public mind with the honoured name
of the Gloucester printer. When Sydney Smith—
fresh from Oxford—set foot in Nether Avon, the good
bishop's zeal had not met in that parish at least with
any response, and it was only when the new clergyman, at the suggestion of the wife of the squire,
took the matter up, that the first Sunday school was
established in the locality.

The squire of Nether Avon, when Sydney Smith
set foot in the parish, was Mr. Hicks-Beach, of Wil-

liamstrip Park, Gloucestershire, and Member of Parliament for the half-forgotten borough of Cirencester. The Beach family first settled in Wiltshire at Fittleton, the adjoining parish to Nether Avon, about the year 1650. William Beach, the last of the male line, purchased in 1760 the estate at Nether Avon, from the Duke of Beaufort, who had used the mansion—Nether Avon House—as a hunting-box. On the death of Mr. Beach in 1790, he was succeeded in the property by Mr. Michael Hicks, who had married, some years previously, his daughter and heiress. Mr. Hicks assumed the additional surname of Beach, and the Right Hon. Sir Michael Hicks-Beach, Bart., M.P., is the great-grandson of the squire who befriended Sydney Smith, and the grandson of the youth whom the latter accompanied to Edinburgh.

Mr. Hicks-Beach, who was himself a shrewd and cultivated man, was not long in discovering the sterling qualities of mind and heart which lay beneath the bright and clever talk of the young Oxford graduate, and whilst he and his family were at Nether Avon House, Sydney had no reason to complain of being dull, though when they were in Gloucestershire, or at their town house in Harley Street, affairs assumed another shape. However, even then, though deprived of cultivated and congenial society, the young clergyman enjoyed at least some of the privileges of the place, and the "Yew-Tree Walk," in the grounds of Nether Avon House, is still pointed out to the visitor as the favourite path where—lost in thought—Sydney Smith was accustomed to pace to and fro, from day to day.

Anxious to do all in his power to improve the condition of the people around him, Mr. Hicks-Beach,

soon after succeeding to the property, requested the
steward of his estates to make some investigations
concerning the poor of Nether Avon. The result of
these inquiries is contained in a curious and lengthy
statement, entitled, " Mr. Verrey, the Steward's List

THE YEW-TREE WALK.

of Nether Avon Poor—1793." This document gives
brief particulars of no less than fifty families or house-
holders, and reveals a deplorable amount of vice, indolence, and abject poverty. Two or three extracts will
suffice to show the state of things which existed :—

No. 14, a young girl, " gets sixteen pounds of

spinning work done a month, which amounts to only four shillings." No. 21, a man aged fifty-five, " is very unhealthy. He works for Mr. Lee, and receives only four shillings per week. Last week young Farmer —— beat this poor old man with a large stick, and had it not been for his having on a great-coat, his daughter reports he would have crippled him." No. 43, a man "with wife and four children (the eldest nine years of age), works for Mr. Lee at six shillings a week," &c. &c. According to the steward's list many of the people were almost dependent on parish relief, and not a man mentioned in that long catalogue was receiving wages amounting to ten shillings a week. Mrs. Beach forwarded this document to Sydney Smith soon after his arrival at Nether Avon, in order that he might go through the list and add his own opinions on any of the cases with which he was personally acquainted. This request elicited the following characteristic comments :—

Mr. Sydney Smith's knowledge of the parish is very limited, but in compliance with Mrs. Beach's desire, he will follow Mr. Verrey's list, and annex a short comment upon those families of which he has had any opportunity of forming a judgment :—

He thinks No. 3 in a wretched condition from mismanagement and extravagance.

No. 4, in a similar state from ignorance bordering on brutality.

No. 6, industrious, and deserving protection.

No. 8, deceitful, but decent, and struggles against her miserable poverty.

No. 14, wretched from their Irish extraction, from numbers, from disease, from habits of idleness.

No. 17. Very deserving.

No. 18. Weak, witless people, totally wretched, without sense to extricate themselves from their wretchedness.

No. 22. Industrious, and, I believe, deserving.

No. 24. Very neat, industrious, and deserving.

No. 25. Aliment for Newgate, food for the halter, a ragged, wretched, savage, stubborn race.

No. 27. Perfectly wretched and helpless.

No. 32. The wife of this man is an object of pity.

No. 38. A good, meritorious woman.

No. 43. A good family, and merit your protection.

No. 49. Good, worthy people; and, as they have no wheat from the farmers, deserve encouragement.

Mrs. H. Beach.

Upon the arrival of this reply Mr. and Mrs. Beach invited him to visit them at Fairford Park, in order that they might confer together on the best methods of helping the poor of Nether Avon. In response to this invitation the following letter was despatched, and it is interesting, as showing the spirit in which the new curate regarded his work:—

[I.]   Nether Avon, July 26th, 1794.

SIR,—I am extremely obliged to you for your kind invitation to Williamstrip. I mean to continue in my present situation for two years, and will certainly pay my compliments to you in Gloucestershire before the expiration of that time; but I am afraid that it cannot be this summer, as I have engagements at Winchester, Weymouth, Bath, and Oxford, and expect my brother at Nether Avon. My stock of theological doctrine, which at present is most alarmingly small, will necessarily occupy a great deal of my time, and I mean to try if I cannot persuade the poor people to come to church, for really at present (as was said of Burke at Hastings' trial) my preaching is like the voice of one crying in the wilderness. You may assure, yourself, sir, that the parsonage-house, owing to the uncommon heat of the summer is perfectly dry. I have suffered a little from the smell of paint, but that is entirely gone off at present.

I am, sir, with the greatest respect, your obliged, humble servant,

SYDNEY SMITH.

Mr. Beach.

As the church and parsonage-house are alluded to in this letter, it may be as well to say a word here about them both. Nether Avon Church is substantially the same as it was in Sydney Smith's time, although the interior has been improved in various ways. Its situation—just below Nether Avon House —is an extremely pretty one, and in the summer it is almost hidden from sight by the surrounding foliage. The chief point of interest is a handsome Norman arch at the west end; the rest of the edifice is of later date. Close by, the placid Avon ripples through the valley, and the river, with the tall trees which fringe its banks, and the quaint old farm-house in the immediate neighbourhood, forms a charming picture. The country all around is bare and open, but the village nestles among the trees which abound in the quiet valley of the Avon.[1] The best description of

---

[1] It is perhaps worthy of passing remark that the Rev. Lancelot

Nether Avon which can, perhaps, be given, is that
conveyed in Sydney Smith's own words, which are
still quoted with a smile in the locality, "A pretty
feature in a plain (Salisbury) face." The present
vicarage was erected some forty-five years ago, and
the parsonage-house which Sydney occupied, and

NETHER AVON HOUSE AND CHURCH.

which was a very inferior building, has long since
vanished.

In the course of the autumn of 1794 he received a
second, and more urgent invitation to visit his new
friends at Williamstrip Park, and the invitation was
accompanied by the offer of a horse, on which to per-

Addison (afterwards Dean of Lichfield) was Rector for many years
of the neighbouring parish of Milston. At this obscure village on
the Amesbury road, his son Joseph Addison, one of the greatest
masters of English prose, was born on the 1st of May, 1672.
Milston and Nether Avon are within three miles of each other, and
though themselves places of no reputation, both are thus associated
with the memory of world-renowned men.

form the journey between **Nether Avon** and **Fairford**, a distance of about fifty miles. The invitation was accepted, but there were still **obstacles in the way**, as the accompanying letter proves; it gives an amusing glimpse of the embarrassments of a journey by road at the end of last century :—

[II.]   Nether Avon, 1794.

DEAR SIR,—If I can get my churches [2] served for one Sunday, I shall have great pleasure in coming to see you at Williamstrip. I rather think I shall be able to effect this; and if I do not write to you to the contrary, I will be with you next Monday night. Your offer of a horse to carry my portmanteau I cannot accept, and for two reasons, which I think will justify me in not accepting it. The first is, you have no horse here; the next, I have no portmanteau. I shall send my things to Bath in a small trunk, from thence by the mail to Fairford, from whence I hope the master of the inn will have ingenuity enough to forward it by a porter to Williamstrip. For this acute and well-contrived scheme of sending my things, I arrogate to myself very little merit; it was chiefly contrived by your charioteer—a man of senatorial gravity and prudence. I beg my compliments to Mrs. Beach.

I am, my dear sir, yours very sincerely,

SYDNEY SMITH.

Michael Hicks-Beach, Esq., Williamstrip **Park**,
       Fairford, Gloucestershire.

---

[2] The curate in charge of Nether Avon had also to conduct a service every Sunday in the neighbouring church of Fittleton at that time.

Sydney Smith's stay at Williamstrip on this occasion was the first of many pleasant visits there, and long after he had emerged from the obscurity of Nether Avon his intimacy with Mr. and Mrs. Beach proved a mutual gratification.

When he arrived at Williamstrip he found his patrons greatly concerned with the condition of the poor of Nether Avon, and willing to do all in their power to elevate the people on their estate, and to help them to help themselves. Various methods were discussed, and, amongst others, the desirability of establishing schools in the parish, so that the children who were springing up might be trained in habits of order, self-reliance, and thrift. The religious condition of the villagers was one of lamentable apathy, and it was therefore determined that the first thing to accomplish was the establishment of a Sunday-school —an institution which at that time had the charm of absolute novelty to the rustic mind. Sydney threw himself heartily into this scheme, and returned to Nether Avon eager to carry it into effect; but "human life," as he afterwards sagely remarked, "is full of tedious and prosaic difficulties which are felt, but cannot be stated," and the consequence was that—in spite of his ardour—the winter rolled away before the Sunday-school became an accomplished fact. A paid teacher had to be engaged, for in those days the principles of Voluntaryism were but little understood by the people; and the curate, with two churches to serve on Sunday, was, of course, unable to instruct the children in person. In the beginning of April he wrote at length to inform Mr. Beach of what had been done, and what was still needed.

[III.]   Nether Avon, April 2nd, 1795.

DEAR SIR,—Upon my return from Bath, I began
to carry into execution your plan of establishing a
Sunday-school at **Nether Avon**. Andrew Goulter,
whom you mentioned as a man likely to undertake it,
is going to quit the place. Bendall, the blacksmith,
Harry Cozens (a tailor and cousin to the clerk), and
Giles Harding have all applied for the appointment.
The last I consider quite out of the question; his wife
cannot read, and he has no room fit to receive the
children. Henry Cozens, in my opinion, is the most
eligible. His wife reads, his brother reads, and his
apprentice reads; he has a good kitchen, some room
in his shop, and his mother next door has a good
kitchen, which may be filled with overflowings of
the school, if it ever should overflow. I have mentioned the salary you arranged with me to the ap-
plicants, namely, 2s. per Sunday, and two score
of faggots. The children will attend on Christmas
Day and Good Friday. Is the master to be paid for
those days? It is impossible to find two rooms in the
same house for boys and girls; if they are put to
different houses, the divided salary will be too small to
induce any reputable man to accept it. The books
that are wanted will be about sixty spelling-books
(with easy lessons in reading at the end), beginning
from the letters, and going on progressively in syllables;
twenty New Testaments, and twenty Prayer-books.
Miss Hannah More's books I think you will like very
much if you look at them. They are 5s. per hundred;
if you will send me down 100 of them, I think I
can distribute them with effect. The people who

D

had sittings in the great pew have given it up, and Munday is going to fit it up for the children. The people all express a great desire of sending their children to the school. The only farmer I have yet had an opportunity of speaking to is Farmer Munday; he will contribute with great cheerfulness. I will talk to the farmers collectively at the vestry, and individually out of it. * * * A few forms will be wanted for the Sunday-school. Will you empower me to order them? In the very hot weather, why might not the children be instructed in the church before and after service, instead of the little hot room in which they would otherwise be stuffed? I shall mention it to the churchwardens, with your approbation. * * * Nothing can equal the profound, the immeasurable, the awful dulness of this place, in the which I lie, dead and buried, in hopes of a joyful resurrection in the year 1796.

I am, my dear sir, yours sincerely,
SYDNEY SMITH.

To Michael H. Beach, Esq., M.P.,
No. 28, Harley Street, London.

The practical common sense of Sydney Smith is evinced in the suggestion that the children during the sultry weeks of summer, should be taught in the cool and spacious church, rather than be crowded into a "little hot room" to their own physical disadvantage, the teacher's discomfort, and the hindrance of the work itself. In the course of a few weeks he wrote a brief note to Mr. Beach, to thank him for attending to his request about the books, and to report the beginnings of the enterprise: "I have received the books—a very ample supply, and thank you in the name of my *sans culottes*. They attend extremely well." One benevolent scheme not unfrequently paves the way (by revealing the necessity) for another; and the Sunday-school had not been long started in Nether Avon, before it became apparent by the bare-footed and ragged condition of many of the children, that other forms of help were also greatly needed. An Industrial School was accordingly established, which met on two or three nights in the week, and into it the girls and young women of the poorest families in the district were gathered, and taught by a competent person the homely mysteries of knitting, sewing, and darning, much to their own subsequent comfort and that of their obstreperous brothers. Taking " short views of life," Sydney did the work that was nearest, lowly though it seemed, and quietly awaited the issue of events. Toiling amongst the poor of a Wiltshire village with cheerful good-will, it was not long ere he convinced all about him, that he had in no mere official sense their interests at heart, but was prepared to do anything which intelligence could suggest, or sympathy inspire to brighten and improve the condition of the people amongst whom his lot had been cast. During this season of busy obscurity there are proofs enough, that self-culture was not forgotten, nor was he to be tempted from his post under ordinary circumstances, except to pay flying visits to Bath to cheer his ailing mother. Meanwhile, all unknown to himself, this period of seclusion was abruptly to cease, and the curate of Nether Avon was to go forth to find elsewhere a wider field for the employment of the talents with which he was so richly endowed.

Sydney Smith was accustomed to advise his friends to " keep in the grand and common road of life," and it was when he himself was patiently treading the grand and common road of present duty, that honourable release from the irksome monotony of a village curacy dawned suddenly upon him. Mr. Hicks-Beach was wishful that his eldest son, Michael Beach Hicks-Beach, should go for a year or two to one of the German universities in order that, under some competent direction, he might there carry on his studies, before proceeding to Christ Church, Oxford. Impressed with the ready scholarship as well as the natural ability of the young curate, whom, moreover, he greatly liked, he asked him to accompany his son on his travels in the two-fold capacity of tutor and friend. The offer was gladly accepted, and Sydney relinquished his curacy in the spring of 1797, and went to spend the summer with his father, who by this time had grown tired of Bath, and had established himself in the neighbourhood of Tiverton.

Mr. Beach had requested Sydney Smith to make inquiries as to the best continental university for his son, and in August he wrote to convey the result of these investigations :—

[IV.]   Beauchamp, Tiverton, Devonshire,
August 23rd, 1797.

MY DEAR SIR,—Since I left you I have occupied myself in procuring, through various channels, information respecting the plan of which we arranged the outline at Williamstrip. I am induced, from the most respectable authority, to prefer Saxe Weimar to any other German university. The duke (who is himself

an extremely well-informed, sensible man), has drawn
to that town some of the most sensible men in Germany,
who have by their example diffused there, a very strong
spirit of improvement. From other accounts that I
have received of this place, I will quote you Sir
Thomas Rivers' :—" If I was to recommend a situation
for a young man in Germany, it would be Weimar.
The duke is an uncommonly well-informed, sensible
man. He has assembled at his court the four heroes
of German literature, Wieland, Goethe, Herder, and
Schiller, besides many other well-informed men of
inferior note. The society is agreeable, and has a
literary turn; the English are very well received.
There is no doubt that a young man well recommended,
who appears anxious to please, and to improve himself," would be readily introduced into any kind of
society; at the same time, a young buck, or a fox-
hunter, would be laughed at and neglected." The
sum you hinted at will do for our expenses extremely
well. Choosing then, if you please, this for our place
of destination, we will let my plan nap a little for the
present. In the meantime I shall attack the German
vigorously, and seize with avidity any information
which may be useful to us. We have begun our
harvest in this part of the world under bad auspices.
The farmers complain they shall not get above twenty
bushels of wheat an acre. I believe you would not be
sorry to compound for this upon the hills. I very
nearly lost my place to Bath by the ingenuity of the
young ploughman who arrived with my trunk through
unknown and unbeaten tracks, about five minutes
before the coach set off. Remember me very kindly
to Mrs. Beach and all the family, not forgetting of

course my intended pupil. Adieu, my dear sir, and
believe me yours very sincerely,

SYDNEY SMITH.

M. Hicks-Beach, Esq., M.P.

Mr. Beach heartily approved of this proposal; but
as there was no particular reason for haste, and public
affairs both at home and abroad were very unsettled,
Sydney's plan was allowed to "nap a little." The
autumn of 1797 glided rapidly away in the midst of
preparations for the proposed journey, and in December, Sydney was invited to Bowood, to marry Bobus to
Miss Vernon, half sister to his friend, Lord Henry
Petty. Meanwhile Europe was full of wars and
rumours of war, and the military genius of Napoleon
was filling the earth with bloodshed and sorrow, and
the minds of men with hatred and alarm. Germany
was not exempt from the general disturbance, and the
plans of master and pupil were in consequence thrown
into confusion. Winter gave way to spring, but the
stormy troubles of the times showed no sign of abatement, and at length driven through "stress of
politics" from all thoughts of scholastic quiet in
Saxony, they were compelled to second thoughts upon
the matter, and eventually Mr. Beach determined that
Michael and his tutor should relinquish all idea of the
Continent, and go to Edinburgh instead. They appear to have started for the north early in May, and
to have proceeded very leisurely on their journey.

Young Beach and his tutor visited Warwick and
Birmingham, and were greatly interested with what
they saw in both places. Sydney was "enchanted"
with Matlock, but thought that the desolation of the

country between Bakewell and Disley was "scandalous." Buxton filled him with supreme contempt, and the jolting of the coach over the roads in its neighbourhood led him to hesitate between suicide and sleep, but fortunately he "unconsciously adopted the latter." The activity and enterprise of Manchester and Liverpool were next duly noted, and then the travellers made their way by easy stages to the Lakes. Here they rambled from place to place, saw the usual sights, and duly climbed Skiddaw. The mountains around Windermere kindled their enthusiasm; but for beauty, Sydney gave Derwentwater the palm, and for grandeur, Ulleswater. They were accompanied in their wanderings by a German courier, named Mithoffer, who had been engaged in prospect of the expedition to the Continent, and who was retained—in the capacity of valet and attendant,—when it was settled that Edinburgh, and not Weimar, should be their goal. They arrived in Edinburgh in the middle of June, 1798;[3] Sydney had just completed his twenty-seventh year, and his pupil was eighteen, when the coach rolled into the picturesque city amid the dust of a midsummer evening.

Sydney Smith could scarcely have set foot in the Northern Athens at a more auspicious hour. During the closing years of last century, and the opening ones of this, Edinburgh was full of keen and varied intellectual life, and at that period it was by no means difficult for a young man of ordinary ability and edu-

---

[3] Lady Holland mentions 1797 as the year; but all the dates given above, as well as others in the early chapters of this narrative, are taken from letters now in the possession of Sir Michael Hicks-Beach, which conclusively determine the point.

cation, to establish himself in the midst of its pleasant and brilliant society. Many of the inhabitants of that " energetic and unfragrant city," as the elder of our two travellers was pleased to term it, were shrewd, hearty, and cultivated, and their hospitality, whilst neither lavish in itself nor pretentious in its forms, was of a nature which imparted not only a singular zest to social enjoyment, but made it an occasion of happy and unstudied mental stimulus. Through a variety of causes, the most prominent of which was the war with France, Edinburgh society from 1795 to 1815 was unusually distinguished and animated. Many cadets of noble English families, such as Lord Webb Seymour, Lord Henry Petty, Lord John Russell, and others, were drawn to its University, partly by the restrictive statutes of Oxford and Cambridge, but still more by the genius and learning of such eminent professors as Dugald Stewart and John Playfair. The city, moreover, was crowded with clever and ambitious young men, whose heads were much better stocked than their purses, and who were ready, with frank good will, to extend the right hand of fellowship, at a moment's notice, to any stranger whose qualifications for the common life were identical with their own. " They formed a band of friends all attached to each other, all full of hope, ambition, and gaiety, and all strengthened in their mutual connection by the politics of most of them separating the whole class from the ordinary society of the city. It was a most delightful brother-hood."[4] Even had it been otherwise, Sydney Smith's

[4] " Memorials of his Time," by Henry Cockburn, p. 176.

fresh and unforced humour, kindly aspect, and attractive manners, would have won a welcome for him
amongst much more stiff and dignified associates than
those who now warmly hailed his accession to their
ranks.

Amongst the men of commanding influence who
adorned the city at the period of his arrival, were
Henry Erskine, Adam Ferguson, Dugald Stewart, and
John Playfair. Scotland, moreover, was still mourning the loss which philosophy and *belles-lettres* had
sustained in the death of Adam Smith, Thomas Reid,
David Hume, and William Robertson; whilst Robert
Burns, one of the greatest and most gifted of her
sons, had then just sunk into an untimely grave.
Amongst the younger men who were struggling into
fame, and with most of whom Sydney Smith soon
became personally acquainted, were Jeffrey, Horner,
Brougham, Murray, Walter Scott, and Thomas Campbell.

The young tutor was keenly alive to the privileges of his new position, and eager to make the most
of the golden opportunities which it afforded. In
after-years he was accustomed to say that contact
with such persons had been the " peculiar felicity of
his early life," and that he regarded " the one earthly
good worth struggling for to be the love and esteem
of many great and good men." Social life in the
Scottish capital eighty or a hundred years ago, was
distinguished by a robust simplicity which contrasts
favourably with some of the more prominent, but less
pleasing characteristics of society both north and
south to-day. People who were not blessed with
much of this world's goods, were not ashamed silently

to avow the fact by offering their assembled friends a frugal but substantial meal, **and there** was a hearty **contempt for** that mischievous **and** unhappy form of social deception **known as living for** appearances.

Scottish life and **character never had a keener critic** than **Sydney Smith,** with the single exception **of Dr. Johnson, three-fourths of whose** supposed hatred of the Scotch (according to one of his admirers) was merely goodhumoured and witty **banter,** whilst **the** remaining fourth was honest prejudice. Sydney loved to catch at the ludicrous **aspects** of Scottish life, and to reproduce them in his own extravagant **but** genial way; but if he played with the odd **foibles and** quaint usages of the people around him, he was equally ready to acknowledge at something like their true value those high **qualities of mind and** heart, **which have made** the Scottish character respected and **influential in every** quarter of **the** globe. His witticisms at the expense of Scotland and the Scotch are almost as well **known as** those **of his** great predecessor **in** the art. **He** speaks **of Scotland, on one occasion, as** the " knuckle-end of England,"[5] and as if that was **not** sufficiently uncomplimentary, adds in the same breath, **and** " garret of the earth." In his day the roads were so villainous, and **the** sanitary arrangements so barbarous, that he declared that to **travel in** Scotland **was** to mortify the body in order to gratify **the mind. And as** for the people themselves, **even if it** required a surgical operation to get a **joke well into a** Scotch understanding,[6] still " no nation has so large a stock of benevolence of

[5] " Memoir of Sydney Smith," chap. ii, p. **18.**
[6] Ibid. p. 17.

heart," and they are so goodnatured that "their temper stands anything but an attack on their climate."

In July, 1798, a week or two after their arrival, Sydney Smith and his pupil took lodgings at 38, South

38, SOUTH HANOVER STREET, EDINBURGH.

Hanover Street, and during their first year in Edinburgh that house was their home. The house stands on rising ground, and is the second building on the west side on approaching from George Street. It is, as the accompanying illustration shows, a well-built city house, and the rooms on the first floor, which were those which Sydney Smith and his pupil occupied, are spacious and lofty, and command a distant view of the Forth. But though the house in South Hanover Street was pleasant and convenient, the landlady was tyrannical and exorbitant, and after their first term at Edinburgh, they deemed it best, on returning to the city, to go further even if they fared worse. They accordingly removed round the corner into Queen Street, and a curious and not very inviting-looking old house there, which still bears the number " 19," became their temporary domicile. Here they seem to have been comfortable; at any rate, we may conclude so, for there is no mention in any of the letters which they regularly despatched week by week to Williamstrip Park of any ground of complaint. From the windows of this house they had a glorious view over the meadows, of the Estuary of the Forth, and of the glittering sea beyond.

Their last residence in Edinburgh and the home to which Sydney Smith brought his young bride in the autumn of 1800, was a neat and attractive little house—not five minutes' walk from either of the others—46, George Street; and that they were thoroughly comfortable and happy in it admits of no question. The letters which were written from that little " main door house" are full of sparkling enjoyment and fun, and evince that the young tutor, in spite of occasional apprehensions about the future—was leading a busy, influential, and happy life. No. 46, George Street is still an attractive-looking house, and now, though hemmed in by warehouses and shops, it has not suffered through the commercial invasion of that once fashionable thoroughfare, to the extent which some of its less favoured neighbours have done; nor is the house as small as it at first sight appears, for both at the front and back there are several handsome rooms, and the drawing-room which looks in the direction of

46, GEORGE STREET, EDINBURGH.

Princes Street is both elegant and spacious. It is now the office of the Educational Endowments Commission, and the apartment in which the young English bride first received her husband's friends, and where Jeffrey and Horner, Brougham and Brown,

became his guests, is now used as the board-room of
the Commission.

Michael Beach, under the genial but firm control of
his tutor, made satisfactory progress with his studies,
and proved himself in other ways neither unmindful
nor unworthy of the advantages which he enjoyed.
The tutor as well as the pupil improved the time at
his disposal by attending the lectures on Moral Philosophy of Dugald Stewart, and by studying the theory
and practice of Medicine. Although Sydney Smith
had come to Edinburgh in a scholastic capacity, his
ability as a preacher soon became known, and was
promptly called into requisition. The chief representative of the Church of England in Edinburgh at that
period was the Rev. Archibald Alison, LL.B., the
author of the well-known *Essays on Taste*, and
father of Sir Archibald Alison, the historian, and
grandfather of the gallant soldier who now bears the
same name and title. The Episcopalians worshipped
in Charlotte Chapel, Rose Street—which runs parallel
with Princes Street; there Sydney Smith officiated
from time to time as an occasional preacher; and there
the great hero of his Edinburgh days—Dugald Stewart
—came to hear him preach. The Episcopalians of
Edinburgh occupy to-day much more imposing buildings than the chapel in Rose Street in which Archibald
Alison and Sydney Smith preached, and now a Baptist
congregation worship there.[1] The chapel has been
re-pewed, and the old pulpit has been replaced by one
more in accordance with the tastes of those who now

[1] The Baptists of Edinburgh purchased Charlotte Chapel in 1818,
and from that period to the present time they have continued to
worship there.

hold possession of the place. There is a schoolroom underneath the building, and there the old pulpit may still be seen, doing duty, doubtless, as the superintendent's desk. Charlotte Chapel has a very deep gallery, which runs along three sides of the building; and an octagonal roof of curious design, with glass lantern in the centre, is probably the only characteristic of the interior which remains unchanged. Externally, however, Charlotte Chapel remains the same; it is a plain but substantial stone building of rather low elevation, and of no artistic merit.

The following amusing note was despatched to Mr. Beach as soon as Michael and the writer were beginning to feel at home amid their new surroundings :—

[v.]
South Hanover Street,
10th Sept., 1798.

MY DEAR SIR,—Michael is in very good health, with an improved complexion, living temperately, bathing constantly, taking regular exercise and regular study, and apparently cheerful and happy. I can say much the same of myself, with the exception of the second article—an improved complexion ; unpardonable nature has, I am afraid, doomed me to eternal coppenr; but even this I could forget if the people of Edinburgh would not gape at my sermons. In the middle of an exquisite address to Virtue, beginning, " O Virtue ! " I saw a rascal gaping as if his jaws were torn asunder. I have a great horror of suicide, and therefore I *yet* live.

Yours, my dear sir, ever most truly,
SYDNEY SMITH.

With Dugald Stewart and Lord Webb Seymour, he was soon on terms of intimate friendship, and they quickly recognized his worth, and introduced him to the best society of the city. Dugald Stewart, a competent and fastidious judge of pulpit oratory, appreciated the new preacher in Charlotte Chapel much more highly than the unknown man who yawned so

CHARLOTTE CHAPEL, ROSE STREET, EDINBURGH.

conspicuously when Sydney was apostrophizing virtue. "Those original and unexpected ideas," declared the Professor, as he left the chapel after hearing him preach, "gave me a thrilling sensation of sublimity never before awakened by any other oratory."[8] An interesting memorial of the Sundays spent in Edinburgh by Sydney Smith exists in a little volume—

[8] "Memoirs of Sydney Smith," chap. iv. p. 69.

which has now become exceedingly scarce—entitled
"*Six Sermons preached in Charlotte Chapel, Edinburgh*, by the Rev. Sydney Smith, A.M., and Fellow
of New College, Oxford. Edinburgh, 1800." The
book is dedicated to Lord Webb Seymour in the following terms :—

My Lord,—I dedicate these few sermons to you,
as a slight token of my great regard and respect,
because I know no man who, in spite of the disadvantages of high birth, lives to more honourable and
commendable purposes than yourself.

I am, my Lord, your most sincere well-wisher,

SYDNEY SMITH.

This was the first appearance of the name of Sydney
Smith in print, and the brief but vigorous preface to
the book opens with the following significant and
characteristic account of its origin :—" I wrote these
sermons in the exercise of my profession—to do good,
and for the same reason I make them public. That
they cannot do much I am well aware, because they
are hasty and imperfect specimens of an unpopular
species of composition. Some little good they may
do, and why should I give way to an immoral vanity,
and do nothing in my vocation, because I cannot do
much ? The sum of public opinion is made up of the
sentiments, as the sum of public revenue is from the
contributions, of individuals; and we become a rich or
a prudent nation, by adding together many trifling
quotas of wisdom and of gold."

The mere titles which follow evince the practical
character and comprehensive spirit of his ministry,
even at this early stage; whilst the sermons themselves

E

display the moral courage as well as the intellectual ability of the ex-curate of Nether Avon. It was, indeed, no easy task for any man to treat in the pulpit such subjects as the "Love of our Country," "Scepticism," the "Poor Magdalene," the "Best Mode of Charity," and "Predisposing Causes to the Reception of Republican Opinions," in a city like the Edinburgh of the end of last century, but Sydney Smith's success was immediate and unmistakable. One extract from a volume so little known, can here be scarcely out of place, especially as the subject is the "Love of our Country:"—"Christianity guides us to another world, by showing us how to act in this; in precepts more or less general, it enacts and limits every human duty. The world is the theatre where we are to show whether we are Christians in profession or in deed; and there is no action of our lives, which concerns the interests of others, in which we do not either violate or obey a Christian law. I cannot therefore illustrate a moral duty, without, at the same time, enforcing a precept of our religion. The love of our country has, in the late scenes which have been acted in the world, been so often made a pretext for bad ambition, and so often given birth to crude and ignorant violence, that many good men entertain no very great relish for the virtue, and some are, in truth, tired and disgusted with the very name of it; but this mode of thinking, though very natural, and very common, is, above all others, that which goes to perpetuate error in the world. If good men are to cherish in secret the ideas, that any theory of duties we owe to our country is romantic and absurd, because bad and foolish men have made it an engine of crime, or found it a source of error; if there is to be this constant action and reaction between extreme opinions; why, then the sentiments of mankind must be in eternal vibration between one error and another, and can never rest upon the middle point of truth. Let it be our pride to derive our principles, not from times and circumstances, but from reason and religion, and to struggle against that mixture of indolence and virtue which condemns the use, because it will not discriminate the abuse, which it abhors. In spite of the prostitution of this venerable name, there is, and there ever will be, a Christian patriotism, a great system of duties which man owes to the sum of human beings with whom he lives; to deny it is folly; to neglect it is crime." [9]

During his residence in Edinburgh, two important events took place in the life of Sydney Smith, the first of which was productive of personal happiness, and the second of public honour. The first of these events was his marriage; the second was the commencement of the *Edinburgh Review*.

In reference to the former, there is in truth but little to tell, little at least which concerns the world at large. It was in June 1800, and therefore after he had been in Scotland for two years, that Sydney Smith—then in his thirtieth year—paid a visit to England in order to be married. The lady—to whom he had been for some time betrothed—was Miss Catherine Amelia Pybus, of Cheam House, Cheam, Surrey, and she had been the friend from early girlhood of his sister, Maria. Miss Pybus was the daughter of the late John Pybus, Esq., of Cheam, and formerly of Greenhill Grove, in Herts.

[9] " Six Sermons preached in Charlotte Chapel, Edinburgh, by the Rev. Sydney Smith," pp. 9, 10.

Born in 1727, Mr. Pybus went to India, where he became a member of the Council of Madras. He was appointed ambassador to the King of Ceylon in 1762, and was the first Englishman received in a public capacity at that prince's court. Returning to England, after an honourable career in the East, he retired to Cheam, where he died in 1789. The monuments of the Pybus family may still be seen in the chancel of the parish church. No traditions of Sydney Smith, although he was a frequent visitor, linger around Cheam, and probably the only memorial of his presence there, beyond the entry of his marriage in the parish register, consists in the following epitaph, which he wrote on the occasion of one of his visits concerning Mrs. Pybus's favourite dog " Nick," which still may be read in the garden of Cheam House :—

POOR NICK.

Here lies poor Nick, an honest creature,
Of faithful, gentle, courteous nature ;
A parlour pet unspoil'd by favour,
A pattern of good dog behaviour.
Without a wish, without a dream
Beyond his home and friends at Cheam,
Contentedly through life he trotted
Along the path that fate allotted ;
Till time, his aged body wearing,
Bereaved him of his sight and hearing,
Then laid him down without a pain,
To sleep, and never wake again.

" Sydney Smith, Clerk, A.M. of New College, Oxford, and Catherine Amelia Pybus of this parish "— so runs the official record—" were married by licence on July 2nd, 1800, in the parish church of Cheam, by

Henry Peach, Rector." Mrs. Pybus had all along
entertained the highest regard for her future son-in-
law, and the union took place in her presence, and met
with her hearty approval. The brother of the young
lady, however, was not by any means so complaisant,
and appears to have imagined that his sister was
making an egregious blunder in consenting thus to
link her fortunes to those of a penniless and unknown
man. Mr. Charles S. Pybus (who was a Lord of the
Admiralty in the Pitt Administration, and at one time
member for Dover), behaved towards his sister in a
very ungracious way, and with something of the lofty
severity of an indignant parent. Fortunately, the
young lady had too much spirit and good sense to
sacrifice her own and her lover's happiness to her
dignified brother's opinions. "I was twenty-two,"
relates the bride-elect in a hitherto unpublished fragment, "and my mother said if I chose to forego the
comforts and luxuries to which I had been born, I
alone was to be the sufferer; and that of my ability to
decide upon that which would best constitute my
happiness there could be no more doubt than of my
right. She had but one wish—that I should be happy.
She had long known and loved Sydney, and if to
marry him was my resolve, she would not oppose it."
Sydney's bride brought him a modest dowry, and he
in turn flung into her lap his entire fortune, which
Lady Holland states consisted of "six small silver tea-
spoons, which from much wear had become the ghosts
of their former selves."

The prospects of the Edinburgh tutor and his young
bride were certainly the reverse of brilliant, and it
must be admitted that on strictly prudential and

worldly grounds, the friends of the lady concerned
were not far from the truth when they roundly asserted that she had not married to advantage. She,
however, was supremely happy in her new life, difficult
though at times it was, and gradually other people
grew more or less reconciled. It was a union which
brought with it peace and gladness, and the glimpses
we shall hereafter get of the cheerful and well-ordered
home of Sydney Smith, are enough to convince all but
the most hopelessly cynical that there are greater risks
in life than those which young people run when they
are rash enough to marry for love. One pleasing incident in reference to this important stage in his
career deserves honourable mention. Mr. Hicks-Beach,
duly grateful for his influence over Michael, came
gallantly to the help of the young couple, and made
two brave lovers profoundly grateful by the opportune
gift of a cheque for 750l. Thus, in spite of Mr. Charles
Pybus and his dismal prophecies, the course of true
love ran almost as smoothly as even Sydney himself
could have wished.

NETHER AVON CHURCH.

CHAPTER III.

1802.

Projection of the *Edinburgh Review*—Jeffrey, Horner, and Brougham:

" I HAVE a passionate love for common justice and for common sense," exclaimed Sydney Smith on one occasion, and he was now to prove before all the world the truth of that declaration. The *Edinburgh Review* was projected in the spring of 1802, and the first number appeared in the following October. In his own off-hand and easy fashion, he has described the origin of that memorable enterprise in words which have become historic :—" Towards the close of my residence in Edinburgh, Brougham, Jeffrey, and myself happened to meet in the eighth or ninth story or flat in Buccleuch Place, the then elevated residence of Mr. Jeffrey. I proposed that we should set up a Review. This was acceded to with acclamation. I was appointed editor, and remained long enough in Edinburgh to edit the first number of the Review. The motto I proposed for the Review was *Tenui musam meditamur avenâ*—' We cultivate literature on a little oatmeal.' But this was too near the truth to be admitted ; so we took our present grave motto from Publius Syrus, of whom none of us had, I am sure,

read a single line; and so began what has since turned
out a very important and able journal. When I left
Edinburgh it fell into the stronger hands of Lords
Jeffrey and Brougham, and reached the highest point
of popularity and success."[1] Even at the risk of being
charged with repeating a twice-told tale, it may not
be out of place to supplement Sydney Smith's account
of the commencement of the Review with the statements of the other two men chiefly concerned, Lord
Jeffrey and Lord Brougham.

Lord Jeffrey gave Dr. Robert Chambers in 1846 the
following account of his recollections of what took
place:—"I cannot say exactly where the project of
the *Edinburgh Review* was first talked of among the
projectors. But the first serious consultations about it
—and which led to our application to a publisher—were
held in a small house where I then lived in Buccleuch
Place. They were attended by S. Smith, F. Horner,
Dr. Thomas Brown, Lord Murray, and some of them
also by Lord Webb Seymour, Dr. John Thomson, and
Thomas Thomson. The first three numbers were
given to the publisher—he taking the risk and defray-
ing the charges. There was then no individual editor,
but as many of us as could be got to attend used to
meet in a dingy room of Willison's printing-office, in
Craig's Close, when the proofs of our own articles
were read over and remarked upon, and attempts made
also to sit in judgment on the few manuscripts which
were then offered by strangers. But we had seldom
patience to go through with this; and it was soon

[1] "Memoirs of the Rev. Sydney Smith," by Lady Holland,
chap. ii. p. 33.

found necessary to have a responsible editor, and the office was pressed upon me."[2]

Lord Brougham has also placed on record his impressions of what occurred :—"I can never forget Buccleuch Place, for it was there one stormy night in March 1802, that Sydney Smith first announced to me his idea of establishing a critical periodical, or review of works of literature and science. I believe he had already mentioned this to Jeffrey and Horner; but, on that night the project was for the first time seriously discussed by Smith, Jeffrey, and me. I at first entered warmly into Smith's scheme. Jeffrey—by nature always rather timid—was full of doubts and fears. It required all Smith's overpowering vivacity to argue and laugh Jeffrey out of his difficulties. There would, he said, be no lack of contributors. There was himself, ready to write any number of articles, and to edit the whole; there was Jeffrey, *facile princeps* in all kinds of literature; there was myself, full of mathematics, and everything relating to the colonies; there was Horner for political economy, and Murray for general subjects. Besides, might we not, from our great and never-to-be-doubted success, fairly hope to receive help from such leviathans as Playfair, Dugald Stewart, Thos. Brown, Thomson, and others? All this was irresistible, and Jeffrey could not deny that he had already been the author of many important papers in existing periodicals."[3]

These three statements, though they differ slightly

[2] "Chambers' Cyclopædia of English Literature," vol. ii. pp. 544, 545.

[3] "Memoirs of the Life and Times of Lord Brougham," vol. i. chap. iv. pp. 251, 252.

in detail, are not difficult to reconcile in more essential points. Lord Jeffrey always acknowledged that Sydney Smith was the first to suggest the idea of the *Edinburgh Review*, and Lord Brougham, in the passage just quoted, not only asserts that such was the case, but also mentions the precise occasion when the ex-curate of Nether Avon first made the proposal. Writing to Robert Chambers after the lapse of more than forty years, Jeffrey states distinctly that he was unable to recall the exact time when the idea was first mooted, though he had a vivid remembrance of the first "serious consultations" which were held to discuss Sydney Smith's proposal. Sydney Smith declared that he first made the suggestion that Jeffrey, Brougham, and himself should set up a review, at the house of the former in Buccleuch Place, at a *chance* meeting with his two friends there, towards the close of his stay in Edinburgh. Lord Brougham not only confirms this statement, but also mentions that it was on a "stormy night in March 1802," that Smith startled Jeffrey and himself with his bold suggestion. Lord Jeffrey, Lord Brougham, and Sydney Smith were, of course, the only three men who could speak with certainty on such a subject; and as Lord Jeffrey did not throw the slightest doubt on Sydney Smith's statement, but simply confessed his own inability —after nearly half a century had elapsed—to recall the precise occasion upon which the subject was first discussed, that statement, confirmed as it afterwards was in so circumstantial a manner by Lord Brougham, may be accepted as conclusive, so far at least as the actual projector of the Review is concerned, and the occasion and place where the idea was first conceived. Jeffrey's dedication of his selected essays to Sydney Smith, as the "projector" of the *Edinburgh Review*, is also worthy of passing notice in this connection.

There are two points, however, in which Sydney

18, BUCCLEUCH PLACE, EDINBURGH.

Smith's statement requires modification. The "eighth or ninth" story of Jeffrey's house in Buccleuch Place existed only in his lively imagination, as all who are acquainted with Edinburgh are perfectly aware; and the expression, "I was appointed editor," is also

slightly misleading. The house which Jeffrey occupied
was No. 18, Buccleuch Place, and his rooms—a handsome suite—were situated on the third floor, and there
seems reason to believe that in the dining-room to the
front, Sydney Smith first broached his scheme. Both
Jeffrey and Brougham have expressly stated that at
the outset there was no recognized editor; the whole
thing was only an experiment, and no such appointment was made until public approval had stamped
the enterprise with success. When the proposal,
however, first took shape, Sydney Smith, as the
originator of the scheme, was naturally appealed to
by his colleagues to read over the articles submitted,
and to see the introductory numbers safely through
the press. He accordingly revised in this informal
way the first articles, and then, on his removal to
London, Jeffrey was duly appointed, though not without
strong misgivings on his own part, to the post of
editor.

The first number of the *Edinburgh Review, or Critical
Journal*, appeared in October 1802, and Archibald
Constable and Co. were the publishers of it. The
contributors were accustomed to meet at Willison's
printing-office in Craig's Close, in the Canongate,
and the narrow, winding passage through which these
literary conspirators used one by one to disappear
remains unaltered. Archibald Constable married Miss
Mary Willison. "One of the trusty workmen of
the printing-office being sent with a sealed packet
of proof to a small lodging-house in the New Town,
was asked by the landlady if he could tell her anything about the lodgers she had got, for, said she,
they were all decent, well-behaved, sober men, but,

although they didn't sleep there, they 'keepit awfu'
unseasonable hours!'"[4] The group of friends entered
into an agreement, according to Lord Brougham, to
guarantee Constable four numbers "as an experiment."
The success, however, was immediate, and transcended
the wildest expectations of the most sanguine of the
contributors, and at one bound the experimental stage
of the enterprise was triumphantly passed. Three
editions were called for in rapid succession, and before
the fourth number was published a wide and reliable
demand was created. Whilst Sydney Smith, Francis
Horner, Henry Brougham, and Thomas Brown were
surprised and elated by the reception thus given to their
venture, Jeffrey, relates one of the group, was " utterly
dumbfounded, for he had predicted for our journal the
fate of the original *Edinburgh Review*, which, born in
1755, died in 1756, having produced only two numbers."[5] It is interesting to learn, on the authority of
Lord Brougham, that Sydney Smith contributed
eighteen articles to the first four numbers, whilst
Jeffrey was represented by sixteen, Horner by seven,
and Brougham himself by twenty-one. When their
venture appeared Francis Horner was preparing to
exchange Edinburgh for London, and the Scottish for
the English Bar, and in April 1803—just after the
third number was published—he carried this resolution
into effect. Sydney Smith followed Horner to the
south three months later, and thus, in nine months,
two of the four principal contributors had quitted

[4] "Old Edinburgh." By James Drummond, Esq., R.S.A.
[5] "Memoirs of the Life and Times of Lord Brougham," vol. i.
chap. iv. p. 253.

Edinburgh, and the burden of undivided responsibility fell upon Francis Jeffrey.

Soon after Horner left Edinburgh, Jeffrey wrote and informed him that Sydney Smith had persuaded Constable and Longman to give 50l. a number to the editor, and to pay 10l. a sheet for all the contributions which the said editor thought worth the money, and added that he felt inclined to accept the responsibility of the post:—"There are *pros* and *cons* in the case, no doubt. What the *pros* are I need not tell you. 300l. a year is a monstrous bribe to a man in my situation. The *cons* are vexation and trouble, interference with professional employment and character, and risk of general degradation. The first I have had some little experience of, and am not afraid for. The second, upon a fair consideration, I am persuaded I ought to risk." [a] The *Edinburgh Review*, Jeffrey declared, stood on two legs, one of which was literature, and the other politics.

It is easy enough to understand what Jeffrey means when he speaks in this connection of the probability of vexation and trouble, and "interference with professional employment;" but we need to remember the despised position of journalism at the beginning of the century before we can at all understand the dreaded opprobrium to which he alludes in the words, the "risk of general degradation;" to write for the press—at least when payment was expected—was regarded ninety or a hundred years ago as derogatory to a gentleman. Men of genius, such as Coleridge, Lamb, and Mackintosh, all of whom were on the staff of a single news-

"Life of Lord Jeffrey," vol. ii. p. 71.

paper, the *Morning Post*, were thus employed, but they recognized the influence of journalism, and bent their energies to its service, in defiance of the public opinion of their times. Writers in the press were regarded half with fear, and half with disdain; they had no acknowledged position in society, and their social claims were usually met with a contemptuous rejection. Even so late as 1808 the " Benchers of Lincoln's Inn made a bye-law excluding all persons who had written for the daily papers from being called to the Bar. More than twenty years afterwards a Lord Chancellor offended the propriety of his supporters, and excited their animadversions, by asking the editor of the *Times* to dinner. The press was regarded as a pestilent nuisance, which it was essential to destroy." [7] It is needless to say that a complete change has passed over public opinion since the time when Jeffrey felt that a " risk of degradation" was involved in the acceptance of an editor's position, and the highest personage in the realm might offer hospitality to a journalist to-day without any fear of hostile criticism. Some credit is due for this altered condition of things to Jeffrey himself, and the statement that he " invented the trade of editorship—before Jeffrey an editor was a bookseller's drudge; he is now a distinguished functionary" [8]—expresses the simple truth, and does no more than justice to the famous reviewer.

It was a fortunate circumstance, alike to Jeffrey and the *Edinburgh Review*, that their mutual friends were shrewd enough to place that bright, energetic, decisive

[7] Walpole's "History of England from the Conclusion of the Great War in 1815," chap. iv. p. 383.

[8] Bagehot's " Literary Studies," vol. i. p. 30.

little man in the editor's chair. He was exactly
the man for the place; and so well did he acquit
himself in it that for years it was next to impossible to
imagine that Jeffrey had existed before the *Edinburgh
Review*, or that the *Edinburgh Review* could exist after
Jeffrey.

It cannot, however, with truth be said that the lines
had fallen to him in pleasant places when the bold project of Sydney Smith suddenly revealed a wide and
influential sphere for the exercise of his powers.

Born in Edinburgh in 1773, and therefore the junior
by a couple of years of his clerical colleague, Francis
Jeffrey had obtained his early education at the High
School of his native city. From Edinburgh High
School he had passed as a lad of fifteen, to Glasgow
University, where he remained for two sessions, and
then returned to Edinburgh, to attend the law classes
of the University. In 1791 he proceeded to Queen's
College, Oxford, where he never really settled, and
only stayed nine months—a period long enough, however, according to Lord Holland, for the Edinburgh
callant to exchange " broad Scotch for narrow
English." In the summer of 1792, chagrined with his
Oxford experiences, he was again in Edinburgh, and
at the unusually early age of one-and-twenty he was
called to the Scotch Bar. His success as an advocate
during the next ten years of his life, was extremely
limited, and it was with difficulty that he was able to
keep poverty at arm's length. Happily, a resolute
young Scotchman of ordinary vigour can cultivate
law as well as literature on a little oatmeal, and
Jeffrey accordingly regarded his straitened circumstances as only a passing phase of existence, and one

from which by manly exertion he was bound, as soon as might be, to set himself free. In order to hasten the process he married, in 1801, his second cousin, Catherine, daughter of Dr. Wilson, Professor of Ecclesiastical History at St. Andrew's. " I am sensible we shall be very poor," he writes in August of the same year to his brother John, in America, " for I do not make 100*l.* a year by my profession. You would not marry in this situation ? Neither would I, if I saw any likelihood of its growing better before I was too old to marry at all. * * * Besides, we trust in Providence, and have hopes of dying before we get to prison." [9] Mrs. Jeffrey died in 1805, just as her husband's fame was becoming established, and his fight with fortune beginning to tell. After the lapse of eight years he married again, and his second wife, Miss Charlotte Wilkes, was an American lady, and the grandniece of the celebrated agitator, John Wilkes.

Sydney Smith was thirty-one ; Jeffrey, twenty-nine, Brougham, twenty-four, and Horner the same age, when the *Edinburgh* under their united inspiration launched out into the deep, and began its long struggle with political and social injustice. We who breathe the free political atmosphere of to-day, and move in the midst of its generous social life, are more indebted to that little group of workers for the cleansed and quickened condition of the once turbid and sluggish current of national thought, than perhaps we are usually inclined to admit. During the first twenty years of its existence—no brief term in the career of magazine or mortal—the *Edinburgh Review* owed its ever-widening

[9] " Life of Lord Jeffrey," by Henry, Lord Cockburn, vol. ii. p. 57.

influence chiefly to the patient ability and skilful management of Francis Jeffrey, and the brilliant wit and bold freedom of speech of Sydney Smith.

There can be no question that Jeffrey worked in season and out for the *Review*, and did more than any other man to bring and keep it to the front of the best thought of the day. He possessed a calm confidence in himself and in the infallibility of his own literary and social judgments which sufficed to shield him from many an anxious hour. Like Lord John Russell, there was literally " nothing that he would not undertake," and linked to this miraculous power to write at demand with an appearance of profundity on all things under the sun, there was also a wonderful degree of tact, and an instinctive perception of character about the " arch-critic " which enabled him to handle with ease all sorts of men, from the irascible and erratic Harry Brougham to the austere and uncompromising Thomas Carlyle. One of the most striking pen-and-ink sketches of Lord Jeffrey which has been given to the present generation is that which Carlyle has bequeathed to the world in the pages of his " Reminiscences;" it would have been equally interesting had Jeffrey left as minute a description of his first impressions of the stalwart if sombre young man who strode into his office armed with Procter's introduction. During the first seven years of his connection with the *Review*, Jeffrey contributed on an average no less than three or four articles to each number ; and during the entire seven-and-twenty years to which his editorship extended he may be said to have written an article for it once in every five weeks. His mode of dealing with the thousand-and-one

topics which in turn engaged his nimble pen was
frequently brilliant, and usually adroit and skilful.
He possessed the happy art of being brief without
being obscure, and few men knew better how to
present the pith of even a bulky or elaborate book,
well within the narrow limits prescribed by the
patience of an indolent reader. Sensible, shrewd,
matter-of-fact, Jeffrey admired precision of thought
and clearness of statement, and grew restless and
uneasy whenever such qualities were denied him. He
liked explicit statements, and felt almost aggrieved
when called to deal with vague aspirations. The
mystical and symbolical aspects of existence lay in a
cloud-capped region of thought to which his spirit
was not sufficiently adventurous to climb.

It need not therefore excite surprise that Jeffrey—
who though a genial man was often a savage critic—
should have written with open scorn the memorable
words, "This will never do," when William Wordsworth
brought the "harvest of a quiet eye," and the rich
treasures of a deeply spiritual and imaginative nature,
and sought the verdict of the great reviewer on his
work. Wordsworth had long noticed and deplored
the lack of sympathy displayed in popular literature
with the ordinary events of life and the common
tasks of men, as well as the wide-spread neglect
of the familiar beauties of the external universe.
Wisely reluctant himself to tread any longer in the
"quiet footsteps of custom," the poet struck out
a path of his own, and was Quixotic enough to run
full tilt against popular taste and the recognized
way of looking at things. But as few men, according to Sydney Smith, possess original eyes and

ears, the majority are apt to resent any rash or violent
departure from accepted canons of taste or ancient
landmarks of opinion. The "Lyrical Ballads" accordingly, notwithstanding the genius of Wordsworth
and Coleridge, made little impression on the public
mind, and were regarded indeed .in many quarters
with a feeling difficult to distinguish from disdain.
Wordsworth's fidelity to Nature offended a generation
of readers who had been trained in an entirely different
school, and the *Edinburgh Review* gave an exaggerated
utterance to the prevailing dissatisfaction.

Jeffrey could not appreciate the mystic element which
pervaded the thought of the Lake School; he knew
nothing about the oversoul with which Wordsworth
held rapt communion as he wandered along the glittering, fern-fringed shore, or roamed through the
eafy woods, or climbed the mountain's purple brow.
The poet dwelt apart with Nature, and she allured
him and spoke to him comfortable words, and told
him those secrets which she entrusts to her lovers
alone; and thus there was nothing from the daisy's
"star-shaped shadow on the naked stone" to the
"light of setting suns" in all her glorious teaching
which missed the way to that reverent and receptive
heart. Jeffrey, however, failed to see, as he sat in his
Edinburgh office, the use of all this fuss and rapture over field-flowers and vernal woods, and rustic
children. And so exclaiming, "This will never do!"
he kicked, as he supposed, the new poet back into
oblivion; and the public, who understood Jeffrey's
philippic much better than Wordsworth's poetry,
overjoyed at the vigorous skill with which the exploit
was accomplished, clapped its foolish hands in merry
approbation. But if Jeffrey was put out, Wordsworth

was not, and, strong in the consciousness of his high vocation and his own **power to fill it**, he went back silently to seclusion, and patiently pursued his mission, sustained by prophetic visions of a triumph he felt sure would ultimately come. When the " Excursion " was published in 1814, Jeffrey returned with characteristic energy to his old task, and presently began to boast with short-sighted complacency that his strictures in the *Edinburgh* had " crushed " the new poem. But there were wiser men in the United Kingdom, in such matters at least, than even this miraculous editor; and one of them, Robert Southey by name, exclaimed with generous warmth and scorn, " Jeffrey crush the ' Excursion ' ! Tell him he might as well hope to crush Skiddaw ! "

Jeffrey, however, could mete out praise as well as censure; and, whatever his opinions were, the honesty with which he held them was as little open to question as the courage with which he avowed them. Not a few of his *ex cathedra* judgments have been reversed by the wider light and more exact knowledge of a subsequent period; but he still stands at the head of his order as a representative man, and is justly regarded as one of the most able, independent, and fearless of critics which English literature has seen.

Francis Horner, the son of an Edinburgh merchant, was born in that city in 1778. Like most lads of the same rank, he was sent to the High School, and proceeded as a mere boy to the University, where he remained until he was seventeen. As he was ambitious to follow the law, and displayed sufficient aptitude to encourage the hope that he might devote himself to it with at least average success, his father placed him under the care of a private tutor at

Shacklewell, in Middlesex ; and after a residence of
two years in England, he returned to Edinburgh in
the autumn of 1797, and began to study equity
with Henry Brougham, and metaphysics and political
economy with Lord Webb Seymour.   Two years later,
when Sydney Smith arrived in Edinburgh as tutor to
young Beach, Horner was already regarded as a man
of singular promise, but his professional advancement
was blocked by the ascendency of the Dundas party,
which looked with jealous and unfriendly eyes on all
men who dared to speak their mind freely in bold and
independent tones, on the grave political questions of
the hour.

The chief facts in Francis Horner's brief but brilliant life are soon told.   Driven in disgust from the
Scottish Courts by the rampant Toryism which prevailed and the sycophancy it induced, Horner trans-
ferred his abilities to London in the spring of 1803,
and was cordially welcomed by many members of
the English Bar.   Sir James Mackintosh, Sir Samuel
Romilly, and Mr. Ward, were among the first to extend the right hand of fellowship to the reserved
but able young Scotchman who now appeared in
their midst.   Horner quickly established himself in
his profession, and justified the generous reception he
had received.   His mastery of financial questions was
so conspicuous, that he was selected as a member of
the Board of Commissioners appointed by the East
India Company for the settlement of the Nabob of
Arcot's debts.   In 1806, through the instrumentality
of Lord Henry Petty, he entered the House of Commons as member for St. Ives, and made steady and
swift progress towards distinction in his new career.
Four years after he entered Parliament, he moved for

OF THE REV. SYDNEY SMITH.

an inquiry into an alleged depreciation of the currency, and in 1811 he was elected a member of the Bullion Committee, and by his remarkable speeches in the House during the debates which followed, he stepped at once into the rank of an authority on that and kindred subjects; and, according to Lord Campbell, he was the first man in England to make the doctrines of political economy intelligible to the House of Commons.[1] Year by year his influence with the aristocratic Whig party rapidly increased, and upon the news of his untimely death in 1817, Parliament suspended its sittings, and voted to his memory a monument in Westminster Abbey. Horner was only thirty-eight at the time of his death, and he rose from obscurity to a position of national importance and honour by the force of his intrinsic merits alone. His premature death was universally deplored, and was looked upon as a public calamity, and probably no young statesman of the Nineteenth century disappeared from the scene of his triumphs, amid more general expressions of deep feeling, until, a generation later, England was called to mourn once more the bright hopes which were extinguished in the early grave of Charles Buller.

The friendship which sprang up between Francis Horner and Sydney Smith at the period of their early struggles was one which grew more intimate and tender with the lapse of each succeeding year. The two men met for the last time in the autumn of 1816, immediately after Horner—far in advance of public opinion—had made his final great speech in Parliament in favour of the recognition of the

[1] "Lives of the Chancellors," vol. viii. Lord Brougham, chap. ii. p. 263.

Catholic claims. With the hand of death upon him, he had gone down to Foston to pay a farewell visit to his old comrade in arms before setting out on that melancholy journey to Pisa, from which he was destined never to return. Sydney Smith was deeply touched with the care-worn and wasted aspect of his friend; but states that even then " there was in his look a calm, settled love of all that was honourable and good—an air of wisdom and sweetness." A few months later, when the blow fell, he told Mr. Leonard Horner, that he did not remember any misfortune of his life which he had felt so keenly as the death of his brother, and added, " I never saw any man who combined together so much talent, worth, and warmth of heart." [2]

As a contributor to the *Review*, Horner never could dash off an article with the bold vigour of Jeffrey or the brilliant ease of Sydney Smith. He worked with great deliberation; he bent over his sentences with patient care; he selected his words with painstaking and often fastidious nicety; his disquisitions smell of the lamp, and suggest the effort they are known to have cost. Horner's knowledge, whilst not in any department profound, was at the same time extensive and exact, and his judgment was remarkably sound. His contributions added a great deal of sober, intellectual strength to the opening numbers of the *Edinburgh Review*, and there was a comprehensive and statesman-like grasp of principles in the views he enunciated on all questions of national policy, which seldom failed to arrest marked public attention.

Henry Brougham, on the other hand, the last in the

[2] " Memoir of the Rev. Sydney Smith," chap. vii. p. 120.

foremost group of Edinburgh reviewers, wrote with
extreme rapidity. His quickness was proverbial, and
he was able to concentrate the whole force of his intellect into the task of the passing hour, and to banish
from his mind with enviable facility all that stood
between him and the conclusion of his work. But if
he was swift, he was the reverse of sure, and was precisely the kind of contributor, provokingly clever and
provokingly fickle—"ill to hae, but waur to want"—
to throw an overwrought editor into despair. Born
in Edinburgh, in the same year as Horner, Brougham's
career extended to more than half a century beyond
the date of his colleague's death. He left the High
School dubbed "prodigy"—a dangerous compliment
in itself, and one which has often retarded less capable
men in their after-endeavours to achieve success. The
reputation of a prodigy remained with Lord Brougham
through life, and in his case its constant application
was justified by the almost unlimited range of his
accomplishments. The work which he mastered when
in the fulness of his fame and strength dazzled his
contemporaries, and seemed to justify the bold paradox
that the more busy a man is, the more leisure he
possesses. "Take it to that fellow Brougham; he
has time for everything!" exclaimed Sir Samuel
Romilly, when requested on one occasion to edit a
forthcoming book.

There seemed, indeed, no bounds to his energy, and
scarcely any to the half-savage impetuosity of his
spirit. In a well-known and extremely clever pen-
and-ink sketch, Maclise has portrayed Brougham as
he appeared in 1834. The restless orator, fresh from
the Lords, is discovered in his chambers, in dishevelled
wig and gown, whilst the clock is on the stroke of

three, hard at work with bent head and flying quill, on
a caustic leader for the *Times*, on the subject of last
night's debate.   Lord Holland once assured Brougham
that he believed that if a new language was discovered
in the morning, he would be able to talk it before
night; and his rival, Lord Campbell, was accustomed
to declare that if Harry Brougham was locked up in
the Tower for a year without a single book, the twelve
months would not roll past ere he had written au
encyclopædia.   Indeed, the impression Brougham
made upon friends and foes alike for aptitude in the
acquisition of knowledge, and versatility in its pursuit,
appears only to have been paralleled in recent years by
that exhibited by M. Guizot, of whom it used to be
said that the knowledge which he had gained in the
morning, he repeated in the afternoon with the air of
a man who had known it from all eternity.   His
vigorous and masculine sense was always at the call
of human freedom, education, and enlightenment; and
if there was much to blame, there was also much to
pity, and still more to respect and admire in the
strange character and stormy career of Henry, Lord
Brougham and Vaux.   The great ability and versatile
accomplishments of Brougham were freely drawn upon
by Jeffrey during the period in which the *Edinburgh Review* won reputation in the long and gallant
contest which it consistently waged against every form
of social and political injustice.

   When we recollect that Lord Brougham was unquestionably one of the ablest and most gifted men
the century has seen, and that his public life, moreover,
was so protracted that young men hardly out of their
teens can recall hearing him speak, it is difficult to
credit the fact that his career as a cabinet minister

had terminated for ever before the death of William IV.
Lord Brougham, unfortunately for himself and for his
country, was blessed with neither reserve nor discretion; he lacked self-control, and was at once too
rash for a leader and too imperious for a partisan.
Arrogant in manner, capricious in temper, and violent
in speech; admired, feared, and shunned; he drifted
rapidly out of the main stream of national life, and
falsified to a deplorable extent the great but just
expectations which his extraordinary powers had done
so much to raise in the common heart of the nation.

CRAIG'S CLOSE, EDINBURGH.

CHAPTER IV.

1798—1803.

Life in Edinburgh as Tutor, Preacher, and Reviewer.

THE remarkable influence which the *Edinburgh Review*
succeeded in gaining was chiefly due to the needs of
the hour, and the fact that the pens of Jeffrey, Horner,
Brougham, and Sydney Smith were enlisted at the
outset, and that its intellectual prowess was augmented
from time to time by such distinguished recruits as
Scott, Carlyle, and Macaulay. These, together with
scores of able men less known to fame, gave the " Buff
and Blue" a position of singular authority in the
political and literary life of the period. Its appearance
was hailed by the friends of progress throughout the
length and breadth of the land, as a cheering sign of
the times, and the decided liberality of its tone infused
fresh courage into the breasts of the despised and
almost discomfited advocates of reform. Questions
which had long lain dormant in men's minds leaped to
the light of public discussion, and the scattered and
broken ranks of the opponents of intolerance and
oppression were reunited for a more vigorous struggle
under the standard which had thus unexpectedly been
uplifted in their midst. " It is impossible," is the

testimony of the friend and biographer of Jeffrey, "for those who did not live at the time, and in the heart of the scene, to feel, or almost to understand, the impression made by the new luminary, or the anxieties with which its motions were observed. * * * The learning of the new journal, its talent, its spirit, its writing, its independence, were all new; and the surprise was increased by a work so full of public life springing up suddenly in a remote part of the kingdom. The effect was electrical."[1]   Jeffrey himself was at first by no means sanguine as to the wisdom of the resolution which had been carried with acclamation over the supper-table in Buccleuch Place, and even on the eve of publication he seems to have dreaded that they had missed the opportune moment and lost the tide that was in their favour.   "We are bound for a year to the booksellers, and shall drag through that, I suppose, for our own indemnification," was his rather dreary and not reassuring statement to an anxious friend.[2]   But the success of the *Review* in spite of such gloomy forebodings, was not only immediate, but went far out beyond the dreams of the most sanguine of its promoters.   Another and more favourable opportunity will occur in the course of this narrative for an estimate of Sydney Smith's share in the work which was thus begun; meanwhile, however, a passing glimpse in this connection at the nature of the gifts which he brought to the common enterprise may not be out of place.

Sydney Smith did not possess the analytical skill of

[1] "Life of Lord Jeffrey," vol. i. p. 131, by Henry, Lord Cockburn.
[2] Ibid., vol. i. p. 120.

Jeffrey, nor the philosophic grasp of Horner, nor the powerful invective of Brougham, but in his own way he was inimitable, and had nothing to fear by a comparison with the most distinguished of his colleagues. In actual knowledge both of literature and the world, Jeffrey was certainly his superior, and probably both Brougham and Horner out-distanced him in this respect; but he possessed in the quality and scope of his native powers a splendid recompense. If it is the perfection of art to conceal art, the art of Sydney Smith approached very nearly to that climax. A master of clear statement, his style is brilliant and yet familiar ; and, whilst singularly bold and adventurous, is marked by great beauty and an unfailing grace of expression. His sentences revive the attention of the most listless, and brighten the dullest eye, not only through their fresh and unconventional structure, but because they are weighted with wisdom and winged with wit. Simple but original, imaginative and yet practical, homely and yet humorous, his writings carry their own credentials, and successfully appeal—with a happy absence of effort—to all sorts and conditions of men, and are, indeed, what Lord Lyttleton once aptly described them, a " most exquisite contribution to the innocent gaiety of mankind."

He was intrepid and unflinching in his investigation of alleged abuses of all kinds, and throughout a protracted career he waged bold and successful warfare— often single-handed—against bigotry, hypocrisy, and superstition. His mind moved quickly, and by his extraordinary insight and powers of expression, he was able to compel everything he handled to reveal itself to the public gaze in what he believed to be its true colours. The reader of to-day who turns to refresh his mind with the mischievous sallies and sparkling common sense of Sydney Smith, hardly knows which to admire most—his vivacity or his vigour, and is equally delighted with the spontaneous flow of his humour and the honesty of purpose by which it is directed and curbed. His humour was genial, frolicsome, and healthy; it ran like a golden thread through all his articles, and lit up in the most unexpected manner subjects of the driest kind, and arguments of the most recondite description. His style is so clear and crisp that he who runs may read, and his illustrations are so felicitous that all who read must laugh. Although his judgment was not by any means infallible, nor his prejudices small, he was as fearless a man as ever held a pen, and there is no exaggeration in saying that he employed it through long years of influence and power to arouse and enlighten public opinion, and to create in the minds of men a sentiment generous to virtue, hostile to vice, and fatal to oppression.

Like Jeffrey, the "master critic," as he styled him, Sydney Smith, the "journeyman critic," as he termed himself, had no love for abstract theories or vague speculations, and tedious inquiries and protracted debates inspired him with undisguised dismay. He liked to get to the point of a question as rapidly as possible, and, having done so, he expressed the result tersely and clearly in words which "stuck and stayed." It is always a pleasure, if one is interested at least in the work which is going forward, to hear the sound of a hammer when every blow strikes the nail on the head, and that is precisely the sensation which a friend of progress obtains from a perusal of Sydney Smith's spirited and generous pages. He laboured in the common cause of liberty and truth in an uncommon way, for he seemed to see at a glance conclusions which less gifted mortals took half a lifetime to discover. With a stroke of that wonderful pen, he was able to coin his opinion into some happy phrase which took the world by storm, and revealed as much to the multitude about the question in hand as a regiment of scholars could have explained in a week. Many a worn commonplace, moreover, renewed its youth, and went on its way rejoicing in the magic transformation accomplished on its behalf, by his extraordinary powers of expression. He appeared to take every one into his confidence, and to address the reader with the perfectly natural and unembarrassed manner of a man who is talking to his familiar friend. People turn to a book of his expecting to be confronted merely with the arguments and opinions of an author, but after they have read a few pages, they discover to their surprise that they have stumbled into the company of a friend. Like all frank people, Sydney Smith has been a good deal misunderstood, and his fearless honesty and candour have been turned into weapons against himself.

It must, of course, be admitted not only that his judgment was sometimes in error, but also that he was a man who never approached certain subjects without displaying the fact that his mind was warped, so far as they were concerned, by invincible prejudice. But although he completely misunderstood the Wesleyan Revival, and grossly caricatured the splendid efforts of the Nonconformist churches of this land to awaken the religious enthusiasm of the people in the work of

Foreign Missions, it cannot be questioned, in spite of such blemishes on his reputation, that his influence as a whole was given steadily and at much personal cost to the advocacy of the very principles of liberty and toleration which have now triumphed to such an extent that his own essays on the Dissenters and their Missionary schemes, are little more than a magazine of exploded fallacies, and read like the records of an archaic period. Sydney Smith misunderstood the evangelical enthusiasm, and refused to separate the chaff of fanaticism from the wheat of self-sacrifice, but his sweeping tirades have long since been refuted by experience, and aggressive work in heathen lands forms now a recognized sphere of activity amongst Christians of every shade of conviction, and—judged by its fruits—is unassailable.

Not unfrequently, moreover, people have spoken and written of Sydney Smith in a semi-patronizing strain as only a jester; and it has almost seemed at times, to those who knew him intimately, as if the brilliancy of his wit had obscured to no small extent the general appreciation of his wisdom and his worth. It is a cherished fallacy with multitudes to imagine that a witty man is always shallow, and Sydney himself was not blind to that fact, for he has declared that the "moment an envious pedant sees anything written with pleasantry he comforts himself that it must be superficial."[3] Perhaps the tears of merry laughter for which he is himself responsible, have blinded even generous eyes to the moral no less than the intellectual stature of an author who habitually used ridicule as a weapon against wrong. Often in

[3] *Edinburgh Review*, vol. xvi. p. 186.

G

this dull world a specially capable man gains a reputation for wit at the expense of one for wisdom, and there are in society at all times, a number of persons who are dense enough to regard a humourist, however subtle or sagacious, as only a kind of educated buffoon, or a modern representative of the court fool of former ages. Unfortunately, however, for the credit of humanity, there are in every circus more clowns outside the ring than within it, and in every theatre— even when the audience is "most select"—there are more knaves present than those who bear that character upon the stage. Sydney Smith often shocked weak and silly people, unable to understand a joke, and held in bondage by extreme notions of propriety and decorum; but all who were able to judge righteous judgment were not slow to discern the earnest moral purpose and wholesome nature of much of his bold and outspoken satire. His wit was indeed but the vehicle for his wisdom, and the aim of his triumphant laughter was itself the best evidence of his commanding common sense. His dreaded powers of ridicule and sarcasm were employed to drive home his argument, and they never appeared without a purpose, and seldom disappeared before they had accomplished it; and their exercise was softened by kindliness of disposition, and restrained by religious principle.

Every one is aware that some of the happiest jokes of Sydney Smith were directed against his own order, but they were concerned with ecclesiastical subjects rather than with anything more sacred. If there was satire in these playful allusions, it was aimed at sins of omission and commission in the ranks of the clergy, which not even the most zealous partisan would dare to defend. Men who scoffed at religion were utterly repugnant to Sydney Smith; in their presence his mirth vanished, and if his wit flashed out for a moment, it was only to assail so unpardonable an offender. There is a story told of a dinner-party at Holland House, at which one of the guests, who had been loudly boasting that he believed in nothing, suddenly fell into a gourmand's rapture over a dainty dish, and asked for another helping of it. "Ah," said Sydney in his driest tones, "I am glad to see that Mr. —— at all events believes in —— the cook!"[4]

In one of the early note-books of Sydney Smith (placed through the kindness of his grand-daughter, Miss Holland, at the disposal of the writer) occurs a short essay which was apparently written during his residence in Edinburgh; and as it is believed that it has not hitherto seen the light, its introduction here may interest many, especially as its theme is one on which he was so well qualified to speak. It bears the somewhat ambitious title of a "Treatise on Wit and Humour," and it is interesting not only in itself, but as the germ of the later reflections on the same subject which were given to the world during the delivery of his Lectures on Moral Philosophy.

A Treatise on Wit and Humour.

Wit is an act of intellectual power evinced in discovering relations between ideas which excite surprise, and surprise only. The pleasure we derive from wit proceeds from our surprise, and at the skill of the discoverer. Surprise is an essential ingredient

---

[4] "Holland House," by the Princess Marie Liechtenstein, chap. iv. p. 102.

of wit, for wit will not bear repetition. We may derive pleasure from repeating to others that wit which first excited our surprise, but this is a pleasure of a very different nature; the sudden joy, the flash of astonishment cannot be re-kindled in our minds, however delighted we may be in witnessing the same excitement in the minds of others. The greater the surprise, the greater the pleasure. Wit is always enlivened not only when no relation is expected between those ideas in which a relation has been discovered, but when it appears to us that the ideas are completely disconnected together, and that they can have no positive relation. Voltaire was praising Haller to a Swiss gentleman. "I am astonished," said the Swiss, "you should speak so well of Haller, for he is outrageous in his abuse of you." "Well, well," replied Voltaire, "I believe the truth is, we have both formed very erroneous notions of each other." Here surprise is excited by the connection discovered between the apparent candour and the real severity of Voltaire. We expect from the first physiognomy of the answer that he is going to say something kind and conciliatory of his enemy, when at the same moment he overwhelms him with the keenest satire. Boileau and his brother were talking over their comparative advantages and disadvantages in life. "I will confess, however, my dear Abbé," said Boileau, "one instance in which fortune has been kindest to you; in point of brothers, you have decidedly the advantage of me. In that respect there can be no sort of comparison between us." Here the surprise is excited by finding that the apparent concession of the poet is a real superiority claimed; we expected a connection between the admission of Boileau and his own inferiority of condition; we find exactly the contrary. The surprise, therefore, is always increased when the notion of a disconnection between the ideas is excited and a connection discovered; or, on the contrary, when the notion of a connection is excited, and a disconnection discovered.

When the surprise excited by the discovery of a new relation between ideas is mingled with any other strong feeling than surprise—when great terror, when strong approbation are excited by the discovery—then the sensation of wit is almost entirely lost, and merges into the stronger accompanying sensations. Sir Isaac Newton discovered a new relation between water and the diamond. When the mind first perceives their affinity to each other in their mode of refracting light and their combustibility, the first sensation excited has some faint analogy to that of wit, but the great approbation of the genius of the discoverer, and a strong sense of the utility and importance of such discoveries, mingle themselves with the feeling of surprise, and the whole effect upon the mind is very different from that of a mere witty relation of ideas. In looking over the various parts of a steam-engine, the mind is repeatedly affected by sensations resembling those of wit— the mode in which the valves open and shut; the connection between the centrifugal force and the slow and quiet motion of the machine in that part called the regulator, are sensations very analogous to those of wit; but at the same moment we begin to speculate upon the importance of the discovery, to reason upon its utility, and the sensation of surprise no longer remains pure and unmixed. In the mind of a child capable of understanding these mechanical discoveries,

the unexpected relation between the parts and movements would excite nearly the same feelings as wit
would do; he would enjoy the pure surprise, and
speculate little, or not at all, upon the matter.

The relationship which existed between Sydney
Smith and Michael Beach in Edinburgh partook rather
of the nature of an intimate friendship than of anything more formal. Sydney Smith treated his companion more as a younger brother than a pupil, and
so fully did he enter into the enjoyments, as well as
the studies of the youth under his charge, that he
quickly secured his affection, as well as his respect.
Two or three letters written at this period by him,
to his old friends at Nether Avon House, reveal not
only the manner of life of the young squire, but also
afford a passing glimpse of events which were happening
in the great world around.

[VI.]   38, South Hanover Street, **Edinburgh,**
                         4th November, 1798.

MY DEAR SIR,—We are all extremely well, and
Michael and myself are very good friends. The courier
is amazingly admired by the Scotch maid-servants,
and takes great pains about his hair, &c. He is an
excellent servant, and saves me a world of trouble.
I congratulate you most sincerely upon our change of
situation for the better. Ireland safe, and Buonaparte
embayed in Egypt, that is surrounded by Beys.
That we should sit under our vines and fig-trees in
safety, I do not expect, for that very excellent reason,
that we have none to sit under; but that we shall sit
round our beef and puddings in security again, I think
there is a very fair reason to expect. This place grows

upon us both, we are **extremely** comfortably situated, and have thoughts of never coming back. We are very much obliged **to you for the** papers which give us a little county intelligence from time to time; of course there **is** no such thing in Edinburgh as an English county newspaper. Some of the French officers are **come here** captured by Captain Moore, **with them is a lady in** blue silk pantaloons, who, I **suppose, was to be the new Queen of Ireland.** My best **regards to Mrs. Beach, and** believe me, my dear sir, yours most sincerely,

SYDNEY SMITH.

To Mr. Beach.

The year 1798 was a critical and anxious period for the English Government ; **for** there were troubles at home as well as abroad, and the Society **of** United Irishmen, led by **a** barrister **of** revolutionary sympathies, was endeavouring, **with** the aid of French bayonets, **to** establish an **Irish** Republic. When Sydney Smith wrote the above letter in November **of** that year, **the fierce** and lawless insurrection **of the** peasantry had been crushed, **and** the **French** invasion under Hoche repelled ; but, **although** Ireland was " safe," and " Buonaparte embayed in **Egypt,"** and the services of the lady in " **blue silk pantaloons** " were no longer needed in British domains, Ireland probably was never more nearly lost to the English crown.

In speaking of their own private affairs, he informs **Mr. Beach** not only that his pupil and himself **are** very much at home in Edinburgh, but also that **so far** as their residence at 38, South Hanover Street is concerned, they **are** " **extremely** comfortably situated." Almost, however, **before this** epistle had time to reach its destination the writer's tranquillity was rudely dis-

turbed. For, with the approach of winter, an invasion
of Edinburgh took place of a very harmless but
annoying kind, and Sydney Smith has related, in a
well-known letter (which was first published in Lady
Holland's "Memoir," and is reproduced in these pages
in facsimile from the original document, through
the kindness of Sir Michael Hicks-Beach), his first
acquaintance with the horrors of a state of siege.

He remained "lord of the castle" until the following May, when he came back to England for the
summer vacation with his pupil; on their return to
Scotland, however, in the autumn of 1799, acting on
the principle of once bitten, twice shy, they made, as
we have already seen, 19, Queen Street their temporary
home. Writing to Mrs. Beach to inform her as to
the time of their journey south, he expresses his regret
at the illness of a lady—one of his former parishioners
at Nether Avon—and adds some general reflections
concerning the courage of women, which most people
will probably be inclined, from their own observation
of character, to endorse.

[VII.]   38, South Hanover Street, Edinburgh,
                             February 21st, 1799.

MY DEAR MADAM,—In May, then, you may expect
to see my goodly personage, with Michael at my heels,
and you will find us both, I daresay, as we are at this
moment, plump, and in good condition. I am sorry
to hear that poor Miss D—— still continues so ill.
The termination of her life, I hope, will be pleasant
and serene, the opening of it has been much otherwise. Yet she seems to bear it extremely well. I
have always said that the heroism and courage of men
is nothing in comparison with these qualities as they

are developed in women. Women cannot face danger
accompanied with noise and smoke and hallooing, but
in all kinds of severe peril and quiet horrors they have
infinitely more philosophical endurance than men.
Put a woman in a boat in a boisterous sea, let six or
seven people make as much noise as they can, and she
is in a state of inconceivable agony. Ask the same
woman on a serene summer evening to drink a cup of
poison for some good which would accrue from it to
her husband and children, and she will swallow it like
green tea. Your character of the Swiss philosopheress[5]
sounds wells. I should like to see her; you know
what a coxcomb I am about physiognomy.

Believe me, dear madam, yours very sincerely,

SYDNEY SMITH.

To Mrs. Beach.

The progress made by his son in his studies was duly
reported from time to time to the squire of Nether
Avon, and every now and then the tutor's wit flashes
out in the most unexpected way. " Michael," thus
he reports in the spring of 1799, " has been learning
to draw for some time. He makes horses and ducks
and trees with Indian ink, as other people do; but I
am, unfortunately, no sort of judge of Indian ink
ducks, though a connoisseur in that species of the
animal so admirably adapted for roasting."

Soon after their arrival in Scotland, Sydney Smith
and his pupil made a short tour in the Highlands
before settling down to their first winter's work in
Edinburgh. They greatly enjoyed this excursion, and
as the summer of 1799 drew on they longed to explore

---

[5] A new governess which Mrs. Beach had just obtained for her
daughters.

some other portion of the country, and eventually they determined, with the sanction of Mr. and Mrs. Beach, to make a tour in Wales before returning to Williamstrip. The pleasure of their former holiday had been lessened by the insecure and draughty condition of the carriages in which they had travelled, and the following amusing letter was despatched to Mrs. Beach, in the immediate prospect of their journey, to beg a favour, which was promptly granted.

[VIII.]   38, South Hanover Street,
                                          May 5th, 1799.

MY DEAR MADAM,—Michael and myself both join in asking a favour of Mr. Beach. We found the inconveniences so extremely great, from not having a carriage with us, that we wish to hire one for the time of our excursion. You are not to form your ideas of chaises in Scotland and the North of England from what you see in the south. The chance is of not getting them at all, or getting them in so mutilated a state that it is not only discreditable and inconvenient, but positively unsafe to ride in them. We were put into chaises with half a bottom, with no glasses to the windows and fastenings to the door, and not unfrequently might have been taken for a party of united Scotchmen on our road to Newgate. I really think, if Mr. Beach could have seen our equipage, he would himself have proposed what we are now requesting. We are all in high spirits to-day at the defeat of the French, an event as unexpected as it is important, for the nearer any nation is pushed to the extremity of its resources, the more critical is any defeat which they may sustain. God send it may be completely true, and well followed up by a numerous progeny of victories. Will you present my best regards to Mr. Beach? and believe me, my dear Madam, most sincerely yours,

SYDNEY SMITH.

The journey through Wales was successfully accomplished, and proved most interesting, and at its close Sydney Smith and his pupil parted, until autumn found them once more together on their way to the north. The following letter belongs to this period, and was written to Michael Beach, in answer to one received from him, in which he gave an account of his holiday doings. There is no date nor heading to the original letter; it was evidently an enclosure in one to Mr. Beach, as it is directed simply " Michael."

[IX.]

MY DEAR COMRADE,—Your friendly letter gave me great pleasure, as it convinced me you were neither forgetful of me, nor of the advice I have taken the liberty of giving you. * * * I shudder, my dear Michael, when I reflect from what you have escaped. Dance at Cheltenham in a pepper-and-salt coat? Do you consider that any two justices might have prosecuted you, and that the law must have taken its course? The papers to-day promise us a new revolution at Paris, but revolutions seem to be as natural to that government as to the heavenly bodies, and I no more augur the dissolution of the one than the other from this cause. Is the wood house begun? You should first recollect exactly the pattern of the house you saw at Lord Douglas's, and then proceed to execute it, which I think may be amusing enough for the summer months. My masterly taste indeed you will want, but figure to yourself, as well as you can,

everything I should advise, and then act directly the
contrary, and by this means your wood house will be
very pretty. Will you be so obliging as to write me
a line when my trunk arrives at Williamstrip, where it
has been sent about two days ago? Your mother has
got my circuit paper, and is acquainted with the
line of my movements. I hope you sometimes take
a book in hand; as I have often told you—to enjoy
the pleasures of doing nothing, we must do something. Idle people know nothing of the pleasures
of idleness; it is a very difficult accomplishment to
acquire in perfection.

My dear Beach, adieu, and believe me,
Yours ever most sincerely,
SYDNEY SMITH.
My best regards to your father and mother.

Michael Beach proceeded to Christ Church, Oxford,
at the close of his second year in Scotland, and so
well satisfied were his parents with the progress he
had made under Sydney Smith's care, that they requested
him to remain in Edinburgh as tutor to their second
son, William Hicks Beach, who afterwards entered
Parliament as member for the town of Malmesbury.
Through the influence, in all probability, of Professor Dugald Stewart, the ex-curate of Nether Avon
was also requested to act in a similar capacity towards
young Mr. Gordon of Ellon Castle; so that Sydney
Smith superintended the studies of three young men
during the five years which he passed in Edinburgh.
His connection, however, with William Beach and
Alexander Gordon was severed by his determination
to follow his friend Francis Horner to London in
1803. Both young men, during the short time they

enjoyed the advantage of his society and advice, endeared themselves to him ; and they in turn, in after-life, ever referred to his influence and example in terms of gratitude and respect. In his intercourse with his pupils he always sought to act in accordance with what he believed to be the true object of education, and so endeavoured to implant, as he himself expresses it, resources that will endure as long as life endures, habits that will ameliorate not destroy, occupations that will render sickness tolerable, solitude pleasant, age venerable, life more dignified and useful, and therefore death less terrible.

The house to which Sydney Smith took his bride—the first home they could call their own—46, George Street—has already been described ; and there they remained from the time of their arrival in Edinburgh in the autumn of 1800, until their removal to London in the summer of 1803. Their home life, which was quiet and simple, was brightened in the spring of 1802 by the birth of their first child, a girl who received the name of Saba ; but long ere the year closed a dark shadow fell across the little household with the tidings of the death of Sydney's mother, to whom he had always been devotedly attached.

Curiosity has often been expressed concerning the origin of a name as strange and mysterious as that of Saba, and there is no reason to conceal any longer the circumstances which led him to bestow it on his daughter. He maintained that parents who were compelled to inflict a trite and dismal patronymic like Smith on their innocent offspring, ought in compassion, and by way of social compensation, to give with it also a Christian name a little less commonplace than the otherwise excellent John or Mary, Thomas or

Sarah. His father—himself plain **Robert Smith**—had
felt the inconvenience of being through life one of an
army of Smiths and **a** regiment **of** Roberts, and he
therefore **resolved in** the case **of his children** that, as
he could not **avert the** primal misfortune, **he** would
not—even for the sake of family traditions—add **to it**
a secondary one.   In harmony **with** this sensible
and kindly forethought, his sons accordingly **became**
Robert Percy, Sydney, Cecil, and Courtenay.

The most distinguished of his children recognized
the wisdom of his ancestor, in this direction at least,
and resolved to follow, **if** blessed with heirs, the
example which his father had **set;** and that is **the**
explanation **of** the names which he **gave** to his eldest
daughter and **her** brothers, Douglas and Windham.
The latter names sprang **out of a** little innocent hero-
worship, and **the** former, though more obscure, **was**
not evolved out of his own inner consciousness, **as**
many people have supposed.   Peculiar **names always**
attracted his attention, and often drew **forth** his **wit,**
and there are many instances **of** the droll manner in
which his **quick** and nimble fancy would seize upon and
play with **a new** idea thus suggested **to his mind.**   He
was determined **that** his little daughter should encounter the world equipped with a distinctive and
original name, and **he** eventually found it in the Prayer-
book version of the Psalms of David : " The kings of
Tharsis **and of** the isles shall give presents : the kings
of **Arabia** and *Saba* shall **bring** gifts" (Ps. lxxii. **10).**

Saba Smith **not only grew** up to womanhood, but
married, in 1834, Dr. **Henry** Holland, and**, as** the sharer
of that distinguished physician's honours, eventually
became Lady Holland.   **She died in** 1866, but not
before she had made the world her debtor by the

charming portrait of her father contained in the pages of the well-known "Memoir of the Rev. Sydney Smith," a book to which the writer of these pages is greatly indebted.

Whilst in Edinburgh, besides superintending the studies of his pupils, and entering with them freely into the social life of the city, Sydney Smith attended the lectures on moral philosophy of Dugald Stewart at the University, and also found time to dabble in medicine, anatomy, and the rising science of political economy. With Dugald Stewart he lived on terms of intimacy, and another of his chief friends at this period was Dr. Thomas Brown, who was a constant visitor at 46, Queen Street, where, indeed, he regularly dined one day in every week. A few months before the *Edinburgh Review* was started, Walter Scott, at that time the youthful Sheriff of Selkirkshire, proposed to Jeffrey, Sydney Smith, Murray, Allen, Brown, and a few other kindred spirits, that they should form themselves into a committee to bring together at a weekly re-union every one in the city who combined literary tastes with social instincts. The idea was heartily received and promptly carried out, and the new association received the name of the Friday Club, from the fact that its meetings were held on that day. Besides the group of men first appealed to, the list of the original members of the club contains the names of Sir James Hall, Dugald Stewart, John Playfair, Archibald Alison, William Erskine, Henry Brougham, Francis Horner, Henry Mackenzie, Henry Cockburn, and Thomas Campbell, who had just risen to fame at one bound by the publication of the "Pleasures of Hope." The club became one of the most delightful resorts in Edinburgh for all who possessed literary

or scientific proclivities, and it materially helped, in
turn, to quicken and elevate the social intercourse of
the capital. " Our club comes on admirably," writes
Jeffrey to his brother, soon after a start had been
made. " We have got Dugald Stewart, the Man of
Feeling,[6] Sir James Hall, John Playfair, and four or
five more of the senior literati, and we sit chatting
every week till two in the morning." [7]

The men who thus met together had, for the most
part, either won distinction in various fields, or were
rapidly advancing towards it; and with them all,
whether distinguished or not, the careless and cordial
hours which they spent at the Friday Club in harmless
pleasantry and animated discussion, remained in after-
years, when scattered far and wide, a happy memory
and a bond of fellowship.

Not the least remarkable figure in the group of
Sydney Smith's Edinburgh friends was John Leyden,
known chiefly to the present generation as an
enthusiastic Oriental scholar, who rivalled Sir William
Jones himself in devotion to the mysterious literature of the East; and as a poet whom Sir Walter
Scott admired and befriended in life, and whose
memory and untimely fate he has enshrined in
some well-known stanzas in the " Lord of the Isles."
It is asserted, and apparently with some degree of
truth, that Leyden, " an awkward, enthusiastic, un-
gainly scholar—as rich in classical learning as he was
poor in current coin," suggested to Scott the character
of the redoubtable Dominie Sampson; and the " prodigious " learning and equal simplicity of the shepherd

---

[6] Henry Mackenzie, author of the "Man of Feeling."
[7] " Life of Lord Jeffrey," vol. i. p. 151.

lad from Teviotdale at least lends colour to the story. Leyden's passion for knowledge knew no bounds; his memory was as retentive as Brougham's, and his mental energy not less extraordinary. Educated for the Presbyterian ministry, he pursued his studies for a time in Edinburgh; but at last, dazzled with Arabic and Persian lore, he grew restless, and determined, cost what it might, that he would pursue his researches in the East. His friends, recognizing his genius and industry, used their influence to obtain from the government of the day an official appointment in India; but a man of Leyden's stamp was scarcely likely to receive much encouragement from the Addington cabinet, and the only result of the strong representations made on his behalf was an offer of the post of assistant surgeon. His friends were chagrined at the outcome of their efforts, but Leyden himself, not at all disconcerted, bent his undivided energies to the acquisition of the necessary knowledge. Amid the mingled amusement and admiration of those who knew him best, in six months the plucky student won his diploma. His difficulties, however, were not yet at an end, for poverty, like an armed man, still stood in his path, and his resources were wholly inadequate to the demands made upon them for the provision of even the most slender outfit for India. From this dilemma he was rescued by Walter Scott, Sydney Smith, and a few others. Sydney— with characteristic generosity—managed to spare 40l. out of a purse that was by no means overflowing, and the learned assistant-surgeon sailed for India in December 1802, with grateful feelings and boyish glee. The poor fellow never saw his native hills again. Nine years later, he was attacked by a

H

fever, and died at the age of thirty-six, but so
splendidly had he redeemed those years that he had
not only risen to the rank of a judge in Calcutta, but
had established a European reputation through his
profound knowledge of the literature of the East.

At a very early stage in their acquaintance Sydney
Smith nicknamed Brougham the " Drum-major," a
title which he had earned by his marvellous command
of high-sounding declamation, and he once told
Moore [a]—in speaking of the fun which they had together at the outstart of the *Edinburgh Review*—that a
certain article appeared in 1803, entitled " Ritson on
Abstinence from Animal Food," which he and the future
Lord Chancellor one night in merry mood concocted.
" We take it for granted " (wrote Brougham), " that
Mr. Ritson supposes Providence to have had some
share in producing him," " though for what inscrutable purpose " (added Sydney), " we profess ourselves unable to conjecture." Jeffrey probably ran
his pen through the audacious sentence, or perhaps
its authors themselves felt that it would not bear the
sober light of day; at all events, the article on Mr.
Ritson's theories duly appeared, without the slightest
allusion to the " inscrutable purpose " involved in
that gentleman's creation. The following unpublished
note to Jeffrey belongs to this period, and it shows
that Sydney Smith felt that he was open to the charge
of " excessive levity," and was preparing himself for
the strictures of his more sober-minded colleague.

[x.]   Burnt Island, July 22nd, 1802.

MY DEAR JEFFREY,—You may very possibly con-

---

[a] Life of Moore, by Lord John Russell, vol. vii. p. 13.

sider some passages in my reviews as a little injudicious and extravagant, if you happen to cast your eyes upon them. Never mind, let them go away with their absurdity unadulterated and pure. If I please, the object for which I write is attained; if I do not, the laughter which follows my error is the only thing which can make me cautious and tremble.

Yours ever,

SYDNEY SMITH.

THE TOLBOOTH, CANONGATE, EDINBURGH.

CHAPTER V.

Arrival in London, and early struggles there.

THE year 1803 was an important one to Sydney Smith, for it witnessed his removal from the Scottish capital to London, which, in an unpublished letter of the same date, he describes as "that pleasing but detestable place." Two of his pupils had by this time finished their studies in Edinburgh, and were on the eve of proceeding to Oxford, whilst the third was rapidly preparing to follow their example. He himself, in spite of the demands of his pupils, the *Edinburgh Review*, the Episcopalians in Rose Street, and an ever-widening circle of friends, had somehow found time to study moral philosophy and to dabble in medicine, and both accomplishments were soon to be called into requisition. It was only after much anxious thought, and not a few misgivings, that he determined to remove to London. His friends at Nether Avon heard of this resolution with sincere regret, and did their utmost to persuade him to remain in Scotland for at least another year, when William Beach would be ready to join his brother at Christ Church. This proposal was, however, promptly though gratefully declined, and on grounds which sensible people like Mr. and Mrs. Beach could not gainsay. "It is a matter of real regret," wrote Sydney, "that I should be compelled to decline any proposal which it would give you pleasure that I should accept. I have one child, and I expect another; it is absolutely my duty that I should make some exertion for their future support. The salary you give is liberal; I live here in ease and abundance, but a situation in this country leads to nothing. I have to begin the world at the end of three years, at the very same point where I set out from; it would be the same at the end of ten. I should return to London, my friends and connections mouldered away, my relatives gone and dispersed, and myself about to begin to do at the age of forty what I ought to have begun to do at the age of twenty-five. * * * I could not hold myself justified to my wife and family if I were to sacrifice any longer to the love of present ease, those exertions which every man is bound to make for the improvement of his situation." [1] He then proceeds in the same letter to allay the natural but needless fears of the anxious parents for their son, and to combat the notion that the youth—whose character he warmly commends—is unfit to stand alone amid the inevitable temptation of a student's life in a city like Edinburgh. After laying down the principle that if a young man at twenty is unable to meet the little world of a university, he will be unable at any age to face the great world outside it, he adds, " To accustom men to great risks, you must expose them when boys to

[1] " Memoir of the Rev. Sydney Smith," chap. iv. p. 57.

lesser ones. If you attempt to avoid all risks, you do
an injury infinitely greater than any you shun." Such
words, revealing as they do a deep acquaintance with
the human heart, and a generous confidence in its free
movements, are worthy of the thoughtful consideration
of all who have the care of youth. To instil right
principles, and then to trust them to the utmost, has
been proved again and again to be the best method
towards ensuring a robust and disciplined character.
The puling virtue which needs a cloister to protect it,
is not that which can overcome the world.

Sydney Smith's resolution to leave Edinburgh was
undoubtedly a wise one. The position of a private
tutor—irksome and precarious in itself—is precisely
one of those occupations which are advantageous
rather as a means than as an end, and which no man
of spirit and ability is ever content—except under
very exceptional circumstances—to regard as a final
goal. A just appreciation of the increased responsibilities which his marriage had imposed upon him,
led him to determine upon some course of action
more likely than his position in Edinburgh, to advance the interests of those whom he loved best.
There are some indications that a more momentous
question than any involved in a severance of present
ties and total change of scene, was occasioning anxious
concern to him at this critical juncture in his affairs.
The *Edinburgh Review* was only beginning its career,
and not even the most sanguine of the group of young
men with whom it originated, and in whose hands its
fortune lay, had the faintest conception of the influence and fame which it was destined by their efforts
and the needs of the hour to gain and keep. Periodi-

cal literature, moreover, had not at that time the inducements to offer, to men of ready and original pens, with
which it tempts the ranks of other professions to-day.

Some of Sydney Smith's critics have said over
and over again that he missed his way in life, and
that he committed a great mistake when he entered
the Church, where, indeed, he was always the round
man in the square hole. From one point of view,
there was not a little, as years rolled on, calculated to
lead Sydney Smith himself to the same conclusion.
Promotion, which at that period at least was not
always by merit, came with very tardy steps towards
a man who is now commonly regarded as one of the
most sagacious and able Churchmen of his age; and he
felt keenly the slow recognition which his abilities
received. In his later years he came, as all the world
knows, into public collision with the Ecclesiastical
Commission, and the form in which he waged warfare
was a series of pungent "Letters to Archdeacon
Singleton," in which he maintained, with his usual
vigour of style and felicity of illustration, that the
commissioners had been invested with too great
power, and that in the exercise of it, the interests of
those who most needed protection and help—the
inferior clergy — had been grievously overlooked.
"You tell me," he exclaims, " I shall be laughed at as
a rich and overgrown Churchman. Be it so. I have
been laughed at a hundred times in my life, and care
little or nothing about it. If I am well provided for
now, I have had my full share of the blanks in the
lottery as well as the prizes. * * * In my grand
climacteric, I was made canon of St. Paul's; and
before that period I had built a parsonage-house with

farm offices for a large farm, which cost me 4000*l.*, and had reclaimed another from ruins at the expense of 2000*l.* A lawyer or a physician in good practice would smile at this picture of great ecclesiastical wealth, and yet I am considered a perfect monster of ecclesiastical prosperity."

When Sydney Smith bade farewell to his friends in the north and prepared to leave Edinburgh, he was rapidly approaching his thirty-third year, and his prospects in his profession were the reverse of satisfactory; as for his means, all that can be said is this, they were as narrow as his views were liberal. His political convictions proved to be a barrier to his promotion in the Church, and because he ventured not only to think for himself, but also to publish his conclusions, he was regarded for a long term of years with coldness and suspicion. He was accordingly left to fight his own way in life, and had the mortification of seeing scores of his intellectual inferiors become, one after another in dismal procession, his ecclesiastical superiors.

The interest which men feel in the progress of Sydney Smith's career is heightened by the glimpse of irresolution which is apparent in his attitude towards his profession in the spring of 1803 ; and the resolution at which he eventually arrived after days of suspense which were marked by "much deliberation," was one which throws into bold relief both his fidelity to duty and the disinterested zeal with which he obeyed its every known behest. Having entered the Church, he felt that its vows were upon him, and therefore, dismissing all dreams of honour in other directions, he elected to remain where he was, and to seek through

" patient continuance in well doing " the elevation of
others, and, in the noblest sense, his own. If, in
arriving at this conclusion, he missed success in life,
or even a degree of it, it must at least be admitted
that he shared such failure in noble company. Men
who enter the ministry are usually supposed—at least
by those who credit them with common honesty—to
be actuated by motives which a shower of gold fails
to satisfy, and to covet better and more enduring
rewards than treasures on earth.

Although the official connection of Sydney Smith
with the Beach family terminated with his removal
from Edinburgh, the closer ties of sympathy and
respect bound him more intimately than ever to his
friends at Williamstrip, and in after-years the intercourse was renewed whenever opportunity permitted.
Mr. Beach had smoothed the path of the young couple
by his kindly gift on their entrance upon their Edinburgh life ; and now that they were about to quit that
city he again came to their help and offered them his
carriage in which to perform the long and tedious
journey to the south. The following note contains
Sydney Smith's acknowledgments of this graceful
act, and reveals the sense of loneliness which the
departure for India of the last of his three brothers
occasioned the struggling young clergyman.

[XI.]   George Street, Edinburgh,
                                       26th April, 1803.

My DEAR SIR,—I am extremely obliged to you for
your kindness in lending us your chaise ; it will be a
great comfort to Mrs. Smith, and she joins me in

acknowledging the obligation. * * * Mrs. Smith and myself intend, if she is well recovered by that time, to be in London by the beginning of September. I have heard of my brother (Bobus) a day's sail from the Land's End, and hardly expect to hear from him again before he arrives in India. I feel quite an exile in England. I am almost tempted to consider India as my native country from the number of relatives I have there.

Believe me, my dear sir,

Your obliged and affectionate friend,

SYDNEY SMITH.

Michael H. Beach, Esq., M.P.

Accompanied by his wife and child, he left Edinburgh on the 8th of August, 1803. They found it hard work parting with so many kind and true friends, and after the last farewell had been uttered they looked long and wistfully at the receding outlines of the Castle and Arthur's Seat. "I shall be," said Sydney, as he thought of the prospect before him, "like a full-grown tree transplanted, deadly sick at first, with bare and ragged fibres, shorn of many a root." His first letter to Jeffrey after his departure from the north affords some indication of what it had cost him to determine on that step :—"I left Edinburgh with great heaviness of heart. I knew what I was leaving, and was ignorant to what I was going. My good fortune will be very great if I should ever again fall into the society of so many liberal, correct, and instructive men, and live with them on such terms of friendship as I have done with you, and you know

whom at Edinburgh." ² In another of his early letters
to the same friend, the warmth of his feelings towards
the beautiful city which he had left behind finds frank
avowal :—" I shall always love Edinburgh very dearly.
I will come and visit it very often if I am ever rich,
and I think it very likely one day or another I may
live there entirely." ³

Sydney Smith knew little of London, and London
knew less of him, when he arrived there to push his
way in life one autumn day, eighty years ago. If,
however, he was still a poor and comparatively an
unknown man, he had already gained the affection of
a small circle of friends, had won a degree of reputation, and was animated moreover by the sense of
conscious power. In spite, therefore, of his protests
to Mr. Beach that he was starting in the world again
at the end of three years, exactly at the same point
from which he had set out, in reality he began his
career in London quickened, enriched, and to some
extent equipped, not less perhaps by the tentative and
half-baffled endeavours than by the accomplished work
of the crucial years of opening manhood. The welcome which he immediately received at the hands of
many good and able men did much to dispel the depression of spirits which his departure from Edinburgh
had occasioned him. Foremost to hail his arrival and
to endeavour to make him feel at home amid his new
surroundings was the Knight of the Shaggy Eyebrows,
as he was accustomed to call his friend Horner. He
arrived in the south just in time to take part in a contested election at Oxford, and Horner went down with

---

² Published Correspondence, p. 288.   ³ Ibid. p. 293.

him to the University, a visit which revived the
memory of his student days at New College.

On their return to town, Sydney Smith appears to
have taken apartments at 77, Upper Guildford Street,
where, however, he only remained for a few months.
Soon after he went there we find him writing in hot
haste and with pardonable pride, to inform Jeffrey that
it is the "universal opinion that our *Review* is uncommonly well done, and that it is, perhaps, the first
in Europe." [4] The same letter contains an amusing
account of Horner, who it seems was inclined to seize
more books for criticism than he could possibly deal
with, and whom his colleague describes as "a sort of
literary tiger, whose den is strewed with ten times
more victims than he can devour."

Life in lodgings, especially in a great city, and
with young children, is not a very exhilarating
state of existence, and it was not long, therefore,
before Sydney Smith established himself in a small
house, No. 8, Doughty Street, Mecklenburgh Square.
It is interesting to know that Charles Dickens, a
generation later, also lived in this street at the
period when *Pickwick* was finished, and *Oliver Twist*
and *Nicholas Nickleby* took the world by storm.
Sydney Smith, always quick to recognize genius, was
one of the first to admit the extraordinary fidelity and
humour which distinguished the portraits which Dickens
drew from life. In his published correspondence there
are several kindly letters addressed to the young novelist,
and the earliest of them was written to the inventor
of Mr. Pickwick, when he was living in Doughty Street,
not many doors off the house which, thirty-five years

[4] Published Correspondence, p. 289.

before, had been the home of the man who made the
English people acquainted with the adventures of
Dame Partington and the opinions of Peter Plymley.
In that letter, Sydney Smith states that the Miss
Berrys have commissioned him to invite Mr. Dickens
to dinner at Richmond, in order that he may meet
"a Canon of St. Paul's, the Rector of Combe-Florey,
and the Vicar of Halberton—all equally well known to
you." [5]   The neighbourhood of Mecklenburgh Square
was, at the beginning of the century, a favourite
locality with lawyers and literary men, and that fact
seems to have induced him to take up his residence in
Doughty Street.

The spring of 1804 was made memorable to the
household in Doughty Street by the birth of Sydney
Smith's eldest son, a child who died in infancy.   Mrs.
Pybus died shortly before the young couple turned
their faces to the south, and she bequeathed to her
daughter Kate her valuable jewels.   Mrs. Smith, with
great good sense, came to the conclusion that such
costly ornaments would be quite out of place in the
personal adornment of a poor clergyman's wife; she
was anxious, moreover, to obtain a little money to
lessen the anxiety of her husband's struggling and
straitened lot.   Almost her first act in London, therefore, was to sell her mother's pearls.   She herself
wrote in her old age the following simple account of
that brave womanly action :—" I took the pearls to
Rundell and Bridges, and sold them for 500*l.*   This
was converting them into a much more useful purpose,
and all we most wanted was obtained."   In itself that

---

[5] Published Correspondence, p. 547.

business visit of the timid young wife's to the famous
jewellers on Ludgate Hill to sell her mother's pearls, was
perhaps only a trivial and not uncommon affair, but it
is at least worthy of passing notice, since it is precisely
by such unobtrusive and matter-of-fact acts of devotion that the beauty and strength of an unselfish
nature leap to light. Both Sydney Smith and his
wife, even in circles where such candour ran the
greatest risk of being misunderstood, had the courage
to confess their poverty at once, and they discovered,
Sydney declared, that in addition to the feeling of independence it gave them, it had the further advantage
of rendering half their wants needless.

Francis Horner was already on the high road to
legal distinction when his old comrade arrived in the
metropolis, and although he still stood somewhat in
dread of the quips and cranks of his reverend friend,
he hailed his advent with much pleasure, and through
his influence Sydney Smith soon found himself welcomed into the midst of a bright and busy circle of
kindred spirits. Sir Samuel Romilly, Sir James
Mackintosh, Dr. Marcet, Mr. Scarlett (afterwards
Lord Abinger), and Mr. Ward (afterwards Lord
Dudley), were probably the most distinguished in the
group of new acquaintances who did their best to
make a man whom Jeffrey called his "beloved and in-
comparable friend," feel at home in his novel surroundings.

Sydney Smith assuredly needed all the encouragement which friends old and new could give him
just then, for he occupied a singular and by no
means an enviable position in the ranks of his profession. Those who were at that time at the head of

affairs in Church and State, so far as they condescended to recognize his existence at all, were provoked by the bold and uncompromising attitude of hostility which the young Edinburgh Reviewer was not afraid to assume towards the public abuses which everywhere prevailed. The consciousness that justice lay at the foot of his quarrel with the existing order of things, did not, under the circumstances, do much towards disarming either their anger or their fear; and Sydney Smith was quickly made to feel that the "universal opinion that the *Review* is uncommonly well done," retarded rather than promoted his advancement in the Church. It was accordingly not long before he realized that he had little to expect beyond coldness and studied neglect from the clerical and official dispensers of patronage. Writing from London, in a somewhat despondent strain, a considerable time after his arrival there, he states, "I have as yet found no place to preach in; it is more difficult than I had imagined. Two or three random sermons I have discharged, and thought I perceived that the greater part of the congregation thought me mad. The clerk was as pale as death in helping me off with my gown, for fear I should bite him." [6] He did not, however, lose heart, and in the midst of his own difficulties and anxieties, he was always ready to cheer others both by precept and example. He felt certain that eventually his abilities would find public recognition, and he did not grudge the sacrifices which he had meanwhile made in the good cause of liberty and progress, and thus he set to all around him an example of manly courage and patient

[6] "Memoir of Sydney Smith," chap. iv. p. 62.

hope. He afterwards taught the same lesson by precept also, and in the accompanying unpublished essay, which he wrote towards the close of his life, some of the things which he had learnt by experience are wittily described. The essay, like several others in this work, is printed from a manuscript in the possession of Miss Holland, through whose kindness it is now made public. It is entitled:—

A LITTLE MORAL ADVICE:

A FRAGMENT ON THE CULTIVATION AND IMPROVEMENT OF THE ANIMAL SPIRITS.

It is surprising to see for what foolish causes men hang themselves. The most silly repulse, the most trifling ruffle of temper, or derangement of stomach, anything seems to justify an appeal to the razor or the cord. I have a contempt for persons who destroy themselves. Live on, and look evil in the face; walk up to it, and you will find it less than you imagined, and often you will not find it at all; for it will recede as you advance. Any fool may be a suicide. When you are in a melancholy fit, first suspect the body, appeal to rhubarb and calomel, and send for the apothecary; a little bit of gristle sticking in the wrong place, an untimely consumption of custard, excessive gooseberries, often cover the mind with clouds and bring on the most distressing views of human life.

I start up at two o'clock in the morning, after my first sleep, in an agony of terror, and feel all the weight of life upon my soul. It is impossible that I can bring up such a family of children, my sons and daughters will be beggars; I shall live to see those whom I love

exposed to the scorn and contumely of the world!—
But stop, thou child of sorrow, and humble imitator
of Job, and tell me on what you dined. Was not there
soup and salmon, and then a plate of beef, and then
duck, blanc-mange, cream cheese, diluted with beer,
claret, champagne, hock, tea, coffee, and noyau? And
after all this, you talk of the *mind* and the evils of life!
These kind of cases do not need meditation, but magnesia. Take short views of life. What am I to do in
these times with such a family of children? So I
argued, and lived dejected and with little hope; but
the difficulty vanished as life went on. An uncle died,
and left me some money; an aunt died, and left me
more; my daughter married well; I had two or three
appointments, and before life was half over became a
prosperous man. And so will you. Every one has
uncles and aunts who are mortal; friends start up
out of the earth; time brings a thousand chances in
your favour; legacies fall from the clouds. Nothing
so absurd as to sit down and wring your hands
because all the good which may happen to you in
twenty years has not taken place at this precise
moment.

The greatest happiness which can happen to any one
is to cultivate a love of reading. Study is often dull
because it is improperly managed. I make no apology
for speaking of myself, for as I write anonymously
nobody knows who I am, and if I did not, very few
would be the wiser—but every man speaks more firmly
when he speaks from his own experience. I read four
books at a time; some classical book perhaps on Monday, Wednesday, and Friday mornings. The "History
of France," we will say, on the evenings of the same

I

days. On Tuesday, Thursday, and Saturday, Mosheim or Lardner, and in the evening of those days, Reynolds' Lectures, or Burns' Travels. Then I have always a standing book of poetry, and a novel to read when I am in the humour to read nothing else. Then I translate some French into English one day, and re-translate it the next; so that I have seven or eight pursuits going on at the same time, and this produces the cheerfulness of diversity, and avoids that gloom which proceeds from hanging a long while over a single book. I do not recommend this as a receipt for becoming a learned man, but for becoming a cheerful one.

Nothing contributes more certainly to the animal spirits than benevolence. Servants and common people are always about you; make moderate attempts to please everybody, and the effort will insensibly lead you to a more happy state of mind. Pleasure is very reflective, and if you give it you will feel it. The pleasure you give by kindness of manner returns to you, and often with compound interest. The receipt for cheerfulness is not to have one motive only in the day for living, but a number of little motives; a man who from the time he rises till bedtime conducts himself like a gentleman, who throws some little condescension into his manner to superiors, and who is always contriving to soften the distance between himself and the poor and ignorant, is always improving his animal spirits, and adding to his happiness.

I recommend lights as a great improver of animal spirits. How is it possible to be happy with two mould candles ill snuffed? You may be virtuous, and wise, and good, but two candles will not do for animal spirits. Every night the room in which I sit is lighted up like a town after a great naval victory, and in this cereous galaxy and with a blazing fire, it is scarcely possible to be low-spirited, a thousand pleasing images spring up in the mind, and I can see the little blue demons scampering off like parish boys pursued by the beadle.

Sydney Smith was always fond of giving "a little moral advice" to his friends whenever opportunity occurred, and as a matter of fact his letters abound in genial and wise counsels for the better regulation of existence. In an unpublished note, written from Foston in 1819, he confides the following prescription to an acquaintance who had complained to him of nervousness :—" REMEDIES AGAINST NERVOUSNESS.—The remedies against nervousness are Resolution, Camphor, Cold Bathing, Exercise in the Open Air, Abstinence from Tea and Coffee, and from all distant views of human life, except when religious duties call upon you to take them."

It is always difficult for a man to possess his soul in patience when every effort seems fruitless, and integrity and talent appear to count for nothing in the eyes of those who have the power to help. Ability, however, when it is linked to good sense and right feeling, seldom fails before long to make its merit known, and to win for itself recognition in some unlooked-for quarter. Not a few of the noblest ministers of the Christian Church have not been cut after the regulation pattern, and, as a rule, such men have fared more hardly in the church than in the world. All through the earlier years of Sydney

Smith's ministry that was precisely his position. His ecclesiastical superiors looked coldly upon him; they were dazzled by his brilliant common sense, and alarmed at the freedom with which he applied it even to such venerable personages as themselves. He was regarded, in the prim and decorous circles of the day, as a dangerous man, and a dangerous man he certainly was to the end of the chapter, so far as all clerical, political, or social pretence and injustice were concerned. But straightforward people, high and low, from earls and marquesses to farm labourers and village children, opened their hearts to welcome a man who placed the precious things of his creed in circulation, not only in good words, but likewise in the more tangible coin of golden deeds.

EDINBURGH CASTLE.

CHAPTER VI.

1805—1807.

Holland House—Preacher at the Foundling Hospital—Lecturer at the Royal Institution—" Peter Plymley "—Gift of Foston by Lord Erskine.

An introduction to Holland House, which Sydney Smith obtained through his brother Robert, who had been an intimate friend from his school days at Eton of its genial and accomplished master, gave the ex-curate of Nether Avon an entrance into the most brilliant society in England. Henry Richard Vassal Fox, third Lord Holland, "nephew of Fox and friend of Grey,"—as with mingled pride and playfulness he sometimes styled himself,—delighted to gather around him in his historic home the most distinguished men and the most beautiful women of his times. Standing in the old court suburb of the town, Holland House, with its charming nooks and corners, its lovely gardens, its weird traditions, its famous pictures, its literary treasures, and its political memories, presents to a cultivated Englishman a galaxy of attractions, which, in their way, are unrivalled through the length and breadth of the kingdom. Here, in the stormy times which preceded the tragic close of Charles the First's reign, the first Lord Holland, whom Clarendon describes as a " very handsome man, of a lovely and winning presence,

and gentle conversation," kept open house for the
troubled friends of the king. Here, in the reign of
Queen Anne, Joseph Addison, having married the
Dowager Countess of Warwick, spent—not very happily,
it is to be feared—the closing years of his life. Here
dwelt the " lass of Richmond Hill," the bewitching
Lady Sarah Lennox, whom George the Third seemed
wishful at one time to make his queen. Here, too, at a
still later period, Charles James Fox slipped through
a somewhat careless and rebellious youth, and duly
emerged into the midst of those fierce political con-
tentions which called forth all the latent powers of
his strong but ill-disciplined manhood. The "nephew
of Fox and friend of Grey," who dispensed with high-
born grace the hospitalities of Holland House when
Sydney Smith first crossed its threshold in 1805, was
himself not unworthy, to some extent at least, of
association with those great servants of the State. He
inherited that peculiar personal fascination—indescribable but most subtle—which led Edmund Burke
to exclaim that his great rival was a man made to be
loved, and he shared, moreover, that generous hatred
of oppression in every shape, which caused tyrants at
home, and slave-holders abroad, to curse the name of
Fox. Nor was Lord Holland unworthy of the confidence of Earl Grey,—the courageous and enlightened
premier of England—who took occasion by the hand,
and consolidated the power and broadened the liberty
of a nation which will ever hold his name in grateful
honour ; for the master of Holland House threw the
whole weight of his social as well as his political influence into the despised cause of the people, and took
his full share of odium as a champion in high places

of the policy of peace, retrenchment, and reform. Another of the great Whig leaders, Lord John Russell, has happily described Lord Holland as a man who "won without seeming to court, instructed without seeming to teach, and amused without labouring to be witty." [1] From the end of last century until the opening years of Queen Victoria's reign, few men in England of liberal proclivities, who had gained renown in art, literature, politics, or science, failed to make acquaintance with Holland House and its genial and patriotic owner. If it can be said with any approach to truth that there was in England in 1806 a ministry composed of "All the Talents," it is equally correct to add that there was before that year, and long after it had run its course, an assemblage of all the talents in the cosmopolitan company which thronged the salons of Holland House in the days when the kindly hand of Vassal, Lord Holland welcomed its guests.

A list of the visitors to Holland House during this period would include the names of half the eminent men in England, from Lord Byron to Lord Macaulay, and would supply ample proof, if that were needed, of the wide sympathies as well as versatile tastes of the noble owner. Political leaders, such as Grey, Russell, Durham, and Lansdowne, met in the Gilt Room or the Library, with poets like Moore and Rogers, and men of science like Sir Humphrey Davy, Count Rumford, or Alexander von Humboldt, or wandering authors from the Great Republic like Washington Irving. The

[1] Preface to vol. vi., "Life of Thomas Moore," by Lord John Russell.

Prince Regent and the Duke of Clarence were not
more at home in that brilliant crowd than Canova the
sculptor and Wilkie the painter. Astute diplomatists
like Prince de Talleyrand or Prince Metternich have
probably leaned across those tables to compare notes
with philosophic students like Bentham, Mackintosh,
or Romilly; nay, it is quite as likely that—for once
off their guard—they may have thrown themselves

HOLLAND HOUSE.

As it appeared before alteration. From an old print.

back in their chairs, convulsed with the humour of
wits like Henry Luttrell or Sydney Smith.

Lord Holland and Sydney Smith had much in
common, and they were therefore soon drawn into
the bonds of a friendship which survived all differences
of opinion and habit, and which death alone was
strong enough to break. In the judgment of his
firend, Lord Holland's career was " one great, incessant, and unrewarded effort to resist oppression, pro-

mote justice, and restrain the abuse of power. He
had an invincible hatred of tyranny and oppression,
and the most ardent love of public happiness and
attachment to public rights."[2]   With Lady Holland
also, Sydney Smith was for years on terms of
close friendship, and many of his wittiest letters
were addressed to her.   Lady Holland was a
beautiful, imperious, and somewhat argumentative
woman, full of strong likes and dislikes, which she
never concealed, and often expressed in bold and sarcastic terms.   It is related of her, that " in the midst
of some of Macaulay's interesting anecdotes she would
tap on the table with her fan and say, ' Now, Macaulay,
we have had enough of this, give us something else.'
She would issue commands to Sydney Smith; but
once he retorted.   Said she, ' Sydney, ring the bell.'
He answered, ' Oh, yes, and shall I sweep the
room?' "[3]   But if Lady Holland was domineering in
manner, and occasionally sarcastic in speech, she had
a kind heart, and was a most loyal friend to all who
gained her esteem, and she was a woman who was
not offended when her attacks were met with weapons
similar to her own.

In John Allen, Lord Holland's factotum, Sydney
Smith had a friend at court at Holland House.   Allen
was so remarkable a personage, and so conspicuous
a figure in the society of Holland House, that no
account, however slight, of Lord Holland or his home,
would be complete without some reference to a man
who was at once his physician, adviser, librarian, and

[2] " Memoir of the Rev. Sydney Smith," chap. x. p. 187.
[3] " Holland House," chap. iv. p. 100.   By the Princess Marie
Liechtenstein.

friend. John Allen was born at Colinton, near Edinburgh, in 1771, the year in which Sydney Smith's
life began. His father, who was a writer to the signet
in Edinburgh, died in embarrassed circumstances when
Allen was a child. His mother married a tenant
farmer named Cleghorn, who gave the boy a good
education, and finally apprenticed him to Mr. Arnot,
an Edinburgh surgeon, with whom another lad, who
afterwards gained fame as Professor John Thomson,
was also an apprentice. Whilst still a very young
man, John Allen became a member of the College of
Surgeons, and of several learned societies in Edinburgh,
where he delivered lectures on Comparative Anatomy
of so much originality and power that no less a man than
Cuvier, greatly interested, was led to make his acquaintance. In 1802 Lord Holland was anxious to secure a
competent physician to accompany him on a long tour
on the continent, on which he was then about to
set out. Lord Lauderdale recommended Dr. Allen as
a suitable man for the post, and the young Edinburgh
surgeon, eager to see the world under such favourable
auspices, gladly accepted the appointment. General
Fox was only a child when Allen came to Holland
House as travelling-companion and physician to his
father, but, young as he was, he never forgot the first
impression which the stranger made upon him. "He
was a stout, strong man, with a very large head, a
broad face, enormous round silver spectacles before a
pair of peculiarly bright and intelligent eyes, and with
the thickest legs[4] I ever remember. His accent

---

[4] This agrees with Sydney Smith's criticism: "Allen's legs are
enormous—they are clerical! He has the creed of a philosopher

Scotch; his manner eager, but extremely good-natured; all this made a lasting impression on me, then a boy of six." Allen was absent from England with Lord Holland for three years, and on his return with the family in 1805 from Lisbon, he settled down at Holland House to a literary life, and soon became a conspicuous and attractive member of the inner circle there. Whilst in Spain he became intimate with Don Manuel Quintana and many other literary men, and he spent much time in studying the early constitutions of the various provinces of that country. The result of these investigations was, that no man in England, at the beginning of the century, was more of an authority on subjects connected with the constitutional history of the Peninsula than Lord Holland's physician. He constantly wrote for the *Edinburgh Review* on constitutional questions and subjects suggested by the early history of France and Spain. He also produced a remarkable summary of contemporary European politics in the " Annual Register " of 1806, and a few years later he published a " Biographical Sketch of Mr. Fox." His principal contribution to literature, however, was his " Inquiry into the Rise and Growth of the Royal Prerogative in England," a book which reveals on every page not only his precision and ease as a writer, but his accurate knowledge and complete mastery of a difficult and abstruse subject.

Allen went abroad with Lord Holland on several occasions, and he never failed to return to Holland

and the legs of a clergyman; I never saw such legs—at least belonging to a layman." Published Correspondence, p. 579.

House after these excursions ladened with intellectual
spoil. Wherever he travelled he carried with him the
enthusiasm of a student, and the trained eye of a
shrewd and intelligent observer ; and the knowledge
which he was thus continually accumulating was at
the service of every visitor to Holland House who
cared to talk with him in a quiet nook of the library
or garden. In theory, John Allen was a republican ; but, though repelled, like every humane man,
by the horrors of the French Revolution, he still
clung to the hope that France would gradually shake
herself free from despotism, bloodshed, and cruelty,
and establish an honest, philanthropic, and peaceful Republican Government. When Napoleon, however, sprang to power, and founded the Empire
by the force of the sword, Allen confessed himself bitterly disappointed, and abandoned the study
of contemporary politics with evident disgust. The
supremacy in England of the ultra-Tories, and the
abandonment of Liberal views by the Prince as soon
as he became Regent, increased Allen's chagrin, and
in despair of progress either at home or abroad, under
such conditions, the baffled politician buried himself
amongst his books at Holland House, and, venting
his spleen in occasional anathemas, devoted his undivided attention to the study of the early history
of the British Constitution, and the Anglo-Saxon
framework of our political principles and laws.

Lord Byron declared that Allen was the best informed, and one of the ablest men he knew. Unlike
Byron, he had little imagination, but he had a memory
which was marvellous in its accuracy as well as its extent, and so tenacious, moreover, that he was able, at a

moment's notice, to give a clear and full outline of the contents of any book which he had read with interest. He was elected Warden of Dulwich College in 1811, and Master in 1820. He occasionally went to reside there, but to all intents and purposes his only home was Holland House, of which he was an inmate for forty years, and where " Allen's Room " is still shown and his memory revered.

After Lord Holland's death in October, 1840, Dr. Allen had increased responsibilities thrown upon him, and he remained, to the close of his own life in 1843, the honoured friend and confidential adviser of the widowed mistress of Holland House. Nothing delighted him more than to welcome his old Edinburgh friends— Jeffrey, Horner, Brougham, Erskine, Brown, and Sydney Smith; and his presence at Holland House was in itself a sufficient magnet to draw them, whenever opportunity offered, to the old court suburb of the town. Though a man of the most simple and lovable character, and full of kindly and generous impulses, John Allen often amazed strangers who met him at Holland House by the unmeasured violence of his speech whenever some such subject as the slave-trade, or the treatment of climbing boys, or the ambition of Napoleon, or the intolerance of the Tories, aroused his anger. Those who knew the goodness of his heart were accustomed to watch with amusement on these occasions, the consternation depicted on the face of some casual guest, by the gentle Allen's sudden outburst of wrath and fiery indignation.

When Sydney Smith was first ushered into the drawing-room of Holland House, he was diffident in speech and embarrassed in manners, and it needed all

Lord Holland's social tact to set the young clergyman at his ease.   But if he was shy when suddenly thrown into the most brilliant society of his times, nothing ever shook the quiet dignity of his bearing, or the manly independence of his views; nor did he allow any considerations suggested by unequal rank or comparative poverty to stand in the way of his full participation in the social privileges and enjoyments of the hour. Mr. George Ticknor relates that Sydney Smith told him in 1838, that he thought as a rule the influence of the aristocracy over men of letters was " oppressive." " I never failed, however," he added, " to speak my mind before any of them.   I hardened myself early."[5]

Into whatever company Sydney Smith was thrown, the force of his character immediately asserted itself, and, whilst genial to a degree, he never for a moment surrendered his independence, or was afraid to utter exactly what he thought.   No doubt the frankness and sincerity which marked his intercourse with the aristocracy heightened its charm to men who at that period at least, were only too well accustomed to be addressed in terms of mock deference and servile flattery.   If Sydney Smith was poor (and poor in a very literal sense he was during the first years of his residence in London), he had the manliness never to be ashamed to acknowledge the fact; for one rule in his life to which he allowed no exception was that which led him never to sail under false colours.   He could not honestly afford the price of a coach when he went to the receptions at that " enchanted palace," as he describes Holland House in one of his unpublished

[5] " Life, Letters, and Journal of George Ticknor," vol. ii. p. 122.

letters, and so he was content to trudge through the streets often in driving rain, and to change his mud-stained shoes on his arrival. The servants, who appear at first to have regarded the advent of so indigent a guest as something very like an unwarrantable intrusion on themselves, if not on Lord Holland, were regaled with flashing pleasantries of so droll a description that not even their official solemnity was proof against the unexpected strain. The only memorial of Sydney Smith at Holland House is a small medallion portrait by Hanning, which hangs in the Journal Room, and bears the date of 1808.

Meanwhile, there was much quiet happiness in a certain unpretending house in Doughty Street, Mecklenburgh Square, and though there was strict economy visible in all its arrangements, fine taste and loving care were equally conspicuous; and if the rooms were small and modestly furnished, they were none the less bright and pleasant places. Sydney Smith kept not willingly, but of necessity, the plainest of tables, yet no man was worthy to share the hospitality of that home who felt inclined to grumble at its simple fare. Once a week, keeping up in London the old custom of his Edinburgh days, he gave a supper-party to his friends; and there was probably more merry laughter behind the closed shutters of No. 8, Doughty Street, on those occasions than in any other house—size at discretion—in the whole of London. Sometimes, however, he was inclined to wish either that "smiles were meat for children, or kisses could be bread," and it was the remembrance of his own early struggles which led him to say on one occasion, with dry humour, " The observances of the Church concerning feasts and fasts are tolerably well kept, upon the whole, since the rich keep the feasts and the poor the fasts!"

Life in London, to Sydney Smith, in spite of the *res angusta domi* which overshadowed it, was gradually becoming more and more attractive, for the spell of the great city was laying hold of his heart. His preaching, moreover, which had been much relished in Edinburgh, now began to be appreciated at something like its true worth in London, and the attention of even careless and captious hearers was arrested by the breadth of view, moral earnestness, and bold freshness of expression which distinguished his pulpit utterances. Sydney Smith was not then, or indeed at any subsequent period of his life, a great preacher, and it is certain that if any one had been foolish enough to describe him as an accomplished theologian, he himself would have been the first to have laughed so preposterous a notion to scorn. He was neither more nor less than a preacher of homely and sanctified common sense, and he lacked the exegetical skill and intuitive spiritual vision which contribute so largely to the best kind of pulpit power.

It appears to have been his mission, and in those days it was not a common one, to reveal the points of contact between the principles of Christianity and the social and political life of the people. His sermons not only abound in robust thought frequently expressed with consummate literary art, but sparkle with generous sentiments, especially towards the suffering and the poor. He was eager to claim for the poorest in the community their rightful share in all the privileges which the march of progress had placed within easy reach of more favoured classes of society, and he never lost an opportunity of impressing the duty of active and personal benevolence on those who by virtue of rank and wealth had time and means at their disposal. Absolutely indifferent to mere prudential considerations, which often weaken and embarrass the testimony of more timid or less conscientious men, Sydney Smith spoke everywhere concerning those great moral precepts of the Gospel which lie at the root of all that is worthy in national, no less than in personal life, and he endeavoured to apply them in all their binding force to the hearts of those whom he addressed. The vigour and freshness of his sermons, and their liberal, outspoken, and practical tone, suggest the higher pulpit teaching of to-day, rather than the more guarded and conventional discourses of sixty or eighty years ago; at the same time, it must be admitted that they do not possess the spiritual beauty, intense fervour, or deep, devotional feeling of the noblest sermons of the present age.

It was whilst Sydney Smith was still only an occasional preacher in the churches of the metropolis, without recognized standing, that Sir Thomas Bernard, charmed and impressed with all that he had heard from his lips, exerted his influence successfully to obtain for him the post of alternate evening preacher at the Foundling Hospital. The records of the Institution show that he held this position for upwards of three years and a half. He was elected on the 27th of March, 1805, and resigned his post on the 26th of October, 1808, the period when he went to reside at Heslington, near York. The stipend attached to the office was the modest sum of 50*l.* a year, but in other respects the position was advanta-

K

geous, as the preachers at the Foundling Hospital
had every opportunity of becoming widely known. It
soon became apparent in the increased attendance
and the revived interest in the evening service, that the
famous and noble charity was not likely to suffer in
public esteem through the choice which the Governors
had made in the occupant of the pulpit. In after-years,
the then forlorn young preacher was accustomed to
recall with lively gratitude, the second start which was
given him in his profession, through the timely aid of
the new friend whom he had now found in Sir Thomas
Bernard. Nothing is known of the relations which
existed between the two men, except the tradition of
their genial intercourse, and unfortunately no memorials of a friendship which on both sides was warm and
appreciative have descended to their living representatives. There were few citizens of London at the
dawn of the present century who equalled in public
spirit or philanthropic devotion the large-hearted and
generous man who helped Sydney Smith at a period
when his fight with fortune was hard. The world is
not only indebted to its great men, but to those unknown people who cheered and upheld them in dark
and adverse hours, and without whose sympathy and
succour they never could have been what they were,
or climbed to the position of honour and influence in
which they stand to-day. The memory of Sir Thomas
Bernard moreover deserves on wider grounds to be
commemorated, not merely in the name of a famous
London street, but also in the grateful remembrance of
every citizen who is able to appreciate protracted,
munificent, and self-denying labours for the public
good. Treasurer for many years of the Foundling

Hospital, he was also one of the founders of the Royal Institution, and laboured likewise with unobtrusive zeal in establishing the City Mission, the Fever Institution, the School for the Blind, the Cancer Hospital, and kindred beneficent associations. In him not only deserted babes found a protector, but poor climbing-boys and brow-beaten factory children a friend and champion.

Lady Holland has related, with a touch of honest pride, an incident which occurred during her father's connection with the Foundling Hospital which is too characteristic of the man to be passed over in silence. He had, it seems, resolved to preach a sermon on a particular Sunday which assailed in no uncertain tones some popular opinions which he believed to be hostile to the best interests of religion. Mrs. Sydney, who had listened to the out-spoken address elsewhere, and had noticed the evident sensation which it produced, dreaded its repetition, as she felt persuaded that it might cost her husband and herself the friendship of one or two people whom they both greatly liked. " Oh, Sydney, do change that sermon," exclaimed the anxious young wife ; " I know it will give such offence to our friends, the F——s, should they be there this evening." " I fear it will," was the gallant response, " and am sorry for it; but, Kate, do you think if I feel it my duty to preach such a sermon at all, that I can refrain from doing so from the fear of giving offence ? " It turned out exactly as Mrs. Smith had dreaded : the people alluded to were of course there ; they duly resented the preacher's remarks as a personal reflection, if not attack, upon themselves, and promptly withdrew their friendship from him. It is pleasant, however, to be able to add, by way of sequel, that years afterwards the grudge was forgotten, and the old intimacy renewed, to the mutual satisfaction of all concerned.

Meanwhile, other opportunities of service in the Church, though still in a somewhat irregular and sub-ordinate capacity, were beginning to present themselves, for the ability of Sydney Smith was of a kind that could not long be hid. He became morning preacher at Berkeley Chapel, John Street, Berkeley Square, and he continued to preach there and at Fitzroy Chapel [6] alternately on Sunday mornings until he quitted London for his Yorkshire living. Berkeley Chapel—in spite of its situation in Mayfair,—was almost deserted when Sydney Smith first appeared in its pulpit, but only a few Sundays had elapsed ere it was densely thronged week after week by the fashionable residents of the neighbourhood. Under ordinary circumstances, power in the pulpit draws people to the pews like a magnet, and ac-cordingly the languid and half-supercilious attention of a congregation which literally consisted of two or three was swiftly exchanged for a crowded church, and every manifestation of deep and reverent interest in its services. Nor was the preacher left, like too many of his order, to shoot his arrows into the air, in anxious ignorance of their effects, for messages and letters— some of them pathetic enough, full of gratitude for counsel given and stimulus received—found their way not unfrequently to the young clergyman in Doughty

* Fitzroy Chapel still exists as a place of worship, though under a different name. In 1864 it was consecrated by the Bishop of London, and became St. Saviour's Church, in the parish of St. Pancras.

Street, as if to prove that the earnest words he uttered on the highest of all themes were not missing their appointed mark.

Sydney Smith was indebted to Sir Thomas Bernard's kindly offices for another appointment which did still more to bring him into fame. Six months before his duties at the Foundling Hospital began, he was invited to deliver a course of lectures at the Royal Institution, of which society Sir Thomas was one of the early patrons and first treasurer. The Royal Institution—which had been founded in March, 1799, at the house of Sir Joseph Banks, by Count Rumford and a small band of scientific men—was at that time struggling into notice, and Sir Humphrey Davy's lectures on the new science of chemistry were beginning to attract public attention to the object and scope of its work. Sydney Smith's subject was moral philosophy, and he gave his first lecture on the 10th November, 1804. The lectures, twenty in all, were continued from that date until the end of May, 1805, and he received for the entire course the sum of 50*l.*, and a complimentary life admission to the meetings of the Institution for himself and Mrs. Smith. Somewhat to his own surprise, the lectures were uncommonly well received, and helped greatly to increase his reputation. Probably the strong desire which the public evinced to see and hear him at the desk of the Royal Institution was heightened by the growing influence of the *Edinburgh Review*, to which it was becoming known he was one of the chief contributors. So great indeed was the interest excited, that the whole of Albemarle Street and part of Grafton Street were blocked by carriages day after day during the delivery of the lectures, whilst every seat, and even the passages and lobbies of the building itself were closely packed by an eager and excited crowd. "You will be amused," wrote Francis Horner, "to hear the account Sydney gives of his own qualifications for the task, and his mode of manufacturing philosophy; he will do the thing very cleverly, I have no doubt. He will contribute, like his other associates of the Institution, to make the real blue-stockings a little more disagreeable than ever, and sensible women a little more sensible."[1] Horner's expectations were not disappointed, for his old comrade did the thing so cleverly that the most competent and critical minds in the assemblage were the first to admit the elevation of thought, originality of illustration, and charm of exposition which distinguished these singularly clear and vigorous addresses. In spite of the approbation he had thus won, Sydney Smith retained a very modest opinion of his own merits as a lecturer, and felt as if he had suddenly been lifted into a false position by the extravagant appreciation of his efforts by the public. In a letter to Jeffrey, written in the spring of 1805, he says, "My lectures are just now at such an absurd pitch of celebrity, that I must lose a good deal of reputation before the public settles into a just equilibrium respecting them. I am most heartily ashamed of my own fame, because I am conscious I do not deserve it, and that the moment men of sense are provoked by the clamour to look into my claims, it will be at an end."[8]

Nearly forty years later, Dr. Whewell, convinced that

[1] "Life of Horner," vol. i. p. 295.

[8] Published Correspondence, p. 295.

a man of Sydney Smith's keen insight and superb common sense must have said many things on " Wit and Humour," " Reason and Judgment," which ought not to be allowed to slip into oblivion by remaining the property of one generation alone, wrote to him on the subject, and received the following characteristic reply :— " My lectures are gone to the dogs, and are utterly forgotten. I knew nothing of moral philosophy, but I was thoroughly aware that I wanted 200*l.* to furnish my house. The success, however, was prodigious ; all Albemarle Street blocked up with carriages, and such an uproar as I never remember to have been excited by any other literary imposture. Every week I had a new theory about conception and perception, and supported it by a natural manner, a torrent of words, and an impudence scarcely credible in this prudent age."[9] The introductory lectures were devoted to a bold and lively sketch of the history of moral philosophy, and in the second of them occurs the famous contrast which he drew between Aristotle and Bacon, whom he described as the two human beings who have had the greatest influence upon the intellect of mankind. The world is indebted to Bacon for an ever-widening extension of its knowledge of the laws of Nature in the external universe ; and " every succeeding year is an additional confirmation to us that we are travelling in the true path of knowledge, and as each year brings in fresh tributes of science for the increase of human happiness, it extorts from us fresh tributes of praise to the guide and father of true philosophy." To the understanding of Aristotle, " equally vast and equally

---

[9] Published Correspondence, p. 587.

original," mankind is "indebted for fifteen hundred years of quibbling and ignorance, in which the earth fell under the tyranny of words, and philosophers quarrelled with one another, like drunken men in dark rooms. * * * Professors were multiplied without the world becoming wiser, and volumes of Aristotelian philosophy were written, which, if piled one upon another, would have equalled the Tower of Babel in height, and far exceeded it in confusion." The account which he gives of Aristotle himself is even more amusing, if not quite so audacious, as his summary of the philosopher's labours: " Some writers say he was a Jew ; others that he got all his information from a Jew, that he kept an apothecary's shop, and was an atheist; others say, on the contrary, that he did not keep an apothecary's shop, and that he was a Trinitarian. Some say that he respected the religion of his country ; others that he offered sacrifices to his wife, and made hymns in favour of his father-in-law. Some are of opinion he was poisoned by the priests ; others are clear that he died of vexation, because he could not discover the causes of the ebb and flow in the Euripus. We now care or know so little about Aristotle, that Mr. Fielding, in one of his novels, says, ' Aristotle is not such a fool as many people believe, who never read a syllable of his works.' " The adroit manner in which the quotation from Fielding is introduced to turn the laugh from Aristotle to those who ignorantly ridiculed his claims, is an illustration of what the lecturer meant when, in another of his addresses at the Royal Institution, he compared true sarcasm to a sword-stick, which at first sight appears much more innocent than it really is, till suddenly there leaps out of it something sharp and incisive, which makes you recoil.

When the lectures, or rather a portion of them, for some had been committed by their author to the flames, were published by Mrs. Smith a few years after her husband's death, a letter written by Lord Jeffrey appeared in the volume, which declared that in his judgment these addresses at the Royal Institution did Sydney Smith " as much credit as anything he ever wrote, and produce, on the whole, a stronger impression of the force and vivacity of his intellect, as well as a truer and more engaging view of his character, than most of what the world has yet seen of his writings." Lord Jeffrey's daughter, Mrs. Empson, afterwards related, that on the evening prior to her father's fatal seizure he stated that it was his intention to write to Mrs. Sydney Smith in order to beg that he might be allowed to correct his old friend's lectures on moral philosophy for the press.

The following unpublished letter, despatched to Jeffrey in the summer of 1805, is interesting, as affording a glimpse of the condition of Sydney Smith's prospects at the time of his unlooked-for triumph at the Royal Institution.

[XII.]   8, Doughty Street, 4th July, 1805.

MY DEAR JEFFREY,—You ask me about my prospects. I think I shall long remain as I am. I have no powerful friends. I belong to no party. I do not cant. I abuse canting everywhere. I am not conciliating, and I have not talents enough to force my way without these laudable and illaudable auxiliaries. This is as true a picture of my situation as I can give you. In the meantime I lead not an unhappy life, much otherwise, and am thankful for my share of good. * * * My kindest regards to all my old friends.

Ever yours, my dear Jeffrey,

With the truest affection,

SYDNEY SMITH.

In 1806 he was urged to continue his lectures, and he appears to have done so with even greater success, for it was found necessary to erect galleries in the hall of the Institution to accommodate the crowds which flocked to hear him. Lord Houghton relates that, in looking back at the popularity of these lectures, Sydney Smith was accustomed to describe them as having been the "most successful swindle of the season." For this second course of lectures he received 120*l*., and this sum enabled him to buy new furniture, and to remove into a better and more convenient house, No. 18, Orchard Street, Portman Square.[1] He remained in this house until he quitted London, and it was the birthplace, in March, 1807, of his youngest daughter, Emily. Douglas was born in 1805, at Doughty Street, shortly before the family removed to their new home.

The years which Sydney Smith passed in London were marked by great and rapid changes in public affairs. The winter of 1804 was full of popular unrest and excitement, for England seemed threatened with immediate invasion. Buonaparte, who had taken

---

[1] The house has witnessed many changes since Sydney Smith called it his home, and its external appearance has been considerably altered. The ground floor has been re-modelled, and the balustrade gives the building a much more pretentious aspect than it originally wore.

to himself the title of the Emperor Napoleon, was
determined to bring down the pride of Britain to the
dust. "Let us be masters of the Channel for six
hours," ran his boast, "and we are masters of the
world." The autumn of 1805 witnessed a succession
of great battles by sea and by land. In October

18, ORCHARD STREET, PORTMAN SQUARE, LONDON.

the heart of England was thrilled by the victory at
Trafalgar, whilst torn at the price at which it had
been won. In December, Napoleon avenged the defeat
which he had suffered at our hands on the sea, by
crushing the combined forces of Austria and Russia
in the bloody struggle of Austerlitz. If the victory of

her arms at Trafalgar cost England the life of Nelson, the defeat of her rising hopes on the plain of Austerlitz deprived her counsels of the presence of Pitt. The great minister was only forty-seven, but his strength was visibly declining when this blow fell, to shatter his plans and break his heart. Austerlitz was fought on the 2nd of December, and seven weeks later, on the 23rd of January, 1806, Pitt breathed his last with the faint cry, " My country, how I leave my country ! " trembling on his lips.

The state of political affairs at home and abroad when Pitt was called from the helm was so compli-cated and critical, that reasonable men of all parties recognized that patriotism demanded from them a strong and united endeavour to uphold the honour of England and to bring the good ship of the State safely through the storms which threatened to overwhelm her. People everywhere realized, and for the moment acted under the spell of that conviction, that in the councils of the nation, no less than in her campaigns, the order which Nelson signalled at Trafalgar to his fleet stood good in every emergency, " England expects that every man will do his duty." Therefore, though many important questions were pressing to the front for solution, and suffering was rife and taxation high, all other considerations sank into insignificance in com-parison with the task of checking the ravages of Napoleon in Europe. At the death of Pitt the tide of popular feeling ran strongly in favour of Fox being called to form the new administration, but the king's rooted antipathy to that bold and brilliant statesman rendered it doubtful whether he would tolerate a Cabinet in which he even found a place. At length, however, the famous Ministry of "all the talents" succeeded to power under the leadership of Lord Grenville.

Fox was too great a man to sacrifice the needs of his country to the disappointment of the hour, and if he was not to have the position in the Cabinet to which his ability and services pointed, he determined to strengthen the hands of a leader who had refused power except on the condition that he shared it with him. Instead, therefore, of retiring gloomily to his tent in Homeric fashion, he ignored the conspicuous slight, and threw all his energies without more ado into the arduous work of the Foreign Office. His influence was soon felt far and wide, and the summer of 1806 was memorable for his splendid efforts to secure the abolition of the slave-trade, and to restore to distracted Europe the blessings of tranquillity. Had he known that his time was short, he could scarcely have laboured in the great cause of liberty and peace with more entire devotion. The year which opened darkly by the grave of Pitt was destined not to run its course ere his only rival was also removed from the scene of his triumphs and the service of his country, and for the second time in nine months England felt that peculiar shock of mingled grief and consternation which in a community is at once the earliest and most honest tribute to departed greatness. Fox died on the 13th of September, and "all the talents" which were left in the Ministry quickly proved themselves unequal to the struggle with the bigotry of the Court, backed as it was by the complacent ignorance which in Parliament and society turned a deaf ear to the petition of the Catholics.

In March, 1807, the Grenville Cabinet proposed to admit officers of Catholic convictions to serve in the army; but this mild concession to justice and common sense so alarmed and irritated the king, whose worst fears seem to have been aroused by the wily Sidmouth, that he demanded an explicit pledge from his ministers that they would under no circumstances introduce measures for Catholic relief, or counsel him in any way upon the subject. The Cabinet had been prepared, in deference not merely to the prejudices of the king, but also of some of its own members, to drop, for a time at least, the obnoxious measure; but no Ministry with a vestige of self-respect could possibly retain office on the humiliating terms thus proffered. Refusing, therefore, to subordinate the responsibilities of ministers to the predilections of the Crown, the Grenville Administration went out of power on the 24th of March, 1807, and for more than a quarter of a century the destinies of England and her Colonies were entrusted to men of the capacity and temperament of Perceval, Sidmouth, Liverpool, and Castlereagh. "It was an awful period for those who ventured to maintain Liberal opinions," said Sydney Smith, as he glanced back upon it in better times; "and there was no more chance of a Whig Administration than of a thaw in Zembla."

Francis Horner wrote the epitaph of the Ministry of "all the talents" in a masterly pamphlet of half a dozen pages, entitled "A Short Account of a late Administration," which was published within a month of the downfall of Government. He contrasts the brevity of the career of the Grenville Cabinet with the greatness of its achievements at home and abroad, and proves beyond all question that, judged by its fruits, the "late Administration" was worthy of the gratitude and confidence of the nation. In less than sixty weeks of power, substantial and permanent benefits had been conferred on the people. The period of service in the army had been shortened, and the character and condition of the common soldier had been raised; the inducements to enter the service had been multiplied, and addressed to a better class of men by the grant of a pension for life at the end of the term of service. A vigorous effort had been made by negotiations with France to restore not to England alone, but to Europe, the blessings of peace. The dangerous misunderstandings which threatened a collision with America had been removed; a system to ensure a more vigilant control of the public money, and to prevent embezzlements on the scale of former years had been framed; a new plan of finance to meet the ordinary expenditure of the war without an immediate increase of taxation had been adopted. The insurrection in Ireland had been quelled without departure from the forms of justice. The *Habeas Corpus* Act had not been suspended, and recourse to martial law had been avoided. An Act had been passed to facilitate the free interchange of every species of grain between Great Britain and Ireland. But even this imposing array of legislative triumphs did not exhaust the list, for the Slave-Trade had been virtually abolished. Well might Horner exclaim, as he proudly left, almost without comment, facts like these to speak for themselves: "These measures were not mere expedients to get through a year; they were measures founded upon large principles, and productive of lasting and extensive effects, and they will form an era in the history of the country."

One of the acts of the " late Administration " which Horner rejoiced at, even if he did not record it, was the presentation of the living of Foston, in York- shire, in the autumn of 1806, to the Rev. Sydney Smith. Foston, as a chancery living, was in the gift of Lord Erskine, and was one of a few pieces of patronage which it fell to his lot to dispense during his brief occupation of the woolsack. He gave pre- ferment to Sydney Smith at the instance of his col- league Lord Holland, who sat in the Cabinet as Lord Privy Seal. The active kindness of Lord Holland at this juncture was never forgotten by Sydney Smith, and it drew into closer friendship two men who were singularly adapted to help and cheer one another. The following letter from Lord Erskine (which has been preserved amongst the family papers) speaks for itself. It was written in response to a grateful acknowledg- ment by Sydney Smith of the gift of Foston.

[XIII.]   Hampstead, Oct. 6th, 1806.

My dear Sir,—I am favoured with your obliging letter, and I should be guilty of insincerity, and be taking a merit with you which I have no claim to, if I were not to say that I should have given the living to the nominee of Lord and Lady Holland without any personal consideration ; at the same time, I can add very truly that I thought myself most fortunate indeed, that the friend they selected was. so de- serving, and one that I should have been happy to have been useful to on his own and his brother's account. I shall feel great pleasure in cultivating your kind acquaintance.

I have the honour to be, dear Sir,

Yours faithfully,

ERSKINE.

The living of Foston was worth 500*l.* a year, and the knowledge that this provision was a permanent one, lifted a load of anxiety from the recipient's mind, and for the first time for many years he breathed freely in reference to money matters. Sydney Smith immediately went down to Yorkshire to inspect his living, and Archbishop Markham gave him temporary exemption from residence, because of his appointment at the Foundling Hospital, and a clergyman from York was engaged to drive over and preach at Foston Church. "My wife and children are well, and the world goes prosperously with me," was the answer Sydney Smith gave at this time to the inquiry of a friend. The little household in Orchard Street was not long in profiting by the improved condition of the family exchequer, for Sydney hired a house at Sonning, near Reading, and established his town-bred children in that beautiful neighbourhood during the four summer months of 1807. "I recollect," relates Lady Holland, "the first breath of air, free from carpet-shakings, that we had inhaled."[2] Whilst at Sonning, Sydney Smith made the acquaintance of Sir William Scott, afterwards Lord Stowell, and elder brother of Lord Eldon. Sir William had married a Berkshire heiress, who had inherited the family seat near Reading. He at once appreciated the remarkable

---

[2] "Memoir of the Rev. Sydney Smith," chap. v. p. 82.

qualities of the young clergyman who was lodging in the village, and told him more than once that his prospects in life would be vastly improved if he would only throw in his lot with the Tory party.

In the autumn of this year, almost before the interest which Horner's pamphlet, in vindication of the Grenville Administration had found time to subside, the first of a series of " Letters on the Subject of the Catholics," addressed " to my brother Abraham, who lives in the country," by Peter Plymley, startled the political world. The sensation created by the first letter was still at its height, when a second dropped, like a bomb-shell into the Tory ranks, and before the end of the year five of these bold and unlooked-for strictures were in circulation, and were galloping through the country as fast as the mail-coach could carry them. Five more of Peter Plymley's letters were published in rapid succession in the opening weeks of 1808, and in a month or two the entire ten were issued as a bulky pamphlet. Before the close of the year this cheap reprint, which was sold at a shilling, was already in its sixteenth edition. Thirty years later, it is curious to relate, the " Letters of Peter Plymley " had become so rare that fifty times that sum was paid for a copy.[3]

With the collapse of " All the Talents " the hopes of the friends of religious toleration were wrecked, and the general election which followed, with its cries of " No Popery!" " Church and King!" and the " Church in danger!" resulted in the return of a Tory and anti-Catholic majority. Mr. Perceval had declared

---

[3] " The work is now (1838) so scarce that we paid for our copy no less than 50s." Dr. Maginn, *Fraser's Magazine*, vol. xvii.

in Parliament that further concessions to the Catholics
were inconsistent with the safety of the State, and his
nominal chief, the Duke of Portland, endorsed the
same narrow and unjust opinions. The Portland-
Perceval Administration was accordingly formed on
the most rigid of Tory lines ; and with a Parliament
which represented an absurd panic in reference to
Napoleon and the Pope, the new ministers, with the
support of the Court, the Church, and even of many
of the Dissenters, inaugurated with little difficulty a
high-handed policy of coercion and oppression. If
religious equality was granted to the Catholics—so
ran the stock arguments of the hour—the Church was
imperilled ; if abuses were removed, or the laws
amended, the constitution was menaced ; Mr. Perceval,
indeed, might have sat for a portrait of the dog in
the manger, so well did he play that time-honoured
part. The Rev. Abraham Plymley was a representative man, and faithfully reflected the opinions and
fears of thousands of his fellow-electors in all parts of
the kingdom. Like many other well-intentioned and
sturdy defenders of the faith, the prejudices of
brother Abraham had been inflamed by the assertion
that there was a widely spread conspiracy against the
Protestant religion, and that even if, as Peter assured
him, writing out of the fulness of superior information
on the subject, the Pope had " not yet landed," there
was still too much reason to dread that he was at
least " hovering about our coast in a fishing-smack."
While dealing tenderly from first to last with
Abraham's prejudices, which even in his ridicule he
respects as the scruples of an honest but misguided
man, he pours supreme contempt on the statesmen

who had led his brother astray, and demolishes with
political irony of the most brilliant and bitter kind
their hypocritical pretensions. The self-constituted
bulwarks of the Reformation in the Cabinet, are casti-
gated with sarcasm of an exceedingly scathing description, and their logical overthrow is complete. Even
though the good taste is not always conspicuous, and
the humour is sometimes forced, and occasionally
coarse, the " Letters of Peter Plymley," with their
marvellous insight into men and motives; their solid
array of facts, which can neither be denied nor met;
their droll pleasantries and inimitable irony; their enlightened and generous sympathies; their unaffected
love of liberty; and their conspicuous common sense,
constitute one of the most powerful and effective
weapons which wisdom and wit have ever forged in
their long warfare with bigotry and superstition.
The " Letters of Peter Plymley" ran like wildfire
through the land, edition after edition was snapped
up, and the whole nation took sides with the Rev.
Abraham, or his audacious and outspoken brother.

The Government were naturally greatly incensed,
and took extraordinary pains to identify the author
of a brochure which had exposed them to public
ridicule, but their efforts in this direction were completely foiled. It seems remarkable that so zealous a
Tory, and so astute a lawyer as Lord Stowell, should
not have suspected that the accomplished young divine
of pronounced Liberal opinions, with whom he argued
in the fields around Reading in the long vacation of
the previous summer, knew more about the subject
than perhaps he cared to confess. No such thought,
however, seems to have crossed Lord Stowell's mind,

and " Peter Plymley " was, for the time at least, as much of a mystery as the man in the iron mask. Meanwhile, it was a fortunate circumstance for the Rev. Sydney Smith that " All the Talents " were not oblivious of his own, and that he received preferment during the brief summer which preceded the long winter of popular discontent. Happily, he was Rector of Foston before the sharp frost of political reaction set in, or his budding hopes in his profession would have been ruthlessly nipped even without the help of Peter Plymley's fearless pen.

THE FOUNDLING HOSPITAL, LONDON.
(*From an old print.*)

CHAPTER VII.

1807—1814.

Removal to Yorkshire—Life at Heslington—Builds Foston
Rectory.

" THE sepulchral Spencer Perceval," as Peter Plymley
described the leader of the House of Commons in the
No Popery Parliament of 1807 was destined, all unknown to himself, to take a prompt revenge for the
ridicule which that lively gentleman had heaped upon
his betters by passing a measure which practically
compelled the mischievous scribe to join his " brother
Abraham in the country." No one will pretend to
deny that the Clergy Residence Bill, which was passed
through the exertions of Mr. Perceval in 1808, was a
much needed measure of reform, or that it produced
very beneficial results in the parishes of England. At
the same time it must be admitted that, like many
other sudden enactments in Church and State, its provisions taxed somewhat unfairly the resources of the
men who were the first to come under its sway.
Sydney Smith's dilemma concerning his Yorkshire
living supplies a case in point. Except on Sundays,
Foston appears to have been a deserted village, so
far as the clergy were concerned, since the reign of
Charles II. Doubtless one pretext for such an in-

excusable state of affairs sprang out of the fact that York, with a society in those days of an eminently clerical caste, was less than a dozen miles away ; and a cathedral city was a much more congenial place of abode to the average parson of the seventeenth and eighteenth centuries than a stagnant village with no society worthy of the name. In the case of Foston, a better plea, though still an insufficient one, was the wretched condition of the parsonage-house, which was mean in all its arrangements and wholly inadequate, except indeed for an elderly celibate of meek disposition and homely tastes who was content to dine with his cook. "A brick-floored kitchen, with a room above it," with a foal-yard on one side, and a churchyard on the other, sums up nearly all that can be said of an ecclesiastical residence, which Lady Holland not inaptly terms a " hovel."

When Sydney Smith came down to look at the place, he asked the local authorities to make a valuation of the parsonage-house. The village carpenter declared it was worth 50l., but the stonemason thought that estimate was rash, and somewhat high. No wonder the rector's heart fell, for the prospect before him was certainly dismal enough ; and the gift of Foston seemed, for the moment, equivalent to that of a white elephant, and to bring his wife and children from their comfortable home in London to such an abode was out of the question. Under the new regulations, however, there was no alternative, except to relinquish the living, or to build a house,—for permission to live at a distance, which Archbishop Markham had granted, was, of course, only a temporary solution of the difficulty. After

various fruitless efforts to exchange Foston for a
benefice nearer town, he determined, though not without some misgivings, to accept the latter alternative,
and the present charming rectory, of which he was
architect as well as occupant, stands as an enduring
monument of his skill as a builder.

Although anxious for a country life, for the sake of
his children, Sydney Smith was reluctant to tear himself so completely away from the social attractions of the
town, as residence in a Yorkshire village implied. The
church at Foston was in almost as dilapidated a condition as the parsonage, and when the new clergyman
went to inspect it he was met by the octogenarian clerk,
a blunt son of the soil, accustomed to speak his mind
with refreshing candour. Lady Holland has sketched
the first interview which took place between the new
rector and the old clerk: " He looked at my father
from under his grey, shaggy eyebrows, and held a long
conversation with him, in which he showed that age
had not quenched the natural shrewdness of the
Yorkshireman. At last, after a pause, he said,
striking his crutch-stick on the ground, ' Muster
Smith, it often stroikes moi moind that people as
comes from London is such fools. But you' (giving
him a nudge with his stick), ' I see you are no fool ! ' " [1]
The verdict thus pronounced by the village oracle on
the strange parson naturally carried great weight
with the rustics of Foston, nor did the old man's reputation for wisdom suffer in after-years, in consequence of the frank avowal of his first impressions

---

[1] " Memoir of the Rev. Sydney Smith," chap. v. p. 85.

concerning his new master. Writing from York to Jeffrey shortly after this amusing episode, Sydney Smith assures his former comrade that, whilst he regrets the prospect of parting with so many friends, he feels the change will benefit his children, and give him greater leisure and more peace. He rejoices, moreover, that in Yorkshire he will be two hundred miles nearer Edinburgh.

Jeffrey, for his part, would have been thankful if Sydney Smith had returned to Edinburgh itself when he was setting out once more for the north, for the responsibility which the conduct of the *Review* imposed upon him at that time was almost more than he could bear. Brougham, Horner, Allen, and Sydney Smith were all at a distance from Edinburgh, and were all immersed in their own special affairs, and Jeffrey despaired of any return of those " careless and cordial hours " which he had once spent in their company. Sometimes, especially in his letters to Horner, in his despair of " copy," he breaks forth into strains of indignant eloquence at the base perfidy of his heartless colleagues. " You seem to treat me a little too much like a common dun, and to fancy that there is something very unreasonable in my proposing anything that is to give you trouble, or cost you a little exertion. * * * I hope you do not imagine that I have any interest in the publication that is essentially different from yours, or Smith's, or that of any of our original associates. * * * When I am deserted by my old associates I give up the concern, and while they are willing to support it I shall feel myself entitled to pester them with the story of our perplexities, and to make them bear, if possible, their full share of my anxieties." [2] On another occasion he exclaims, with a sigh of relief, "This number is out, thank Heaven, without any assistance from Horner, Brougham, Smith, Brown, Allen, Thomson, or any other of those gallant supporters who voted their blood and treasure for its assistance." [3] If Jeffrey dunned his colleagues, they were not slow to return the compliment, as the following very straightforward note from Sydney Smith sufficiently attests : —

[XIV.]   Orchard Street, Nov. 18th, 1807.

MY DEAR JEFFREY,—Upon the receipt of this, compute diligently what thou owest me for reviews in the three last numbers, and send me the money. When does Constable mean to raise his prices, or does he mean to do so at all? I ask, because (to be honest) I have three motives for writing reviews. First, the love of you. Second, the habit of reviewing. Third, the love of money ; to which I may add a fourth, the love of punishing fraud and folly. All the money I get in reviewing, I spend in books. Mrs. Smith and the children are in perfect health.

SYDNEY SMITH.

The motives which "Peter Plymley" thus gives for his work as a reviewer, are about as reliable as the statement which, years afterwards, he made to a lady concerning what he termed his threefold pretensions to do well with the world : "First, I am fond of talking nonsense. Second, I am civil. Third, I am brief." [4]

[2] "Life of Lord Jeffrey," vol. ii. p. 83.   [3] Ibid. p. 96.
[4] Published Correspondence, p. 424.

Almost the last playful passage of arms which Sydney
Smith had with Jeffrey, ere he quitted London for
Foston, occurs in an unpublished fragment penned in
Orchard Street in 1808. After referring to Jeffrey's
position in Edinburgh society and the reputation which
the growing influence of the *Review* was beginning to
give him, he adds the characteristic comment : " As
you live on the spot, you take out the payment half in
money, and half in homage and fraudulent smiles ! "
It would be interesting to have heard Jeffrey's retort,
but, alas, there lives no record of reply.

When Sydney Smith went back to town and met his
friends there, the prospect of being immersed in a
village like Foston did not grow more inviting. Nothing
would have pleased him better than to have become
rector of Sonning or Cheam, or some country parish
which he knew and within easy reach of the society he
delighted in and adorned ; but a removal to an obscure
and almost inaccessible village like Foston was a very
different matter, and involved a complete change in the
habits and associations of his life. Many a man, under
such circumstances, would have thrown up his profession in disgust, especially if he was conscious that he
possessed gifts which episcopal hands could never impart, and which were enough and more than enough to
win him a position of influence and emolument in the
world, if not in the Church. But Sydney Smith had a
deep sense of duty, and he struggled successfully to
obey it through the whole course of a life which was
one of more than common temptation. When the
desolate church and ruinous parsonage-house of Foston
presented themselves to him as the allotted scene of
his labours, he was in the full maturity of his powers,

and had already proved, first in the metropolis of
Scotland, and next in that of England, the high qualities of mind and heart which met in his strong and
courageous nature.

Seventy or eighty years ago, moreover, the difficulty
and hazard connected with the removal of a family
from London to York was quite equal to that which is
experienced to-day in a voyage from Liverpool to
Quebec. The danger, to say nothing of the discomforts,
of the old coaching days—for which a few sentimental
people still affect to sigh,—were neither few nor incon-
siderable, and, as a matter of fact, those who are old
enough to remember the practical working of the
former system of locomotion, are usually the last to
regret its disappearance. It is at least certain that
the ordinary discomforts of such a mode of travelling
(to say nothing of the delay) more than counterbalanced
its chance delights, and as for the romance of the road,
that, even now when distance has begun to lend en-
chantment to the view, is not worthy to be set against
the real and ever increasing gain of the victorious iron
horse.

Soon after his return from Yorkshire, he published
two volumes of sermons, for which he received from
Messrs. Cadell and Davies—itself a passing testimony
to the position he had won—the sum of 200*l.*;
this amount solved for the time the vexed question
of ways and means, and early in June, 1809, the
dreaded removal from Orchard Street was accomplished. "With heavy hearts we quitted London,"
relates Mrs. Smith in a hitherto unprinted record of
her experience, " and never shall I forget the heart-
sinking pain I felt on arriving on a hot June evening

at a dirty inn in York. Within a week, Sydney hired a house at Heslington, two miles from York, and from there he was able to serve his church twice on Sunday, returning to a late dinner; the distance was about twelve or thirteen miles. We had bought a little phaeton for the journey from London, and in this little vehicle with one horse, Sydney drove over every Sunday."

It was on the evening of Midsummer Day, 1809, that they arrived in York, and a fortnight later the house at Heslington was taken, in order to give them time to look round for a more convenient place of abode. Heslington was not on the road to Foston, and Sydney Smith was at least two miles further from his work in that village than if he had settled in York itself. But the house suited him, the neighbourhood was pleasant, and so he remained there until Foston Rectory was built. The house at Heslington, which thus became the first Yorkshire home of Sydney Smith and his family, is an unpretentious, old-fashioned, red-brick dwelling, standing within a few yards of the wide and straggling village street. Heavy iron railings of a pattern common enough in the Georgian era, enclose a well-stocked shrubbery, and a short flight of broad steps leads up to the door. There is a spacious passage running through the centre of the dwelling, and ordinary rooms of moderate dimensions open into it on either side. Behind the house there is a delightful old garden, in which Sydney Smith was accustomed to wander to and fro. There are no memorials of the great wit to be seen, and indeed, whilst everybody in York can point out to a stranger where Lindley Murray once lived, few of the citizens appear to be aware that

Sydney Smith spent the greater part of five eventful years in a house which, curiously enough, has now become the vicarage of the modern parish of Heslington. One tradition still lingers around the house. The lofty bay-windows which flood the vicar's study with morning light are said to have been added by Sydney Smith, and as they correspond almost exactly to some of the windows which he afterwards put into his homes at

SYDNEY SMITH'S HOUSE AT HESLINGTON, NEAR YORK.

Foston and Combe-Florey, there seems no reason to doubt the statement. Sydney Smith occupied this house until the new rectory at Foston was completed in the spring of 1814.

It was at Heslington, living as he said in "great seclusion, happily, and comfortably," that he watched with secret glee the hue and cry against the Perceval Administration, which the "Letters of Peter Plymley" evoked through the length and breadth

of the kingdom.   It was here that he wrote some of
the most powerful of his political and social essays for
the pages of the *Edinburgh Review*.   And it was here
that Dugald Stewart, Jeffrey, Sir James Mackintosh,
Brougham, Horner, Murray, Sir Samuel Romilly, and
other distinguished men became his willing guests.   In
a letter written to Lady Holland in the autumn of
1809, he states that, whilst he is not leading at Heslington precisely the life he would have chosen, he is
resolved to like it, and to reconcile himself to it, as
such a course he esteems more manly than to pretend
that he is thrown away in the country, or to send up
complaints by the post of being desolate, &c., &c.
" If it be my lot to crawl," is his sensible declaration,
" I will crawl contentedly; if to fly, I will fly with
alacrity; but, as long as I can avoid it, I will never be
unhappy.   If, with a pleasant wife, three children, a
good house and farm, many books, and many friends who
wish me well, I cannot be happy, I am a very silly,
foolish fellow, and what becomes of me is of very
little consequence." [5]

Heslington is still a quiet village; but when Sydney
Smith took up his residence in it, there was an air
of primitive simplicity about the place.   Old Major
Yarburgh, the lord of the manor, lived in a stately
Elizabethan mansion in the outskirts, and seldom
stirred far from the village street.   The squire was an
ardent lover of field-sports, and his breed of grey-
hounds was the admiration of the whole countryside.
Heslington was the major's little kingdom, and he
reigned over it with autocratic but goodnatured sway.

[5] Published Correspondence, p. 331.

A squire of the good old sort, he had a cheery word
for old and young, and an unfailing supply of silver
sixpences for the beggars who clamoured or cringed
at his gate. His horses were even more renowned
than his dogs, and they carried his colours to the
winning-post in many a famous race.

The squire at first regarded the clergyman from
London, who had taken up his quarters in the village, as a questionable, if not an undesirable intruder.
He had heard it whispered that his new neighbour
held the most dangerous and extreme opinions on
political and social subjects. The squire could not
tolerate men of that description, and accordingly
gave the stranger a stern glance and a wide berth.
After an interval, however, finding that nothing of
a revolutionary character had occurred to convulse
the life of the village, the feelings of the major
underwent a change, and one fine morning he even
went so far as to bow to the parson. The ice once
broken, the exchange of courtesies became the rule
instead of the exception, and presently the squire
arrived at such a pitch of confidence in his new friend,
that he hurried him off one day in a transport of
enthusiasm to see his dogs. From that day forward
their intercourse was cordial and unembarrassed, and
the two men understood each other completely.

The old squire was not the only friend whom
Sydney Smith made at this period, for other and more
distinguished men began at Heslington to cultivate
his acquaintance. His intimacy with Earl Grey dates
from a flying visit which he paid to Howick in the
autumn of 1809, and for many years he made an
annual visit there on his way from Yorkshire to Edin-

burgh. The close friendship which existed between
Lord and Lady Grey and Sydney Smith continued
without any interruption till the last, and was a source
of constant pleasure to all concerned. The present Earl
Grey states that he can still recall the great pleasure
which, when he was a boy, the visits of Sydney Smith
gave to his father and the whole circle at Howick,
and adds that he was most kind to every member of
the family, and delighted to amuse the young people
around him in his own inimitable way. Lady Georgina
Grey also " well remembers how much we all loved,
admired, and respected him." The home life of the
great Whig statesman, whose name is indissolubly
linked with the Reform Bill of 1832, was simple,
bright, and unassuming, and all who stayed at
Howick quitted its hospitable walls with sincere
regret, and with a heightened respect for its master.
Sir James Mackintosh—a mutual friend of Lord
Grey and Sydney Smith—after spending a few days
on one occasion there as the guest of Lord and
Lady Grey, jotted down in his diary a note to the
effect that he had passed that week in the best ordered
family, and amongst some of the purest people he had
ever seen.[6] It is certain that some of the happiest
hours in the life of Sydney Smith were spent at Howick
and Portman Square in frank and cordial intercourse
with Lord Grey and his family, and some of the most
sprightly epistles he ever wrote were dashed off in the
freedom of perfect confidence to Lady Grey. In one
of the earliest of these letters he gives an amusing
account of his fellow-passengers in the coach, and

[6] " Life of Sir James Mackintosh," vol. ii. chap. iv. p. 259.

their outspoken but friendly criticism of the character
and means of his noble host at Howick. On reaching
Heslington, he states that he found everybody very
well at home, and various schemes laid, which he duly
intends to aid and abet, for keeping Christmas, 1810,
in joyous and worthy fashion.

He did not, however, always find everybody very
well at home on his return from his northern visits, or
his annual trip to town. Sometimes he is compelled
to confess that he discovered on these occasions " some
illness and much despondency, of which, if my absence
was not the cause, my return has been the cure."
Many a man who has shone before the world as a
social wit, has been gloomy and morose at home ; but
there was no spot on earth where Sydney Smith was
more gay or welcome than at his own fireside. He
was not only the friend, but the playfellow of his
children, and nothing delighted him more than a merry
romp through the house with his little ones laughing
and shouting at his heels. He encouraged his children
to talk freely to him, and to make him a confidant in
their little schemes ; and he was accustomed to listen
with the greatest patience and good-humour to any
question which was not wholly thoughtless.

At the same time, mere idle and foolish questions,
which they could have answered for themselves by a
moment's reflection, were not received with the same
complaisance. However busy he might be, he could
always find time to smooth difficulties out of the way
of a puzzled child, and by every means in his power
he sought to quicken and enrich their opening minds.
Neither conversation nor music needed to be hushed
when he sat down to his desk, and his pen moved as

swiftly in the midst of a happy family group as the tongues of his children. Both at Heslington and Foston the children's hour, on all ordinary occasions, was duly observed, and was looked forward to by them and remembered in after-years with unmixed pleasure. In an evening, he would sit in the twilight with his children on his knees or at his feet, and thrill them with the sorrowful or laughable adventures, as the case might be, of old world heroes and their lady-loves. With the magical wand of imagination he was able at will to conjure up before the delighted minds of his children the brave little men and bright little women who frolic to their hearts' content in the shadowy glades of Fairyland. No wonder Saba, when a child of eight, should have exclaimed one day when the house was quiet and her mother seemed depressed, "Why, mamma, I'll tell you what the matter is: you are so melancholy and dull because papa is away; he is so merry that he makes us all gay. A family doesn't prosper, I see, without a papa." [7]

Sydney Smith's good-will to children went far beyond the limits of his own household. It mattered not where he was—in the cottages and lanes of Foston or Combe-Florey, or the picture-gallery at Castle Howard, or the library at Bowood, he always noticed the children, and gave them a pleasant smile and a kind word. Towards the close of his life, as he one day watched from a rustic seat his daughter's little ones scampering round the garden in the morning sunshine, wild with glee, his words were, "Attend to

[7] Letter of Mrs. Smith to Francis Jeffrey, Esq., Heslington, 1810. "Memoir of the Rev. Sydney Smith," p. 330.

the happiness of children. Mankind are always happier for having been happy, and a happy childhood is the last remembrance which clings to us in old age. I have always regretted that I had no such recollections."[8] "You have no idea," said he on another occasion, " of the value of kindness. Pleasure is very reflective, and if you give it you will feel it, and pleasure which you give by a little kindness of manner returns to you with compound interest."

Dr. Vernon Harcourt—who succeeded Dr. Markham, and was the last of the Prince Archbishops of York—soon discovered the rare qualities of the man upon whom Lord Erskine had conferred the obscure living of Foston. Probably the Archbishop of York felt, like the squire of Heslington, a little shy of his new neighbour, but it was not long before that shrewd and vivacious prelate recognized the worth as well as the wit of the genial clergyman who had been placed through the influence of Lord Holland under his crosier. Dr. Harcourt was a man who could appreciate at something like their true value the peculiar talents of Sydney Smith ; and the unconventional freshness of his conversation, as well as the extent and variety of his information on all the questions of the day, called forth his admiration, and secured his friendship.

Sydney Smith on his visits to Bishopthorpe frequently acted as croupier at the archbishop's table, and several amusing anecdotes used to be told of his

[8] One immediately recalls the case of a brilliant leader of society, Harriet, Lady Ashburton, the friend of Sydney Smith, Thomas Carlyle, and a host of other distinguished men. "She often alluded," relates Lord Houghton, "to the hard repression of her childhood, and its effects : 'I was constantly punished for my impertinence, and you see the result.'" "Monographs : Literary and Social," p. 227.

conduct in that capacity. Dr. Harcourt had a rooted
aversion to bores of every description, but he particularly dreaded the attentions of scientific and erudite
guests, as he had discovered, through many a doleful
experience in the past, that they were addicted to long-
winded and tediously minute explanations. One day
an entomologist, full of enthusiasm for his hobby, and
eager to impart what he knew of insect ways to his
reluctant host, sat at the right of the archbishop. A
momentary lull in the conversation, which up to this
point had been general, gave the admirer of beetles his
coveted chance, and straightway he plunged into the
midst of his subject, until the goodnatured prelate,
who cared for none of these things, was rendered
supremely miserable by a complicated and confused
account of a department of knowledge with which he
had never intermeddled. The archbishop frankly
avowed his ignorance, and did so in such significant
terms, that his indifference likewise stood confessed.
The student of things which creep, was either blind or
remorseless, and accordingly pursued his way through
larvæ, antennæ, and the like, with dangerous animation.
The master of the banquet tried to turn a deaf ear
to the maddening persistency of his misguided visitor,
who told a tale as interminable, but not as interesting,
as that with which the " Ancient Mariner " detained
the wedding guest, whilst the host sat at the head
of his table like a picture of injured innocence. At
the other end, Sydney Smith, a delighted spectator
of the scene, awaited his opportunity to rescue the
disconsolate prelate from his embarrassing dilemma.
By-and-by he heard the man of science declare that
the eye of a fly was larger in proportion to its body
than that of any other creature. At once, in tones

of lofty authority, not unmingled with contempt, the croupier struck in and met the statement with a flat denial. Indignant at such a contradiction on ground of which he felt sure, the entomologist proudly fell back on facts, and demanded visual proof. The whole company was now on the alert, and began to settle down to the expected controversy. With much deliberation and precision, Sydney proceeded to call attention to the great sources of all truth, and argued that it must be admitted that the common judgment and knowledge of mankind lay treasured in the bardic measures and nursery rhymes of antiquity. "What then, how does all this bear upon the present case?" demanded the naturalist somewhat stiffly. In overwhelming recitative came the familiar words, "I, said the fly, with my *little* eye, I saw him die!" The *reductio ad absurdum* was complete, and Archbishop Harcourt was free.

At another banquet at Bishopthorpe, a reverend and learned antiquary led the conversation into dry and dusty by-paths, untrodden by the feet of ordinary mortals, and, lost in the mazes of the mind, and blind to all hints, persisted in wandering deeper and deeper into the intricacies of obsolete periods and problems. The archbishop darted a glance, in which entreaty struggled with despair, at Sydney Smith, and sank back wearied in his chair. Presently, in a confidential but clear undertone, loud enough to be distinctly heard by all at table, Sydney thus addressed an immediate neighbour, "How he is annoying the worthy archbishop! It is easy to see where he is; as usual, he is in the Persian War: yes—now he is at Darius Hystaspes. Ah! he has presumed too much; his grace is waking up. "Darius Hystaspes? I never heard of that horse before.

What is his pedigree, sire and dam ?" It is needless to say that the pedantic bore was silenced, and rational table-talk resumed its sparkling and easy sway.

If Sydney Smith addressed his immediate neighbour on that occasion, it was not his usual custom to do so, at least at large dinner-parties. He, of course, talked a little with the people at his side, but he usually endeavoured at the outset to place the conversation on a wider basis, so as to elicit the powers and secure the interest of every member of the company. He accordingly, as a rule, talked across the table, and if the person opposite proved too sheepish or stupid to respond, some one a little lower down was certain to return his balls. He was not only a superb talker, but an attentive listener, and in this respect his bearing in general society contrasts favourably with that of many less brilliant men. He believed that brevity was the soul of wit, and a piece of advice which he was fond of giving was, " Take as many half-minutes as you can get, but never talk more than half a minute without pausing and giving others an opportunity to strike in." One thing he disliked exceedingly, and that was the half-whispered tones in which so many people speak at feasts as well as at funerals, and he declared that so far as his observation went, most London dinners evaporated in whispers to one's immediate neighbours.

The early years which Sydney Smith spent in Yorkshire formed a somewhat restless and anxious period in his career, for whilst he diligently attended to his duties at Foston, he was still far from reconciled to the prospect of being immured indefinitely in that obscure and sleepy village. As late as the beginning of 1812, he appears to have cherished the hope of exchanging his living for one nearer London, but as the year mentioned passed with no likelihood of that hope being realized, he finally abandoned it, and set himself seriously to consider how best he could provide a suitable home for his family at Foston.

When once this decision was taken, life at Heslington became more pleasant, and the last two years of his stay there glided swiftly away amid literary and parish work, occasional visits to town, and more frequent visitors from it, the superintendence of Douglas' education, and the cultivation of the farm and erection of the parsonage-house at Foston. In September, 1813, his second son was born at Heslington, and he wrote with sly humour to one of his friends to say that he meant to call the new arrival Grafton, and to train him up as a Methodist and Tory. The child received a very different name, however, for he was called Windham, after the great statesman whom England had just lost, and whom Dr. Johnson regarded as the model of a true English gentleman. Three months before the birth of his son, Sydney commenced to build his house, and he describes himself as having spent the autumn of that year " trowel in hand."

The following account of the building of Foston Rectory was written in her old age by Mrs. Sydney Smith for the information of her grandchildren. Some portions of this statement have been reproduced in the narrative of Lady Holland, but the greater part (which is now printed by the kind permission of Miss Holland) has hitherto remained in the manuscript pages of a family record :—

MRS. SYDNEY SMITH'S ACCOUNT OF THE BUILDING
OF FOSTON RECTORY.

Sydney sent for an architect, told him the sort of

house he wanted, and begged for plan and estimate. It was three thousand pounds. We both knew what we wanted, and the number and size of the rooms which we wished to have. " Cannot you take your rule and compass, and so arrange these by a scale that we can do without this great man ? " said Sydney. This I did. We sat in judgment over our plan, hired an excellent carpenter and mason, and our house was begun : when finished we had not made one mistake. On the glebe was some fine clay. A skilful bricklayer from Leeds was sent for to pass sentence upon it. It was declared to be of the best quality. Large heaps were dug up to be tempered by the winter's frost. A hundred and fifty thousand bricks were burnt : they were not worth a rush ! The old parsonage just made the foundation of the new house. Grandfather bought four oxen to carry the bricks—Tug, Lug, Hawl, and Crawl; he was soon tired of these slow, unexcitable animals. The roads were utterly neglected. There was a mile of very deep sand close to the village. These heavy beasts, Tug and company, little relished this at the end of their journey with the bricks. Their remedy was to lie down and roar ! Grandfather said he found them too expensive ; they required ' a bucketful of sal volatile ' daily. He gave up his oxen to a farmer for fattening, and set up a more manageable team—of horses.

All seemed to be prospering. The first stone of the parsonage was laid in June, 1813. Windham was born in the following September. A tremendous winter and long-continued frost for eight weeks stopped all the work both within and without the house. Our hired house at Heslington was let at the coming Lady Day, March 25th, 1814, and our furniture, of course, was

to be removed. The never-ending frost was a serious
affair, but there was no help. In its half-finished state
we were obliged to flit, and such a flitting it was! The
bedding—the last thing left at Heslington (with two
or three chairs and a table)—we slept upon on the
ground the last night, for the bedsteads had been
carried off the day before to Foston. All up at five—
a cold March morning—to liberate the bedding, which
was to be removed to Foston for the next night. A
close carriage was hired to convey me and Windham
(now six months old, but never before out of the house
in which he was born), and the three other children,
with Annie Kaye. Some waggons had gone early,
others followed us.

We set out after the children's dinner at one
o'clock. Windham slept soundly till we were half-way
up the sandy road (the scene of Tug's afflictions),
when he set up an awful noise. We had made our
way about half-way up to the house, when it seemed
very likely that we should get no further. The field
—there was at that time no road up to the parsonage,
or only a rough one—had been so much cut up by constant carting that the carriage stuck fast. I got out
with the baby in my arms, but soon lost my shoe in
the stiff clay, and so walked on without. There were
no doors to the drawing-room, but I remember, in spite
of it all, there was a very merry tea-making upon
some of the boxes piled up in the drawing-room.

———

It is not difficult to picture the scene. The toils
and adventures of the day over, and thick gloom
closing rapidly in upon the cold March afternoon.
Outside, the shouting of the waggoners, and the
neighing of the horses. Within, the unexplored won-

ders of the strange house, and the hurrying servants
flitting to and fro through the dimly-lighted corridors.
The blazing fire in the drawing-room casting a ruddy
glow on the tear-stained faces of the tired but excited
children, and sending dark shadows to dance fitfully
against the vacant walls. The kind mother busily
preparing a hasty meal for the hungry young travellers,
while her husband arranges boxes and bedding for
its luxurious enjoyment, laughing gleefully meanwhile
over the episode of the lost shoe, and mischievously
pretending to be grateful for his wife's escape from
imaginary pitfalls of a more alarming kind. Thus,
amid homely domestic cares and happy household
mirth, the eventful Lady Day of 1814 drew near to
its welcome close; yet it did not vanish into the past
until it had ushered in an altered phase in Sydney
Smith's experience of life.

PORCH OF FOSTON CHURCH.

CHAPTER VIII.

1814—1817.

Life at Foston—The Church, the Rectory, and the People—Kindness to the poor as "village Parson and Doctor"—Fondness for children—Popularity with servants.

MANY of the best years of Sydney Smith's life were spent in the village of Foston. When he took possession of his new rectory, he was forty-two years of age, and he was fifty-seven when he exchanged Foston for Combe-Florey. In one respect at least, the fourteen years which cover his experiences in Yorkshire were uneventful, for neither birth nor death occurred under his roof during that period. Windham, the youngest member of the family, was a babe of six months when Foston Rectory became his home, and the first break in the circle—the death of Douglas —did not take place until the happy and tranquil Yorkshire days were recalled as a sunny memory over the fireside at Combe-Florey.

The new house was a great success, in spite of the dismal predictions which some of his London friends made to the architect, that he would lose his own health in it, or ruin that of his children. A month after he entered it, he was able to tell Allen, who had sent him a letter of medical advice on the subject of damp walls, " I am very much pleased with my house.

I aimed at making a snug parsonage, and I think I have succeeded." [1] No one who has actually visited Foston Rectory will be inclined to quarrel with that statement, for the house, though plainly built and simple in style, is the perfection of comfort. It has been the fashion to commiserate Sydney Smith over his life at Foston, and probably the habit has grown around a too literal interpretation of his own language concerning it; most people, however, who know that charming spot are more inclined to envy than to pity him. No doubt before the roads were properly made, or the rectory built, life in such a village, especially to a man accustomed to move in the best London society, would naturally appear somewhat uninviting; but when these difficulties were vanquished, and the preacher at the Foundling Hospital himself grew bucolic in his tastes, the aspect of affairs must soon have assumed a more attractive shape. The roads in the neighbourhood were little better than bridle-paths, and between the deep mud of winter and the dangerous ruts of summer, locomotion was usually irksome, and often perilous.

Castle Howard is in the immediate neighbourhood, and the Earl and Countess of Carlisle were amongst the first to welcome Sydney Smith to Foston.[2] Their first visit to the rectory was accomplished under rather awkward conditions, for their coach and four stuck fast in the mud which had tried so sorely the mettle of Sydney's unfortunate oxen twelve months ago. The eldest son of the Earl of Carlisle, Lord Morpeth, had been a companion of Bobus Smith at Eton, and

---

[1] Published Correspondence, p. 360.

[2] The fifth earl; the friend of Charles James Fox and George Selwyn, and the kinsman and guardian of Lord Byron.

through Lord Grey and other mutual friends, the
doors of Castle Howard were thrown open to Sydney
Smith.   The intimacy which thus began, continued—
like almost every friendship Sydney Smith made—
until it was broken by death.   What Holland House
had been to him in his early struggles in London,
Castle Howard became when the scene was shifted to
Yorkshire; and though he was never as closely
associated with Lord and Lady Carlisle as with Lord
and Lady Holland, he experienced from them almost
equal kindness, and regarded them as a man regards
friends whose loyalty has been proved in time of need.
The knowledge that a welcome always awaited him at
Castle Howard, took the sting out of his comparative
isolation at Foston, whilst access to cultivated society,
and to an extensive library which was thus placed
within his reach, swept away half the disadvantages
of a country life before the age of steam.   At a sharp
turn in the road between Foston and Castle Howard,
the palatial seat of the Earls of Carlisle comes suddenly
into sight; the view from this point is magnificent,
and Sydney Smith accordingly named the spot, Exclamation Corner.   "You have no idea," he was accustomed to say to his noble friends, "how splendidly lugu-
brious Castle Howard appears when you are all away."

Other friends, from far and near, gradually found
their way to the rectory, but those who came from a
distance sometimes completely missed the route, partly
through the insignificance of the village, and partly
through the atrocious condition of the roads by which
it was approached.   In order that the exact locality
of Foston might be better understood by prospective
travellers, some of whom appear to have imagined

that it was situated in barbarian fastnesses, he had
bills (foolscap size) printed in bold type containing
directions as to the roads, and stating the distances
in the following fashion: York is ten miles from
Foston Rectory. Malton is eight miles from Foston
Rectory. Castle Howard is four miles from Foston
Rectory," &c. After these directions were circulated,
the " Rector's Head," as he sometimes styled his
house, became well known, and people no longer
missed their way to its hospitable shelter. The roads
in the district, moreover, by his exertions, were in
course of time much improved, and another difficulty
was thus greatly lessened.

A visitor to Foston in these days knows nothing, of
course, of such obstacles, for, taking a seat at York in
the Malton train, he alights at the wayside station
of Flaxton, and is at once directed to the rectory,
which is some two miles away. The traveller in
the Scarborough express, who seats himself with his
back to the engine in the right-hand corner of the
carriage, will catch a passing glimpse of Sydney's
Smith's parsonage, with its bay windows and red-tiled
roof, standing amongst the trees, at a distance of
three or four fields, when the train is running between
Kirkham Abbey and Flaxton. The nearest way for
a stranger from Flaxton station to Foston, is through
the fields; a winding path, which it is impossible to
miss, will lead him for a mile through undulating
meadows, until, leaving Foston Hall to the left, he
strikes the main road again, and finds himself close
to the church, which is within two minutes' walk of
the gate through which he has just passed, and stands
on rising ground to the right of the turnpike road.

Foston Church is one of the oldest ecclesiastical buildings in the north of England, and though a plain and unpretending structure, it presents several points of considerable interest. The present rector of the parish (the Rev. Francis Simpson, M.A.), after long-continued research, states that he is unable to give any reliable information as to the date of erection, but a close investigation shows that every portion of the building bears marks of great antiquity. The chancel arch and that over the porch are both remarkable features in the building; the latter is singularly curious, a Norman arch, with Scripture subjects carved on each stone. Some of these representations have crumbled away through age, but on one stone David playing on the harp, and on another Abraham offering up Isaac, can still be distinctly traced; whilst on the keystone of the arch, a carving of the Last Supper is visible.

The building is exceedingly small, and the interior is disfigured by a narrow gallery which runs across the end and up one side of the church. In this gallery, the village children, have from time immemorial been seated at morning service on Sundays; and there is an old man still in attendance at the church, who sat there regularly sixty years ago, when Sydney Smith was rector. He states that Mr. Smith, when he was preaching, kept a sharp eye on the more restless of the lads, and sometimes gave them a significant shake of the head in the course of his sermon, which they knew to mean—" You must give an account of yourself at the close of the service." Along the front of the gallery there is a row of unsightly wooden pegs, upon which the people in the pews below were accustomed to hang their hats and coats. Under the gallery, at the far end of the building is a heating apparatus, and the flue-pipe connected with it is carried outside through an aperture made for that purpose in the west window of the church.

INTERIOR OF FOSTON CHURCH.

The pulpit is stuck up in a corner opposite the side gallery; below the pulpit is a reading-desk, and above it a large sounding-board is fixed to the ceiling. The pulpit hangings are faded and worn, and the whole church looks desolate and neglected;

N

it will seat, including the gallery, from one hundred and
fifty to one hundred and seventy people. Perhaps a
better idea of the smallness of the place in which Sydney
Smith preached for twenty years may be gathered when
it is stated that between the door (which is near the
end gallery) and the front of the pulpit, there are only
four pews. There is neither stained window nor memorial tablet to the memory of Sydney Smith, and so far
indeed as Foston Church is concerned, there is not a
line to show that he ever entered its pulpit. On the
28th of May, 1883, when the writer wandered amongst
its tombs, the burying-ground around the church was
equally forlorn, whilst that portion of it which lies at the
back of the building was little better than a bed of
nettles. It is to be hoped—for the credit of the whole
diocese of York—that this state of affairs will not be
allowed to continue much longer. Local munificence
may perhaps be inadequate to the task of restoring this
venerable church, but the sentiment of the nation, if
rightly invited, may be trusted to respond to an appeal
on behalf of a building as closely associated as Foston
Church with the life and labours of a clergyman of
the Establishment who proved himself by voice and
pen the powerful friend and helper of the entire
English people.

There are two or three cottages in the neighbourhood
of the church, and a few more are scattered by the
roadside a little further on, but there is no village of
Foston in the ordinary sense of the word. A mile
beyond the church, a small school-house stands on the
opposite side of the road, and just behind the school-
house is the gate to Foston Rectory. A well-kept
drive, winding through park-like grounds, leads up to

the house; half-way between the turnpike road and
the parsonage a second gate is passed, which bears the
curious name of the "Screeching Gate." Sydney
Smith, it need scarcely be said, gave it that name, and
it received it not on account of any infirmity of its own,
but because of an infirmity apparent in his wife and
daughters. The master of the house had learnt by
experience that on Sundays, when on his way with his

FOSTON RECTORY.
(*Built by Sydney Smith in* 1814.)

family to church, one or other of the ladies was certain
to cry out at this stage of the journey that she had
forgotten this or that, and to run back in sudden haste
to the house to secure it, and so the "Screeching Gate"
received its name. There is not much, either in the
house or around it, to call for special remark. The
flower-beds are tastefully laid out, and fringed with
woodland trees; and behind the house is a well-

stocked kitchen-garden and orchard. An extensive range of barns, farm-buildings, and stables adjoins the back premises, but is partially hidden by a belt of trees.

The house has not been altered to any material extent since Sydney Smith built it, and the picture on the preceding page—which was drawn a few months ago on the spot—is a correct representation of its present appearance. In the bay on the ground floor is the drawing-room, and above it Sydney Smith's bed-room. The dining-room, which is bright and spacious, is on the same side of the house as the conservatory; the open window to the left of the bay is Sydney Smith's study, justice-room, and surgery. The principal rooms, both upstairs and down, are shut off from the rest of the house. York is about eight miles from the rectory as the crow flies, and from the drawing-room window on a fine day the majestic towers of the Minster can be distinctly seen through a break in the trees. "I like my new house very much," wrote Sydney in a letter to Jeffrey in the autumn of 1814; "it is very comfortable. I would not pay sixpence to alter it; but the expense of it will keep me a close prisoner here for life." [3]

A few steps beyond the gates of Foston Rectory the pretty village of Thornton-le-Clay—consisting of some thirty or forty houses—straggles up the hilly turnpike road; and most of the people who attend Foston Church live in Thornton. In the distance, on the crest of a wooded hill to the right, stands the stately column erected in the grounds of Castle Howard to the memory of the famous Lord Carlisle.

[3] Published Correspondence, p. 362.

Seventy years have rolled away since Sydney Smith built Foston Rectory, and more than half a century ago he ceased to call it his home. There are, accordingly, exceedingly few persons now living who remember the place in his days, and probably only two or three who experienced his hospitality there. One of the last of his Yorkshire friends has recently departed this life in the person of Mr. Egerton Vernon Harcourt, a Deputy-Lieutenant and Justice of the Peace of the East Riding. Mr. Harcourt (who died on the 19th of October, 1883) was a son of Dr. Edward Vernon Harcourt, formerly Archbishop of York, and was uncle to the present Home Secretary, Sir Wm. Vernon Harcourt, M.P. A few months before his death, Mr. Harcourt—at the instance of Lady Elizabeth Grey—penned the following account of visits paid in his youth to Foston, and placed it at the disposal of the writer.

RECOLLECTIONS OF SYDNEY SMITH AT FOSTON.

Whitwell Hall, York, July 2nd, 1883.

The Rev. Sydney Smith was very intimate with my father, the Archbishop of York, and his family, and used frequently to visit at Bishopthorpe. When, by gift of the Lord Chancellor, he took possession of the living of Foston, there was no house for the clergyman, and the Sunday duty had been done by a former incumbent from York, which was ten miles distant; but after consulting my father, he determined on residing in his parish, and so built himself a good plain brick house in an open field adjoining Thornton, the principal village in his parish, though at the distance of a mile from the church. In this house, both when a boy at Westminster School (to which his eldest son went), and afterwards when I was a student of Christ Church, Oxford, I was frequently invited to visit him; and most pleasant visits they were, not only on account of the amusement afforded by his exuberant flow of wit, but also from his conversation in graver hours being full of sound sense and ability. Besides which his two daughters made the evenings pass very agreeably by their singing, in which he sometimes took a part.

I never passed a Sunday in his house, but he seemed to be always attentive to his parishioners, and he had a dispensary at home, to which they resorted for his medical aid, which he was quite competent and desirous to give. Considering Sydney Smith's previous habits of literary intercourse with distinguished men in Edinburgh, I used to wonder at his living so contentedly in his very quiet rural nest. In those days the services of clergy were frequently put in requisition for acting as magistrates, and he took a useful part on the neighbouring bench of petty sessions. His well-known affability and kindness made him popular among the poor as well as the rich.

E. V. HARCOURT.

Mr. Harcourt mentions Sydney Smith's medical attentions to his parishioners, and his services in the locality as a county magistrate. Reference has already been made to the "study" at Foston Rectory, and that room is associated not only with the composition of sermons, but with the examination of patients and prisoners. Physic and justice were alike dispensed

in a room which was known to some as the "surgery,"
to others as the "justice-room," and to the master of
the house as the "study." Here he kept his surgical
instruments and appliances, and did his best to relieve
the sufferings of the old and infirm who came to him
for advice. The knowledge of medicine which he had
acquired in Edinburgh was thus called into requisition,
and his skill in the healing art soon proved itself far
from contemptible. He was kind to the villagers in a
variety of ways, and his memory is still cherished in
Foston with affectionate respect. One act of charity
which was greatly appreciated was the gift of a quart
of milk daily to a number of poor people in the parish.
In order that each might get exactly the same, and
thus jealousy be avoided, he provided cans for the
purpose of equal capacity, and they were all marked
with his initials. He soon made himself at home with
his parishioners, and sought to brighten the lives of
the people around him in various ways. He was a
great pedestrian at this period of his life, and moved
freely about amongst the cottages of Foston and
Thornton, where many traditions of his kindliness and
consideration still linger.

The distress amongst the poor throughout the
country at the close of the Peninsular War was
aggravated by the failure of the harvest of 1816, and
the people of Foston shared the common privation
which ensued. Bad and insufficient food reduced
many to the verge of the grave, and fever of a malig-
nant type prevailed that winter in the village, and
carried off some of the inhabitants,—and "Sydney
visited them all constantly, every day," was the testimony of his wife in a forgotten letter to a friend, which

has just come to light. In the midst of all this misery
and suffering he went to and fro, calmly and kindly,
and did everything in his power by medical skill and
clerical ministrations to relieve or lessen the troubles
of the poor, and his attitude at this crisis in the little
world of Foston in which he now moved, gave him a
hold upon the affections of the people which he never
lost.

Adjoining the rectory grounds there are a number
of small gardens, filled with well-grown fruit-trees, '
and these gardens were planned, stocked, and given to
the villagers at a merely nominal rent by Sydney
Smith. The people still speak gratefully of "Sydney's
Orchards," as they are termed, and last spring the
gnarled branches of the old trees were richly laden
with pink and white blossoms, which, seen from the
village street, against the dark-green background of
the rector's plantation, with the red-tiled roof of the
parsonage beyond, peeping through the foliage, formed
a pretty picture. The shrubberies around the house
were designed by Mr. and Mrs. Smith, and the
ornamental flower-beds on the lawn attest the fine taste
which reigned at the rectory, and was apparent in
every detail of its arrangements.

The living of Foston was chiefly derived from land,
and one farm of three hundred acres close to the rectory
he himself cultivated, and did so with a considerable
degree of success, in spite of his own assertion about
not knowing the difference between a turnip and a
carrot. He kept a sharp eye on the labourers, and
part of his stock-in-trade as a farmer was a ship
captain's speaking-trumpet and a large telescope. He
was thus able to watch from his study window opera-

tions in the neighbouring fields, and, standing on the steps of the rectory, he could speak in commanding tones of authority to the distant ploughman. He was a strict master, and could not tolerate careless and idle people around him, and sometimes the revelations of his telescope were of a nature to ruffle his temper. One day, for example, a lad at work in the fields lay down in the furrow, and spread out his arms in order to teach his companions how to swim. In the midst of the lesson, Sydney came suddenly from behind a hedge, and after gazing for a moment in amazement at the scene, ordered the culprit to come to the " justice-room " in the evening. The poor boy was, however, too much afraid to venture until he was sent for, but the sequel proved that he had little to dread. His master reproved him for stealing his time, and told him never to be such a simpleton again as to try and swim on dry land. He was then goodhumouredly dismissed to the kitchen with a shilling in his pocket, and a recommendation to the cook. On another occasion a man on the farm blundered to such an extent that his master completely lost his temper, and called him a fool. " God never made man a fool," growled the transgressor. " That is quite true, sir," was the immediate retort ; " but man was not long in making a fool of himself."

He was particularly fond of children and young people, and liked to have them around him at the rectory. He used to contrive all sorts of little services in order to keep the village lads out of mischief, and whilst he always had a kind word and pleasant smile for the industrious and respectful, those who were idle or impertinent became the object of sarcastic remarks which usually had the desired effect. A number of the children, both boys and girls, were employed for a few hours a day in gathering sticks in the plantation, sweeping the fallen leaves from the lawn, weeding the flower-beds, or helping in the work of the farmstead. The children, in almost every case, were proud to work for the rector, for he took such a lively interest in them, and in all that they did, that they felt him to be their friend as well as their master. In his dealings with their parents, he seemed always anxious to deepen the sense of responsibility to the children, and he encouraged them by every means in his power to forward, by personal self-denial, the future advantage of their families. " The haunts of Happiness are varied," he would sometimes say, " but I have more often found her among little children, home firesides, and country houses, than anywhere else." [4]

Occasionally, it must be confessed that he was unduly harsh and inconsiderate with the little work-people in the rectory grounds, and there were times when he seems scarcely to have measured the force of his words, or realized the strength of his fingers. For instance, to stand all day on the lawn with a large placard with the word " Thief" printed boldly upon it, was a heavy punishment to award to a little girl for biting a fallen peach; and to pinch an urchin's ears so vigorously that they tingled in old age at the remembrance of the episode, was a severe penalty to incur for the high crime and misdemeanour of falling into a brown study under an apple-tree, and betraying undisguised admiration for the tempting fruit, and too keen an interest in its ultimate fate. It was not uncommon

---

[4] " Memoir of Sydney Smith," chap. x. p. 194.

for Sydney Smith, on second thoughts, to see that he had regarded such venial offences in too serious a light, and he was not too proud a man to acknowledge an error of judgment even to a village lad. It is only fair to add that in both the cases mentioned, and in others of the same kind, he managed, by subsequent acts of kindness and consideration, to convince the delinquents themselves that they had no truer friend in the parish than the rector. Towards the younger children he was extremely indulgent, and as he passed to and fro through the village, the little ones hastened to the cottage doors to greet him. The people of Foston still relate that young children felt no fear of him, but were accustomed to run after him on the road, "pulling at his coat tails," and roguishly clamouring for the sweets which they knew he always carried in their interests.

Sydney Smith's journeys to Malton and York, and even much further afield, were usually performed in that "ancient green chariot, supposed to have been the earliest invention of the kind," which he discovered in the "back settlements of a York coachmaker," and of which he has given in the following words so graphic a description : " I brought it home in triumph to my admiring family. Being somewhat dilapidated, the village tailor lined it, the village blacksmith repaired it; nay, but for Mr. Sydney's earnest entreaties, we believe the village painter would have exercised his genius upon the exterior; it escaped this danger, how-ever, and the result was wonderful. Each year added to its charms; it grew younger and younger; a new wheel, a new spring; I christened it the *Immortal*." [5]

[5] " Memoir of Sydney Smith," chap. vii. p. 115.

Long after the "Immortal" had rumbled out of
Foston for the last time, the "village tailor," Thomas
Johnson, used to relate an incident connected with the
lining of the chariot which might have brought his
own career, as well as Sydney Smith's, to an abrupt
termination. It seems that the man had received his
orders from Mrs. Smith, and, according to his statement, they were strictly carried out. When Mr. Smith
inspected the carriage after the work was finished, he
declared somewhat sharply that the tailor had not
followed his instructions. The man maintained the
contrary with corresponding warmth, and in the course
of a fruitless altercation on the subject, the rector and
the tailor both lost their tempers. The tailor, indeed,
who was naturally very impulsive, at length went so
far as to cry out that if Mr. Smith ventured to say that
his work on the "Immortal" was not according to
instructions again, he would throw his scissors at his
head. The challenge was at once accepted, and the
statement emphatically repeated. Wild with passion,
the tailor hurled his heavy scissors with such force
across the room that they stuck fast in the opposite
wall, and if Sydney had not seen his danger and darted
instantly aside, the consequences would have been
distressing. After rating the man in angry terms for
his obstinate folly and ungovernable temper, in high
dudgeon the rector stalked rapidly home, leaving his
opponent, whose wrath had found some relief in the
flight of the scissors, still in a sullen and defiant
frame of mind. Presently, to the tailor's intense surprise, the rector reappeared, and began to address him
in friendly and apologetic tones. They were both
right it seemed. Sydney was right in declaring that

the work was not in accordance with the instructions
he had given ; the tailor was right in maintaining that
he had lined the carriage in the way he had been told.
The missing link between the rector's wish and the
tailor's work was found in a mistake which Mrs. Smith
had made. Mutual explanations and protestations duly
followed, and with perfect good humour on both sides,
and the gift of half-a-crown on the rector's, the
awkward episode ended.

During the entire period of his life in Foston,
Sydney Smith was, to quote his own words, " village
parson, village doctor, village comforter, village magistrate, and Edinburgh Reviewer," [6] and more than one
of these distinctions was recognized even by the juve-
nile population of the place. " I was walking with
him one day," relates his wife in an unpublished
fragment, " and we met a little round-faced, cherry-
cheeked boy. Sydney stopped and gave him a sugar-
plum. 'Now, what's my name?' 'Don't naw.' 'Not
know? Why, you little rogue, you do know my
name quite well. Tell me what it is.' After a little
hesitation—'Doctor, the parson!' Another sugar-
plum."

Sydney Smith lived on the most friendly terms with
the poor of his parish, and had a kindly word or a
smile of recognition for every one he met. Mrs. Smith
established a singing class at the rectory for the young
women of the neighbourhood, and won the hearts of
the poor girls by helping them to make bonnets. The
rector conducted a Bible-class for youths, and there
are still one or two old men in Foston who gratefully

[6] " Memoir of Sydney Smith," chap. vii. p. 115.

recall the instruction in the Scriptures which they
received sixty years ago from the Rev. Sydney Smith.

The Rector of Foston was a great favourite with his
servants, and their allegiance to him was close and
loyal, and such as mere money can never obtain.
Lady Holland assures us that her father hardly ever
lost a servant except from marriage or death. " People
complain of their servants," are his own words ; " I
never had a bad one ; but then I study their comforts—that is one recipe for securing good servants." [7]
The memory of Sydney Smith is still cherished with
reverent affection by the children, and nephews and
nieces of the old servants at Foston, and here a " present from the master " is shown, and there a bundle
of faded letters written by Mrs. Smith and the young
ladies from Combe-Florey to their humble friends in
Yorkshire ; and yonder, a quaint portrait of Windham,
aged five, a veritable " little boy blue," hangs on the
parlour wall.

From many incidents, in themselves too trivial to
relate, the impression of Sydney Smith as a kindly,
genial, quick-tempered, large-hearted man, full of
authority, but equally full of good-will, is strengthened and confirmed. The household at Foston
consisted for many years of Mr. and Mrs. Smith,
their four children, the cook, housemaid, lady's-
maid, laundry-maid, the girl " Bunch," and the
man " Jack Robinson." A kind-hearted old Yorkshire
woman, energetic and practical, Molly Mills by name,
reigned supreme in the adjoining farmstead, and was
deservedly a great favourite not only with her master,

[7] " Memoir of Sydney Smith," chap. xi. p. 244.

but with every one about the place. The lady's-maid was Annie Kaye, a noble and devoted servant, of a type which now, alas, seems almost obsolete. She remained thirty years under Sydney Smith's roof, and " ended by nursing her old master through his long and painful illness night and day." [8] She filled various offices in the household both at Foston and Combe-Florey, and eventually rose, like most faithful servants, into an undefined position of the utmost trust and influence.

In his celebrated account of his establishment at Foston, Sydney Smith states that he " caught up a little garden-girl, made like a milestone, christened her Bunch, put a napkin in her hand, and made her my butler." [9] Bunch was a very robust and broad-set girl, and doubtless that fact accounts for the sobriquet she received from her master. Her real name was Rachel Masterman, and her duties were to wait on Sydney Smith at table, to attend to the justice-room, to bring the hot water in the morning, and, in a word, to make herself generally useful. In process of time Bunch became cook, and accompanied the family in that capacity to Combe-Florey, where she married the coachman. Her last days were spent in York, and she died there a considerable time ago. When Bunch was promoted to the position of cook at Foston, another little girl was " caught up " by Sydney Smith, and installed in the vacant place as his personal attendant. The second little girl, in old age, still survives at Helperby, near York, and is the only

[8] " Memoir of Sydney Smith," chap. vii. p. 117.
[9] Ibid. chap. vii. p. 114.

one now living who can speak from personal knowledge of the ordinary life at Foston. She recalls with
manifest pleasure long forgotten acts of kindness, and
is able to relate characteristic little incidents which
help to explain the attachment which Sydney Smith's
servants felt for their master. Her duties, like
Bunch's, were to attend to her master's wants, night
and morning, to fold his large white cravats in a particular way, to mix his lather for shaving in a huge
wooden bowl, and to run to and fro through the house
at his summons. Unlike her predecessor, she had not
to wait upon her master at table; for when Bunch
was promoted, the family circumstances had improved,
and a man-servant was then engaged.

   The master of the house took a mischievous delight
in making his servants laugh in the presence of
visitors, and the more solemn their aspect, the more
eager he appeared to excite their risible faculties.
Passing testimony to this odd habit is given by Lord
Brougham, who states that he has seen him at dinner,
at Foston, drive the servants from the rooms with the
tears running down their faces in peals of inextin-
guishable laughter.[1] Even before a regular man-
servant was engaged, Bunch seems only to have waited
at table when the family were alone; at all events,
when company arrived another famous personage
was called upon the scene as chief butler in " Jack
Robinson," the carpenter. Everybody has read in the
pages of Lady Holland, Sydney Smith's own statement in reference to this man, and his services in
providing the new rectory with furniture. " I had

---

[1] " Memoirs of Life and Times of Lord Brougham," vol. i. chap. iv.

little furniture, so I bought a cart-load of deals; took a carpenter (who came to me for parish relief), called Jack Robinson, with a face like a full moon, into my service; established him in a barn, and said, ' Jack furnish my house.' You see the result!"[2] When this statement first appeared in print, some of Sydney Smith's acquaintances in Yorkshire poohpoohed the whole story, and were inclined to treat it as a sheer romance. The matter was, however, exactly as he himself stated. When he made Foston his home, he had "little furniture," in comparison, at least, with the size of his new house, and "Jack Robinson' set to work to fit up the vacant rooms. An interesting sample of Jack Robinson's handiwork at Foston Rectory is now in the possession of the writer in the shape of a comfortable arm-chair of rough make and old-fashioned design. The chair was formerly the property of William Kilvington, of Foston, and it had been in his cottage there ever since it was left behind by Sydney Smith on his removal to Combe-Florey. Kilvington was coachman to Sydney Smith during the last five years of his residence in Yorkshire, and he married the cook whom "Bunch" succeeded. Kilvington, who had often driven his master in the "Immortal" on long and short journeys, was able to tell the writer, in the summer of 1883, many episodes concerning those far distant days. The chair (of which a representation is given at the close of this chapter) stood for a number of years in Sydney's justice-room, where it was in constant use; it finally found its way into the kitchen, and was given by Sydney Smith to Mrs. Kilvington at the sale which

[2] "Memoir of Sydney Smith," chap. vii. p. 114.

O

preceded his removal to the south. His old servant was sitting on the chair at the sale, when the rector came forward to say good-bye. As he turned to leave her, Sydney Smith said, "Take that chair home, and keep it in memory of me." For more than half a century the chair remained by the fireside in Kilvington's cottage, close to the gates of Foston Rectory.[3]

Three years after Sydney Smith settled in York-shire, "Bobus" paid him a visit, and gathered whilst at Foston that his brother was anxious to secure for his eldest boy Douglas the advantage of a few years' training at a public school. The building of the rectory had seriously crippled his income, and for some years afterwards he had to practise the utmost economy. Douglas and Windham both received in consequence their early education from their father, whilst Mrs. Smith acted as governess to Saba and Emily. During his stay at Foston, in 1817, Bobus offered to send his eldest nephew to Westminster School. The proposal was gladly accepted, and it was arranged that Douglas, now a fine lad entering his teens, should go there in the spring of the following year.

Lady Holland has described a journey which Sydney Smith and his family took, soon after their settlement at Foston, to Manchester, in order to visit Mr. (afterwards Sir George) Philips, at that time a well-known Lancashire manufacturer. The visit proved so pleasant to all concerned, that it was often repeated, and the acquaintance between Sir George and Sydney Smith soon ripened into a firm friendship. The "Immortal" was called into service

---

[3] Mrs. Kilvington died many years ago. William Kilvington,— an intelligent and handsome old man,—died a few months since.

on these expeditions, and proved itself a comfortable though somewhat slow and inelegant travelling coach. Sir George Philips lived at Sedgley Hall, Prestwich, near Manchester, and it was there that Sydney Smith was frequently his guest between the years 1815 and 1827. Sir George Philips was on intimate terms with some of the best families in Lancashire and Cheshire; and it is believed by those who are most likely to be informed on such a point, that it was through his visits to Sedgley Hall that Sydney Smith became acquainted with the Stanleys of Alderley, the Davenports of Capesthorne, the Leycesters of Toft, the Wilbrahams of Delamere, and others of the Cheshire aristocracy. Sydney Smith's published letters, and others which have passed through the hands of the writer, conclusively prove that he was a guest on several occasions at the charming seats in Cheshire of the ancient families named, and the Leycesters and Wilbrahams, and probably also the Stanleys and Davenports, were entertained by him at Foston and Combe-Florey.

Sydney Smith's visits at the country houses of his friends were usually extremely short, for he was a firm believer in Miss Ferrier's dictum, that country visits should seldom exceed three days—the rest day, the dressed day, and the pressed day. There are no traditions at Alderley Park, Toft Hall, or Capesthorne of the visits which he paid to those places in the earlier years of the century, for those who entertained him have, of course, long since passed away. The writer has, however, seen a somewhat severe criticism which Sydney Smith one day, whilst a visitor at Toft, scribbled in a then popular romance; and he has also read in his own journal the brief entry: "Sunday, 10th October, 1824. Preached on Hatred at Alderley."

In a letter to Lady Mary Bennett (daughter of his friend, the Earl of Tankerville) which Sydney Smith wrote from Sedgley Hall, Manchester, January, 1817, he states, "I am going to preach a charity sermon next Sunday. I desire to make three or four hundred weavers cry, which it is impossible to do since the late rise in cotton." [4] Whether the preacher succeeded in his attempt to make the weavers cry, cannot now be discovered, but there was a young girl present in Prestwich Church, Manchester, on Sunday morning, January 12th, 1817, who still remembers in old age how fast her tears fell during that sermon. Miss Laura Leycester, of Toft, was herself a guest at Sedgley Park when Sydney Smith, accompanied by Douglas, arrived there on a visit to Sir George Philips. Miss Leycester had not previously met the famous Edinburgh Reviewer, whom she afterwards knew intimately as a visitor to her father's houses at Toft and London. Sydney assured the young lady that he would certainly make her cry that day at church, and she maintained with equal decision that he would accomplish no such thing. "As I came down stairs to go to church," relates Miss Leycester, "I heard him call to his son: 'Douglas! look for my sermon-book—it is under the mat at the bottom of the stairs!'" The charity sermons of Sydney Smith were always very impressive, and full of moving appeals, and now and then of heart-rending facts with which he was personally acquainted. At Prestwich Church on that far off Sunday, he seems to have

---

[4] Published Correspondence, p. 371.

put forth all his powers, and one of his hearers at least forgot all else, and could hardly look at the pulpit through her gathering tears, for, in her own words, " He drew some very touching pictures of destitution." An hour later, at Sedgley Hall, the preacher looked up and said, " I succeeded in making you cry, Miss Leyces-ter ;" and that lady's confession to the writer to-day is, " He certainly did."

Some of his impromptu sayings reveal his humour very happily, and they appear to have flashed to the surface of his ordinary talk in a remarkable manner. The pages of Lady Holland's life of her father contain many illustrations of his droll power of expression, and his ever-flowing wit, and the following examples are taken almost at random from it, and from other reliable sources of information. It was at his brother's house at Farming Wood that he told the child who was stroking the tortoise to "please it," that he might as well stroke the dome of St. Paul's to please the Dean and Chapter. The difficulties con-nected with placing wood pavement around the Cathedral were according to him easily solved, for when the subject came up for discussion in the chapter-room of St. Paul's, he is reported to have said in his most matter-of-fact tones, and with his usual innocent look, " If my reverend brethren here will but lay their heads together, the thing will be done in a trice !" As a critic of pictures, his verdict occasionally seems to have been more accurate than artistic, and it is not difficult to understand the virtuous indignation con-veyed in the " look that ought to have killed me," when, standing before a small landscape at Bowood with a distinguished connoisseur, he met the glowing

admiration which found expression in the words,
"Immense breadth of light and shade!" with the
apparently obtuse, and certainly provoking rejoinder,
"Yes; about an inch and a half!" He seemed able
to hit off in a phrase the characteristics of the
people whom he knew. "Lady L—— is a remarkably
clever, agreeable woman, but Nature has made one
trifling omission—a heart!" "Yes, Mr. —— has
great good sense; but I never met a manner more
entirely without frill." Nothing could be more gallant, and scarcely anything more graceful, than his
response to a beautiful young lady who exclaimed,
"Oh, Mr. Smith, I cannot bring this flower to perfection!" "Then let me lead," said he, as he took
her hand, "perfection to the flower." "You must
take a walk on an empty stomach," Rogers declares
was the advice of Sydney Smith's medical man to him
on one occasion. The patient quietly looked up with
a glance of inquiry, and naively uttered but one
word—"Whose?"

A CHAIR FROM FOSTON RECTORY.

CHAPTER IX.

1818—1824.

Family Changes—Attitude on Public Questions—The Treatment of Prisoners—The Game Laws—An Accession of Fortune— Busy Life at Foston.

THE departure of Douglas in the spring of 1818 to Westminster School, was the first break in the circle at Foston, and although the separation was inevitable, it was none the less keenly felt on that account. Sensible, kindly, and bright, the lad had endeared himself to all who knew him, and was daily becoming more and more of a companion to his father in his favourite recreation—a long country walk. It would be absurd to say that Sydney Smith was ever " buried alive " at Foston ; nevertheless, the first five or six years of his life there were spent in great retirement, and month after month sometimes rolled away without bringing him any society other than that which an obscure agricultural village afforded. He had little time, however, to cultivate despondency, or to wring his hands over his hard fate. He was a county magistrate, a gentleman farmer, an Edinburgh Reviewer, and the village parson and doctor rolled into one ; and what between the Law and the Gospel, Edinburgh and Foston, his books and his bottles, his family and his farm, his time was filled up with honest work, which ability made a delight, and to which variety lent a zest. Every now and then, there are indications, however, that the isolation of his position oppressed him ; but there are no signs whatever that he allowed the sense of loneliness to unfit him for the energetic discharge of the common duties which confronted him with each new day. "Pray, send me some news," he writes on one occasion ; "it is very pleasant in these deserts to see the handwriting of an old friend—it is like the print on the sand seen by Robinson Crusoe." The consolations of a student were an unfailing resource to the rector of Foston on long winter nights, when the snow lay on the silent, untrodden fields, and the household gathered

> " Around the radiant fireplace, enclosed
> In a tumultuous privacy of storm."

He was accustomed to declare that he was at a loss to understand how any reflecting man could trust himself in the solitude of the country without clinging to the love of knowledge as his sheet anchor. He held that, though the best books were apt to become a little languid and soporific at times, there was at least this advantage over conversation, that a man and his book generally kept the peace with tolerable success, and that if they did quarrel, the man could at all events shut his book and toss it into a corner of the room— an action not always quite so safe or easy to do in the case of a living folio.

It was but seldom that the "Immortal" in those earlier years at Foston travelled so far as Cheshire, and beyond an annual trip to town by the mail coach, and

an occasional visit to York to meet his old friends of
the Northern Circuit, or a few days at Scarborough
with Bobus, Sydney Smith was compelled, by the flat
refusal of sixpence to do the work of a shilling, to stay
at home and content himself with such interests as he
could find or invent amid his pastoral surroundings.
His success as a farmer was not immediate, and never
overwhelming, and like every one else, he had to buy
his experience. The outlay upon Foston Rectory kept
him a poor man for several years, and it was not until
1821, when his circumstances were improved by an
unexpected legacy, that his financial anxieties were
ended. The following statement was made by him to
a friend, and it is now published for the first time, as
it gives a graphic account not only of the exact condition of Foston when he came to it, but also recounts
the changes which he had been able to effect there in
the course of a very few years :—

" When first I was presented to the Chancery living
of Foston, there had been no resident clergyman for
upwards of one hundred and fifty years. I had a
cottage valued at 50*l*. by way of parsonage-house, three
hundred acres of glebe-land entirely exhausted, stiles,
gates, &c., &c., all in ruins, and not a single farm-
building for my tenants. From my foolish moderation
and ignorance of country matters, I received 30*l*. for
dilapidations. I have built a very handsome parsonage-house, barns, farm-buildings, stables, and agricultural buildings of every kind, at an expense of above
4000*l*. I have brought a hundred acres into excellent tillage, let the rest to responsible tenants, and
have constantly resided upon my parsonage. The
living is 600*l*. a year, so that (100*l*. deducted for what

the salary of a curate would be, and my age (fifty) considered), I have spent upon the living more than it is worth.

SYDNEY SMITH.

Foston, July 29th, 1820.

Strict economy marked all the arrangements of the household at Foston between the years 1814 and 1820, and the inclination of the rector to move freely about amongst his friends was held in check by the constant strain on a slender purse of ordinary expenditure. Writing to Jeffrey to thank him for an invitation to visit Edinburgh, he states that nothing could give him more pleasure, but frankly adds, "Poverty, agriculture, children, clerical confinement, all conspire to put such a pleasure out of my reach."[1] His friends were beginning to find out his fondness for the spoils of the chase, and his letters abound in quaint allusions of this sort to their kindness, "Lord Tankerville has sent me a whole buck—this necessarily takes up a good deal of my time."[2] His acknowledgments of such presents were always characteristic, as the accompanying note —besides many already published—reveals :—

[xiv.]   Foston, Sept., 1817.

DEAR DAVENPORT,—You have no idea what a number of handsome things were said of you when your six partridges were consumed to-day. Wit, literature, and polished manners were ascribed to you—some good quality for each bird. You never met with a more favourable jury. I conclude the *éloge* with my best thanks for your kind and flattering attention. We all, however, objected to your equipage ; longevity is

---

[1] Published Correspondence, p. 382.   [2] Ibid., p. 386.

incompatible with driving two horses at length. Man
is frequently cut off even in buggies; an inch to the
right or the left may send you to the Davenports of
ages past, and put half Cheshire in mourning.

Ever most truly yours,
SYDNEY SMITH.

Edward Davenport, Esq.

In February, 1818, the Earl of Ossory died, and
left his estates in Bedfordshire to his nephew, Lord
Holland. The vacant living of Ampthill went with
the property, and Lord Holland instantly seized the
opportunity to offer it to his friend, but as it could not
be held with Foston, it was gratefully declined.

The following letter—written a month or two later
to Lady Holland—has reference to an approaching
visit to town to see Douglas settled at school :—

[xv.]   Foston, April 22nd, 1818.

MY DEAR LADY HOLLAND,—There is no place more
agreeable to me, or to anybody else, than Holland
House; but I have a great deal to do in town about
Douglas and Westminster, and till he is fairly housed
there it will be quite impossible for me to be absent
from London. For this reason, I must postpone my
visit to you, though of course I shall come to see you
as soon as I am landed, which will be next Tuesday or
Wednesday. I am delighted to see country gentlemen
rebelling against the Government upon any occasion;
they had better do right in the wrong place than not
at all.

I remain always,
Dear Lady Holland,
Affectionately yours,
SYDNEY SMITH.

Lady Holland,
    Kensington.

At first all went well with Douglas at Westminster, and his father was able to report that the lad had "fought his first battle, come off victorious, and is completely established."[3] But in the autumn he fell dangerously ill of fever, and his mother hastened to London to nurse him. A visit which had been planned to Lord Grey at Howick for November, had in consequence to be abandoned, and it was determined instead that the whole family should spend Christmas in London with the young patient, who by this time was fortunately convalescent. Lord Grey was wishful that Sydney Smith should accompany him to Lambton Castle, and break his homeward journey there in order that he might become better acquainted with Mr. Lambton, M.P. (afterwards first Earl of Durham). Mr. Lambton had married Earl Grey's eldest daughter two years previously, and Lady Louisa had of course known Sydney Smith as her father's friend all through her girlhood, and was eager now to welcome such a guest to her husband's stately home on the banks of the Wear. The following letter was written to Mr. Lambton, when his son's illness compelled Sydney Smith to relinquish his contemplated visit to the north; it was found with two or three others written to him, which occur in these pages, in an interesting collection of autograph letters at Lambton Castle, and it is here inserted with the permission and through the kindness of the present Earl of Durham :—

[XVI.]   Foston, Saturday, Dec. 5th, 1818.

MY DEAR SIR,—Lord Grey—who from his serious turn of mind always desires to have a clergyman of

---

[3] Published Correspondence, p. 388.

his parties—had planned to smuggle me into Lambton, and had the arrangements taken place this week, it would with your kind connivance have been effected; but I am going with all my family to London at the end of next week, and though you perform this with as much ease as a ball quits a cannon, you cannot conceive the blunders and agony, the dust and distraction, the roaring and raving with which a family like mine is conveyed through three degrees of latitude to its place of destination. The 7th will be too late, and render my visit quite impossible. I hope to be more fortunate on some other occasion. It will be very agreeable to me to pay a visit to Lady Louisa and yourself, and

I remain, my dear Sir,

Very truly yours,

SYDNEY SMITH.

J. G. Lambton, Esq., M P.

In January, Douglas was not only well again and at school, but had worked himself to the head of his class, and a month later Sydney Smith, having paid in the interval a brief visit to Bath, to see his father, was back at Foston, and in the thick of his work once more.

The condition of the prisons of this country began to excite general attention at the close of the Peninsular War, and the devoted labours and tragic fate of John Howard at last bore fruit by awakening the public mind to the nameless horrors of the existing system. The heart of the nation was touched, moreover, by the story of Elizabeth Fry's ministry to the degraded women of Newgate, and by the marvellous influence she exerted over the most abandoned through her womanly kindness and Christian sympathy. In the year 1818, there were committed to the jails of the United Kingdom upwards of 107,000 persons, and the felon convicted of the most atrocious crime and the untried stripling charged with some venial offence were left unmolested together. No wonder that Sydney Smith should declare that there existed " in every county in England, large public schools maintained at the expense of the county for the encouragement of profligacy and vice, and for providing a proper succession of housebreakers, profligates, and thieves." The sanitary state of the prisons was almost as bad as their moral condition, and in both senses they were disgraceful and pestilential places. Lady Holland relates that her father, who was deeply interested in the published accounts of Mrs. Fry's noble and humane efforts, obtained permission to accompany her on one occasion, to Newgate. He afterwards declared that he " never felt more deeply affected or impressed than by the beautiful spectacle he there witnessed ; it made him, he said, weep like a child." [4]

In the spring of 1819, the question of the Reform of the Criminal Law was before the House of Commons, and that fact led him to write the following unpublished letters to the Marquis of Lansdowne, who, as Lord Henry Petty, had been, like himself, a friend and pupil of Dugald Stewart's, in distant Edinburgh days. The suggestions reveal not only his intimate acquaintance with the subject in all its details, but also the humane and practical spirit in which he approached its discussion.

[4] " Memoir of Sydney Smith," chap. vii. p. 118.

[XVII.]   Foston, March 25th, 1819.

DEAR LORD LANSDOWNE,—On all such occasions there are generally too many suggestions instead of too few. The few rules I send proceed from evils I have observed. It is very singular to find the public so humane and reasonable that they will listen to these subterraneous miseries, and very good and wise in you to derive from this spirit a law of permanent humanity which will outlive it.

       I remain, my dear Lord Lansdowne,

            With great respect and regard, yours,

                 SYDNEY SMITH.

Pray do not think of answering my letter; it requires none.

PROPOSED RULES FOR PRISONS.

I. The names of the visiting magistrates and their places of abode to be printed and stuck up in all rooms where prisoners are confined, under penalty to jailors.

II. Names of visiting magistrates to be called over by the clerk of the peace, or clerk of assize, in open court, on the first day of any assize and quarter sessions, and the judge or chairman to ask in open court whether they have visited the prisons, and have any observation to offer upon their state and condition. Penalties to clerk of the peace and of assize.

III. A book to be kept by the jailor, noting down the visits of magistrates to the prison, to be read in open court in the same manner.

IV. More power to visiting magistrates to make alterations between session and session, subject to the approbation of magistrates assembled at quarter sessions or assizes.

V. Divisions of accused and committed, young and old offenders.

VI. Neither beer nor spirits without order of the apothecary, or permission of magistrates in visiting. Heavy penalties.

VII. No Roman Catholic or Dissenter compellable to attend the prison worship if he objects to do so, and expresses himself willing to attend a clergyman of his own persuasion.

VIII. Power in two magistrates to confine for two or three days in solitary confinement any refractory prisoner.

IX. No prisoner to be locked up in sleeping-room for more than ten hours at night. N.B.—They are now locked up in small rooms in winter from four in the evening till eight in the morning, without fire or candle, to avoid the trouble and expense of watching, lighting, and warming them.

X. No male prisoner after conviction to have less than two pounds of bread per day, if their diet is bread alone; women, a pound and a half. Prisoners before conviction to have per day not less than this, and twice a week one pound of meat each.

XI. Money allowance to be put upon a more rational footing.

A second letter on the same subject, with two or three additional hints suggesting more stringent regulations in reference to prison fare, soon followed the first :—

[xviii.]   York, May 31st, 1819.

DEAR LORD LANSDOWNE,—Spirituous liquors are forbidden under heavy penalties ; fermented liquors are not so in jails, consequently they are introduced publicly, so are all sorts of meats which felons can pay for. Coarse men should be made sorrowful and penitent by plain food. A jail is not an object of terror if men have friends who send them money, and so purchase roast veal and porter. Spirituous liquors and dangerous tools are let down from the windows of debtors. The weekly allowance is meant for food, but spent in a very different way. If you are sitting in a committee watching a Bill, these hints—if they have not already occurred—may be of some consequence; if they have, you will see my motive, and forgive the useless intrusion upon your time.

Ever yours, dear Lord Lansdowne,

Very sincerely,

SYDNEY SMITH.

1st. No fermented liquor of any sort after trial.

2nd. A good wholesome allowance of food, and no other food but what is allowed.

3rd. No windows of the apartments of debtors to look into the felons' yards.

4th. Washing allowed, and no money allowance.

In the course of the summer another letter, in which criticism and gossip are amusingly blended, found its way to Lord Lansdowne :—

[XIX.]   July 24th, 1819.

DEAR LORD LANSDOWNE,—I am much obliged by your intention of sending me the Prison Report. I have no doubt it will embrace all the important points, but the great difficulty will be to frame a law that will be executed, and not become a dead letter, as the last statute upon prisons. To do this effectually, a person should be well acquainted with all the subor-

P

dinate machinery, but such persons, of course, Lord Sidmouth has about him.

There is a prodigious jealousy among the landed gentlemen of Tory principles respecting this humanity to prisoners, but it will bear down all folly before it. In the meantime, B—— is married to the widow. They would have been married a long time since, but for the depreciated state of the currency. She vowed she would not change her situation till the bank question was settled. We hear a great deal here of the miseries and discontents of the clothing counties, but are so purely agricultural that we are affected by nothing but showers and sunbeams.

I hope you have studied Lord Carlisle's pamphlet upon colouring and wrapping up poisons. What are we to do for our boot-tops, which are cleaned by oxalic acid, if we may not purchase oxalic acid but when coloured by rose-pink? Are we to walk about with rose-pink boots? Did any government ever yet prescribe a colour for boots, and if a colour, such a colour?

Walter Scott seems to me the same sort of thing laboured in a very inferior way, and more careless, with many repetitions of himself.[5] Caleb is overdone. Sir W. and Lady Ashton are very good characters, and the meeting of the two coaches and six the best scene in the book. The catastrophe is shocking and disgusting.

Pray present my kind regards to the Hollands

---

[5] Sydney Smith was nevertheless a great admirer of Sir Walter Scott, and used to declare that when he got hold of his novels "turnips, sermons, and justice-business were all forgotten." When *Ivanhoe* appeared, he wrote in hot haste to Constable: "Pray make the author go on. I am sure he has five or six more novels in him, therefore five or six holidays for the whole kingdom."—"Constable and his Literary Correspondents," vol. iii. p. 134.

and the Morpeths. I quite agree in all you say of the heirs-apparent. Henry Fox is a very remarkable boy. George Howard is full of every good quality which his father and mother could wish, or infuse, by their own example.

I am always, dear Lord Lansdowne,

Yours very truly,

SYDNEY SMITH.

The "heirs-apparent," to whom Sydney Smith refers in the concluding words of this letter, both lived to succeed to their ancestral titles and estates, though neither of them left sons to inherit the family honours; for one died childless, and the other was never married. Henry Fox became fourth and last Lord Holland on the death of his father in 1840. He lived much abroad, and was at one time British minister at Florence, and he died at Naples in 1859. The last master of Holland House was worthy of its best traditions, and the kindliness of his nature, and the refinement of his tastes survive as pleasing memories amongst all who, in his day, shared the hospitality of the picturesque and renowned old house at Kensington.

George Howard, who, like Henry Fox, was born in 1802, became seventh Earl of Carlisle in 1848, but, as Lord Morpeth, he had been long and honourably known, both throughout the realm and in the House of Commons, as a man of brilliant scholarship, high moral sensibility, and cosmopolitan sympathies. He entered the Upper House with the reputation of being a supporter of the Anti-Corn-Law League, and such a circumstance did not enhance his welcome in that assembly in the year 1848. Twice Viceroy of Ireland,

Lord Carlisle did all that a capable and disinterested man of persuasive lips and generous instincts could accomplish to pacify the people of that distracted country, and though no one can claim for him the reputation of a great statesman, he will still be remembered as a man whose heart was in tune with the purest and best tendencies of his time, and who used without ostentation and continuously the influence which rank and ability gave him to knit all classes of the community more closely together, and to promote the public good.　He died at Castle Howard in 1864.

The two " heirs-apparent " were youths of seventeen when Lord Lansdowne and Sydney Smith exchanged favourable opinions concerning them. " George is a fine manly, sensible, straightforward young man, full of right feelings and opinions," was the verdict which Sydney Smith pronounced a year or two later on the " heir-apparent " of Castle Howard.　He continued to take the liveliest interest in young Howard's development. " I wish George," he writes in an unpublished note, " would read Mr. Wilkes' speech at the meeting of Protestants for promoting the principles of toleration—a fine and affecting piece of eloquence, and full of such principles as I hope he will always display in public life."　To Lady Georgiana Morpeth,[6] the mother of the youth whose early career he watched with so much hope, he wrote as follows in the autumn of 1819 :—

[xx.]　　　　　　　　　　　　Foston, Sept. 5th, 1819.

DEAR LADY GEORGIANA,—Everybody is haunted with spectres and apparitions of sorrow, and the imaginary

---

[6] Daughter of the fifth Duke of Devonshire, and afterwards Countess of Carlisle, as wife to the sixth earl.

griefs of life are greater than the real. Your rank
in life rather exposes you the more to these attacks.
Whatever the English zenith may be, the horizon is
almost always of a sombre colour. * * * I like in you
very much that you are a religious woman, because,
though I have an infinite hatred and contempt for the
nonsense which often passes under, and disgraces the
name of religion, I am very much pleased when I
see anybody religious for hope and comfort, not for
insolence and interest. About the nature of your
complaint, I hope and trust you are wrong; if you
are right, I shall pity you as much as I please, and
show that I do so as much as you please. Your
praise and approbation are very grateful to Mrs.
Sydney and Saba; as for me, I will promise never to
quiz you, that is, only a very little, and to your face,
and in a low voice, and not before strangers; and for
the rest, you will always find me a discreet neighbour
and a sincere friend.

SYDNEY SMITH.

Constable, the publisher, about this time launched
a new literary journal, entitled the *Farmer's Magazine*,
and in the course of the year 1819 an amusing letter
appeared in its pages, in which the Rector of Foston
gave a graphic account of the vagaries of a flock
of Scotch sheep, which, in his admiration of northern
mutton, he had rashly introduced to his Yorkshire
farm. Scotch mutton, he was still of opinion, was a
great luxury, but he declared that he would rather
renounce the use of animal food altogether, than obtain it at the cost of so much anxiety and care.
Ten times a day the ploughmen were hastily sum-

moned from their work to chase the Scotch sheep
out of his neighbour's wheat. They leaped over
gates, or crawled through hedges which seemed too
closely set for a rabbit to break. Five or six times
they laid their heads together, and forthwith proceeded briskly on their return journey to the north.
"My bailiff took a place in the mail, pursued them,
and overtook them half way to Newcastle!" All
efforts to fatten them were in vain. They devoured
the turnips in winter, and nibbled the clover in
summer, but still remained provokingly lean. Nor
was he more successful with his oxen, for in the same
letter he states that they were twice as ravenous as
the same number of horses, were awkward in descend-
ing a hill, and could not plough in hot weather.
Moreover, "It took five men to shoe an ox. They
ran against my gate-posts, lay down whenever they
were tired, and ran away at the sight of a stranger.
I have now got into a good breed of English sheep
and useful cart-horses, and am doing well." [7]

The treatment of prisoners was not the only burning social topic of the hour, which Sydney Smith,
in the intervals between his clerical and bucolic
labours, found time to discuss. His experiences as a
country clergyman and a county magistrate had
opened his eyes to the iniquitous condition of the
Game Laws, and in the pages of the *Edinburgh Review*
he employed all his powers of reason, ridicule, and
persuasion to bring about the repeal of their obsolete
and unjust enactments. The criminal code of the
country was harsh and oppressive, and the sacredness

---

[7] "Constable and his Literary Correspondents," vol. iii. chap.
vii. p. 131.

of human life counted for little when brought into collision with the sacred rights of property.[8] Sydney Smith was not opposed to the Game Laws in general, for he held that game ought, in common fairness, to belong to those who feed it. His contention was that, whilst these laws were constructed on a " basis of substantial justice," there was a great deal of folly and tyranny mixed up with them, and a " perpetual and vehement desire on the part of the country gentlemen to push their provisions up to the highest point of tyrannical severity." With indignant sarcasm he denounced the cruel and unworthy expedient of spring guns and man-traps as vindictive and immoral, and impeached such efforts to protect the interests of the lord of the manor in the wider interests of humanity.

The ferocity with which the Game Laws were administered, demoralized the peasantry without put-

---

[8] " Every class strove to have the offences which injured itself subjected to the extreme penalty. Our law recognized 223 capital offences. Nor were these mainly the legacy of the Dark Ages, for 156 of them bore no remoter date than the reigns of the Georges. * * * If a man injured Westminster Bridge, he was hanged. If he appeared disguised on a public road, he was hanged. If he cut down young trees; if he shot at rabbits; if he stole property valued at 5s.; if he stole anything at all from a bleachfield; if he wrote a threatening letter to extort money; if he returned prematurely from transportation, for any of these offences he was immediately hanged. * * * Judge Heath avowed from the bench the theory which seemed to govern the criminal policy of the time. There was no hope, he said, of regenerating a felon in this life. His continued existence would merely diffuse a corrupting influence. It was better for his own sake, as well as for society, that he should be hanged. In 1816 there were, at one time, fifty-eight persons under sentence of death. One of these was a child ten years of age." " The Nineteenth Century : a History," by Robert Mackenzie, book ii. chap. i. pp. 77, 78.

ting an end to the trade of the poacher. As late as
the year 1816, an Act was pushed through Parliament, which punished with seven years' penal ser-
vitude every person discovered at night in any
open ground, armed with net or gun for the purpose
of snaring or killing any kind of game. England
lay under the blight of the Corn Laws, and not
bread alone, but almost all the necessaries of life
were burdened with excessive taxation, and as a
consequence the privations of the working classes,
both in town and country, made existence almost
unendurable.   No wonder that the people, rankling
under the sense of injustice, grew restless and discontented with their lot, and were ready to lend
themselves to any wild scheme which the first wandering agitator might propound. With the growth of
commerce, luxury spread, and there were soon rich
merchants and manufacturers in every town in the
kingdom who were wishful to purchase the game of
the landed gentry for their tables; but in 1820 it was
not only against the law to sell game, but every one
who ventured to buy it ran the risk of a heavy fine.
One illustration, in passing, is perhaps enough : " An
unfortunate householder, who bought a brace of
partridges for his dinner, was liable to a penalty of
10l." [9] Such enactments were of course constantly
set at defiance, and Sydney Smith, who held that
nothing will ever separate the wealthy glutton from
his pheasant, demanded free trade in game.

In 1820 an Act was passed for the summary punishment of all persons who wilfully or maliciously

* Walpole's " History of England from the Conclusion of the
Great War in 1815," vol. iii. chap. xii. p. 64.

damaged or trespassed upon any public or private property. By this Act the offender was immediately seized by the first man he met, taken before a magistrate, and heavily fined; or in default of payment, sent to gaol for three months. But to so sweeping a rule there naturally was an exception, and, as usual, it was made in favour of the privileged classes. All damage done in hunting was accordingly excluded from the operations of the Act, and every man duly qualified to carry a gun might ravage his neighbours' fields with impunity. Sydney Smith pounced like a hawk on this glaring act of injustice, which was worthy of the ancient forest laws which the Norman kings established in this country; and was too obvious a specimen of class legislature to pass unchallenged even sixty years ago. He denounced it as the " most impudent piece of legislation that ever crept into the statute-book," and demanded, " Is there upon earth such a mockery of justice as an Act of Parliament pretending to protect property, sending a poor hedge-breaker to gaol, and specially exempting from its operation the accusing and the judging squire, who, at the tail of the hounds, have that morning perhaps, ruined as much wheat and seeds as would purchase fuel for a whole year to a whole village ?" Like Charles Kingsley of a generation later, Sydney Smith had not only convictions, but the courage of them, and surrounded though the " village parson " was on all sides by landed proprietors and squires who, for the most part, held political opinions the very opposite of his own, he never hesitated to avow his sentiments in any company, and, if occasion demanded, to defend them.

As a magistrate, when called upon to deal with crimes of violence, or cases of brutality, assault, or desertion, he was not accustomed to spare the offender, but his clemency was extended towards a half-starved man who snared a hare or shot a pheasant. One who knew him intimately when he was Rector of Foston, and always looked up to him with admiration as the poor man's champion and friend, declares that he " used to plead like a lawyer " with his brother magistrates at Malton on behalf of the poacher. His sympathies were not limited to any section of the community, and his services were at the call of all who appealed to him on the ground of misery, injustice, or oppression. He had nothing but indignation and contempt for those " profligate persons who are always ready to fling an air of ridicule upon the labours of humanity, because they are desirous that what they have not virtue to do themselves shall appear to be foolish and romantic when done by others." He despised men as guilty of a still higher degree of depravity who sought "to regulate humanity by the income tax, and deemed the wretchedness and tears of the poor a fit subject for pleasantry." He was one of the earliest advocates of a more merciful treatment of the insane, and he pleaded that it was surely high time that kindness took the place of chains. Upwards of twenty years before Parliament interfered on their behalf, he championed in the pages of the *Edinburgh Review* the cause of the poor climbing-boys, and in various other directions, small and great, he gave his services without stint, and often in the face of bitter ridicule and angry opposition, to the desolate and the oppressed.

The summer of 1819 was marked in many of the great towns by ominous symptoms of general discontent, and political feeling of the most bitter type everywhere ran high. As August was drawing to a close, the nation was thrilled with the tidings of the wanton attack on the unarmed reformers at Manchester, in public meeting assembled, by the local military; and the news of the " Peterloo Massacre," as men came to call the cowardly and disgraceful affair, drew forth the most indignant protests against so harsh and ill-timed a display of power. Strong resolutions, denouncing the conduct of the magistrates at Manchester, were passed in all parts of the kingdom, and the Prince Regent's approbation of the "firmness of the local authorities" did not heighten the admiration of the people for their future Sovereign. Yorkshire, always bold and out-spoken on critical occasions, vindicated its position by a vast and enthusiastic indignation meeting of the county, which was called by the High Sheriff on requisition.

Earl Fitzwilliam placed his name to the requisition, and was also present at the meeting, and for these offences, which were construed into an act of defiance of Government, he was abruptly dismissed from his post of Lord-Lieutenant of the West Riding. The noble family at Castle Howard naturally took a lively interest in the renewed controversy which this arbitrary act of power gave rise to, and Lady Georgiana Morpeth wrote to Sydney Smith on the subject, as she knew that he, with his strong love of justice, would be in full sympathy with all who recognized in Lord Fitzwilliam's dismissal an attempt to intimidate men in high official places from the free expression of

their convictions on the gravest questions of the hour.
His reply was as follows :—

[XXI.]   Foston.

DEAR LADY GEORGIANA,—Excuse my making a
short reply to your politics. If a very important
privilege in a free government appears to have been
flagrantly violated, and if such violation is approved
by the administration, it is high time that the people
should meet together, express their sense of the
apparent wrong, and call for inquiry. If I were a
politician, and found the people remiss in meeting on
such occasions, I would be the first to rouse them. If
they met of their own accord, I should think it the
most important of all duties to be amongst them, that
I might enlighten their ignorance, repress their presumption, and direct their energy to laudable purposes.

For these reasons I think Lord Fitzwilliam has acted
like a virtuous and honourable man. I am no more
surprised at his dismissal than you are. It is a blow
aimed at the manly love of reasonable liberty, the
natural recompense which a profligate prince requires
from those to whom he delegates his power. As for
your confidence in the times, I hope it is as well
founded as it is agreeable ; but if the revenue continues
to decay, and commerce and manufactures do not
soon revive, I think you will not find the sufferers and
the enjoyers to remain upon the same friendly terms
which you kindly suppose them to be upon at present.
When I state my opinion about the meetings of the
people, of course I acknowledge that honest and
enlightened men may arrive at conclusions entirely
opposite. I would punish neither line of conduct,

but if either, then **I** would dismiss lord-lieutenants who had *not* called meetings.

Ever, dear Lady Georgiana,

Very truly yours,

SYDNEY SMITH.

A sudden accession of fortune came to him early in 1820, when he was entering his fiftieth year, through the death of his father's sister, Miss Mary Smith, and to his own surprise he then discovered that, through her thoughtfulness for her clerical nephew, his income was permanently increased to the extent of 400*l.* a year. No one rejoiced more heartily at this improvement in his circumstances than his noble friend and neighbour, the Earl of Carlisle, who, in writing to congratulate him, paid a well-deserved tribute to the good management which had marked through straitened years the household of Foston. " In neatness and ostensible comfort, Foston," remarks Lord Carlisle, " will hardly perceive the benefit of this addition to your income, but I trust this augmentation will extend to objects of nearer interest to you. I have ever regarded the establishment at Foston with admiration and surprise, not being above knowing to a shilling the monthly consumption and expenses of Castle Howard." This addition to his income was a great relief, and kept the closing years at Foston free from pecuniary anxieties; it also left Sydney Smith, who never at any period of his life would gratify himself at the expense of others, at liberty to cultivate the society of his friends in various parts of England. Almost the first use he made of his improved financial position was to take his wife and children down to

Somerset, in order that they might pay a visit to his father, who had at last settled, after many wanderings, at Bishop's Lydiard, near Taunton. Bishop's Lydiard, where Mr. Robert Smith died in his 88th year in 1827, curiously enough is within three miles of Combe-Florey; and two years later his son became rector of the latter place, and thus spent the closing years of his own life within an easy walk of the house in which his father lived and died.

His friendship with the Earl and Countess of Car-lisle, and with Lord and Lady Morpeth was a source of constant gratification to him, and the kindness and respect which he continually received from all the members of the family at Castle Howard helped to cheer him not a little amid that enforced seclusion at Foston from which he was beginning—through the improvement in his circumstances—at length to emerge. Learning from Lady Georgiana Morpeth that she was suffering from depression, he wrote in reply a letter, which other sufferers from the same complaint may be glad to possess, and which contained the following :—

ADVICE CONCERNING LOW SPIRITS.

[xxii.]   Foston, February 16th, 1820.

DEAR LADY GEORGIANA,—* * * Nobody has suffered more from low spirits than I have done—so I feel for you. 1st. Live as well as you dare. 2nd. Go into the shower-bath with a small quantity of water at a temperature low enough to give you a slight sensation of cold, 75° or 80°. 3rd. Amusing books. 4th. Short views of human life—not further than dinner or tea. 5th. Be as busy as you can. 6th. See as much as you can of those friends who respect and like you.

7th. And of those acquaintances who amuse you. 8th. Make no secret of low spirits to your friends, but talk of them freely—they are always worse for dignified concealment. 9th. Attend to the effects tea and coffee produce upon you. 10th. Compare your lot with that of other people. 11th. Don't expect too much from human life—a sorry business at the best. 12th. Avoid poetry, dramatic representations (except comedy), music, serious novels, melancholy, sentimental people, and everything likely to excite feeling or emotion, not ending in active benevolence. 13th. *Do good*,[1] and endeavour to please everybody of every degree. 14th. Be as much as you can in the open air without fatigue. 15th. Make the room where you commonly sit, gay and pleasant. 16th. Struggle by little and little against idleness. 17th. Don't be too severe upon yourself, or underrate yourself, but do yourself justice. 18th. Keep good blazing fires. 19th. Be firm and constant in the exercise of rational religion. 20th. Believe me, dear Lady Georgiana,

Very truly yours,

SYDNEY SMITH.

In the autumn of 1820, Sydney Smith was again a visitor at Sedgley Hall, near Manchester, and took the opportunity, according to his own statement, of studying the field of Peterloo. Earl Grey's son-in-law, Mr. Lambton, M.P., wrote early in October, proposing to pay a flying visit to Foston, but when the

---

[1] The italics are of course Sydney Smith's, and are rendered the more significant by the fact that, in looking through several hundred autograph letters, the above is almost the only instance of their usage which I have found.—S. J. R.

letter arrived the rector was already the guest of Sir
George Philips, and from there he despatched the
following reply :—

[XXIII.]   Philippi, Manchester, October, 1820.

My dear Sir,—I left Foston on the 27th, with my
family, on a visit to Marcus Tullius Philips, from
whence I write thanking you for your kindness in proposing that Lady Louisa and yourself should pay us a
visit at Foston, and assuring you that it would have
given Mrs. Sydney and myself the greatest pleasure to
have seen you. * * * I was glad to extort from Lord
Grey a confession that the climate of Devonshire is
superior to that of Northumberland, and that Lady
Grey was better. I now consider that my prediction
to Lady Grey is in a train of being accomplished—that
she will live till past eighty, and die intensely fond of
cribbage and piquette. Everything here is prosperous
beyond example. Philips doubles his capital twice a
week; we talk much of cotton, more of the fine arts,
as he has lately returned from Italy, and purchased
some pictures which were sent out from Piccadilly on
purpose to intercept him. If Lady Louisa wants anything in the calico line—happy to serve her.

Yours, my dear Sir,
Most truly,
Sydney Smith.

J. G. Lambton, Esq., M.P.

Another of his friends, Mr. Davenport of Capesthorne,
hearing that he was in Manchester, wrote to urge him
to pay him a visit on leaving Sedgley, and in reply he
gives an amusing account of the reasons which prevented him accepting the invitation.

[xxiv.]   Foston, Nov. 8th, 1820.

DEAR DAVENPORT,—Your letter dated the 5th followed me here, where I arrived on the 4th, having left Mrs. Sydney and my family at Sedgley, who do not return till the 14th, or thereabouts. I should have had great pleasure in spending a day with you at Philips'. I am much pleased with the kindness of Mrs. Davenport in inviting us to Capesthorne, and I should have liked very much to have gone there, but human life is full of tedious and prosaic difficulties, which are felt, but cannot be stated. For instance, we come down to the Philips' for a certain time every two years, bag and baggage, including this year, among other articles, a large, bouncing girl of thirteen, between nursery and parlour, and a little boy with a sore ear; to bring such a party into Capesthorne would have been an outrage against every law, human and divine; to have converted Philippi into a depôt for our heavy baggage, while we were absent ourselves, would not have been pretty behaviour—so that we had no alternative. As for the Queen, my only fear was that they would be candid, and stop the Bill. It has now pleased Divine Providence to give them up to our hands, and we shall smite them with the edge of the sword.

Ever very truly yours,
SYDNEY SMITH.

Jeffrey had often clamoured for his presence in the north, but hitherto, with the exception of a flying visit in 1811, he had not been in Edinburgh since 1803. His friends in Scotland understood the reason of his absence, and knew that it arose from poverty and not

Q

apathy. He had laughingly promised Jeffrey, so far
back as the struggling years of his London life, that if
ever the portion of goods which fell to his share should
outstrip his immediate needs, he would hasten to renew
his acquaintance with Edinburgh and its genial citizens.
He was now in a position to redeem his pledge, and
his gratification was enhanced by his ability to take
his wife and children with him. Setting out in
November, they broke the journey in going at Howick,
where they spent a few most agreeable days with Lord
Grey, and in returning Sydney halted at Dunbar, in
order to visit Lord Lauderdale, and then went forward
to Lambton Castle, where he was the guest of Mr.
J. G. Lambton, M.P. In his own graphic and inimitable way he describes the changes which had come
over the appearance and life of Edinburgh, since the
days he had spent there as tutor to Michael Beach.
" I found a noble passage into the town, and new since
my time; two beautiful English chapels, two of the
handsomest library-rooms in Great Britain, and a
wonderful increase of shoes and stockings, streets and
houses. When I lived there very few maids had shoes
and stockings, but plodded about the house with feet
as big as a family Bible, and legs as large as port-
manteaus. I stayed with Jeffrey. My time was spent
with the Whig leaders of the Scotch Bar, a set of very
honest, clever men, each possessing thirty-two different
sorts of wine. My old friends were glad to see me;
some had turned Methodists, some had lost their teeth,
some had grown very fat, some were dying, and, alas !
alas ! many were dead; but the world is a coarse
enough place, so I talked away, comforted some, praised
others, kissed some old ladies, and passed a very

riotous week." [2] Several of the most distinguished of
Sydney Smith's Edinburgh friends had but recently
passed away when he thus renewed his acquaintance
with the society of the Scottish capital in 1820.
Francis Horner and Henry Erskine died in 1817, Dr.
John Gordon in 1818, and Lord Webb Seymour and
his bosom friend, Professor John Playfair, in 1819.
The loss of these five men, whom Lord Cockburn
calls "the delight and pride of the place," [3] threw
a gloom over the most cultivated circles in Edinburgh, and diminished the social attractions of the
city.

When Sydney Smith left Edinburgh, in the beginning
of December, a great meeting organized by the Whigs,
in order to call attention to the political condition of
Scotland, and to petition the Crown for the dismissal
of the Liverpool Cabinet, was rapidly approaching.
The gathering was held on the 19th December, 1820,
and it was long afterwards known as the "Pantheon
Meeting," from the name of the building where the
agitators met. The speeches and the petition on that
occasion constituted the first open challenge which the
Whig party in Scotland had ventured to make to their
Tory oppressors for nearly a quarter of a century.
The city was filled with political enthusiasm, and it
was easy to forecast the success of the demonstration,
when Sydney Smith was compelled reluctantly to turn
his face to the south. In the following note to Mr.
Lambton, written while he was the guest of Lord
Lauderdale, he gleefully depicts the chagrin of the
Scotch Tories as they witnessed the fervour which the

[2] Published Correspondence, p. 425.
[3] "Life of Lord Jeffrey," by Lord Cockburn, vol. i. p. 257.

Q 2

Whig manifesto had kindled in the breasts of the great majority of the citizens :—

[xxv.]   Dunbar, Dec. 11th, 1820.

MY DEAR SIR,—I am much obliged to you for your kind letter. I shall be at Lambton before dinner on Wednesday. The Tories in Edinburgh are in despair. Some are taking poisoned meal, others scratching themselves to death, others tearing their red hair and their high cheek-bones, and calling on the Scotch gods, Scabies and Fames.

> Ever yours very truly,
> SYDNEY SMITH.

J. G. Lambton, Esq., M.P.

Eight days after this note was written the " Pantheon Meeting" took place, and the petition to the king was signed by about 17,000 persons. Jeffrey, who had spoken with great effect at the meeting, over which Moncrieff presided, received a week later the first public recognition of his services to Scotland in his installation as Lord Rector of the University of Glasgow.

From Dunbar, Sydney Smith proceeded to Lambton Castle, the country seat of his friend Mr. Lambton. The ardent love of liberty which marked the future Lord Durham, his advanced political opinions, and his chivalrous interest in the welfare of the people, met with a ready response in the breast of his guest, and the two men rapidly discovered that they were thinking along the same lines, and already had much in common. Lambton Castle was one of the first mansions in the country to be lighted with gas, and Sydney Smith was greatly impressed on his arrival there with the brilliant success of the experiment. " Dear lady," writes he to one of his Chillingham friends, " spend all your fortune in gas apparatus. Better to eat dry bread by the splendour of gas, than to dine on wild beef with wax candles. The splendour and glory of Lambton make all other houses mean." [4] Such sentiments would have been very coldly received at Dunbar, for Lord Lauderdale had conceived the most inveterate prejudice against gas, and had even gone so far as to record his " formal protest" upon the introduction of the first Gas Bill into Parliament.[5] The noble lord believed that multitudes would lose their money by mad speculations, and that a "most important branch of trade, our whale fisheries, would be ruined." Sydney Smith, on the contrary, had no such fears, but at once welcomed the new discovery as a great addition to the comfort of mankind; and as he always had his own sitting-room " lighted up like a town after a great naval victory," he was glad to know of a less costly and troublesome method of illumination than that afforded by a cluster of wax candles.

At the close of 1820 he was back once more at Foston, and cherished the pleasing expectation—at least if we are to believe his own statement—that the rest of his life was destined to be spent in that rural retreat.

Fresh from the political excitement of Edinburgh and the society of kindred spirits there, Foston, with its scattered cottages and lowly church, must have looked exceedingly quiet to Sydney Smith as he hastened once more in the waning December afternoon, along the familiar road which led to the rectory. No

[4] Published Correspondence, p. 426.
[5] Walpole's " History of England," vol. i. chap. i. p. 97.

man could possibly have been more popular under his
own roof than he was, and not merely his wife and
children, but the servants, old and young, were accustomed to look forward wistfully, on the occasion of his
visits to the great people of the land, to his return to
his own fireside.   His animated tones and merry laugh
as he recounted at table the adventures of his journey,
or bustled to and fro about the house and grounds,

FOSTON CHURCH.
(The scene of Sydney Smith's ministry for twenty-two years.)

inquiring what had happened in his absence, seemed
to infuse new life into the whole household, and to
make everybody in it more active and cheerful.   It
was, moreover, impossible to mistake the genuine
gratification with which his humble parishioners
welcomed him back on Sunday to the church, and saw
him again installed in his own pulpit.

Early in the following year Sydney Smith despatched

the accompanying letter to a young gentleman of fortune, who was wishful to enlighten the readers of the *Edinburgh Review* as to the true causes of the " Peterloo Massacre " [6] at Manchester, and who had appealed to him to revise his manuscript. This request drew forth an exceedingly frank reply, which there is no longer any reason to suppress, though, for obvious reasons, the name of the gentleman to whom it was addressed is still withheld :—

[XXVI.]

I hope you will not be angry with me, but I would not reduce your manuscript to order for the best living in Lord Crewe's gift. I figured to myself a neat article that would print to about twelve pages, in a clear German text hand, written over by the village schoolmaster, with intervals of white paper for interlineation as broad as gravel walks in a garden. The interlineations are so numerous, and the writing frequently so illegible, that I would really much sooner write ten articles upon the Manchester Massacre than reduce your manuscript to lucid order. If it had been a phrase to recast here and there, to shorten a redundant or expand a dwarfish sentence, I would have undertaken it with the greatest pleasure, but in its present state there is nobody but Reginald Heber who could encounter it. What I *can* read is very well written in point of style, but much too long for any subject. All that people would read about the murdered weavers would be about eight *Edinburgh Review* pages of calm and candid observation. ·

This criticism seems to have chilled the literary

[6] Manchester, 16th August, 1819.

enthusiasm of the young scribe; at all events, the article on " Peterloo" never appeared in the pages of the *Edinburgh Review.*

The accompanying note is thoroughly characteristic, and gives a humorous passing glimpse of his home surroundings at the close of 1821.

[XXVII.]   Foston, Dec. 1st, 1821.

MY DEAR LADY GEORGIANA,—How is Lord Carlisle? Pray do not take it for inattention that I do not call oftener, but it is rather too far to walk, and I hate riding. Next year I shall set up a gig, and then I shall call at Castle Howard twice a day all the year round, like an apothecary. I have just finished Miss Aitkin's " Memoirs of Queen Elizabeth," a pretty book, which I counsel you to let your daughters read, if they have not read it five years ago. I am in low spirits about the Malton road. I must go over to Malton so often, and it will be so troublesome. All my hay-stacks and corn-ricks are blown away by this wind, two of my maids are married, and the pole of my carriage broken! These are the sort of things which render life so difficult.

Yours, dear Lady Georgiana,
SYDNEY SMITH.

Though a lover of horses, he had good reason to " hate riding," for his falls were frequent, and occurred with a regularity which was both startling and ominous. "I left off riding"—is his own confession—" for the good of my parish and the peace of my family; for somehow or other, my horse and I had a habit of parting company. On one occasion I found myself suddenly prostrate in the streets of York, much to the delight of the Dissenters. Another time Calamity flung me over his head into a neighbouring parish, as if I had been a shuttlecock, and I felt grateful it was not into a neighbouring planet!"[7] His visits to the market-town of Malton were constant during the later years of his residence at Foston, and they arose chiefly out of his duties as a county magistrate on the bench there; and with such engagements he permitted nothing to interfere. The gig to which he alludes in the letter to Lady Morpeth was duly "set up" in the course of the following year, and the troubles which he anticipated on the Malton road turned out, as the following incident proves, to be not entirely imaginary. Some of the farmers and their labourers in those days were rather lax in the manner in which they allowed the waggons and carts under their charge to go along the turnpike roads. The horses were often imperfectly harnessed, and frequently were without reins; and Sydney Smith, as a justice of the peace, always drew up and expostulated with the drivers wherever he encountered them proceeding in so careless and dangerous a way. If the caution thus given was treated with contempt, or the offence repeated, the law was quickly enforced, and the men or their masters fined. One day, as he was returning in his gig from a meeting of magistrates at Malton, he overtook, near Kirkham, a half-witted fellow called Jack Storey, who was in the employment of a farmer there. The man's mental deficiencies were unknown to Sydney Smith, and as he was riding in a

---

[7] "Memoir of the Rev. Sydney Smith," chap. vii. p. 122.

cart and driving without reins, he ordered him to get down and walk at the horse's head. Jack, who did not at all relish the stranger's sudden assumption of authority, was not long in setting it at defiance, for hardly were the words uttered ere he growled out in reply, " Get down, and walk thee sel' ! " The order was repeated still more emphatically ; he was to leave the cart instantly, and walk at the horse's head ; but it was again met with the same clownish response, " Get down, and walk thee sel' ! " The cart went rumbling along through the dust, and the gig, with its now indignant occupant, kept closely at its side. Presently the order was again repeated, and still more sternly ; but the third time of asking was not more effectual than the first, and the same aggravating rejoinder was once more insolently hurled back. At length, thoroughly exasperated, Sydney Smith threatened to lay his whip across his shoulders, where-upon Jack, roused to frenzy, roared out, " If thee disent get on al stean thee ! " Almost at this moment a heap of small stones for mending the road came into sight, and no sooner was the cart opposite to them than Jack jumped out, and instead of going to the horse's head, ran to the stones and began to pelt his tormentor with them. He was a good marksman, and his vigour, for the moment at least, was unbounded, and Sydney Smith received some hard blows, and was shrewd enough to see that he was in the way of get-ting more. He, accordingly, was obliged to set his horse at a gallop, and so escaped ignominiously from the scene. It need scarcely be added that Jack's hare-brained condition soon became known to the rector, and prevented reprisals, and Sydney Smith

was forced laughingly to confess that in one contest, at
any rate, he had been compelled to retreat ingloriously
from the field of battle.

His life during the next two or three years
glided smoothly along, and, though filled with multi-
farious work, was devoid—like many of the happiest periods of existence—of special incident. It
was "cut up," to use his own expression, "into little
patches;" and he was still schoolmaster, farmer,
doctor, parson, author, justice, &c. Occasionally he
was accustomed, as already seen, to slip the collar
which such duties imposed, in order to dip into society,
or to renew his acquaintance with friends north and
south. Mackintosh, Brougham, Wishaw, Jeffrey, and
other men of their stamp were glad to avail themselves
of the vicinity of Foston to York, to look in at the
"Rector's Head," where a genial welcome ever awaited
them, and where they were regaled in a manner which
made them recall the merry supper-parties of Orchard
Street, where they were accustomed to gather a dozen
years before.

In 1823 his second son, Windham, through the
influence of Archbishop Harcourt, went to the Charterhouse, and the same year also witnessed Douglas' triumph in his election as captain of Westminster School.
Whilst in town about Windham, Sydney Smith dined
one day at Rogers', with a distinguished party.
Moore, who was present, records the fact that he was
particularly amusing: "His imagination of a duel
between two doctors, with oil of croton on the tips of
their fingers, trying to touch each other's lips, was
highly ludicrous. Have rather held out against Sydney
Smith hitherto; but to-day he has conquered me, and

I 'am now his victim in the laughing way for life." [8]
The success of Douglas was all the more creditable
to the lad, as his health was uncertain, and he had
been compelled to lay aside his studies more than once
in consequence of serious illness. In the autumn he
proceeded to Christ Church, Oxford, with the ultimate intention of studying for the law.

The " Rector's Head " was often a veritable " inn
of strange meetings," as people of the most opposite
attainments, tastes, and pursuits not unfrequently
met within its walls. But the host had the art of
making all and sundry feel at home. " There is one
talent," he was accustomed to say, " which I think
I have to a remarkable degree. There are substances
in nature called amalgams, whose property is to
combine incongruous materials; now I am a moral
amalgam, and I have a peculiar talent for mixing up
human materials in society, however repellant their
natures." [9]

Amongst other visitors at this period were Lord
and Lady Grey, who had long been anxious to see
Foston. Lady Grey, however, with her usual kindliness, was somewhat apprehensive that the resources
of the parsonage might be overtaxed if they halted
with a retinue of servants on their journey from
Howick to London. Her fears on that score were
quickly set at rest, for Sydney Smith wrote back
immediately to express his pleasure at the prospect of
seeing Lord Grey under his own roof; and added,
" We can hold you, heavy baggage and all. The following was the cavalcade of the Leycesters : five
horses, three men-servants, two maid-servants, four

[8] Moore's " Memoirs and Correspondence," vol. iv. p. 53.
[9] " Memoir of Sydney Smith," chap. viii. p. 147.

Leycesters, and we had other persons in the house, so you need not be afraid." One of the party thus referred to, Miss Leycester, still retains some recollections of her stay at Foston Rectory, and of that goodness of heart and charm of manner which rendered Sydney Smith's company so delightful to his guests. The unusual arrangements of the place impressed and diverted her as a girl not a little, such as a very large store-room in the house, which contained almost everything that could be wanted by the whole village, as they were very far from any shops. His thoughtfulness extended even to dumb animals, and he did not think it beneath him to promote their comfort; for "I remember," adds Miss Leycester, "that there were at Foston pieces of wood joined together placed at intervals in the grounds for the cows to scratch themselves upon."

Honours in his "own country" and in his own profession now began to fall to his lot, for in 1824 Sir John Johnstone, then High Sheriff, appointed him his chaplain, and in that capacity he preached two remarkable sermons of unconventional type—one on the lawyer who tempted Christ, and the other on the Unjust Judge—in York Minster, before the Judges of Assize.

In the summer of that year he also paid a farewell visit to Sir George Philips at Sedgley Hall, Manchester, and from thence he went to the Leycesters of Toft, the Stanleys of Alderley, and the Davenports of Capesthorne. The Countess of Camperdown states that her grandfather, Sir George Philips, "was driven away from Sedgley by the smoke of Manchester, owing to the rapid increase of the town." He accordingly left the neighbourhood and settled in Warwickshire, where he built Weston House, Shipston-on-Stour, and there Sydney Smith was frequently his visitor. Lady Camperdown has vivid recollections of the manner in which, in her childhood, her grandfather's guest proved himself again and again the friend of three bashful little maidens, who stood somewhat in awe of him. Eventually he won their hearts, and they grew quite fond of him, for he was accustomed to chase them through the hall, and round the picture-gallery, and to enter into their pastimes, more like a frolicsome elder brother fresh from school, than a grey-haired and dignified old clergyman. The three little girls afterwards became respectively, the Countess of Camperdown, Lady Carew, and the Countess of Caithness, and the eldest of them once more calls Weston House her home.

YORK MINSTER.

CHAPTER X.

1825—1829.

Sydney Smith and the Catholic Claims.—Appointed Canon of Bristol
by Lord Lyndhurst.—Farewell to Foston.

THE year 1825 witnessed a memorable struggle in
Parliament in connection with a question which was
at last coming rapidly to the front for settlement—
the long-neglected claims of the Catholics. The conduct of the English in Ireland in the eighteenth century,
must ever be regarded by all who believe that no man
should be subjected to civil incapacities on account of
religious convictions with feelings of shame and de-
testation. George III. was violently opposed to all
concessions to the Catholics, and obstinately refused
to countenance any effort to repeal those unjust and
tyrannical statutes which, in previous reigns, had
imposed civil disabilities on no less than five-sixths of
his subjects in Ireland. In spite of the obstinacy of
the king, backed as it was by the ignorant intolerance
of an unreformed Parliament, and the miserable
bigotry of an apathetic Church, which reserved what
zeal it possessed for purposes of obstruction, the first
quarter of the present century was marked by many
gallant but unsuccessful endeavours to revoke a code
of laws which were an insult to Ireland, and a scandal

to England. If George III. had been impervious to argument, and blind to the signs of the times, no man had questioned the sincerity of the old king's motives, for it was well known that he unfortunately conscientiously regarded the proposal to grant relief to the Catholics as a violation of his coronation oath. Selfish, dissolute, and trifling, his successor was a man of a different stamp; and bent on personal gratification alone, George IV. turned a deaf ear to the grievances of his people, and made no attempt to conceal the fact that, Gallio-like, he cared for none of these things.

Pitt, Grenville, Grattan, Plunket, and Canning attempted one after another to induce Parliament to investigate the Catholic claims, but in spite of the growing support of the English people, the subject was again and again contemptuously dismissed. In 1825, the Irish, exasperated by the repeated failures of the Catholic cause, seemed on the eve of rebellion, and the political horizon was darkened by angry and threatening clouds. O'Connell, who knew better than most men that union is strength, threw himself with characteristic ardour into the work of the Catholic Association, and sought by every means in his power to knit the people together in indignant remonstrance at the common wrong. "Agitate, agitate, agitate!" was O'Connell's constant cry, and nobody could accuse the great orator of preaching what he did not practise. "I always go on repeating," was his frank declaration, "until I find what I have been saying coming back to me in echoes from the people."

The Catholic Association cherished no visionary or revolutionary scheme, but, like the Anti-Corn League

twenty years later, simply sought a practical measure
of relief, and one which had been urged upon the
Legislature by the foremost statesmen of the time, and
the justice of which was beyond all challenge.   In
1823, the network of the Association had spread itself
over the whole of Ireland, and embraced most of the
Catholic nobility, gentry, priesthood, and peasantry
of the sister isle.   From that year until its sup-
pression, the Catholic Association assumed the attributes of a national Parliament.   It held its sessions
in Dublin, appointed committees, received petitions,
directed a census of the population to be taken, and
levied contributions in the shape of a Catholic rent
upon every parish in the land.   Its stirring and im-
passioned proclamations were placed in the hands of
the priests, and were read by them to their flocks
from the altar.   Its debates, abounding in fiery de-
nunciations against the British Government, were
published in every newspaper, and were thus scattered
broadcast over the land.   The oratory of such men as
O'Connell and Sheil could not fail to arrest public
attention, and the whole movement accordingly began
to assume proportions which filled its supporters with
enthusiasm and hope, and its foes with alarm and
dismay.   Lord Eldon, on whose judgment as confidential adviser, the king placed implicit reliance, was
filled with inveterate hostility to the Catholics, and the
Tories, from their leader, Lord Liverpool, downwards,
repeated with dismal unanimity the "No Popery" cry.

It soon became quite obvious that the demands of
O'Connell and his followers must be granted, or the
clamour of the Catholic Association silenced.   The
Tory Government was not prepared for the former

alternative, and determined therefore in 1825, to introduce a Bill to suppress the Catholic Association
for three years. The measure, which was open to
the gravest constitutional objections, was strenuously
resisted, and naturally excited the utmost indignation throughout Ireland ; and though it became law,
the progress of the Catholic cause was accelerated by
the very means which were taken for its repression.
Whilst this measure was still under consideration,
Sir Francis Burdett, taking advantage of the general
feeling in the Liberal ranks against the tyrannical
policy of the Government, raised the whole question
of the Catholic disabilities, and carried a motion to go
into committee to investigate their claims. Eventually,
after a series of splendid debates, in which many
waverers were won over to the side of toleration, a
Bill, which granted a considerable degree of relief,
was sent up to the Lords. The antipathy of the Court
to Sir Francis Burdett's proposals was evinced by an
extraordinary speech which the heir-presumptive, the
Duke of York, delivered in his place in Parliament,
and in which he made no secret of his personal inten-
tions in reference to the question in the event of his
accession to the throne. Petitions for and against the
Bill were despatched in hot haste to Westminster, but
it was thrown out in the Lords on the second reading
by a majority of forty-eight.

The author of " Peter Plymley " was no idle spectator of a struggle in which he had already played
so important a part, but used whatever influence he
possessed to further the cause of civil and religious
liberty. As far back as 1808, when the vast majority
of the nation held very different opinions, he had had

the courage to declare that the treatment of our Catholic fellow-subjects reflected " indelible disgrace upon the English character, and explained but too clearly the cause of that hatred in which the English name has so long been held in Ireland." [1] The clergy of the English Church, almost to a man, were hostile to the Catholic claims, and clerical gatherings were, as a consequence, held in different parts of the country in 1825 to petition against Sir Francis Burdett's motion. In March a crowded meeting of the clergy of Cleveland was held at Thirsk, and on that occasion Sydney Smith made his first appearance on a political platform. Beginning his speech with the unexpected declaration that he had never even attended a public political meeting before in his life, he proceeded in a genial vein of pleasantry to ridicule the childish prophecies of danger which filled the air, and to protest against the false and mischievous assertions of a number of loyal but foolish Churchmen, who seemed to imagine, if any conclusion at all could be gathered from their language, that the Church of England, instead of being, as he believed, the " strongest, wisest, and best establishment in the world," was the " most fainting, sickly, hysterical institution that ever existed in it." If the meeting was determined to address Parliament on the subject, he ventured to submit a petition which, in deference to the opinions of others, he had endeavoured to render as moderate and mild as possible, requesting the House of Commons to inquire whether the opportune moment had not arrived for the immediate repeal of the laws which

---

[1] *Edinburgh Review*, vol. **xi.**

affect the Roman Catholics of Great Britain and
Ireland. Sydney Smith had been in advance of the
public opinion of the nation in 1808, when the " Letters
of Peter Plymley" startled the community; and in
1825, when he made his first political speech at the
" Three Tuns," Thirsk, to help the cause of civil and
religious liberty, he was still in advance of the public
opinion of the clergy. His petition received only two
signatures, those of Archdeacon Wrangham and the
Rev. William Vernon Harcourt; and an address of a
very different character was adopted by an overwhelming majority.

On the 11th of April, a similar meeting of the
clergy of the East Riding of Yorkshire was held at the
Tiger Inn, Beverley, for the purpose of petitioning
Parliament against the emancipation of the Catholics; and the Rector of Foston again protested in
even more emphatic terms against the injustice of
such a proceeding. " If you go into a parsonage-house
in the country, Mr. Archdeacon," said he, addressing
the chair, " you see sometimes a style and fashion of
furniture which does very well for us, but which has
had its day in London. It is seen in London no more;
it is banished to the provinces; from the gentlemen's houses of the provinces these pieces of furniture,
as soon as they are discovered to be unfashionable,
descend to the farm-houses, then to cottages, then to
the faggot-heap, then to the dung-hill. As it is with
furniture, so it is with arguments. I hear at country
meetings many arguments against the Catholics which
are never heard in London; their London existence is
over—they are only to be met with in the provinces,
and there they are fast hastening down, with clumsy

chairs and ill-fashioned sofas, to another order of men. But, sir, as they are not yet gone where I am sure they are going, I shall endeavour to point out their defects, and to accelerate their descent." In spite, however, of argument, statistics, common sense, and wit, his words were of no avail, and at the close of the meeting he was in a minority of one. Even his curate opposed him, and stood there " breathing war and vengeance on the Vatican." The curate, it appears, had felt some doubt about the propriety of voting against his rector, but he was met by the assurance that he need fear no animosity, but might expect instead, as a tribute to his courage, increased good-will and respect. " I assured him that nothing would give me more pain than to think I had prevented in any man the free assertion of honest opinions." A half-humorous, half-pathetic incident took place in connection with the meeting, which Sydney Smith thus records : " A poor clergyman whispered to me, that he was quite of my way of thinking, but had nine children. I begged he would remain a Protestant." The following amusing note was written to Mr. Davenport, M.P., a few days after the Beverley meeting.

[XXVIII.]   Foston, April 20th, 1825.

MY DEAR SIR,—In return for my speech at the " Tiger " which I sent you last week, pray frank the enclosed letter for me. I slept at the Tiger Inn the night before, and asked the servants of the inn what they thought of the Catholics and Protestants. I must inform you of the result. The chambermaid was decidedly for the Church of England. Boots was

for the Catholics.   The waiter said he had often (God
forgive him) wished them both confounded together.

I am, dear sir,
Very truly yours,
SYDNEY SMITH.

D. Davenport, Esq., M.P.,
28, Lower Brook Street, London.

Shortly before the question of Catholic emancipation
had reached this phase, the Duke of Devonshire, at
the instance of the Earl of Carlisle, gave the Rector
of Foston the family living of Londesborough to hold
until his nephew, the Hon. W. G. Howard (the present
Lord Carlisle), came of age.   The living, which was a
valuable one, was within driving distance of Foston,
and it was held by Sydney Smith until 1832.   Londesborough is a pretty village, sheltered by lofty trees,
and built high up on the western edge of the breezy
wolds of the East Riding.   From the rising ground
beyond the church there is a splendid view of the vast
and cultivated plain which lies below, and in one
direction the Humber may be traced against the dark
background of the Lincolnshire hills; whilst in an
opposite direction, but much nearer at hand, the stately
towers of York Minster gladden the eye.   Londesborough has a quaint little hospital or almshouse,
founded and endowed two hundred years ago, for twelve
poor people, by the first Earl and Countess of Burlington, who at that time lived in an ancient mansion
close by, of which the only memorial now is a broken
flight of broad and ornamental steps which rise above
the uneven turf, under which all else that remains of
Londesborough Hall lies buried.   The ancient family
of the Cliffords had lived at Londesborough for

generations before one of their number built the hospital. On the chancel-floor of the church there is an inscription which links the name of John, Lord Clifford, who was slain at the battle of Towton, and upon whom Shakespeare hurls deserved odium as " bloody Clifford," and his son Henry, the noble-hearted " shepherd lad," the charm of whose romantic story has been heightened by the genius of Wordsworth. The third Lord Burlington, the friend of Alexander Pope, is also buried in the church, and in his day many celebrated men visited Londesborough, including Pope and Garrick. At the death of the third Earl in 1753, in default of male issue, Londesborough became the property of the fourth Duke of Devonshire, who had married a few years previously the heiress of the house of Clifford.

Sydney Smith never lived at Londesborough, but was accustomed to drive over two or three times a year from Foston. He was, however, very efficiently represented by the curate in charge, a Mr. Mayelstone, who resided at the rectory, and whose name suggests what is probably the only authentic anecdote of Sydney Smith at Londesborough. On one of his few visits to the place he encountered a young rustic on the village street who, startled by the apparition of a stranger in broadcloth, unconsciously halted, and gave him the full benefit of an uncompromising stare. " Where are you going, my boy ? " inquired the rector in his blandest tones. " To't Sunday-school," answered the lad, with his eyes still fixed upon him. " Who do you think I am ? " " I dun' noa." " Am I Mr. Mayelstone ? " The answer came with ill-concealed contempt. " Noa ! " " Am

I Mr. Mayelstone's mother!" "Noa!!" "What do you think I am, then?" The stony stare disappeared in a merry twinkle as the boy replied, "I think you're maist like one of them chaps that gangs aboot wi' knives and razors!" The rector was delighted with the shrewd retort, and pulled out half-a-crown in payment on the spot. As for the lad, his words were not as far from the truth as at first sight appears, and it was undoubtedly a fortunate thing for society that the polished knives and razors of Sydney Smith's trenchant satire and incisive wit were employed not against, but in the interests of the English people. Possibly he was thinking of this Londesborough incident, when long afterwards he declared, "The whole of my life has passed like a razor—in hot water or a scrape." As the rector seldom appeared in Londesborough, except to preach an occasional sermon, few traces of his presence remain in the place, and the parish registers contain no record concerning him. It is related, however, apparently on good authority, that one Sunday he announced his subject, in a somewhat slipshod fashion, as " Putting one's hand to the plough and looking back," and then calmly referred the congregation to one of the Epistles for his text. There is another tradition of Sydney Smith which rests on good authority, and which illustrates his occasional absent-mindedness not only when in church, but also when on his way to it. One of his intimate friends in the neighbourhood of Heslington used to relate that he once arrived late at Naburn Church, near York, where he had arranged to take the service. He excused himself by saying to the anxious officials who greeted him with reproachful glances on his tardy arrival, that he had started from home on his pony, but dismounting had thrown the bridle over his arm and walked on in front of the animal, conning over his sermon. Meanwhile, the pony had taken advantage of the situation, and had slipped the head-gear over its ears, and quietly trotted home, so that when the astonished rector turned round, he found that he had only the bridle behind him! He added, in sly allusion to the Yorkshire adage, " Give a tyke a bridle, and he will soon have a horse," that he was not enough of a Yorkshire man yet to get himself a steed in time, and therefore had been compelled to walk the rest of the way. It was his custom, both at Foston and Londes-borough, to hasten out of the vestry as soon as the service was over, to talk with the farmers about the health of their families, or the prospect of their crops.

The Rev. William Vernon Harcourt, son of the late Archbishop of York, and father of the present Secretary of State, was one of Sydney Smith's Yorkshire friends, and a brother clergyman with whom he had much in common. Canon Harcourt was moreover one of two clergymen who ventured to sign Sydney Smith's petition to Parliament, in 1825, in favour of Catholic emancipation, and his attitude then was only in keeping with the liberality and courage which marked his treatment of other great questions of the day. On the occasion of his friend's marriage, the Rector of Foston wrote some exceedingly witty lines, which hitherto have remained unpublished, and which are now transcribed by kind permission of Sir William Vernon Harcourt, M.P. It is scarcely necessary to add that Canon Harcourt was a distinguished geologist; his ardent devotion to science led Sydney Smith, in inviting him, a few years later to visit Combe-Florey, to urge as an additional attraction, "We are on the old red sandstone."

[XXIX.]

ON MR. AND MRS. WILLIAM HARCOURT PASSING THEIR HONEYMOON AT THE LAKES.

'Mid rocks and ringlets, specimens and sighs,
On wings of rapture every moment flies,
He views Matilda, lovely in her prime,
Then finds sulphuric acid mix'd with lime!
Guards from her lovely face the solar ray,
And fills his pockets with alluvial clay.
Science and Love distract his tortured heart,
Now flints, now fondness, take the larger part,
And now he breaks a stone, now feels a dart.

SYDNEY SMITH.

A friendship which he had formed with Mr. and Mrs. Beilby Thompson—afterwards Lord and Lady Wenlock [2]—brightened the closing years of Sydney Smith's residence in Yorkshire, and proved a source of gratification throughout the remainder of his life. Unfortunately for him, Escrick Park was not so accessible from Foston as Castle Howard, but lay more than fifteen miles away; nevertheless, he was an occasional visitor there, and his new friends were

[2] The first Lord Wenlock, Paul Beilby Lawley, was a younger son of Sir Robert Lawley, of Canwell, in Staffordshire. He assumed the surname of his mother on the death of his uncle, Richard Thompson, Esq., of Escrick Park, York, to whose fortune and estates he succeeded. His wife—to whom several very cordial letters in the published correspondence of Sydney Smith are addressed—was the daughter of Richard, Lord Braybrooke. Lady Wenlock died in 1868; her husband sixteen years earlier.

always delighted to see the familiar gig drive up to their door. The intimacy between Sydney Smith and his friends at Escrick was deepened by the delicate and respectful sympathy evinced by the latter on the death of Douglas. Whilst Lord and Lady Wenlock enjoyed as much as any one the high spirits and exuberant fun which marked the ordinary appearances of Sydney Smith in society, and concerning which so much has already been said and written, they never failed to recognize the generous and lofty qualities of his character, and the deep reverence for the good, the beautiful, and the true, which always curbed his mirth, and rendered his conversation in quiet hours and serious moods eminently helpful and suggestive to his friends. Towards the close of his life when, as he expressed it, he lived with one leg in Combe-Florey and the other in London, few things pleased him better than to meet his friends from Castle Howard or Escrick in town, and to renew in intercourse with them his many pleasant recollections of his Yorkshire days. The Hon. Mrs. J. Stuart Wortley, daughter of Lord Wenlock, was a young girl when he left Foston, but she met him frequently in London when he was Canon of St. Paul's, and as the child of his valued friends at Escrick as well as on personal grounds, was always received by him with even more than his usual kindness. It is interesting to be able to place on record in these pages the impression created on the mind of one so well qualified by intimate acquaintance to speak on such a subject as the nature of Sydney Smith's influence, as Mrs. Stuart Wortley :—

[xxx.]

I was still too young when the Rev. Sydney Smith

removed from Yorkshire to remember the Foston days,
but I was continually hearing of them, and well knew
how he was missed. My dear parents were never
weary of recalling the brilliant days when he was with
them, when they "ached with laughing" at the wealth
of fun and nonsense which he poured forth when he
was in high spirits. They were, however, not less
fond of dwelling on the fact that in their view this
joyousness never impaired his excellence as a clergyman, or infringed on his perfect charity and gentleness
to all mankind. I like to give this as *their* testimony
because their standard was an especially high one.
They saw him, moreover, both in sorrow and in joy,
and I have heard my mother speak of how she visited
them at the time of the death of their eldest son.

Comparing my own personal recollections with their
accounts, I incline to the belief that Sydney Smith
never quite recovered the loss of Douglas, or in his
London days ever quite equalled the abundant hilarity
of his earlier years. When I now recall his conversation, I see what he meant when in one of his published
lectures at the Royal Institution, he mentions surprise
as the principal element in wit. No mortal could
conceive the unexpected turns of his fancy. His talk
was like a stream of fireworks, brilliant, incessant, and
perfectly harmless. He kept, for instance, a whole
party, of which I was one, laughing at his droll way of
announcing the appointment of Dr. Vowler Short to
the Bishopric of Sodor and Man. "Vowler Short is
to be Sodor and Man. Mrs. Vowler Short and all the
little Shorts are now trying on short cassocks, and
saying, ' This is what papa will wear when he is Sodor
and Man ! ' " His manner was so funny and yet so kind

that it never occurred to any one to think the slightest
disrespect could be inferred, but the antithesis of the
double names amused him, and he proceeded to twist
them about very comically. I wish anything could
reproduce his talk in a manner which would reveal all
the depth of his feeling, as well as the brightness of
his fancy; but it is quite indescribable.

His tenderness and kindness left a very lasting
impression upon me; he certainly had a marvellously
deep well of human sympathy in his heart.

JANE STUART WORTLEY.

16, Clarges Street, Piccadilly, W.
31st May, 1884.

The year 1826 opened in England with a commercial panic of almost unparalleled severity,—some
seventy banks suspended payment and were closed,
and Sydney Smith declared that henceforth he should
keep his money in a hole in his garden! The causes
of the disaster cannot be traced in these pages; it is
enough to chronicle the fact, and to recall the wide-
spread privation and discontent which the famine-price
of bread, and the scarcity of water, produced amongst
the poor during that tropical summer. In the manufacturing districts the starving masses, mistaking the
introduction of machinery for the cause of their distress, destroyed the power-looms. In Blackburn, on one
Sunday alone a thousand power-looms were wrecked
by an infuriated mob; and from Bradford, Manchester,
Liverpool, Hull, Norwich, and Bethnal Green, news of
riots and disturbances were continually coming to
hand. A general election took place in the course of
the summer, and the Corn Laws and the Catholic

emancipation were the chief questions of the hour, whilst the abolition of slavery was also earnestly demanded by an influential section of the nation.

The anti-Catholic feeling in the country seemed to revive under the pressure of the times, and Lord John Russell, Lord Howick, Henry Brougham, and other prominent Whigs failed at first to secure seats in the new House of Commons. Sydney Smith seized the occasion of the general election to issue his famous " Letter to the Electors upon the Catholic Question," and as a political pamphlet it went far and wide, and its noble plea for justice made a deep impression on the public mind. He urged the electors to vote for " a free altar," and advised them to have nothing to do with those " modern chains and prisons for a man's faith under the name of disqualifications and incapacities, which are only the cruelty and tyranny of a more civilized age." He maintained that civil offices should be open to all loyal subjects, whatever their religious convictions might be, and for himself was not at all afraid of a Roman Catholic alderman or a Wesleyan justice of the peace. He pleaded that there might be no longer any " tyranny in belief, but an open road to Heaven, and no human insolence hallowed by the name of God." The " Letter to the Electors" bristles with facts and arguments, and it proved an armoury from which many resolute champions of toleration drew fresh weapons of attack. The humour of Sydney Smith is perhaps less conspicuous in this manifesto than usual, but the plea advanced for the delay of concessions is demolished by a peculiarly happy bit of satire: " Every man in trade must have experienced the difficulty of getting in a bill from an unwilling paymaster. If you call in the morning, the gentleman is not up; if in the middle of the day, he is out; if in the evening, there is company. If you ask mildly, you are indifferent to the time of payment; if you press, you are impertinent. No time and no manner can render such a message agreeable. So it is with the poor Catholics; their message is so disagreeable that their time and manner can never be right."

In the course of the summer, Macaulay was in York, at the Assizes, and spent a Sunday at Foston, and in a letter to his father (dated July 26th, 1826) he describes his impressions of the place:—" On Saturday, I went to Sydney Smith's. His parish lies three or four miles out of any frequented road. He is, however, most pleasantly situated. 'Fifteen years ago,' said he to me as I alighted at the gate of his shrubbery, 'I was taken up in Piccadilly and set down here. There was no house, and no garden; nothing but a bare field.' One service this eccentric divine has certainly rendered to the Church. He has built the very neatest, most commodious, and most appropriate rectory that I ever saw. All its decorations are in a peculiarly clerical style; grave, simple, and gothic. * * * We passed an extremely pleasant evening, had a very good dinner, and many amusing anecdotes. After breakfast next morning, I walked to church with Sydney Smith. The edifice is not at all in keeping with the rectory. It is a miserable little hovel with a wooden belfry. It was, however, well filled, and with decent people, who seemed to take very much to their pastor. * * * Sydney Smith brought me to York on Monday morning in time for the stage-coach which runs to Skipton. We parted with many assurances of good-will. I have really taken a great liking to him. He is full of wit, humour, and shrewdness. He is not one of those show-talkers who reserve all their good things for special occasions. It seems to be his greatest luxury to keep his wife and daughters laughing for two or three hours every day." [3]

The same year Sydney Smith paid a visit to Paris, a city which he had often desired to see, and there he renewed his acquaintance with Prince Tallyrand, and was introduced by Lord Holland, who was in the French capital at the same time, to a number of distinguished statesmen and literary men. The universal civility of the French, the taste and ingenuity displayed in their shops, their propensity for explaining things which do not require explanation, and their mastery of the art of furnishing, were all duly noticed. The profusion of mirrors in their rooms comes in for a word of praise, and the brilliant aspect which they give to large apartments is also mentioned. "I remember entering a room with glass all round it, and saw myself reflected on every side. I took it for a meeting of the clergy, and was delighted of course." [4] Soon after his return from Paris, his friends Wishaw and Jeffrey came for a short time to Foston, and during their stay he realized, according to his own statement, his idea of good society. The hot weather of 1826 tried him not a little, though his health, as a rule, was exceedingly good; probably the cause of his physical distress during the sultry months of that oppressive

---

[3] "Life and Letters of Lord Macaulay," by his nephew, George Otto Trevelyan, M.P., vol. i. chap. iii. p. 147.

[4] "Memoir of Sydney Smith," chap. xi. p. 243.

summer, is to be found in the naive confession which
he made, when it was running its course, in a letter to
one of his correspondents, "I am, you know, of the
family of Falstaff." [5]

In February, 1827, Lord Liverpool was struck with
paralysis, and it was soon apparent that his political
career was absolutely at an end. He had been called
to the head of affairs upon the assassination of Spencer
Perceval in 1812, and his tenure of power forms one of
the darkest and most discreditable epochs in modern
history. Lord Liverpool was succeeded by the Right
Hon. George Canning, who had been Foreign Secretary
since the suicide of Castlereagh in 1822. Canning had
long been in favour of Catholic emancipation, and so
far back as 1812 he had supported Grattan's motion
on the subject. The friends of religious liberty, therefore, hailed his accession to power, and their satisfaction
was increased when it was immediately followed by
the retirement of Lord Eldon. The withdrawal of
the Lord Chancellor was followed by the resignation
of the Duke of Wellington, Mr. (afterwards Sir Robert)
Peel, and four other members of the late Cabinet.

The attitude of the "no-surrender" Tories towards
the new Premier was one of undisguised hostility,
and Canning could never have held his own against
them but for the support of a section of the Whigs.
Lord Lansdowne and Mr. Tierney entered the Cabinet, and Brougham, Burdett, and others supported
the Ministry in the House of Commons. Although
in favour of Catholic emancipation, Canning was
opposed to the repeal of the Test Act, and had little
sympathy with the gathering cry in the country for

[5] Published Correspondence, p. 456,

S

Parliamentary reform. Lord Grey accordingly held aloof from him, and the position of his Government was still further imperilled by the strength of ultra-Tory sentiments in the House of Lords. Probably Albany Fonblanque expressed the general opinion of the Whigs on Canning's accession to power with tolerable exactness, when he declared himself glad to admit that, in "the substitution of Canning's rule for that of his late bigoted and despised colleagues, a comparative benefit of great value is obtained by the nation. He is not all that we wish ; they were all that we hate."[6] Sir John Copley was raised to the woolsack in place of Lord Eldon, and entered the House of Lords as Baron Lyndhurst. The new administration was of singularly brief duration, for Canning had scarcely reached the pinnacle of his ambition when, to the great sorrow of the nation, death surprised him in August, 1827. A feeling akin to consternation passed over friends and foes alike when it became known that a minister, whose courage, eloquence, and ability had produced a deep impression on the public mind, had been struck down by death at the very moment when a great career seemed dawning upon him. His administration had not lasted four months when Canning expired on the 8th of August at the Duke of Devonshire's house at Chiswick, in the "very room in which Fox had died twenty years before."[7] A few days later he was laid, amid every demonstration of respect, in an honoured grave, close to Pitt and Fox, in Westminster Abbey. In spite of the shortcomings of the "last of the rhetoricians," as Canning was styled by a distinguished

[6] "England under Seven Administrations," vol. i. p. 16.
[7] "Walpole's History of England," vol. ii. chap. x. p. 459.

contemporary, his death was deplored by every oppressed race in Europe, for his foreign policy had made his name abroad synonymous with liberty itself.

Although the death of Canning robbed the friends of Catholic emancipation of the hope of immediate repeal, nothing could arrest the steady and triumphant progress of the movement, and all who were not blinded by fanaticism clearly perceived that the claims of justice must shortly prevail. Sydney Smith's last contribution to the pages of the *Edinburgh Review*, by a happy though undesigned coincidence, was on the subject of the Catholic claims, and with a final protest in the interests of civil and religious liberty, his long and honourable connection with periodical literature ceased. The article, which appeared in March, 1827, concludes with a few words of advice addressed to the different opponents of the Catholic question : " *To the No-Popery Fool.*—You are made use of by men who laugh at you, and despise you for your folly and ignorance; and who, the moment it suits their purpose, will consent to emancipation of the Catholics, and leave you to roar and bellow ' No popery ! ' to vacancy and the moon. *To the No-Popery Rogue.*—A shameful and scandalous game to sport with the serious interests of the country in order to gain some increase of public power. *To the honest No-Popery People.*— We respect you very sincerely, but are astonished at your existence. *To the Base.*—Sweet children of turpitude, beware ! the old anti-popery people are fast perishing away. Take heed that you are not surprised by an emancipating king, or an emancipating administration. Leave a *locus pœnitentiæ !* prepare a place for retreat; get ready your equivocations and denials. The dreadful day may yet come, when liberality may lead to place and power. We understand these matters here. It is safest to be moderately base, to be flexible in shame, and to be always ready for what is generous, good, and just when anything is to be gained by virtue. *To the Catholics.*—Wait. Do not add to your miseries by a mad and desperate rebellion. Persevere in civil exertions, and concede all you can concede. All great alterations in human affairs are produced by compromise." [8]

The danger of a mad and desperate rebellion in Ireland was the reverse of a remote contingency when these closing words were written. Exasperated beyond endurance by the unrelieved misery of their condition, and by the cool insolence with which arguments and appeals alike had been set aside, the Irish people were ripe for revolution, and the popular leader O'Connell was dangerous to the public peace, not chiefly through his splendid oratorical gifts, but because of the sense of outraged justice which helped to wing his words, and caused them to awaken responsive echoes in the hearts of the impressionable crowds which flocked around him wherever he went. Sydney Smith saw clearly, in 1827, that, repugnant though the Catholic claims might be to George IV. and his advisers, no Government could much longer exist in this country, however tyrannical, which did not deal with the question on the lines marked out by policy and prudence, as well as justice and mercy; and it was because he perceived the issue so distinctly that his last words to the

people of Ireland on the subject were to stay their
hand and await the issue of events, and the swift and
peaceful triumph of a cause which had always been
righteous, and had at length grown irresistible. In a
private letter to a friend in the course of the same
year, he thus depicts the aspect of political affairs:
" Jesuits abroad—Turks in Greece—No poperists in
England—A. panting to burn B.; B. fuming to roast
C.; C. miserable that he cannot reduce D. to ashes;
D. consigning to eternal perdition the three first
letters of the alphabet." [9]

On the death of Canning the country dreaded the
immediate return to power of Tories trained in the
narrow school of Lords Eldon and Liverpool; the
King, however, summoned Lord Goderich, and entrusted him with the difficult task of constructing a
new administration. Lord Lansdowne and other influential Whigs determined to accept office under
Canning's successor, but they were speedily disheartened in their allegiance by the King's refusal to
acknowledge by Cabinet rank the brilliant services of
Lord Holland. Lord Goderich passed the autumn in
futile endeavours to reconcile the differences in his
Cabinet, and the year ended with the ignominious
downfall of the new administration; and on the 8th
of January, 1828, the Duke of Wellington was called
to the head of affairs. The Coalition Ministry of Lord
Goderich did not, however, disappear into the gulf of
Toryism, without some recognition, on the part of the
more liberal-minded members of it, of the public
services of Sydney Smith.

[9] Published Correspondence, p. 459.

Lord Lyndhurst, who, though a political antagonist, was a personal friend, nominated the Rector
of Foston to a vacant stall at Bristol; and probably
the influence in the Cabinet of his old and attached
friend Lord Lansdowne, who admired Sydney Smith
both on public and private grounds, had also much
to do with the promotion which he thus received.
Sydney Smith was on intimate terms with Lord
Lyndhurst; and soon after the latter became Lord
Chancellor, he was present at a dinner-party at
his house, when the conversation turned to the
custom in India of widows burning themselves on
their husband's funeral pyre. For the sake of argument, he began to defend the practice, and asserted
that no wife who truly loved her husband could
wish to survive him. "But if Lord Lyndhurst
were to die, you would be sorry that Lady Lyndhurst should burn herself?" was the sudden and
embarrassing question of one of the guests. "Lady
Lyndhurst," came the deliberate reply, "would, no
doubt, as an affectionate wife, consider it her duty to
burn herself, but it would be our duty to put her out;
and, as the wife of the Lord Chancellor, Lady Lyndhurst should not be put out like an ordinary widow.
It should be a state affair. First, a procession of the
judges, then of the lawyers." "But pray, Mr. Smith,
where are the clergy?" Instantly came the sly
response, "All gone to congratulate the new Lord
Chancellor!"

The year 1828 opened eventfully to Sydney Smith,
for, on the 1st of January, his youngest daughter,
Emily, was married; and a few days later a letter
arrived at the rectory, informing him that he had been

made a Canon of Bristol. It was a sad day to the villagers of Foston when their friend and helper, "Miss Emily" went away; and there are still two or three old folks in the locality of her early home who recall with an affection which the lapse of more than half a century has not dimmed, the kindliness and sympathy with which the young girl laboured for their good. Beautiful, gentle, and accomplished, Emily Smith was greatly beloved by those who knew her, and throughout a long life she endeared herself to all around her, and rich and poor alike continually felt the attraction of her sunny and benevolent nature. Her husband was Mr. Nathaniel Hibbert, a young barrister, and the son and heir of George Hibbert, Esq., of Munden House, Watford, Herts. After an honourable career at the Bar, Mr. Hibbert succeeded in 1841 to the family estate, and the last twenty years of his life were spent at his charming seat amid the ordinary avocations which mark the pleasant life of an active and scholarly country gentleman. Mr. Hibbert, who was for many years a magistrate for Hertfordshire, and in 1855 High Sheriff of the county, died in 1865. Mrs. Hibbert, who resembled Sydney Smith in character more closely than any of his other children, died at Munden in 1874. A good conversationalist as well as a good woman, she was a special favourite with her father's friend, Lord Jeffrey, who had known her since she was a child at Heslington, and always referred to her in terms of warm affection.

The marriage of Emily Smith was celebrated at Foston Church, and the Archbishop of York drove over and performed the ceremony.

Foston, January 6th, 1828.

DEAR LADY HOLLAND,—I have received congratu-
lations from various quarters on being presented to a
Prebend of Bristol, as I have done before on being
Rector of St. George's, Bloomsbury. All that I can
say is, no intelligence of these elevations has reached
me. Our wedding went off to admiration. The
dinner was well-dressed, the day not bad, the Archbishop was tall, good-natured, and obliging. The
bridegroom and his bride looked happy.

Ever your obliged and affectionate friend,

SYDNEY SMITH.

It was perhaps well for Sydney Smith that his
thoughts were turned into fresh channels by tidings
of preferment, for Foston Rectory was robbed of much
of its brightness when Emily left it as a bride. Three
days after his daughter's wedding he confessed to a
friend, "I feel as if I had lost a limb, and were
walking about with one leg; but nobody pities this
description of invalids."[1] In February he went to
Bristol, and was duly installed in "an extremely comfortable prebendal house, which looks to the south,
and is perfectly snug and parsonic."[2] Bristol has
always been a stronghold of Nonconformity, and the
Rector of Foston quickly discovered that, ecclesias-
tically at least, the atmosphere of the city was much
more bracing than anything which he had experienced
in the north. The services at the Cathedral were in
a very languishing condition, and the Church seemed

[1] Published Correspondence, p. 466.   [2] Ibid. p. 466.

to have lost its hold on the reverence and affection of the people. The citizens, of course, were aware of the bold and brilliant advocacy of the Catholic claims, which had distinguished the new Canon of Bristol; and if some narrow churchmen resented Sydney Smith's arrival, and many timid ecclesiastics shook their head at his appointment to a position of so much influence, there was a distinct movement of the popular mind in his favour, and the more intelligent inhabitants were not slow to recognize that a renowned champion of liberty had appeared in their midst.

In March he occupied the Cathedral pulpit for the first time, and the manly and rational tone of his vigorous and pointed sermons at once arrested public attention, and the most hostile, as well as the most indifferent, were compelled to acknowledge that in the Rev. Canon Smith, Bristol had secured a preacher who reached the people, not only on account of his popular sympathies, but also because he appealed to motives which they felt, and addressed them in language which they could understand. Towards the close of his life he was accustomed to declare that he had only one illusion left, and that was the Archbishop of Canterbury; and whilst at Bristol he seems to have been taken aback by the diminutive stature of the Bishop of the diocese, whose aspect was all the more startling when contrasted with his stately friend, Dr. Harcourt, of York, to whom as his ecclesiastical superior he had literally been looking up for many years. Conversation between the two prelates must certainly have been carried on under rather embarrassing conditions; for, according to Sydney Smith, " the Archbishop of York was forced to go down on his knees to converse with the Bishop of Bristol, just as an elephant kneels to receive its rider." [3]

The movement for Catholic emancipation made steady progress through the political storms which marked the opening year of the Duke of Wellington's tenure of p wer, and Brougham maintained in August that the question was as good as carried. " I never, however, think myself as good as carried," was Sydney's comment, " till my horse brings me to my stable-door."[4] The Mayor and Corporation of the city of Bristol, were accustomed to pay an annual state visit to the Cathedral on the anniversary of Gunpowder Plot, and the clergy were accustomed on the same occasion to dine with the civic authorities at the Mansion House. The 5th of November was accordingly a time when loyal sentiments concerning Church and State were publicly exchanged by the ecclesiastical and civic dignitaries, and the whole city was supposed to be ablaze with patriotic fervour.

The new canon was appointed to preach before the Mayor and Corporation on the first anniversary after his promotion, the 5th of November, 1828. Writing to inform one of his friends of this approaching duty, he states, " All sorts of bad theology are preached at the Cathedral on that day, and all sorts of bad toasts drunk at the Mansion House. I will do neither the one nor the other, nor bow the knee in the house of Rimmon." [5] He kept his word, and preached what he styled an " honest sermon " on those " Rules of Christian Charity, by which our opinions of other sects

---

[3] Published Correspondence, p. 466.   [4] Ibid. p. 468.
[5] Ibid. p. 468.

should be formed." He took for his text Colossians iii. 12, 13, and delivered a noble and closely-reasoned plea for toleration in reference to the religious scruples of others. The sermon, as might have been expected, gave great offence, for the Corporation of Bristol included at that time many rigid and uncompromising Tories, and though some of them must have realized that the cause of bigotry was already lost, that fact increased rather than lessened their animosity towards a preacher who had compelled them for once to listen to a clear and dispassionate statement of the facts of the case.

The mortification of the civic authorities was complete; and they expressed the irritation which they felt by discontinuing for many years the custom of a state visit to the Cathedral, and it was only about twenty years ago that they forgave their grudge and resumed attendance; their annual visit now, however, takes place at another time of the year. Bristol Cathedral was crowded during the delivery of Sydney Smith's sermon, and so great was the interest which it excited that he seldom stood in that pulpit again without looking down on a sea of upturned faces. The preacher became the talk of the town, and he was urged to print a discourse, which seemed for the moment to have divided the whole community into two hostile camps. It promptly appeared in print, with a brief preface in which the author claimed only to have given utterance to the plain rudiments of common charity and common sense. The newspapers took up the controversy, and in leading articles and letters the old warfare was waged. Sydney Smith was attacked at public dinners, and declaimed against from the pulpit, but when the storm was past it was apparent that the cause of justice had been strengthened.

The distance of Foston from Bristol, and the desire also for a warmer climate than that of Yorkshire, led to various proposals for migration to the south or west, and in October he even wrote to the Earl of Carlisle to inform him that he had resolved to take the living of Corse in Gloucestershire, which he describes as being in a very beautiful country, in exchange for that of Foston; eventually, however, this idea was abandoned, and fortunately, for—unknown to himself—other and more congenial prospects were in store for him.

The winter of 1828-9 was the last which Sydney Smith spent at Foston, and it glided tranquilly onwards amid a round of congenial duties, but as spring drew near the shadows of approaching loss fell over the household. Douglas had been for some time in a delicate state of health, and his condition now began to excite the gravest misgivings. He had never been robust, and his strength had been overtaxed in the strain of a gallant and successful struggle for the post of captain of Westminster School. From Westminster he had proceeded to Christ Church, Oxford, and his ambition was to equip himself for the profession of the law; but at the age of twenty-four, to the great sorrow of all who knew him, he died in London on the 15th of April, at the very moment when the kingdom was ringing with rejoicings over the final triumph, two days before, of the Catholic Emancipation Bill. Sydney Smith heard the tidings of the victory, which he had done so much to win, as he watched by the deathbed of his eldest son. Douglas Smith was buried in Kensal

Green Cemetery, and his grief-stricken father, who sleeps beside him now, placed the following tribute on his tomb : " His life was blameless. His death was the first sorrow he ever occasioned his parents, but it was deep and lasting."

In a letter to a friend, written soon after Catholic Emancipation had been won, he declares, " I rejoice in the temple which has been reared to toleration ; and I am proud that I worked as a bricklayer's labourer at it —without pay, and with the enmity and abuse of those who were unfavourable to its construction." [6]

With his stall at Bristol, the new canon had received the small living of Halberton, near Tiverton, and the death of Douglas seemed to supply an additional reason for removal to the south—for there was not a room in the rectory, or a tree in its grounds that did not suggest to his sorrow-stricken parents the lost presence of their son, and all the hopes that had vanished in his early grave.

Lord Lyndhurst again came to his assistance, and eventually it was arranged that he should exchange the living of Foston for that of Combe-Florey, in Somerset. Combe-Florey, the " sacred valley of flowers," as he was afterwards accustomed to call it to his friends, is a beautiful village some seven miles distant from the pleasant old county town of Taunton. It was hard work leaving Foston, the scene of so much quiet happiness, and a place where every field and building had grown familiar, and where friends old and young, rich and poor, wise and simple, had gladdened the rectory with their presence. But if

[6] Published Correspondence, p. 479.

it was difficult at last for the rector and his family to
tear themselves away from Foston, it was still more
painful to the villagers to watch the dismantling of the
house, and all the bustle of departure, and it was impossible to mistake the genuine distress with which old
people who had themselves never been given to change,
regarded the removal of their pastor, adviser, and
friend. The inhabitants of Foston and Thornton-le-
Clay had learnt to love as well as to respect Sydney
Smith, and there were not a few ready to declare when
the last farewells had been uttered, and midsummer
found the rectory silent and deserted, that "better
would never come into the place."

BRISTOL CATHEDRAL.

CHAPTER XI.

1829—1832.

First impressions of Combe-Florey—His manner of life there—
Appointed Canon Residentiary of St. Paul's by Earl Grey—
Takes part in the struggle for Reform—Dame Partington's
combat with the Atlantic.

THE country around Combe-Florey possesses that quiet
charm of wooded hills, and shady lanes, and rich and
cultivated fields, which belongs to the most characteristic
bits of English scenery, and to none more fully than to
the lovely vale of Taunton. The few cottages which
make up the little village fringe the short stretch of
road which winds between the rectory and the church,
and, except for the beauty of its situation and the
attraction with which Sydney Smith's presence has
invested the spot, there is nothing of special interest
about Combe-Florey itself. In July, 1829, the family,
accompanied by as many of their Yorkshire retainers as
they could persuade to leave Foston, arrived on the
scene, and Annie Kaye and David Leef were soon
installed in their new quarters, and proved invaluable
in helping to carry the old methods into the new home,
and in interpreting their master's odd ways and strange
commands to the more stolid and less quick-witted
servants of the west of England.

The rectory, a roomy house standing in the midst of a beautiful garden, was in a somewhat dilapidated condition, and as Sydney Smith was now tolerably well off, he determined to remodel and enlarge it. Some thirty masons and joiners were accordingly set to work, and under the rector's supervision such rapid progress was made, that ere long he was able to write to a friend, " My place is delightful ; never was there a more delightful parsonage ! Come and see it. Be ill, and require mild air and an affectionate friend, and set off for Combe-Florey."[1] It was a fortunate circumstance that the summer and autumn of 1829 were filled with new interests and spent amid fresh scenes, for the death of Douglas had cast a deep shadow over the entire household, and the thought that he would never behold Combe-Florey, not unfrequently occasioned a thrill of pain. Adjoining the parsonage garden is a little wood, and in its secluded nooks the rector was accustomed to ramble. Most people who have visited the spot will not feel inclined to quarrel with the truth of Sydney Smith's statement concerning it : " The country is perfectly beautiful, and my parsonage the prettiest place in it."[2] Combe-Florey was in nearly every respect a great contrast to Foston, and the climate proved so relaxing that, accustomed to the bracing winds of Yorkshire, he used to say that the air of Somerset felt as if it had been boiled. The following note was written to a friend in the East Riding soon after his removal to the west of England :—

[XXXII.]   Combe-Florey, 13th August, 1829.

MY DEAR SIR,—I am very sorry to lose so many

---

[1] Published Correspondence, p. 478.   [2] Ibid. p. 476.

good friends in Yorkshire. The only acquaintance I have made here is the clerk of the parish, a very sensible man, with great *amen-ity* of disposition.

SYDNEY SMITH.

Philip Howard, Esq.

Two or three weeks later, in reply to a request from Lord Lansdowne that he would spend a few days at Bowood, he gave the following account of his plans for the summer :—

[XXXIII.]   Combe-Florey, August 22nd, 1829

DEAR LORD LANSDOWNE,—About the 25th of this month I am expecting Jeffrey and his family. Lady Lyndhurst and the Chancellor, as I learn from her ladyship, intend calling here on their way to Lord Morley's. I have told her that she will be covered with bricks and mortar, but that, if she will come after such warning, we shall be most happy to see them. Till she says she will or will not come, I am in duty and gratitude bound to attend to that engagement. Lastly I am bound by oath to go down to Lady Morley to meet the Chancellor and Lady L., the end of this or beginning of next month. It would have given us all very sincere pleasure to have come to Bowood but for the reasons I have stated, and we feel very much obliged by your good nature and kindness in inviting us.

I am delighted with this parsonage and this country. It is, by common consent, the prettiest place (I am speaking of the residences of holy men) in one of the finest counties of England. To leave old friends and acquaintances is always an evil, but in all other respects I have materially improved my residence, and shall make a very good, comfortable house, better, I think,

T

than that of Foston. It would give us great pleasure to receive in it Lady Lansdowne and yourself. That you are fond of excursions I know from the testimony of the most fashionable baronet in England, who met you the other day in Lancashire.

I take up my residence in Bristol on the first day of

A GLIMPSE OF THE RECTORY, COMBE-FLOREY.

the new year. I shall be very pleased to be considered as your neighbour; seven or eight hours brings me to your door, and I would with pleasure employ double the time for such an object. We get from here to Bath in five or six hours.

Sir Thomas L—— cannot keep the friendship of

the Pope and that of the county of Somerset at the same time; he is almost certain, I think, of being ejected at the next election. He is as absurd in his political capacity as he is amiable and obliging in all the relations of private life in which he shines.

I have very few years to live, and therefore I cannot afford to waste time in building. I have ten carpenters and ten bricklayers at work. Part of my house has tumbled down, the rest is inclined to follow. We sleep upon props; an enemy or a dissenter might saw me down in the night-time. Pray tell Moore when my house is finished he must come and see me—it is really a place for a poet.

I remain, dear Lord Lansdowne,
Very sincerely yours,
SYDNEY SMITH.

The visit of Jeffrey alluded to in this letter duly took place in the closing days of August, and Lady Holland has given us a glimpse of her father and his old Edinburgh comrade, sitting on the lawn at Combe-Florey amidst the rafters and timbers of the broken house, enjoying the pleasant weather and the lovely scenery. The summer of 1829 was a memorable period to Jeffrey as well as to Sydney Smith, and a new phase of life was opening to both men. Long delayed professional honours were at last beginning to fall, and the Rector of Foston's preferment to a prebendal stall was soon followed by the announcement of his friend's appointment as Dean of the Faculty of Advocates.[3]

[3] It was in reference to this peculiarly Scottish title that Sydney Smith once startled a lady from beyond the Tweed with the alarming announcement, "In England, our Deans have no faculties."

Jeffrey received this appointment (which Lord Cockburn declared was the highest honour of the kind that can be conferred in Scotland) at the beginning of July, and he immediately resigned the editorial chair of the *Edinburgh Review;* the ninety-eighth number, which appeared in June, 1829, was the last for which he was responsible, so that his control of the great Whig organ of public opinion was not continued more than two years after the retirement of his brilliant clerical colleague. Having thus in the most honourable manner slipped the collar of responsibility, almost the first use to which Jeffrey turned his recovered leisure was to visit Sydney Smith in his new home at Combe-Florey. He was delighted with the place, and being out of harness, was exactly in the spirit to enjoy it; in the following year he entered Parliament, and, in recognition of his services to the Liberal Party, was made Lord Advocate of Scotland in the Grey Administration. In 1834 he was raised to the Scottish Bench, and from that period to the close of his life in 1850, he was known by the courtesy title of Lord Jeffrey. It was in prospect of his friend's elevation to the Bench, and in allusion to his diminutive stature, that Sydney Smith observed, " His robes will cost him little ; one buck-rabbit will clothe him to the heels."[4] As a judge, Jeffrey was distinguished by his capacity to take pains and to follow with close attention the details of each case brought before him, and the rapidity with which having done so, he arrived at a final decision. His unfailing courtesy and inflexible integrity increased the respect with which his judgments were from first to last received. The exigencies of public life, added

[4] Publ'shed Correspondence, p. 477.

to the distance between their homes, prevented Lord Jeffrey from ever renewing his acquaintance with Combe-Florey, though he appears to have met from time to time, in London and elsewhere, his old literary associate, its genial rector. It is pleasant to know that almost the last letter he wrote—three days before his fatal illness—was addressed to the widow of his life-long friend, and expressed even heightened admiration for his wisdom and his worth.

Jeffrey's sojourn at Combe-Florey was a gratification to the whole household, and his intimate acquaintance with the missing member of it enabled him fully to sympathize with the feelings of the bereaved parents. The spirit of fun was not, however, exorcised either then, or at any subsequent period of Sydney Smith's career, and the old banter was wont to creep slily into the midst of the most earnest discussion; and it is not even difficult to imagine him repeating one of his mischievous Scotch jokes for the benefit of his friend. "Mr. Jeffrey," he writes to Lady Grey, "wanted to persuade me that myrtles grew out of doors in Scotland, as here. Upon cross-examination, it turned out they were prickly, and that many had been destroyed by the family donkey."[5] In an unpublished note to Lady Holland, he writes: "I sit in my beautiful study, looking out upon a thousand flowers, and reading agreeable books, in order to keep up my arguments with Lord Holland and Allen." His books were an unfailing resource, and he held that the only way to read to advantage was to read so heartily, "that dinner-time comes two hours before you expected it."

---

[5] Published Correspondence, p. 474.

The kindliness which had marked Sydney Smith's intercourse with the people of Foston was equally conspicuous at Combe-Florey, and the same active and practical benevolence marked all his dealings with the suffering and the poor. He was most regular and attentive in visiting the aged and the sick, and seldom came empty-handed to the bedsides of the poor. His improved position at Combe-Florey enabled him to do more for those who were in want than had ever been in his power whilst at Foston, and he was accustomed to assist the poor around him in delicate and generous ways. In cases where nourishing and tempting viands were required, the parsonage kitchen was called into requisition, and the listless hours of recovery were brightened in many a poor man's cottage by the pleasant books the rector laid upon the table when he went away. A room in the rectory was fitted up as a dispensary, and simple remedies for common ailments were there prescribed and distributed. He was doctor to all the village, and at the call of every one whom he had power to help. In cases of serious illness, he would order out his carriage and drive to Taunton and back, a distance of more than a dozen miles, to bring his own medical man, Dr. Liddon,[6] to the relief of some poor labourer. There are only two or three persons now living in Combe-Florey who were intimately acquainted with Sydney Smith, but they confirm all that has ever been said or written concerning the goodness of his heart, and his practical interest in the welfare of his parishioners. One man recalls the rector's attention to his father during a long and

---

[6] Dr. Liddon, a well-known practitioner in Taunton, was uncle to the Rev. Canon Liddon of St. Paul's.

dangerous illness, and states that he was accustomed
to see him almost every day, when he would pray with
him, and read to him, and by gay and cheery conversation divert his thoughts.

During the earlier years of his residence at Combe-
Florey, Sydney Smith was continually walking about
the parish, and it was remarked that he seemed fond of
wet weather, for whenever it rained he was sure to be
seen trudging manfully along the muddy lanes beneath
the shelter of a huge umbrella. He was a general
favourite both with old and young, and he never passed
any one on the road whom he knew without a good-
natured joke, a kind word, or a pleasant smile. Towards the close of his life he was accustomed to drive
about the village in a low chaise drawn by two donkeys
named " Jack and Jill," whilst " Monk," his black
Newfoundland dog, trotted lazily in the rear. " Jack
and Jill," by the addition of branching antlers of
formidable aspect and imposing magnitude, were on
state occasions transformed into " foreign deer," and
sent to scamper on the lawn, to the mingled amazement
and admiration of the guests assembled at the drawing-
room window! Sometimes it happened that the
" foreign deer " called attention to their own charms
in unmistakable tones, and then the master of the house
would gravely say—" Perhaps, ladies and gentlemen,
you recognize their voice." There still survives at
Combe-Florey a worthy old man, who recounts with a
smile the glee with which he was accustomed in the
days of his youth to obey his master's orders to
decorate the donkeys.

He was particularly anxious to encourage habits of
thrift amongst the farm labourers of the village, and

frequently, when setting out for Taunton, his carriage would stop at the cottage doors of the more frugal, in order that he might volunteer to take their savings'-bank books into the town that they might be posted up and brought back. He had personally a great horror of outstanding debts, and was always glad to pay at once the accounts of tradespeople.   He kept at Combe-Florey all paid bills in pigeon-holes in one of his rooms, and seemed to derive a measure of satisfaction whenever he glanced round on these discharged liabilities. When at home, he never paid any bill, except by cheque, and even accounts of a few shillings were settled in this way, so that he avoided the risk of paying twice over.   "A balance at your banker's," he was accustomed to say, " is a source of happiness ; you may have sickness, family trials, and a thousand aches and pains, but a balance at your bankers, taking care that the balance is your *own*, is a great relief." His own experience during the first five or six years at Foston had taught him the misery of a struggle with debt, and though he was now in a very different position, and had little reason to fear for himself, his visits to the cottages of the labouring men for their savings'-bank books were prompted by the desire that they too might share, to some extent at least, the " great relief " which springs out of money in hand.

Sydney Smith's connection with Halberton—the living which was attached to his Bristol stall—was little more than nominal, and he appears to have contented himself with an annual visit, and to have left the work of the parish to the curate in charge.   At the first vestry meeting after his appointment, he proposed to exercise the customary right of nominating a vicar's churchwarden. His authority, however, was challenged by the parishioners, who evidently regarded the proposal as an invasion of what they had come to regard as their rights. After inquiry, the matter was left by the new vicar in abeyance, and the parishioners for a term of years duly elected all the churchwardens. The controversy was, however, renewed when the Rev. Edward Girdlestone, M.A. (now Vicar of Olverston, and Canon of Bristol), succeeded to the living. Canon Girdlestone carried the question to the Court of Queen's Bench, and established, at a cost of 1750*l.* to his opponents, the vicar's right in perpetuity to nominate a churchwarden. The following letter was written to the vestry by Sydney Smith, when he felt powerless in the matter, and unable to establish his case :—

[XXXIV.]   Combe-Florey Rectory, Taunton,
                                 March 3rd, 1830.

GENTLEMEN,—It has always been a rule with me through life to be as firm and tenacious in the maintenance of my just rights, as I am willing to sacrifice those to which I am not entitled. I must in candour confess that from all the evidence I can collect—and I have employed two active solicitors in the search—I cannot find that the clergyman of Halberton has been in the habit of nominating a churchwarden. I shall therefore not attempt to exercise that power this year at the ensuing Easter. If, from any fresh evidence I can collect, I should see reason to alter my opinion another year, I reserve to myself the full right of doing so; but, that I may not take the parish by surprise, I engage to give two months' notice of such an intention. In the selection of churchwardens, I submit to you

whether it is not right that they should be members
of the Church of England, and if my wishes were consulted, I should desire Mr. Manley to be one of them.
I have nothing to do, nor will I ever have anything to
do with any dissensions which may take place in the
parish, but Mr. Manley appears to me to be a gentleman of sense and respectability, and a good Churchman. However, as I have said before, the choice is
with you and not with me. If I could have satisfied
myself that I possessed the right, I would have contested it at any expense, but I am not so satisfied, and
I give it up as I said I would.

   I am, gentlemen, your obedient servant,
         SYDNEY SMITH.

The Rev. Canon Tinling, of Gloucester, was for
several years curate to Sydney Smith at Halberton,
and through his exertions national schools for the boys
and girls of the parish were erected. Mr. Tinling
states that when he wrote to ask the non-resident
vicar's assistance in this effort, he received a donation
and with it the characteristic reply : " Four walls and
a thatch roof are sufficient ; but I cannot refuse, as I
never oppose a proposition unless I am prepared to
move an amendment." There is a tradition current
in Halberton to this day to the effect that when Mr.
Smith paid his annual visit to the church, he always
preached from the same text—" I die daily."

Parliamentary reform was a question in which
Sydney Smith took a keen interest, and in the struggle
which was now impending he played a manly and
gallant part.

The death of George IV., in June, 1830, was re-

garded as a positive relief by the great majority of
his subjects, and as soon as his oppressive influence
was withdrawn, the popular cause came rapidly to the
surface of the national life. The sympathies of the
Duke of Clarence, who, as William IV., succeeded his
unhappy brother on the throne, were known to be
towards the Whigs, and that fact strengthened the
new king's popularity in the country, and increased
the demand for immediate reform. The accession of
William IV. was quickly followed by the downfall of
Charles X., and this second revolution in France
excited the masses still further, and threw the nation
itself into a condition of turbulent agitation. Fifteen
years had rolled away since Waterloo, and during
that interval thousands of intelligent men in every
part of the kingdom, had become convinced that
good government could only be secured by a change,
which amounted to a revolution in the system of
Parliamentary representation. The Duke of Wellington was, however, blind to the signs of the times,
and when Lord Grey expressed the hope in the new
Parliament, which met in the autumn, that the Cabinet
would prepare " to redress the grievances of the people
by a reform of the Parliament," he went so far—in
spite of the unenfranchised thousands of Birmingham,
Manchester, and Leeds—as to declare that the representation could not be improved. From that moment,
the Wellington Administration was doomed, and on the
16th of November it ignominiously collapsed before a
rising storm of public indignation, and within a week,
Lord Grey, having expressly stipulated that reform
should be a Cabinet measure, was at the head of affairs,
with the nation at his back. " It will seem very odd

to me," was Sydney Smith's reflection soon after
the news of the popular triumph arrived, "to pass
through Downing Street, and to see all my old friends
turned into official dignitaries."' The new Premier
announced that "Peace, Retrenchment, and Reform "
would be the objects of his policy, and the presence in
his administration of a Radical of the earnest and uncompromising type of Lord Durham, was everywhere
accepted by the populace as a hopeful omen. The
tendency to outbreak was checked by the confidence
which the people reposed in the Grey Administration,
and the wanton destruction by night of corn-ricks,
which had disgraced the months of September and
October, ceased with their accession to power. The
hopes of the nation were centred in Lord Grey and his
colleagues, and the popular enthusiasm ran so high,
that, even ere it closed, 1830 was declared to be the
year one of the people's cause.

The Government promptly redeemed its pledges,
and Lord John Russell introduced the Reform Bill on
the 1st of March, 1831. The Bill was more comprehensive than either the friends or the foes of Reform
had been led to expect, and proposed "a measure
which could never be withdrawn without a deadly
struggle, nor stand without becoming a dividing line
between the old history of England and the new." [8]
Representation, and not nomination, was the principle
of the Reform Bill, and even a partial application of
this principle excluded fifty-four rotten boroughs at
a sweep, and deprived thirty obscure towns of one
of their representatives. The Government proposals

[7] Published Correspondence, p. 487.
[8] Martineau's History of the Peace, book iv. chap. iii. p. 418.

had been awaited with great anxiety by the people, and though the more advanced Radicals were disappointed that the ballot had not been included in the ministerial programme, they, in common with the distressed and unrepresented classes, did all in their power through the press, the platform, and petitions, to strengthen the hands of the great Liberal Premier. Whilst the first memorable debate on the Bill was in progress in Parliament, meetings were held all over the country in support of the demand for reform, and at a political gathering at Taunton on March 9th, "to address the King and both Houses of Parliament in approval of the measures proposed by ministers for Parliamentary reform," Sydney Smith attended and delivered a vigorous and eloquent speech, in the course of which he denounced as monstrous the fact that a retired merchant should be able to go into the market and buy ten shares in the government of twenty millions of his fellow-subjects !

His attitude on this occasion was in strict consistency with the liberal convictions which he had held for nearly half a century, and which he had never scrupled to avow, even when to do so meant the sacrifice of his prospects in life. The clergy, with a few honourable exceptions, were as hostile to the reform movement in the spring of 1831 as they had been to Catholic emancipation in the summer of 1825, and therefore general surprise was excited in the minds of all who had not closely watched the bold and independent career of the Rev. Sydney Smith, when he, a dignitary of the Church, was one of the foremost to rush into the fray. But in so acting he was loyal to the one principle of public conduct, which he was never tired of urging on

others, and which marked his own career from first
to last, "Do what you think right, and take place and
power as an accident."

On the 22nd of March the Reform Bill passed
the second reading by a majority of one; but
exactly a month later, after a Government defeat on
General Gascoigne's amendment that the number of
members for England and Wales ought not to be
diminished, and an extraordinary scene in the Lords,
the King was persuaded suddenly to dissolve Parliament, and an appeal to the country was immediately
made by the Grey Administration. Sydney Smith was
accustomed occasionally to write to the local papers on
the questions of the hour, and no sooner had General
Gascoigne's amendment in the Commons, and Lord
Wharncliffe's proposition in the Lords brought about a
crisis which was favourable in the highest degree to
the party of progress, than the following political squib
appeared in prominent type in the columns of tho
Taunton Courier of May 4th, 1831 :—

GAZETTE EXTRAORDINARY. GLORIOUS VICTORY !

[xxxv.]   Admiralty, Friday, April 22nd.

A despatch has been this day received announcing
a glorious victory gained by Admirals Grey and Al-
thorp, commanding the Constitutional squadron, over
the combined flotilla of the Anti-Reformers and
Boroughmongers in St. Stephen's Bay.

On board His Majesty's ship *Reform*.
Anchored off Thorney Island, April 22nd.

I have the honour to communicate (for the information of the friends and supporters of the British

Constitution) the details of a splendid victory gained over the combined flotilla of the Boroughmongers, under the command of Admirals Peel and Wharncliffe, in St. Stephen's Bay.

At 6 p.m., on the 21st of April, Admiral Wharncliffe, having formed the *Mansfield* advice-boat, the *Carnarvon* steamer, the *Newcastle* trader, and the *Londonderry* fire-ship, in order of battle, with a flotilla of small craft in the rear, I directed the *Richmond* and *Burdett* to watch the enemy's movements. At half-past six Admiral Wharncliffe hoisted signals for a general attack on the vessels under my command, and endeavoured to annoy the *Royal William*, the leading ship of our squadron.

Seeing the intended manœuvre could not succeed during the night, I worked up to windward, and in the morning I had the weather-gauge of the enemy. The *Royal William* having taken a fine position for the purpose of bearing down and breaking the enemy's lines, I despatched the *Lord Vaux*, the *Lansdowne*, and *Melbourne* to act as tenders, and support the Royal standard.

Admiral Wharncliffe, finding himself to leeward, and in a desperate position, commenced a running fire. The *Londonderry* made sail at the same time to get alongside the *Richmond*, but in the attempt was nearly blown out of the water by the skilful pointing of the *Richmond's* guns. The *Londonderry*, endeavouring to exhibit a *coup d'état*, found she was only making a *coup d'éspoir*, and finally received a *coup de jarnac*. The *Richmond* and *Clanricarde* were engaged yard-arm and yard-arm with the Boroughmongering flotilla, when the *Lord Vaux* ran in and fired a dreadful broadside upon the enemy. She then tacked and stood off again for a more combined movement.

The *Londonderry* (rushing with too much precipitancy into the heat of action) blew up, and her guns going off at the same time, the explosion, which was heard far from the scene of action, struck terror into the enemy.

The *Mansfield* opened a cross-fire, and endeavoured to parley, but was silenced by the *Royal William*, which came up in gallant style to put an end to the engagement. The thunder of her guns soon made the Boroughmongers run from their quarters, and hide in holes and corners. Victory finally crowned the brave Reformers, and the enemies of the Constitution were crushed to rise no more.

Another party of the Rotten Borough craft, having commenced hostilities in the lower creek of St. Stephen's Bay, the commander, Admiral Peel, was defeated, and one of the bombs, the *Vyvyan*, sunk.

The coast of Westminster is now cleared of the marauding cruisers, so long employed by their corrupt owners, and whilst the *Royal William* remains on the station a stopper will be put upon their unconstitutional practices.

All the Reformers under my command have done their duty.

I have the honour to be, &c.

GREY.

(Further particulars.)

The following is a return of the flotilla defeated and destroyed in the above memorable engagement :—

The *Hero of Waterloo*.[9]—An excellent troopship;

---

[9] The Duke of Wellington.

was formerly employed in the war against Buonaparte. Just before the action she sustained great injury by running her head against the rock of Reform, and remaining immovable.[1]

The *Cotton Spinner*.[1]—Launched from the University Dock, and towed into Tamworth. Veers about like a dog-vane in a shift of wind, and cannot keep a straight course. Timbers rotten. It is expected the *rats* will leave her, as these vermin know by instinct when a ship is not trustworthy.

The *Gascoigne*.[2] —An old Liverpool trader, only fit to form a masked battery against the Constitution; has been many years employed to transport money out of the pockets of the people, and carry on the slave-trade.

The *Honest Charlie*.[3]—Almost a total wreck. In her attempt to escape from Reform Roads she fired many random shots, but was left a log upon the water.

The *Southwark Fly Boat*.[4]—This vessel has seen much service, and was famous for hoisting signals to deceive the friends of Buonaparte. She carried off Lavalette; annoyed the Government during the funeral of Queen Caroline; carried off the people's subscription-money; and finally carried herself off with a flowing sheet from St. Stephen's Bay at the moment when the Reformers required her assistance.

The *Preston Wheeling Cock*.[5]—It is difficult to describe the mould and trim of this craft. She is painted

---

[1] Sir Robert Peel, M.P. (Tamworth.)
[2] General Gascoigne, M.P. (Liverpool.)
[3] Mr. C. W. Wynn, M.P. (Montgomeryshire.)
[4] Sir Robert Wilson, M.P. (Southwark.)
[5] Mr. Henry Hunt, M.P. (Preston.)

U

with false ports to deceive both friends and enemies. She has not been closely examined, and it is uncertain at present whether she belongs to the Boroughmongers or the Reformers. She steers without compass, and has no ballast to keep her steady.

The *Banks of Dorset.*[6]—This is a heavy-sailing lug boat. Its owners belong to Corfe Castle. During many years she has made part of the Rotten Borough flotilla. In the late action she succeeded in cutting off the supplies required by the *Royal William.*

The *Wharncliffe.*[7]—A vessel of the first class, built in the reign of George IV. She is only remarkable for her late attack on the friends and supporters of the Constitution.

The *Derry-Down.*[8]—This fire-ship appeared in the fight of the 22nd, like a volcano, vomiting terrible combustibles. Even the vessels of the Boroughmongers were compelled to sheer off from the flames. She would have grappled the *Richmond*, had not the *Tabella Rock* (which rises in the middle of St. Stephen's Bay) separated them. The *Derry-Down* is a crazy, ungovernable vessel, and it will be long before she is in a condition to resume offensive operations. She is in the Newcastle trade, and brings coals to London. She may meet a *Tempest* in the north, but must avoid battles with Reformers on the banks of the Thames.

The *Mansfield.*[9]—This packet carried advice to the *Royal William*, and struck upon the shoal of Presumption. She tried to back off with a revolutionary wind, but could not stir; she sank in the mud, and there she must remain. * * *

---

[6] Mr. W. Bankes, M.P. (Dorset.) [7] Lord Wharncliffe.
[8] The Marquis of Londonderry. [9] The Earl of Mansfield.

This brilliant victory over the Boroughmongers is of the highest advantage to old England. Like the piratical corsairs of Algiers, they not only robbed the people of their property, but of their liberty and constitutional rights. The good ship *Britannia* has long been kept on the wrong tack, but, with Reform for a pilot, she will put about, steer for free and fair Representation, and sail with a fair breeze into the harbour of Public Prosperity. Our present helmsman knows how to keep her steady by avoiding the rocks and quicksands of Corruption, which obstruct the channel through which the Reformers must navigate. Riding at last in smooth water, and clear of the dangers spread by her enemies, she may again protect commerce, and excite the admiration of the world.

Popular indignation was everywhere aroused by the treatment which the measure had received, and "the Bill, the whole Bill, and nothing but the Bill," became the election cry. Not only in the great towns, but in rural districts as yet untraversed by the iron horse, the daily newspapers, or the electric telegraph, the keenest political interest was excited, and the possessor of the week's sevenpenny newspaper found himself beset whenever he stirred abroad by anxious-looking men who implored him to tell them the probable fate of the Bill.

The new Parliament met in June, and the glad tidings ran quickly through the land that the Reformers were in a great majority—out of eighty-two county members returned, only six were hostile to the Bill; and all but the most short-sighted of men began to realize that, for good or for evil, the political life of England was on

the verge of a revolution which it was no longer possible to arrest. The speech from the Throne advised
the Commons to set their house in order, and three
days later Lord John Russell (now justly rewarded
by Cabinet rank) introduced the second Reform Bill
—which was substantially the same as the first—
and the measure was carried rapidly through its preli-
minary stages, and passed the second reading on the
8th of July by a majority of 136.

In Committee, however, the Government was met
night after night by a succession of irritating and
trivial objections, and whilst Parliament wrangled over
clause after clause of the Bill, the people, afraid that the
Scotch moors would prove irresistible to jaded legislators in the sultry days of August, became alarmed
and indignant, and from various parts of the kingdom
came ominous testimony to the growing impatience
of the masses. At length the tactics of the Opposition
were exhausted, and the Reform Bill passed the House
of Commons, and was sent up to the Peers. The
"lords spiritual and temporal" made short work of
the measure, for on the 7th of October, by a majority
of forty-one, the Bill was contemptuously thrown
out.

The people, now thoroughly exasperated, gave
utterance to their wrath by alarming threats and
stormy meetings in every part of the kingdom,
and it was only the confidence they reposed in
their leaders, and the certainty they felt in the
speedy and complete triumph of their cause, which
restrained a general outbreak of violence. Even as
it was, riots of the most disquieting and turbulent
kind took place at Bristol, Derby, and elsewhere,

and Nottingham Castle was set on fire by an infuriated mob, as if to convince the Duke of Newcastle that it was not always advisable for a man to " do what he liked with his own."

In the midst of all this political turmoil and excitement, Lord Grey, who had long been anxious to acknowledge the obligations which the Whig Party were under to his friend, the Rector of Combe-Florey, gladly availed himself of a moment's lull in the fray, and an unexpected vacancy in the Church, to appoint Sydney Smith a Canon Residentiary of St. Paul's. A few weeks previously it seemed probable that a stall at Westminster, and not one at St. Paul's, would have fallen to his lot, for Dr. Bell, one of the chapter at the Abbey, was then thought to be dying, and Earl Grey wrote to Sydney Smith to say that, if a vacancy occurred, he should receive the appointment. It was St. Paul's, however, and not Westminster, which was henceforward to be associated in men's minds with the name of Sydney Smith, as the accompanying letter will show :—

[XXXVI.]   Downing Street, Sept. 10th, 1831.

MY DEAR SYDNEY,—You are much obliged to Dr. Bell for not dying, as he had promised. By the promotion of the Bishop of Chichester to the See of Worcester, a Canon Residentiary of St. Paul's becomes vacant. A snug thing, let me tell you, being worth full 200*l.* a year. To this the King, upon my recommendation, has signified his pleasure that you should be appointed, and I do not think it likely that you can be *dis*-appointed a second time by the old bishop coming to life again, like Dr. Bell. Mr. Harvey, tutor to Prince George of Cambridge, will have your stall at Bristol.

> I am, my dear Sydney,
>> Yours very sincerely,
>>> GREY.

P.S.—I must take care that your appointment is placed out of the possibility of being recalled—before we are turned out!

The appointment was gratefully accepted, and the Rev. Sydney Smith read himself in at St. Paul's on the 2nd of October, and his visit to London for that purpose enabled him to watch the reception of the Reform Bill by the House of Lords. He had reached the age of threescore before he received this recognition of his services, and, although his career extended until 1845, no higher preferment was bestowed upon him; and this neglect was the more remarkable, as men who were both his political and personal friends held office during most of those years.

The Whigs have been blamed not a little for the languid appreciation which they showed towards their ablest clerical supporter, and they have been somewhat thoughtlessly charged with ingratitude in not rewarding so bold and consistent a champion of justice and liberty with episcopal rank. Some of Sydney Smith's admirers resented this supposed slight rather warmly, and when it was observed to one of them, on the occasion of an offer of a place in the ministry to O'Connell, that the Whigs, after all, could forgive and forget, the retort was immediate,—"Yes; they forgive O'Connell and forget Sydney Smith!"

There is evidence enough to prove that the new

Canon of St. Paul's was at one time ambitious of higher ecclesiastical position than that to which he attained; but "whether I get preferment or not," was his quiet remark to a friend, "I shall always be the same, and, like the patent flannel at seven shillings a yard, will never shrink in heat or cold!" In the ranks of his profession he had fought almost single-handed on behalf of the rights of the people, and had endured no small share of obloquy and reproach—during a struggle which extended over the best years of his life—for his resolute adherence to what was then the despised cause of civil and religious liberty. It is easy, therefore, to understand why a man who had borne the burden and heat of the day should feel annoyed when Liberals of the eleventh hour were awarded positions which were altogether out of proportion to their deserts. "It is perhaps of little consequence to any party, whether I adhere to it or not," was his statement in an unpublished letter to Lord Holland, "but I always shall adhere to the Whig party, whoever may be put over my head, because I have an ardent love of truth and justice, and they are their best defenders." It is no use, however, attempting to disguise the fact that Sydney Smith, notwithstanding his ability and goodness, lacked some of the essential qualifications for a bishopric, and the best friends, both of the witty Canon and the Church of England, can scarcely have desired to see the author of Peter Plymley and Dame Partington in lawn sleeves.

If, instead of being appointed Canon of St. Paul's, he could have been appointed Dean of Westminster, he would have received the most appropriate, and probably the most acceptable, recognition of his splendid services to the nation. People who urge his claims to a bishopric appear to be oblivious of the fact that before it was in the power of his political allies to offer him such preferment, he was already an old man, with growing physical infirmities, and was scarcely in a condition to cope with the inevitable anxieties and increased responsibilities which must in the very nature of things always accompany the control of a diocese. There is, moreover, conclusive proof that he himself lost all desire for exalted office in the Church soon after the Whigs returned to power, and, influential and happy in his work at St. Paul's, and in his relationship with his humble parishioners at Combe-Florey, it is certain that nothing would have induced him to sever ties which grew closer and more alluring with the lapse of years.

After reading himself in at St. Paul's, the new Canon returned at once to Somerset, and writing from Combe-Florey on the 6th of October, he stated that as the coach rolled westwards he found " public meetings everywhere, and the utmost alarm at the idea of the Bill being thrown out ; coachmen, ostlers, inside and outside passengers, barmaids and waiters, all eager for news." [1] Two days later the worst fears of the people were verified, for on the 8th the Lords rejected the measure. Sydney Smith had predicted that any attempt of the Lords to throw out the Bill would be the signal for the most energetic resistance from one end of the kingdom to the other, and as soon as the news spread through the country on that memorable Saturday immediate steps were taken by the people

[1] Published Correspondence, p. 491.

to reassert their claims in bolder terms than ever. Several of the leading Liberal newspapers appeared in mourning, and all of them hotly resented the action of the Peers. Muffled peals were rung in some instances on the bells of the churches. Riots and disturbances began again, and in almost every town crowded and enthusiastic meetings were held to support the Government.

On the following Tuesday, the 11th of October, a meeting was held at Taunton to petition the king to retain the ministry, and to express unabated confidence in Lord Grey and his colleagues; and it was on that occasion that Sydney Smith delivered the famous speech in which he compared the efforts of the House of Lords to restrain the rising tide of Democracy to the ludicrous endeavour of Mrs. Partington to sweep back the waves of the Atlantic from her door.

The meeting was summoned for the hour of noon, and it was announced that it would be held in the usual place of assembly, the Guildhall. When the time arrived, however, the people had gathered in such numbers from far and wide that the idea of the Guildhall had to be abandoned, and it was determined that the meeting should be held in the Assize Hall, which was capable of holding ten times the number, and which was immediately filled to overflowing. Sydney Smith's speech was short, but telling. He began by deploring the collision which had arisen between the two Houses of Parliament, and hid so on the ground that it impeded the public business, and diminished the public prosperity. He declared that, as a Churchman, he blushed to see so many dignitaries of the Church arrayed against the

wishes and happiness of the people. As for the loss
of the Bill he cared little, and that for the best of all
possible reasons, because he had not the slightest idea
that it was lost. He felt as certain that the Bill would
pass in the course of a few months as that the annual
taxes would be gathered.

Then followed, in two or three words, the inimitable sketch of Mrs. Partington's unequal combat with
the ocean: "As for the possibility of the House of
Lords preventing ere long a reform of Parliament, I
hold it to be the most absurd notion that ever entered
into human imagination. I do not mean to be dis-
respectful, but the attempt of the Lords to stop the
progress of Reform reminds me very forcibly of the
great storm of Sidmouth, and of the conduct of
the excellent Mrs. Partington on that occasion. In
the winter of 1824 there set in a great flood upon that
town—the tide rose to an incredible height—the waves
rushed in upon the houses, and everything was
threatened with destruction. In the midst of this
sublime and terrible storm, Dame Partington, who
lived upon the beach, was seen at the door of her house
with mop and pattens, trundling her mop, squeezing
out the sea-water, and vigorously pushing away the
Atlantic Ocean. The Atlantic was roused. Mrs.
Partington's spirit was up; but I need not tell you
that the contest was unequal. The Atlantic Ocean
beat Mrs. Partington. She was excellent at a slop or
a puddle, but she should not have meddled with a
tempest. Gentlemen, be at your ease—be quiet and
steady—you will beat—Mrs. Partington." The description of Mrs. Partington's adventure was received
with peals of laughter; and when the closing sentence

brought the application, the enthusiasm of the great assembly knew no bounds.

The wit of Sydney Smith was never put to a better purpose than on that occasion; for the story of Dame Partington's unequal battle with the Atlantic immediately caught the public fancy, and, as the press carried it everywhere, did more than argument or entreaty to relax the savage temper of the nation, and to turn defiant hostility, which threatened a breach of the peace, into good-natured contempt, which made patience possible. There are now very few persons living who were present when the Rector of Combe-Florey told this story; but Mr. R. A. Kinglake, J.P., of Taunton, who has enriched the closing chapters of this book in many ways, has kindly furnished some

PERSONAL RECOLLECTIONS OF SYDNEY SMITH'S REFORM SPEECH.

[XXXVII.]   (Taunton, Oct. 11th, 1831.)

Sydney Smith was no unfrequent guest at the house of my uncle, Dr. Kinglake, who was among the first to congratulate him on his taking possession of his new preferment, Combe-Florey, that paragon of parsonages, abounding in sunshine and roses, and free from the blasts of the unkind east wind. I remember as if it was but yesterday the excitement that prevailed in the town and neighbourhood on the occasion of the great Reform Meeting, at which he described, as no other man could have done, the immortal duel between Dame Partington and the Atlantic Ocean. On that exciting day carriages of every shape and size, and horses of every breed were urgently requisitioned. The county squires, the farmers, the clergy, county

voters, and a sturdy band of Nonconformists and
Church-rate Abolitionists, mingled indiscriminately
with the 'buffs and blues' of the ancient borough of
Taunton, as they rushed on to the old Castle Hall.

It was no obscure structure in which the unrivalled
wit was to address the assembled multitude, but a
grand building, built by a Saxon king, and rich in
historic interest. Within its walls the illustrious
Robert Blake must have often taken counsel with his
faithful followers, whilst defending with the genius of
a strategist the unfortified town against a powerful
Royalist army. Here, too, the ferocious Judge Jeffreys,
the murderer of the gentle Alice Lisle, held his Bloody
Assize; and in calmer days Henry Fielding, the father
of the English novel, might have been heard addressing a West-country jury of more than ordinary stu-
pidity; and the great William Pitt, moreover, first displayed his powers of oratory within these ancient walls.

On that October morning, long before Sydney
Smith had entered the town, every seat was taken in
the hall. The Bailiffs of the Borough, and other prominent inhabitants, occupied the platform, where also
seats were reserved for a few ladies of position in
the county and town, including the beauteous Lethbridges of Sandhill Park, kind neighbours and faithful
friends of Sydney Smith. In those days the Iron
King was not visible in the West of England, and I
well remember hearing that extraordinary pressure
was put on the postal authorities with a view of getting the speech despatched with all possible celerity to
Printing-House Square, soon to be read with eager
eyes by his friend, Earl Grey, and other members of
the Whig Cabinet.

More than half a century has passed away, yet
I see before me now the familiar figure of one whom
"wise men loved, and even wits admired;" as I
beheld him entering the hall, I was struck with the
calm dignity of his manner; the people respectfully
made way for him as he passed, and seemed, I thought,
awed by his noble presence. Many of those who
were present wore silver medals, on one side of which
was engraved a portrait of Earl Grey, and on the
other a bundle of sticks, with the motto, "Union is
strength." The majority of those who were present
did not share the calmness of Sydney Smith, for
they had not the same vision of triumph, and some
even feared that the country was on the verge of
civil war.

Just before Sydney Smith rose to speak, a foolish and violent reformer in the hall started to his
feet, and cried out in a loud voice, "If we don't
have Reform directly, we will pull down that
church!"—pointing to the beautiful Church of St.
Mary Magdalen, the gem of Somerset—"we will pull
it down and repair the roads with its stones." No
sooner were the words uttered than Sydney Smith
calmly rose from his seat, and walked deliberately
across the hall, and looking the man straight in the
face, said in perfectly distinct and freezing tones of
scorn, "Your language, sir, is highly indecent."
The man immediately subsided, and I never afterwards saw him again in public.

His speech was delivered in a clear and musical
voice, and with all the fluency and grace of an accomplished orator; from first to last, he had complete
command over his audience, and no one ventured to

laugh until he issued his mandate. The introduction
of the Partington storm was startling and unexpected,
but as he recounted in felicitous terms the adventures
of the excellent dame, suiting the action to the word
with great dramatic skill, he commenced trundling
his imaginary mop and sweeping back the intrusive
waves of the Atlantic, with an air of resolute determination, and an appearance of increasing temper.
The scene was realistic in the extreme, and was too
much for the gravity of the most serious; and even
the staid brethren in drab were convulsed with uncon-
trollable mirth. The house rose, the people cheered,
and tears of superabundant laughter trickled down
the cheeks of fair women and veteran Reformers.

> ROBERT ARTHUR KINGLAKE, J.P.
>
> Haines Hill, Taunton, 7th March, 1884.

There is little need to dwell on the subsequent
stages of the great agitation for Reform, for practically the victory was already won, and though there
were still obstacles to be encountered, the consciousness that the nation was at their back armed the
Ministry then, as it must always do, with invincible
strength. "Pray beg of Lord Grey to keep well,"
wrote Sydney Smith to the Countess, when the third
Reform Bill was fighting its way in the spring of 1832,
"I have no doubt of a favourable issue. I see an
open sea beyond the icebergs."[2] The last of the icebergs was safely past, and the good ship of the State
went out into the "open sea," on the 7th of June,
1832, when the Reform Bill became law amid the

---

[2] Published Correspondence, p. 496.

rejoicings of thousands whom it had emancipated from political thraldom. "There are two methods of making alterations," remarked Sydney Smith when the struggle was over, "the one is to make concessions which are always too late; the other to see at a distance that the thing must be done effectively and at once. The merit of this latter method belongs to the administration of Lord Grey; he is the only Minister I know who has conceded at the beginning of twenty years what would have been extorted at the end of it."

THE CASTLE HALL, TAUNTON

(*Where the Dame Partington Speech was delivered*).

CHAPTER XII.

1832—1839.

Combe-Florey and London—Old friends and new—Letters to Archdeacon Singleton—Republishes his contributions to the *Edinburgh
Review*.

THE summer of 1832 brought a succession of visitors
to Combe-Florey, and amongst them came Lord John
Russell—one of the heroes of the hour. "My butler,"
relates Sydney Smith, "said that he should let the
country people peep through the shutters at Lord
John for a penny a piece. I wonder what he would
charge for Lord Grey, if he should come here."[1]   He
declared that the people were disappointed by the
extreme smallness of "Lord John Reformer," and
that he turned it off by assuring them that he was
once much larger, but had diminished from extreme
political anxiety.

   The beautiful coast scenery of North Devon possessed a great attraction for Sydney Smith, and the
romantic neighbourhood of Lynton drew forth his
special admiration. Set completely at ease in his
circumstances, he felt at liberty, now that he was on
the shady side of sixty, to lead a more leisurely life;
but whilst he successfully endeavoured, as he said,

[1] Published Correspondence, p. 499.

"to grow old merrily," and to enjoy the fair aspects of nature which were now within his reach, no consideration of personal pleasure or ease was ever permitted to interfere with his work amongst his parishioners at Combe-Florey, for, though he was generally gay, he was never careless, and unfailing devotion to everything which he esteemed a duty was not the least prominent or honourable trait in his character.

The death of a friend of his youth—Sir James Mackintosh—which took place as the summer was dawning, was an occurrence which he severely felt. The two men, although their fortunes in life lay far apart, had always held each other in affectionate regard, and there were few more welcome guests at Foston than the absent-minded, but warm-hearted, Sir James. It was of Mackintosh—whom Horner was accustomed to term his own "Intellectual Master"—that Sydney Smith declared "he could not hate; he did not know how to set about it. The gall-bladder was omitted in his composition." [2] Amongst more recent friendships which did much to cheer the closing years of Sydney Smith's life, was one which he had formed with the Earl and Countess of Morley, and as their seat at Saltram was comparatively near, he was a frequent visitor.[3] Some of his most characteristic letters in the published collection, including the famous one on the mysterious subject of Quaker babies, were addressed to the lively and accomplished countess, who was herself a woman of wit and a recognized ornament of

[2] "Life of Sir James Mackintosh," vol. ii. chap. viii. p. 564.

[3] The tidings of his preferment to a canonry of St. Paul's reached him whilst Lord Morley's guest at Saltram.

society. Mr. Abraham Hayward, writing in 1855 in
the pages of the *Edinburgh Review*, declared that the
" death of Lady Morley was the greatest loss which
English society had sustained since it lost Sydney
Smith."   Lady Morley greatly relished the peculiar
humour of Sydney Smith, and her own vivacious re-
torts called forth in conversation his most brilliant
powers. A close friendship sprang up between the
canon and the countess, and no one appreciated more
highly than the former the many claims to admiration and honour which met in Lady Morley,—   .

> " Whose laugh, full of mirth, without any control
>   But the sweet one of gracefulness   rang from her soul."

Most of the letters to the countess have already
been published, but two or three characteristic notes
are here inserted with the permission of the present
Earl of Morley, the grandson of Sydney Smith's correspondent.

[XXXVIII.]   Combe-Florey (1832).

MY DEAR LADY MORLEY, — Excuse my tenderness
in asking you how you do, because I heard from Mrs.
Villiers you were not so well as all your friends
wished you to be. Don't consider this merely as a
summer hotel. We do a good deal of business in the
winter, and are as warm as a stove, so be so good as
to come here on your way to London. I am going to
Cambridge, London, and twenty places, but shall return in a fortnight. * * * We are all obliged to Dr.
Erica for keeping you clear of cholera—a dangerous
disease, but a shabby and insignificant epidemic. Our
soups had the full approbation of Luttrell; he

declared himself last year perfectly satisfied with the fish department. I hope Lord Morley is on his legs again ; my kind remembrance to him.

Ever, my dear Lady Morley,

Very truly yours,

SYDNEY SMITH.

The sly reference to Luttrell suggests a passing remark, as he was a prominent figure in the society of Holland House. A man of wit and fashion, and a celebrated diner-out, his company at table was greatly sought, and his criticism of the viands sometimes feared, as he was a connoisseur of the first rank, and a judge of dainty dishes, whose verdict was final. It was Luttrell who was responsible for the saying that the man who does not like a good dinner must be either a fool or a liar, and, as every one is aware, his notion of the English climate was, " on a fine day, like looking up a chimney; on a rainy day, like looking down it." [4] Rogers declared that he knew no man in London society who could slide in a brilliant thing into general conversation with equal readiness. It was Luttrell who detested the sight of monkeys, and based his objection on the plea that they reminded him too vividly of poor relations.

[XXXIX.] Combe-Florey, Jan. 25th, 1833.

MY DEAR LADY MORLEY,—What is deferred is not lost. We shall hope to see you in better weather, and when this beautiful country has put on its fine clothes. * * * I am convinced Brighton is the place for November, December, and January. If I could live

[4] Russell: " Memoir, Journal, and Correspondence of Thomas Moore " (May 22nd, 1828).

where I pleased, there I would then live; then London till the middle of June, then four months of the country. What a reasonable man I am; but always sincerely

Yours,
SYDNEY SMITH.

Lady Morley had expressed a wish to hear the Rev. Edward Irving preach, and Sydney Smith at once volunteered to accompany her. On inquiry, however, he found that the famous Scotch preacher was just setting out for the north, and he therefore wrote in the following terms to postpone the engagement:—

[XL.]   20, Saville Row, Bond Street (1833).

DEAR LADY MORLEY,—Touching this discourse which we intended to hear, it is my duty to inform you that the preacher goes out of town to-night. * * * Let us, therefore, dear Lady Morley, be content with the hebdomadal truisms, the tranquil logic, and the undeniable positions of our parish priests, and restrain, if you please, that pungency of remark, and that sharpness of distinction, which characterizes you in secular things. Lower your spirit, prostrate your talents, be like other ladies till church is over, and only till then, or you will lose the homage of

SYDNEY SMITH.

The Earl and Countess of Morley paid a visit to Combe-Florey in the course of the summer of 1833, and Lady Davy, the wife of the great chemist, followed them in September.

[XLI.]   Combe-Florey, Sept. 7th, 1833.

MY DEAR LADY DAVY,—We shall be heartily glad

to see you on the 14th. We dine at half-past six, and
are six miles and a half from Taunton, where our inn
is the London Inn. The artiste (who is instructing
our lady cook) is not despicable; but his forte seems
to be culinary architecture. He has done Solomon's
Temple in red sugar, and Somerset House with
Powlett Thomson [5] looking out of the window, in
chocolate.

Ever sincerely yours,
SYDNEY SMITH.

His duties at St. Paul's called him frequently to
London, and whilst there in November he wrote an
amusing note to a gentleman who made the not
uncommon request for a good place at a forthcoming
service of special interest :—

[XLII.]   November 22nd, 1833.

DEAR GUILLEMARD,—To go to St. Paul's is certain
death. The thermometer is several degrees below
zero. My sentences are frozen as they come out of
my mouth, and are thawed in the course of the
summer, making strange noises and unexpected assertions in various parts of the church; but if you are
tired of a world which is not tired of you, and are
determined to go to St. Paul's, it becomes my duty
to facilitate the desperate scheme. Present the enclosed card to any of the vergers, and you will be well
placed.

Ever truly yours,
SYDNEY SMITH.

On his return to Combe-Florey he despatched a letter

_____
[5] Afterwards first Lord Sydenham.

to Lady Morley, in which he gives some account of
his past movements and future plans :—

[XLIII.]   Combe-Florey, Dec., 1833.

MY DEAR LADY MORLEY,—I have been to London
for a month without fogs, with many friends and very
agreeable. * * * I am returned to the *via monotone* till
the middle of February, when we are all going to
London; some say we are going to be married, but
I know nothing about it. I never saw Lord Grey
better; he has no more notion of resigning his place
than I have of resigning St. Paul's. I taxed Lady
Holland roundly and plainly with being a good deal
better, and after much shuffling and evasion, she was
forced to confess that she was better. I promised not
to tell.⁶ Read 'Hamilton's America,' it is quite excellent. Brougham's brother died of a complaint of
very old standing, mismanaged in the country where
all complaints are mismanaged, but many prevented.
* * * I suppose you will not be in London till the
supra fines begin to assemble, and yet there will be some
bloody battles in the Lords. We have been surrounded all summer by scarlet fever, and have buried
one-fourteenth of our population; our average burials
are two and a half, and we have buried this year
twenty-one; the same thing happened a hundred and
fifty years ago.

God bless you, dear Lady Morley.

Although Sydney Smith was not "going to be
married," his eldest daughter, Saba, was about to

---

⁶ Lady Holland, towards the close of her life, afforded her friends
mingled amusement and concern by her whimsical anxiety concerning
her health.

become the wife of Dr. Henry Holland, and in the spring of 1834 the marriage duly took place. "It makes my old age much happier," were his words, "to have placed my amiable daughter in the hands of so honourable a son."['] When he was informed that his daughter's marriage was announced in the London papers under the heading of "Fashionable Intelligence," he exclaimed, with a merry twinkle in his eye, "How absurd!—why, we pay our bills!" The marriage of his daughter deprived him of one who had been a constant companion for many years, and as it was followed by a summer of sickness, the loss was all the more keenly felt. Gout, which he was accustomed ruefully to declare was the only enemy he did not wish to have at his feet, was laying siege to him, and occasionally he was also troubled with violent pain in the eyes.

In July, Lord Grey resigned his position at the head of affairs, but not before he had carried the abolition of colonial slavery, the abolition of the East India Company's monopoly, and the Poor Law Amendment Act, through the first reformed Parliament. A few weeks after Earl Grey's retirement, Sydney Smith wrote to the countess in the following terms :—

[XLIV.]   Combe-Florey, 26th August, 1834.

My dear Lady Grey,—Tired of groaning alone on a sofa in London, and unwilling that Mrs. Sydney should quit her flower-garden in July and come to town, I set off with the gout in both feet, and got home without being the worse for the effort. Before the gout left me here, I had a sharp attack of

['] Published Correspondence, p. 509.

ophthalmia, and am now recovering fast, though a
little blind and a little lame. Your letter gave me
great pleasure. Lord Grey has met with that reception which every honest and right-minded man felt to
be his due. If I had never known him and lived in
the north, I should have come out to wave my bonnet
as he passed. He may depend upon it, he has played
a great part in English history, and that the best part
of the English people entertain for him the most
profound respect. And now for the rest of life let
him trifle and lounge, and do everything which may
be agreeable to him, and not be too severe in
criticizing himself. God bless you.

SYDNEY SMITH.

He had now been a canon residentiary of St. Paul's
for upwards of three years, and his ability as a
preacher, which had long been admitted by the more
cultivated and thoughtful in the nation, was at length
fully recognized on all sides, and became one of the
chief attractions to that fickle, and somewhat limp and
unsatisfactory crowd, which in every great city runs
hither and thither on Sundays to catch the words of
well-known men. If, as not unfrequently happened, a
passing stranger half carelessly followed the multitude
into the cathedral, attracted by their eagerness and
its magnificence, his apathy vanished when the sermon
began, and the discovery was made that he was
listening to the voice of a man of strong and original
character, who spoke with an air of authority, and in
accents of conviction. The freshness and variety of
the preacher's language was not more remarkable than
the vigorous thought and generous sympathy which

marked his utterances, and the favourable impression thus created was deepened by his familiar yet dignified manner, and the evident sincerity and naturalness of the man himself.

Strangers entering St. Paul's on such an occasion, in the year 1834, would have witnessed a burly but active-looking man of sixty-three, of medium height, with dark complexion and iron-grey hair, ascend the pulpit. When he stood up to preach, the shapely and well-carried head, the fine eyes, with their quick and penetrating glance, the expression of thorough benevolence which lit up the sensitive yet boldly chiselled features of the strong and intellectual face, would all contribute to heighten favourably the first general impression concerning a man whose every movement suggested intelligence, determination, and kindliness. One who was not by any means a stranger to Sydney Smith has given a brief description of a service at St. Paul's when he was the preacher, in the year mentioned ; and the following passage from the journal of so shrewd an observer as Mr. Greville will be read with interest :—

" December 1st, 1834.—Went to St. Paul's yesterday evening to hear Sydney Smith preach. He is very good ; manner impressive, voice sonorous and agreeable, *rather* familiar, but not offensively so, language simple and unadorned, sermon clever and illustrative. The service is exceedingly grand, performed with all the pomp of a cathedral, and chanted with beautiful voices ; the lamps, scattered few and far between throughout the vast space under the dome, making darkness visible, and dimly revealing the immensity of the building, were extremely striking.

The cathedral service thus chanted and performed is my *beau idéal* of religious worship,—simple, intelligible, and grand, appealing at the same time to the reason and the imagination." [8]

One of the most interesting men in London society at this period was Mr. Richard Sharp, M.P., a prominent figure in the social life of the capital from the days of Johnson and Burke, to those of Mackintosh and Byron. He had amassed a large fortune in trade, and had managed at the same time to acquire accurate and extensive information on a great variety of subjects. He was a splendid talker, and that fact led his friends to give him the name by which perhaps he is best known to the present generation—" Conversation Sharp." One of Luttrell's best jokes was made at the expense of Sharp. "I was mentioning," relates Moore, " that some one had said of Sharp's very dark complexion, that he looked as if the dye of his old trade (hat-making) had got engrained in his face." ' Yes," said Luttrell, " darkness that may be *felt !*" Sharp was an intimate friend of Sydney Smith's, and they constantly met in the society of Holland House; he died in 1835, and one of the most charming letters in the published correspondence of his clerical friend was written to him during the long illness which preceded his death.

With men like Luttrell, Rogers, Moore, and Sharp, Sydney Smith was in his element, and their gay fancy and lively wit called forth some of his most sparkling sallies. One day, the conversation ran on the subject of pluralities in the Church, and

[8] Greville, " Memoirs and Journals," vol. iii. chap. xxv. p. 166.

Luttrell told an anecdote concerning an Irish clergyman who hotly resented the application of the term to
himself. He protested against being described as a
"pluralist," and added impetuously, "if you don't
take care what you are saying, you will find me a
duellist." Sydney immediately caught up the idea,
and said, "I suppose there is scarcely a clergyman in
Ireland who has not *been out*. I am told they settle
these matters when the afternoon's service is over. I
myself have seen a parson's challenge—'Sir, meet me
on the first Sunday after Epiphany.'"

On another occasion, he entertained his friends with
a laughable account of the difficulties in the way of
introducing trial by jury into Australia ; the colonists
up-country were beset with obstacles of a kind of which
we at home did not so much as dream, and he ended
up a statement to that effect by putting the following
words into the mouth of an embarrassed and reluctant
juryman : "I cannot come and serve upon your jury ;
the waters are out, and I have two miles to swim.
If I leave, the kangaroos will break into my corn. My
little boy has been bitten by an ornithorhynchus para-
doxus. I have sent a man fifty miles with a sack
of flour to buy a pair of breeches for the assizes,
and he has not yet returned."

Sydney Smith's efforts to soothe the ruffled feelings
of a friend were not always successful, and were sometimes hardly of a nature to warrant the hope that they
would produce that result. A worthy baronet, who
dabbled in politics, came to him one day very much
irritated. "What is the matter ?" was the immediate
question. "Are any of our institutions in danger ?"
"No, but I have just been with Brougham, whom I

sought out for the purpose of making an important communication, but upon my word, he treated me as if I was a fool!" "Never mind, my dear fellow," said Sydney, in his most sympathetic tones, "never mind, never mind, he thought you knew it!"

The letters which he wrote at this period, especially during his visits to London, reveal his keen enjoyment of the ordinary intercourse of life, and sometimes even so common-place a production as an invitation to an evening party becomes in his hands amusingly frank and explicit, as the accompanying note to his valued friend Miss Harcourt proves:—

[XLV.]   18, Stratford Place, March 21st, 1835.

DEAR GEORGIANA,—Our rout generally consists of half a dozen highly respectable old women, and the same number of greasy philosophers, the Ladies H—— (the only little bit of nobility we can raise) and Colonel ——, who represents the amorous part of the community. There are also half a dozen young ladies, unquestionably the plainest in Europe, and, indeed, I might extend my geographical limits for the purposes of this comparison.

All this is out of your line. Think of the wilderness of a drawing-room where in the whole horizon there is not a duchess or a countess to be seen!

Having thus fairly warned you, we have nothing to add, my dear Georgiana, but that Mrs. Sydney and I shall be very glad to see you and Anne, if at any time you have a fancy to come.

Yours ever,
SYDNEY SMITH.

The following unpublished note also belongs to this

period, and will explain itself. It was written to satisfy some qualms of conscience experienced by Mrs. Smith, after she had acceded to the request of a somewhat bold and troublesome person for an introduction to Lord Lansdowne.

[XLVI.]

MY DEAR LORD LANSDOWNE,—"Pray introduce me to Lord Lansdowne." When this is said by a very forward person to a lady, you know how extremely difficult it is to say "No." Mrs. Sydney was in this predicament yesterday when Mr. —— made this petition to her. She has been tormenting herself about this, but I said I would explain it, and told her that you must have been subjected repeatedly to these accidents, and must perfectly understand them as almost inevitable. Even I have had persons desirous of being introduced to me, and it is not every one who could make as good an answer as the late Mrs. Humphrey Mildmay. Croker said to her, he wished particularly to be introduced to me. "Yes," she said, "that may be agreeable to you, but are you sure it would be equally agreeable to Mr. Sydney Smith?"

Ever yours,
SYDNEY SMITH.

Combe-Florey, to quote his own expression, "bound up well with London," and as the roads to the west were good, the journey to and fro, even before the age of steam, was not an arduous one—at least when gout was in abeyance. His periodical visits to town seem to have enhanced his love of the country, and his letters bear witness to the continual charm of his surroundings in Somerset. In a letter to Dr. Holland, written at midsummer from his rural retreat, he implores his medical son-in-law to turn his attention to that "little curse," the hay-fever, of the effects of which he gives the following amusing description: "Light, dust, contradiction, an absurd remark, the sight of a Dissenter—anything sets me sneezing; and if I begin sneezing at twelve, I don't leave off till two, and am heard distinctly in Taunton (when the wind sets that way), a distance of six miles. * * * If consumption is too powerful for physicians, at least they should not suffer themselves to be outwitted by such little upstart disorders as the hay-fever."[9] He usually spent February, March, and July in London, as his duties at St. Paul's occupied him during those months; in July, 1835, he states that he travelled home in his carriage "with a green parrot and the 'Life of Mackintosh.'" "I think," is his criticism in a note to Lord Murray, "Robert Mackintosh has done his father's life very well; done it by putting in as little mortar as possible between the layers of stone." At the close of August, he writes to another correspondent: "We have had charming weather; and all who come here, or have been here, have been delighted with our little paradise,—for such it really is,—except that there is no serpent, and that we wear clothes."[1]

In the autumn he was able to fulfil a promise of long standing by taking Mrs. Smith to Paris. They were accompanied by their daughter Emily, and their son-in-law, Mr. Hibbert. They crossed the Channel

---

[9] Published Correspondence, p. 513.   [1] Ibid. p. 518.

in a hurricane, and Sydney Smith relates that, wrapped in a cloak, he lay on the deck, and reflected that as he had now " so little life to lose, it was of small consequence whether he was drowned, or died like a resident clergyman, from indigestion." [2]   Between Calais and Paris they travelled—such at least is the statement of the vivacious chronicler who was at the head of the party—at the primitive speed of five miles an hour, and, like everybody else, they were delighted with the magnificence of the Gothic churches at Rouen, and with the dreamy beauty of the quaint old Norman city.   They found Paris full of English people, most of whom were eager to welcome so distinguished a countryman as Sydney Smith, and the visit was full of enjoyment, especially to Mrs. Smith, who had never seen the French capital before. " I suspect," he wrote from Paris, " the Fifth Act of life should be in great cities ; it is there, in the long death of old age, that a man most forgets himself and his infirmities ; receives the greatest consolation from the attentions of friends, and the greatest diversion from external circumstances." [3]

After a short stay in London, during which he took on lease a house in Charles Street, Berkeley Square, just across the street from Berkeley Chapel, where, as a young man, he had so often preached, and " five minutes from the Park, and ten from Dr. Holland," the beginning of December found him safely ensconced in winter quarters at Combe-Florey. The journey home was not without incident, in spite of his own statement that few are the adventures of a canon travelling gently over good roads to his benefice.   In

<hr>

[2] Published Correspondence, p. 520.   [3] Ibid. p. 521.

a letter to his eldest daughter descriptive of his experiences in the Bristol coach, he states that, oddly enough, the mayor of that city in 1829, whom he had so mightily offended by his sermon in the cathedral on the Catholic claims, was his fellow-passenger. Times had changed since then, and the worthy alderman had grown more tolerant with them, and condescended to exchange civilities with the militant churchman, who was terribly afraid lest he should stop at the same inn at Reading. However, as a loyal man, he stayed at the " Crown," and Sydney confesses that, being a rude one, he went on to the " Bear." The letter concludes with an amusing episode, which he thus recounts : "Being, since my travels, very much gallicized in my character, I ordered a pint of claret; I found it incomparably the best wine I had ever tasted; it disappeared with a rapidity which surprises me even at this distance of time. The next morning, in the coach by eight, with a handsome valetudinarian lady, upon whom the coach produced the same effect as a steam-packet would do. I proposed weak warm brandy and water; she thought, at first, it would produce inflammation of the stomach, but presently requested to have it warm and *not* weak, and she took it to the last drop, as I did the claret." [1]

Notwithstanding his frequent absence from Somerset, he kept up neighbourly intercourse with many of the leading families in and around Taunton. One of his acquaintances in that town was Dr. Blake, a well-known medical man, and an ardent politician of the Radical type. The doctor in religion was a staunch Unitarian. Hearing that he was unwell, the Rector

---

[1] Published Correspondence, p. 524.

OF THE REV. SYDNEY SMITH.

of Combe-Florey looked in as he passed through the town, to inquire after his health. "Oh, Mr. Smith," exclaimed Dr. Blake, "I am far from well. I have got a cold, aguish feeling all over me, and though I sit by a good fire, I cannot keep myself warm." "I can cure you, doctor," said his visitor as he prepared to go; "cover yourself with the Thirty-nine Articles, and you will soon have a delicious glow all over you!"

On another occasion, dining one summer evening in the neighbourhood of Combe-Florey at the house of a friend, where a pleasant party had been invited to meet him, a youthful and somewhat conceited officer of the Scots Greys, a troop of which regiment was at that time quartered in Taunton, was of the company. It was a beautiful and sultry evening, and as the repast proceeded, the buzzing of a bee which had dropped in at the open window—attracted doubtless by the fruit and flowers—greatly disturbed the young soldier's peace of mind. Turning to a lady who sat next to him, he exclaimed in peevish and affected tones, "If there is one thing more than another that I hate, it is the buzzing of a bee at dinner-time." Sydney Smith immediately remarked in an undertone to his fair neighbour, "I suppose, madam, if a hornet came in the captain would *sell out !*"

He often drove over to Taunton, where the Combe-Florey successor to the "Immortal," a much more stylish equipage, was a familiar object in the streets of the town. The following recollections of his visits there, though slight, are characteristic and amusing :—

[XLVII.]   Rolls Park, Chigwell, Essex, May 29th, 1884.

Very distinctly do I recall the portly figure of

Y

Sydney Smith seated in his large yellow chariot—then a fashionable style of carriage—the full-sized head, the face indicative, as it now presents itself to my mind's eye, of mental power, of kindliness, and of the spirit of humour which possessed him.

My father, who was a timber merchant in Taunton, took a deep interest in politics through the exciting days of the Reform agitation of half a century ago, working hard with Sydney Smith, Sir Thomas B. Lethbridge, and others on the Liberal side.

I can just remember the delighted and exultant state of mind in which he returned from the county meeting at Taunton, at which Sydney Smith produced the far-famed fable of Dame Partington and the Atlantic. He had stood close to the speaker's elbow, and in after-years he often described in vivid words the telling action with which the old lady's energetic but futile mopping was illustrated.

This brilliant man was not brilliant only ; there was in his character, as I conceive, an unusually substantial basis of sound common sense. This was not only visible in his writings, but also prominent in his practical life. When in residence at Combe-Florey, his calls on business at my father's wharf were not unfrequent, and it used to be a matter of common remark how definite and clearly expressed his instructions always were.

Even under such circumstances he sometimes found food for his fun. In my father's employment was a queer old fellow, a sawyer, out of whom Mr. Smith one day discovered that some amusement was to be obtained. This fact was not forgotten when he came again, until at length " Brooks " got quite frightened, and kept as

far as possible out of the way.   I remember one day
the old man's catching sight of the well-known chariot
nearing the wharf gates, and, twitching up the waist-
band of his breeches, bustling off to the shelter of his
saw-pit with the cry, in tones of almost agony,
" There's Sir Sydney a-coming !   There's Sir Sydney
a-coming ! "

EDWARD A. BALL.[5]

At no period were absent friends in the north forgotten ; and although year by year his powers of locomotion became more and more impeded by recurring
and most weakening attacks of gout, he always availed
himself of any chance opportunity of renewing the
delightful intercourse of former years.   Sometimes,
when writing to those with whom he was perfectly at his ease, he would enclose a set of verses
which he had composed for their amusement and his
own.   The following unpublished lines were presented
by him to the Hon. Mrs. Henry Howard, and bear in
his own handwriting the title of

[XLVIII.]   THE POETICAL MEDICINE CHEST.

With store of powdered rhubarb we begin ;
(To leave out powdered rhubarb were a sin),
Pack mild magnesia deep within the chest ;
And glittering gum from Araby the blest ;
And keep, oh lady, keep within thy reach
The slimy surgeon, blood-devouring leech.

[5] Mr. Ball, to the regret of a wide circle of friends, who justly
esteemed him, died suddenly a few weeks after the above letter was
written.

Laurel-born camphor, opiate drugs prepare,
They banish pain, and calm consuming care.
Glauber and Epsom salts their aid combine,
Translucent streams of castor-oil be thine,
And gentle manna in thy bottles shine.
If morbid spot of septic sore invade,
By heaven-sent bark the morbid spot is stayed ;
When with black bile hepatic regions swell,
With subtle calomel the plague expel.
Anise and mint with strong Æolian sway,
Intestine storms of flatulence allay,
And ipecachuana clears the way.
I know thee well, thou antimonial power,
And to thee fly in that heart-rending hour,
When feverish patients heave their laden breath,
And all is sickness, agony, and death !
Soda and potash change the humours crude,
When hoven parsons swell with luscious food.
Spare not in eastern blasts when babies die,
The wholesale vigour of the Spanish fly.
From timely torture seek thy infant's rest,
And spread the poison on his labouring breast.
And so, fair lady, when in evil hour
Less prudent mothers mourn some faded flower,
Six Howards valiant and six Howards fair,
Shall live and love thee, and reward thy care.

                                        SYDNEY SMITH.

Some of his brief notes to his friends, dashed off
quickly, in the midst of more engrossing occupations,
are very bright and witty. Most people will recall,
for example, the famous excuse which he sent to
Mr. Longman, the publisher, in reply to an invitation
to dinner : " I cannot accept your invitation, for my

house is full of country cousins. I wish they were once removed." [6] The following notes, which have not hitherto been published, are characteristic examples of his style, and bear witness to the high spirits which usually marked him :—

[XLIX.]   18, Stratford Place, June 6th, 1833.

Dear Georgiana,—You use me very ill in not sending me the receipt for the lemon-peel water. I verily believe I should have recovered two days ago if I had received it. My premature decease will be entirely attributable to you.   Yours truly,

SYDNEY SMITH.

MY EPITAPH.

This horrible slaughter
Was entirely owing to the Archbishop's daughter,
Who would not give him the receipt for lemon water.

Miss G. Harcourt.

[L.]   33, Charles Street, June 27th, 1836.

Dear Lord Lansdowne,—Many thanks for the two books of Hallam's, which I return this day, having received from them a good deal of instruction, clear of every particle of amusement.

Ever yours,

SYDNEY SMITH.

In reply to an invitation to dinner, which he was unable to accept, instead of the usual hackneyed " previous engagement," he despatched this graceful little note to his friend, Lady Davy :—

[LI.]   33, Charles Street, Berkeley Square,
February 25th, 1837.

Dear Lady Davy,—Our tastes (pardon my vanity) are so similar that I like to meet all whom you like to

[6] " Life of the Rev. R. H. Barham," vol. i. p. 283.

invite. My inclinations, however, must remain un-
gratified on the 4th, as I am engaged to dine with
Lord Tankerville.

> Body and mind will thus divided be,
> I dine with Tankerville, and think of thee.

SYDNEY SMITH.

Early in 1837 the " Letters to Archdeacon Singleton
on the Ecclesiastical Commission " began to appear,
and in them he exerted all his remarkable powers of
reason, wit, and satire against measures which he
stigmatized as rash, foolish, and imprudent. The
Commission, which had been originated by Sir Robert
Peel, and was supported by the Whigs under Lord
Melbourne and Lord John Russell, aimed at bringing
about some much-needed ecclesiastical reforms. Many
glaring abuses in the Church were exposed through
its investigations, and a number of sinecure offices
connected with the cathedrals were abolished. The
incredible inequalities which existed between some of
the sees (the Bishop of Durham had a revenue of
19,480*l.*, whilst the Bishop of Rochester had to be
content with 1400*l.*) were diminished, and the wealth
of the Church underwent, to some extent at least, a process of redistribution. The boundaries of each diocese
were revised, questions arising out of the growth and
removal of the population were fully considered, and
the new sees of Manchester and Ripon were founded.

The incomes of deans were also brought into
greater conformity with each other, and the number of canons attached to the cathedrals was
reduced. The funds which accrued to the Ecclesiastical Commissioners were applied by them to the

augmentation of small livings in populous parishes, to the building of churches in the working-class suburbs of manufacturing towns, and in any other way which might seem desirable in order to make Church work more efficient. The Commissioners were also instrumental in bringing about a much-needed reform—the abolition of the right of one clergyman to hold two livings unless they were within a distance of ten miles of each other.

Sydney Smith did not for a moment deny the need of ecclesiastical reform; on the contrary, he was of opinion that it was absolutely necessary, and ought not to be postponed. He objected, however, to the constitution of the Commission, and to the exclusion from a council which was to deal with every branch of churchmen,—bishops, dignitaries, and parochial clergymen,—of the two lower orders of the clergy. He regarded many of the proposals of the Commissioners as short-sighted in policy and hostile to the best interests of the Church, and he looked upon a scheme which provided for the wants of the poor clergy by lessening the rewards to which they might hope eventually to climb, as a singular evasion of duty.

He maintained that the curates themselves, all of whom hope to draw great prizes, did not care for a paltry improvement of their poverty if it could only be gained by the wholesale confiscation of cathedral property and the chief rewards of the Church. He declared that, as a matter of fact, the great emoluments of the profession were already within the reach of the lowest ranks of the community, and that butchers, bakers, and publicans were constantly seeing their clever children elevated to the mitre. In support of this statement, he drew a rapid sketch of the triumphant rise and progress of young Crumpet's fortunes as he advances from his father's bakehouse step by step until he is safely landed in an episcopal palace : "Let a respectable baker drive through the city from the west-end of the town, and let him cast an eye on the battlements of Northumberland House; has his little muffin-faced son the smallest chance of getting in among the Percies, enjoying a share of their luxury and splendour, and of chasing the deer with horn and hound upon the Cheviot Hills? But let him drive his alum-steeped loaves a little further till he reaches St. Paul's Churchyard, and all his thoughts are changed when he sees that beautiful fabric; it is not impossible that his little penny roll may be introduced into that splendid oven. Young Crumpet is sent to school—takes to his books—spends the best years of his life, as all eminent Englishmen do, in making Latin verses—knows that the *crum* in crumpet is long, and the *pet* short—goes to the University—gets a prize for an essay on the Dispersion of the Jews—takes orders—becomes a bishop's chaplain—has a young nobleman for his pupil—publishes a useless classic and a serious call to the unconverted—and then goes through the Elysian transitions of prebendary, dean, prelate, and the long train of purple, profit, and power." [7]

He contended that the whole mass of property which the Commission proposed to confiscate would only make the poor clergy a trifling degree less poor, whilst it destroyed in almost every case the powerful stimulus

[7] Second Letter to Archdeacon Singleton.

of hope in the breasts of young ecclesiastics. He ridiculed the idea of a Christian bishop proposing in cold blood to create a thousand new livings of 130*l.* a year each; in other words, "to call into existence a thousand of the most unhappy men on the face of the earth, the sons of the poor, without hope, without the assistance of private fortune, chained to the soil, ashamed to live with their inferiors, unfit for the society of the better classes, and dragging about the English curse of poverty, with the smallest hope that they can ever shake it off." [*]

The Commissioners, of course, expected to secure for 130*l.* a year a thousand good and enthusiastic men, each of whom combined in himself all moral, physical, and intellectual advantages. Without exception, each one of the thousand—so ran the official dream—was to be "a learned man, dedicating himself intensely to the care of his parish, of charming manners and dignified deportment, six feet two inches high, beautifully proportioned, with a magnificent countenance, expressive of all the cardinal virtues and the Ten Commandments, and it was asked, with an air of triumph, if such a man as this will fall into contempt on account of his poverty?" Sydney Smith was prepared to say, "Certainly not, if you can get the men for the money," an achievement which he however regarded as rather difficult. But substitute for this ideal personage "an average, ordinary, uninteresting minister—obese, dumpy, neither ill-natured nor good-natured, neither learned nor ignorant, striding over the stiles to church, with a second-rate wife, dusty and deliquescent, and four parochial

* Third Letter to Archdeacon Singleton.

children, full of catechism and bread and butter," and
how rests the question then?

He declared that the smaller livings in the Church
were held, as a rule, by young men who looked forward to a college or family living, or were the sons
of people of substance, and these young men were
paid " once by money and three times by hope." If,
however, the legitimate rewards of the profession were
seriously reduced both in number and in value, young
men of family would not feel the same inclination to
enter the Church, and divinity students would have to
be gathered wholesale from the ranks of the poorer
and less educated classes.

He protested against the notion that deans and
chapters had made a worse use of their patronage
than bishops; and he argued that it was eminently
unfair to exclude the former from the Commission in
the first instance, and next to confiscate their revenues.
He pointed out that the Prelate Commissioners, in spite
of their new-born zeal to provide for the spiritual
destitution of the masses, were careful not to sacrifice a
shilling of the aggregate income of the episcopal order
to that purpose, but were eager to relieve it with property to which they had no claim . " Is not this as if
one, affected powerfully by a charity sermon, were to
put his hands in another man's pocket, and cast, from
what he had extracted, a liberal contribution into the
plate?" It was a little too bad, he thought, for these
stately ecclesiastics to want to sacrifice with other
men's hetacombs, and at the same time to enjoy the
twofold character of personal disinterestedness and
martyrdom to unjust spoliation. Idle prebendaries of
Canterbury or St. Paul's might make the Church un-

popular; but why not, he asked, as the existing prebendaries vanished from the scene, annex their stalls to some large and populous parish, and so compel their successors to combine labour with wealth? The Ecclesiastical Commissioners, moreover, aimed at abolishing many offices in the Church, which he deemed might, with a little care and thought, have been turned to purposes of national utility and education.

Sydney Smith has frequently been accused of having had interested motives in the opposition with which he met the Ecclesiastical Commission, but such a charge is more easily made than proved; and those who look with unprejudiced eyes at the circumstances of the case are likely to arrive at precisely the opposite conclusion. He was old and wealthy, and had neither sons nor near relatives in the Church, and therefore there was no selfish end concealed beneath his attacks, and it is not more certain that his opposition was mistaken than that the motives which prompted it were pure. No such evils as he dreaded have fallen upon the Church; and if its worldly value as a profession has declined, its true honour as a spiritual vocation has been correspondingly advanced. Sydney Smith approached the question too much on the temporal side, and not even his powers of wit and eloquence were sufficient recompense for that fact; nevertheless, it remains true that " as long as the English language endures, the memory of the Ecclesiastical Commissioners will be handed down in the humorous and argumentative letters of their great antagonist." [9]

[9] "Canon Molesworth's History of England, 1830-74," vol. i. chap. vi. p. 391.

When the question had arrived at a further stage, and various modifications of the original proposals had been made, he wrote as follows to the Marquis of Lansdowne :—

[LII.]   Taunton, Sept. 14th, 1838.

DEAR LORD LANSDOWNE,—Do what you like with the Church, it will never make the smallest alteration in my respect and regard for you. All that I require is full permission in shilling pamphlets to protest that we are the most injured, persecuted, and ill-treated persons on the face of the earth. Against Lord Holland and you personally I could not, and would not, write a single syllable, and of course you must both laugh at such nonsense as I put forth from time to time.

After all, the Residence and Plurality Bill was (as it came out of the Commission) a very bad Bill. I could point out eleven or twelve very material points, bearing strongly upon the happiness of the parochial clergy, which have been omitted or completely changed in the passage of the Bill through Parliament; to all of these I objected, and though I do not of course imagine that I had weight and authority to produce these changes, yet it shows that my hostility was not frivolous and vexatious.

The Bill is now a very good Bill. The original Bill was bad, because John Russell, legislating on what it is not likely he could understand, took his information from bishops, who were sure to mislead him because they consulted their own power. In the same way I am sure that his Dean and Chapter Bill may be very materially improved, and that the errors it contains proceed from the same source.

Many thanks for the venison, which arrived here safely to-day, and apparently in very good condition. We have had a great run of blue-stocking ladies here this summer, and are expecting more. I have had a fit of the gout, which I chased away speedily with colchicum. Are you going to make your promised tour to Lynton? If so, pray come and see us, you and yours.

I am very much obliged by your good-natured and sensible letter, which gave me great pleasure and satisfaction; for I should have been heartily sorry that my defence of my profession should have been construed into the most distant intention of ill-will and hostility to *you;* and to show you how little I consider the venison as deprecatory, I will put into my next pamphlet any abuse of yourself which you choose to dictate, but decline entirely to insert any of my own.

Ever sincerely yours,
SYDNEY SMITH.

A few days later he wrote to Miss Harcourt, to give her the benefit of his own and the parish clerk's opinion of a certain well-known preacher who had made a passing appearance in the pulpit of Combe-Florey Church :—

[LIII.]   Combe-Florey, Taunton, Sept. 30th, 1838.

MY DEAR GEORGIANA, —— will have described to you our place, and described it, I hope, in a manner that will give you a disposition to visit it when an opportunity offers. You know that you are a great favourite here, but that is a position which has no novelty for you. Mr. Hodgson, of the Bounty Office, is here; we sigh over the temporal prospects of the Church, and that state of labour and poverty which the Whigs are preparing for us, and for which erroneous reasoners suppose we were intended.

We like your Boreal Bourdaloue. If he will limit himself to thirty minutes, and carry up a book into the pulpit in conformity with our well-known habits, he would beat all the popular preachers in London. My clerk said to me, " Your honour is not fit to light a candle to his honour ! " He is a handsome man also, and has a kind of Ten Commandments look about him, which is very suitable to a preacher.

God bless you, dear Georgiana,

Your sincere friend,

SYDNEY SMITH.

In the early part of the following year he republished, in a collected form, most of his contributions to the *Edinburgh Review;* the articles which were thus given anew to the world were sixty-five in number, and they cover the period between October, 1802, and March, 1827. Scarcely a number of the great northern quarterly appeared during the first quarter of the century in which Sydney Smith had not something racy and original to say concerning the topics which in those years engaged public attention. There is great variety in the subjects which he passes under review, and not a little versatility is shown in their treatment; and whilst it must be frankly admitted that his wisdom is not always conspicuous, or his judgment infallible, his wit never flags, and the strength and beauty of his style continues undiminished to the end. Whether the subject was Mr. Fox or

Dr. Parr, Hannah Moore or Madame D'Epinay, Botany Bay or Palestine, Irish Bulls or English Man-traps, the Poor Laws or the Poor Clergy, Climbing-boys or the Treadmill, the Catholic Claims or Methodists and Missions, Caleb in search of a Wife or Female Education, Mad Quakers or Persecuting Bishops, he was always humorous, manly, matter-of-fact, and independent.

There can be no question that Sydney Smith did more during the period of his connection with the *Edinburgh Review* for the extension of civil and religious liberty than most people even now are prepared to admit. Against nearly all the abuses of the time he protested with straightforward and honest boldness, and sought to broaden public opinion on social questions, and to evoke a sentiment in the breasts of the people of brotherly kindness and manly self-respect. Writing to Jeffrey, he dwells with just pride on the stand which they had together made against many forms of political and social oppression. "It must be to you," are his words, "as I am sure it is to me, a great pleasure to see so many improvements taking place, and so many abuses destroyed; abuses upon which you with cannon and mortars, and I with sparrow-shot, have been playing for so many years."[1] When his "Contributions to the *Edinburgh Review*" were republished, it is pleasant to find him in the narrow limits of one brief letter to a lady declaring that his old literary chief is "one of the best as well as one of the ablest men in the country. Jeffrey's friendship is to you—honour, safety, and amusement."[2] Then, after a graceful allusion to a presentation copy

---

Published Correspondence, p. 442.　　　[2] Ibid, p. 533.

of the book, which he begs his fair correspondent to accept, he adds an explanatory sentence in regard to it of wider and more permanent interest : " I printed my reviews to show, if I could, that I had not passed my life merely in making jokes, but that I had made use of what little powers of pleasantry I might be endowed with to discountenance bad, and to encourage liberal and wise, principles." " Ah, Mr. Smith," exclaimed a Romish dignitary to Sydney after one of his quaint sayings had bounded forth never to be forgotten, " you have such a way of putting things !" Let it be remembered by all who know how to appreciate fearless and disinterested labours for the public good, that Sydney Smith habitually and without stint employed his wonderful " way of putting things"—to put things right.

COMBE-FLOREY CHURCH.

CHAPTER XIII.

1839—1843.

Politics—Society—Wealth—Fame

" THE success of my pamphlet has been very great. I always told you I was a clever man, and you never would believe me," [1] wrote Sydney Smith to one of his friends in the spring of 1839. The pamphlet to which he alludes was that on the " Ballot," and it was the last he ever wrote. On the subject of the ballot as a panacea for political corruption, philosophical Radicals like George Grote, and wild Chartists like Feargus O'Connor, were of one mind. The Radical Party were greatly disappointed, because of its omission, when Lord John Russell introduced the Government proposals for reform; and it is a matter of history that, if Lord Durham could have had his way in the Grey Cabinet, the question would have been settled in the affirmative half a century earlier than was actually the case. Mr. Grote, whom Sydney Smith described as an honest and able man who would have proved an important politician if the world had been a chessboard, pressed the question year after year upon the attention of Parliament, and the revela-

---

[1] Published Correspondence, p. 547.

z

tions concerning bribery and corruption which were constantly coming to light did more than speeches and arguments to convert the nation to the principle of secret voting, which thousands, however, persisted in regarding as an un-English mode of procedure. For many years the present Premier opposed the introduction of the ballot, and it was not until the exposures which followed the general election of 1868 that Mr. Gladstone gave in his adhesion to the scheme.

Sydney Smith was too wise a man, and had too much faith in human advancement, to regard the triumph of the Reform Bill as an end of all controversy. He wanted, however, a little breathing-time for the country and himself after the bloodless revolution of 1832, and he deemed that the generation to which he belonged should not rush off into battle again, but be content with securing the magnificent spoils which had already fallen to their swords, leaving other victories to be won hereafter by " those little legislators who are now receiving every day after dinner a cake or a plum, in happy ignorance of Mr. Grote and his ballot." The majority of the Liberal Party in 1839 shared his convictions, and only the practical working of the Reform Bill at last convinced statesmen of the necessity for adopting more stringent precautions against political intimidation.

He maintained that a tenant dismissed for a fair and just cause often endeavoured to make a martyr of himself with the public, and having ploughed badly, and paid badly, went about declaring that he had been turned adrift because of his vote. He believed that inquisition into the political opinions of tradesmen was very rare, and that shopkeepers as a class were apt to cry out before they were hurt. " A man who sees after an election one of his customers buying a pair of gloves on the opposite side of the way, roars out that his honesty will make him a bankrupt, and the country papers are filled with letters from Brutus, Publicola, Hampden, and Pym." He ridicules the idea that the ballot will put an end to canvassing, and he regards it as tyrannical to compel those persons to conceal their votes who hate all concealment, and who glory in the cause they support. " Who brought that mischievous profligate villain into Parliament? Who opposed the man whom we all know to be one of the first men in the country? Are these fair and useful questions, to be veiled hereafter in impenetrable mystery?"

The compulsory application of the ballot to all electors seems to him as if a few cowards, who could only fight behind walls and houses, were to prevent the whole regiment from showing a bold front in the field. " What right," he asks, " has the coward to degrade me who am no coward, and put me in the same shameful predicament with himself? It is really a curious condition that all men must imitate the defects of a few, in order that it may not be known who have the natural imperfection, and who put it on from conformity. In this way, in former days, to hide the grey hair of the old, everybody was forced to wear powder and pomatum." The conclusion at which he arrives is that, if the ballot is adopted, the controlling power of Parliament is lost, and the members are at the mercy of the returning officer; and therefore to institute secret voting is to apply a very dangerous

z 2

innovation to what he considers is after all only a temporary evil.

Soon after the pamphlet on the ballot had appeared, he wrote an amusing note on the subject to Lord Durham in reply to an invitation to dinner :—

[LIV.]   33, Charles Street, Berkeley Square,
                                        March 3rd, 1839.

DEAR LORD DURHAM,—I dine with Sir Francis Chantrey on the 13th, or should have great pleasure in dining with you. Lady Grey writes me word that my pamphlet on the ballot made Lord Grey laugh heartily, which is to me the pleasantest thing I have heard about it. When I come out with my universal suffrage, I hope to put him in convulsions.

                                Ever sincerely yours,
                                      SYDNEY SMITH.

The summer of 1839 brought with it an unexpected accession of fortune, and for the remainder of his life Sydney Smith was a wealthy man. Twelve years before, in a letter to a friend, he had remarked, " The Smiths are a stiff-necked generation, and yet they have all got rich but I. Courtenay, they say, has 150,000*l.*, and he only keeps—a cat!"[2] By the sudden death of Courtenay, without a will, he found himself entitled to a third of his brother's fortune, and thus he was recompensed at last for the sacrifice which he had made as a youth, in far-off Oxford days, to pay a certain little spendthrift's Winchester debts. He immediately took a large and handsome house in Green Street, Grosvenor Square, and it continued to be his

---

[2] Published Correspondence, p. 463.

London home until his death. It was to this house, which he declared to be the essence of all that is comfortable, that he was accustomed to welcome many rising men of a younger generation, towards all of whom his attitude was one of unfailing kindness and goodwill.

The art of the novelist did not find excessive favour in his eyes, but Charles Dickens completely won his heart with "Nicholas Nickleby;" and he told Sir George Philips, in 1838, that he stood out against Dickens as long as he could, but that he had been conquered by him at last. One of the most amusing notes in his published correspondence was addressed to Dickens in the following year, and in it he states that the Miss Berrys had commissioned him to request the novelist to dine with them in order that he might meet three clerical gentlemen, "all equally well-known to you—a Canon of St. Paul's, the Rector of Combe-Florey, and the Vicar of Halberton." [3]

About this time allusions to Macaulay, whom he describes as that "book in breeches," begin to appear in his letters, and there are references also to Carlyle, about whom he feels "very curious." He admired Macaulay's versatility, and believed that he had a genuine love of his country. "He is certainly more agreeable since his return from India. His enemies might, perhaps, have said before (though I never did so) that he talked rather too much; but now he has occasional flashes of silence that make his conversation perfectly delightful. * * * Oh, yes! we *both* talk a great deal, but I don't believe Macaulay ever did hear my voice! Sometimes, when I have told a good story, I have

[3] Published Correspondence, p. 547.

thought to myself, Poor Macaulay ! he will be very sorry some day to have missed hearing that."[4]

Macaulay undoubtedly merited the sly hit, for he was apt to monopolize conversation, and his talk was frequently too pedantic and academical for general society. It must at the same time be confessed that Sydney Smith himself was also inclined to take the lion's share of conversation, but, unlike Macaulay, he talked in his inimitably sparkling and witty fashion of the passing events of the hour, or else seized upon a more serious subject in which every one in the room might reasonably be expected to feel a degree of interest.

The two men met now and then at the house of Samuel Rogers, " that anomalous personage, a rich —poet ! " as Leigh Hunt was accustomed to describe the author of the " Pleasures of Memory ;" and on such occasions the host's brilliant collection of piquant anecdotes was frequently crowded out by the sonorous vivacity of his guests. " Nobody can get a word in when *you* are here ! " was the muttered growl with which the eclipsed poet relieved his overcharged feelings when the room rang with laughter at one of Sydney Smith's droll remarks. But if Sydney Smith sometimes exasperated Rogers, Macaulay quite as frequently ruffled the composure of Sydney Smith, for Mrs. Malcolm relates that she heard the latter declare to Rogers at a breakfast party at the poet's house, " I wish I could write poetry like you, Rogers. I would write an Inferno, and I would put Macaulay amongst a number of disputants, and gag him ! "

Society in the country, especially as age crept on,

"Memoir of Sydney Smith," chap. xi., pp. 234—236

bored him at times not a little, as the following note, written in the winter of 1838-39 to his friend Mrs. Austin, will show :—

[LV.]   Combe-Florey.

MY DEAR MRS. AUSTIN,—I have been dining out two or three times in the country—a state of some suffering, but it reminds you of the value of your own society, and prevents a great deal of anger and heart-burning which the seclusion of any individual produces among his neighbours. You, who are re-velling in the luxuries of Mayfair, may spare a moment of commiseration for diners-out in West Somerset-shire. Mrs. Sydney has recovered her general health, but her eyes are become very weak. How far the virtuous patience of women exceeds that of men! The Hibberts and their children are with us, and as we have every luxury and comfort which can keep off the evils of life, we shall, I hope, get through the winter tolerably well. To see you again will be like the re-surrection of flowers in the spring. The bitterness of solitude (I shall say) is past.

God bless you, dear Mrs. Austin,

SYDNEY SMITH.

During the closing years of his life, when his fre-quent residence in London made him more accessible to general society, men of all ranks and conditions eagerly availed themselves of the privilege of his com-pany, and his house in Green Street became a well-known political and literary resort. Occasionally, in conversation over the breakfast or dinner-table, he would relate to his guests charming snatches of his experience in former years, and sometimes it chanced that George Ticknor or Henry Crabb Robinson was present to play to the best of their ability the part of James Boswell. Ticknor states that at one little breakfast-party at Sydney Smith's, at which Hallam, Tytler, and himself formed the guests, their host told them he would never be a contributor to the *Edinburgh Review* on the common business footing. "When I wrote an article, I used to send it to Jeffrey, and waited till it came out; immediately after which I enclosed to him a bill in these words, or words like them.: 'Francis Jeffrey, Esq., to Rev. Sydney Smith: To a very wise and witty article on such a subject, so many sheets, at forty-five guineas a sheet,' and the money always came."[5]

It is not too much to say that there is scarcely a biography or volume of reminiscences, which deals with the period represented by the closing years of Sydney Smith's life, which has not something to tell concerning his happy sayings and doings, and which does not reflect the mingled admiration and affection which those who knew him best entertained towards him.

The year 1840 opened brightly, and as the days began again to lengthen he declared it was the only sensible spring which he remembered—"a real March of intellect." When any one asked after his health he would exclaim, with a smile, "I am tolerably well, but intolerably old!" "We do not go to town," he wrote to Lady Morley, "until after the Queen's marriage, in order that we may avoid hymeneal and

[5] "Life, Letters, and Journals of George Ticknor," vol. ii. chap. v. p. 123.

bridesmaid conversation." The illness of Mrs. Smith, however, took him to Brighton early in the summer, a place which he advised all rich and rational people living in the metropolis to take small doses of from time to time. In July he was back at Combe-Florey, and at work amongst his parishioners, and in August he was cheered by a visit from his friend, Mr. Monckton Milnes (Lord Houghton).

MRS. GROTE'S SKETCH OF COMBE-FLOREY RECTORY.

Mrs. Grote also came to Somerset at the end of the month, and it was on the occasion of this visit that she made the accompanying sketch of the parsonage, and in the foreground she has depicted her host engaged in animated conversation with one of his faithful retainers. The original picture is a beautiful water-colour drawing, and it is here reproduced by per-mission of Miss Holland. On the back of the frame

of the picture Mrs. Grote has herself inscribed the
following words, "Drawing made by Mrs. Grote in
1840, of Combe-Florey Parsonage, near Taunton, the
incumbent at that date being the Rev. Sydney Smith,
Canon Residentiary of St. Paul's Cathedral.   Presented by Mrs. Grote to his granddaughters, December 24th, 1872, in memory of their great and good
ancestor."   Mrs. Grote, whom he sometimes styled
" the Radical Queen," amused herself, he declared,
with horticulture and democracy—the most approved
methods of growing cabbages and destroying kings.[6]
The autumn found him in great physical distress
from a severe attack of gout, to which complaint was
now added an unwelcome companion in the form of
violent asthma; Mrs. Smith also seemed to be losing
rapidly the good effects of the sea-breezes at Brighton,
for, in a letter to Sir Roderick Murchison, he says,
" Mrs. Sydney has eight distinct illnesses, and I have
nine. We take something every hour, and pass the
mixture from one to another."[7]   One day, when Murchison was dilating in grave tones on recent scientific
discoveries, his friend, the canon, met him with the
unexpected remark, " Your Silurian system is all very
well, Murchison, but I shall think nothing of you till
you have discovered a woman in granite ! "

The death of Lord Holland, which occurred at the
end of October, was an event which moved him deeply.
His own references to the removal of one who had
been a true friend to him for more than thirty years
were very touching, " It is indeed a great loss to me ;
but I have learned to live as a soldier does in war,

⁶ Published Correspondence, p, 558.   ⁷ Ibid. p. 557.

expecting that on any one moment the best and dearest may be killed before his eyes.[*]

The winter of 1840 was spent at Combe-Florey, and as his children and grandchildren gathered around him, and he had also "two months' holiday from gout," the dark days passed rapidly on in the society of his family, and in the midst of his work. His delicate sympathy with the poor, and his diligence in visiting the sick, knew no abatement, and his return to the parsonage from London was always hailed with gladness by old and young. His practical concern for the welfare of the people was manifested in a variety of ways, and nothing which was for the advantage of his poor neighbours was beneath his notice. As a country clergyman he had witnessed the very great hardships inflicted upon the poor through the defective weights and measures of dishonest shopkeepers, and he accordingly addressed a petition to the Somerset magistrates assembled at quarter sessions to rectify this abuse. The matter was at once taken up, and the law was enforced, and the poor labourer's loaf, in years when corn was dear, was no longer habitually under weight.

The spring found him once more in active duty at St. Paul's, and eager also to renew his intercourse with his friends.

[LVI.]   March 12th, 1841.

DEAR MOORE,—I have a breakfast of philosophers to-morrow at ten punctually; muffins and metaphysics, trumpets and contradiction. Will you come?

SYDNEY SMITH.

[*] " Memoir of Sydney Smith " chap x. p. 186.

It is easy to understand the alacrity of the poet's
response to such a summons, for Moore was a great
admirer of his clerical friend, and used to declare that
as a conversational wit he vanquished all the men he
had ever met; indeed, he agreed with Mrs. Jameson
that Sydney Smith's wit generally involved a thought
worth remembering for its own sake, as well as for
the brilliant vehicle in which it was conveyed.

During the last few years of Sydney Smith's life,
the Athenæum Club formed one of his favourite
resorts, and there he might frequently have been seen
chatting pleasantly with friends old and new. The
chief literary club of the metropolis, with its noble
library and unusual social advantages, had naturally
powerful attractions for such a man, and, being himself of an eminently "clubable" disposition, he was
extremely popular within its walls. The social intercourse which he enjoyed in London was rendered still
more agreeable because it was in marked contrast
with his ordinary life at Combe-Florey; and the
quietude of a country life in a secluded Somerset
parsonage—which to a lively man with flagging
physical powers must otherwise have grown irksome
and monotonous—was brightened on the dullest day
by the recollection that in the course of a month or
two his work at St. Paul's would take him back once
more to the crowded town. Sydney Smith felt as
much at home in Piccadilly as Dr. Johnson was in
Fleet Street, and he sympathized with the great
moralist's sententious verdict, that the man who is
tired of London is tired of life. "I have no relish
for the country," is his amusing confession to a
lady friend, "it is a kind of healthy grave. I am

afraid you are not exempt from the delusions of
flowers, green turf, and birds; they all afford slight
gratification, but are not worth an hour of rational
conversation; and rational conversation in sufficient
quantities is only to be had from the congregation of
a million of people in one spot." [9]

Some snatches of his conversation—floating straws
which reveal how the stream ran—are here added to
those which have already been published, as they are
thoroughly characteristic both of the man and of his
method. "Ah! you talk very lightly of common
sense, but you forget, as I said in my lectures, that
two thousand years ago common sense was not invented, and that philosophers would be considered as
inspired by the gods, and would have altars raised to
them for the advice which a grandmother now gives
to a child six years old." "Keep doing, expect little
from others, but cherish confidence in their good-will.
Be thankful." "Great care must be taken that life
does not become wearisome before it is time to
depart." "Nothing convinces me more of the fine
nature of man than the undoubted pleasure derived
from benevolent actions—it seems to be the right way
of living." "Respect for the past is not bigotry, and
we are to beware of the danger of changing too much,
as well as that of not changing at all." "A few
scraps of victory are thrown to the wise and just
in the long battle of life." "Every political eminence is a Tarpeian Rock." Such remarks, uttered
for the most part in casual conversation, afford a
passing glimpse of the wisdom of Sydney Smith;

* Published Correspondence, p. 542.

and the two or three which follow exhibit with
equal clearness the sly and sparkling nature of
his wit. One day the conversation turned upon an
obstinate man who was full of prejudices. Sydney
Smith, who knew his character and opinions, expressed despair,—"You might," said he, "as well
attempt to poultice the humps off a camel's back!"
Preferment in the Church, like fortune in the world,
has a tendency to make men more conservative, and it
was in allusion to this well-known social fact that he
observed drily, "The liberality of churchmen generally is like the quantity of matter in a cone—both
get less and less as they move higher and higher."
"Benevolence is a natural instinct of the human mind.
When A sees B in grievous distress, his conscience
always urges him to entreat C to help him!" "I will do
human nature the justice to say," were his words on
another occasion, "that we are all prone to make *other*
people do their duty." To one who expressed a very
strong opinion, and justified it on the ground that he
was "only a plain man," he retorted that he was
"not aware what the gentleman's personal appearance
had to do with the question." With equal ease he
was able to hit off in some happy phrase the strength
or weakness of the people around him:—"He is like
a barometer, the more you press him the higher he
rises." "His understanding," so runs his criticism
of another man, "is as small and as pinched as the
foot of a Chinese woman." He expressed his admiration of a woman whom he admired, by declaring that
"her looks are the natural food of my soul;" and of
a man, "in his conversation there are the furrows
of long thought." A distinguished American, Mr.

Edward Everett, perhaps pronounced the best criticism on the table-talk of Sydney Smith, when he declared, after listening for a while to his conversation, that "if he had not been known as the wittiest man of his day, he would have been accounted one of the wisest." [1] No more kindly humourist ever breathed than Sydney Smith, and the fact that though he was armed with so sharp a weapon, he went through life surrounded by the love as well as admiration of those who knew him best, says a great deal not only for the goodness of his heart, but also for his habitual self-restraint. [2]

About this period a clergyman from the north of England, who afterwards rose to eminence in the Church, was attracting great attention by his eloquence as an occasional preacher in London. Sydney Smith had heard him refer in the pulpit to the "brilliant reptile's venomed fang," and in the following note to Miss Harcourt, he applies that curious

[1] "Memoir of Sydney Smith," chap. xii. p. 258.

[2] Sydney Smith is reported to have written the following witty lines, but the evidence of his authorship is not quite complete, and therefore they are given in this note with the accompanying traditional account of their origin:—The occasion was an animated discussion at a friend's house on the folly of spending money in jewellery, whereupon a lady retorted that her husband spent twice as much and twice as foolishly at the club; soon after, whist was introduced, and Sydney Smith wrote the following on the back of a card :—

> "We think not that all pleasure fades,
>   Regardless of the knave of *spades*,
>   The sexton and his subs. ;
> We thus as partners play our parts,
>   Our wives on *diamonds* set their *hearts*,
>   We set our hearts on—*clubs !*"

expression in a manner which probably would have surprised the preacher had he heard it.

[LVII.]

56, Green Street,
April 30th, 1841.

DEAR GEORGIANA,—The necessity at a rout of talking to five or six persons at the same time confuses an understanding not remarkable for light and arrangement; but I believe our contract was that I am to call for you in my carriage at eleven o'clock, to encounter the " brilliant reptile's venomed fang," and this I shall do, unless I hear to the contrary.

Yours, dear Georgiana,
Very truly,
SYDNEY SMITH.

Miss G. Harcourt.

" Strange commotion in the political world," wrote Sydney Smith to Lord Carlisle in May, "and I trace all the evil to the attack upon—Cathedrals."

There are one or two significant allusions in the letters which he wrote in the course of this year, which indicate the religious and social changes of the times. " Everybody is turning Puseyite," he writes to Mrs. Crowe ; " having worn out my black gown, I preach in my surplice ; this is all the change I have made, or mean to make." [3] Railway communication had just been made between London and the West of England, and Combe-Florey and the metropolis seemed at one stride to have become near neighbours. " We are just nine hours from door to door," he informs Lady Grey ; " I call this a very serious increase of comfort. I used to sleep two nights on the

[3] Published Correspondence, p. 561.

road, and to travel with a pair of horses is miserable work." [4]

Robert and Sydney Smith were through life devotedly attached to one another, and it is a matter of regret that scarcely any memorials of their brotherly intercourse have been preserved. The accompanying letter from Bobus is therefore valuable, as affording a passing glimpse of the attitude in which the two brothers stood to each other.

[LVIII.]   Cheam, September 5th, 1841.

My dear Sydney,—I go on as most old fellows do, *nec recte nec suaviter!* I should like to be with you at Combe-Florey, but I have not energy enough to go. The number of hours matters little; it is the preparation and the displacement. * * * I am not sorry the Whigs are out. The country was tired of them, I think, and always will be after a short time. There is too much botheration in their politics for our people, who, though they have reformed more than all the nations of Europe put together, do not like scheming and planning reforms when the work is not in hand, and called for by some pressing occasion; they have something else to do, and talking about reform disturbs them. I do myself think the state of things best suited to our condition is a Tory Government, checked by a strong opposition, and under the awe of a tolerably Liberal public opinion. That is pretty near what we shall have if Peel can keep his army in order. But who will answer for that? I am glad to hear so good an account of

[4] Published Correspondence, p. 565.

A a

you all.   God bless you, dear Sydney !   Love to your wife.

Your affectionate brother,
ROBERT SMITH.

In the autumn Sydney Smith was at Munden House, Watford, on a visit to his daughter, Mrs. Hibbert, and as the cold weather returned he retired to his winter quarters at Combe-Florey. " I pass my life in reading. The moment my eyes fail I must give up my country preferment." [5] His habits in the country were always most methodical, and the household arrangements went with the regularity of clock-work. He had prayers at nine, a carriage drive at ten, lunch at one, dinner at eight, prayers at ten, and went to bed at eleven. The services on Sunday were in the forenoon at eleven, and in the afternoon at three. The Sacrament was administered once a month. His sermons seldom exceeded twenty minutes in length; they were plain, pointed, and impressive.

A gentleman, now occupying a prominent position in the world, who, as a child, accompanied his parents on a visit to Combe-Florey, states that he has a vivid remembrance of Sydney Smith's kindness towards him during the delightful days which he spent under his roof. The speaking-trumpet, through which he used to give his orders to the ploughman at Foston, was used by him at Combe-Florey to call the children in to dinner, and the little boy from London was not likely to forget in after-days such a summons. He states that on Sunday at church " he made me weep bitterly by his sermon,

<hr>

[5] Published Correspondence, p. 571.

the only sermon at which I ever wept. The subject
of it, or, at any rate, of the part which moved me,
was the duty of obedience to parents." The present
Rector of Combe-Florey, the Rev. Edward A. Sanford,
M.A., who immediately succeeded Sydney Smith in
the living, adds the additional testimony that, "he

INTERIOR OF COMBE-FLOREY CHURCH.

performed the service in church in a loud, clear, and
reverent voice. His sermons were simple, short, and
practical. He wrote a very illegible hand,[6] so much
so that sometimes he was unable to read his own

[6] Readers of Lady Holland's book will remember Sydney Smith's
own confession on this point: "My writing is as if a swarm of
ants, escaping from an ink bottle, had walked over a sheet of
paper without wiping their legs." Chap. viii. p. 135.

writing. This caused him to employ a shoemaker, who was also his clerk, to copy his sermons, and other manuscripts. For some time after I came here this same man, Thomas Lovelace by name, continued to act as clerk, and more than once after my sermon he would tell me that he had copied one for Mr. Smith on the same text as that on which I had preached. The parish school in Mr. Smith's time was not large or well attended. Still there was one, kept by a dame in a cottage, and I am told that both Mr. and Mrs. Smith took much interest in it, and continually visited it."

The same spirit which animated him at Combe-Florey was conspicuous also in his ministrations at St. Paul's. As a preacher at the Cathedral he was greatly liked; and the plain, direct, and rational character of his sermons, and the deep religious feeling which always seemed to accompany their delivery, caused them to be heard with rapt and reverent attention. One who frequently heard him at St. Paul's speaks of the character of his sermons in almost the same words as those which have already been employed to describe his appearance in the village church of Foston : " His discourses were pointed and practical; they seldom, or never, exceeded twenty minutes in delivery ; and usually, even in the crowded congregations which he drew, the silence was so complete that you might have heard a pin drop." The same lady,—the daughter of an intimate friend of Sydney Smith's—in speaking of the bold attitude which he took in reference to the High Church movement, which was beginning to make its influence felt towards the close of his life, states that she was in the Cathedral when he preached a sermon on the Vestments question, and she recalls hearing him exclaim, "I cannot tolerate," or words to that effect, "this bowing to the east, bowing to the west, and kindred absurdities!" The Tractarian movement, or the " Newmania," as he sometimes termed it, after its real leader, seemed to Sydney Smith distinctly retrogressive in character and dangerous in tendency, and his masculine common sense revolted at the insidious attempt to bring about a revival of what he, as a staunch Protestant, maintained was effete and mawkish superstition.

He was too honest and too courageous a man to conceal the hostility which he felt to a movement which casts a slur on the Reformation, and distracts with its vestments and vain shows the thoughts of men from the chief end of Religion—a life of practical righteousness. "I believe I shall be burned alive by the Puseyites," are his words to a friend on the Continent; " nothing so remarkable in England as the progress of these foolish people. I have no conception what they mean, if it be not to revive every absurd ceremony and every antiquated folly which the common sense of mankind has set to sleep. You will find at your return a fanatical Church of England, but pray do not let it prevent your return. We can always gather together in Park Street and Green Street a chosen few who have never bowed the knee to Rimmon."[1] If Sydney Smith had been ten years younger when the Puseyite movement sprang into existence, it would have had to reckon with the opposition of one of the ablest Church-

[1] Published Correspondence, p. 577.

men of this century—a man who had gained the ear
of his countrymen to an extent to which few ecclesiastics ever gain it, and one to whom the English
people were prepared to listen, not only because of his
unrivalled powers of expression, but also out of the
confidence inspired by unselfish devotion to their good.
He was, however, as the following letter to Miss
Martineau reveals, already an old man, harassed with
increasing physical infirmities, and no longer equal to
the strain of prolonged controversy, and the Puseyites
and their Ritualistic successors have reason to congratulate themselves on that fact, although, as we
shall presently see, they did not entirely escape the
satire of a·man who regarded their teaching with
indignation and their practices with contempt.

[LIX.]   Combe-Florey, Dec. 11th, 1842.

DEAR MISS MARTINEAU,—I am seventy-two years
of age, at which period there comes over one a
shameful love of ease and repose, common to dogs,
horses, clergymen, and even to *Edinburgh Reviewers.*
Then an idea comes across me sometimes that I am
entitled to five or six years of quiet before I die. I
fought with beasts at Ephesus for twenty years. Have
not I contributed my fair share for the establishment
of important truths, and for the discomfiture of quacks
and fools? Is not the spirit gone out of me? Can I
now mix ridicule with reason, so as to hit at once every
variety of opposition? Is not there a story about Gil
Blas and the Archbishop of Granada?

I am just come from London, where I have been
doing duty at St. Paul's, and preaching against the
Puseyites—1. Because they lessen the aversion to the

Catholic faith, and the admiration of Protestantism, which I think one of the greatest improvements the world ever made. II. They inculcate the preposterous surrender of the understanding to bishops. III. They make religion an affair of trifles, of postures, and of garments.

Nothing is talked of in London but China. I wrote to Lord Fitzgerald, who is at the head of the Board of Control, to beg, now that the army was so near, that he would conquer Japan. I utterly deny the right of those exclusive Orientals to shut up the earth in the way they are doing, and I think it one of the most legitimate causes of war. But this argument we will have out when we meet.

I believe **Peel** to be a philosopher disguised in a Tory fool's-cap, who will do everything by slow degrees which the Whigs proposed to do at once. Whether the delay be wise or mischievous is a separate question, but such I believe to be the man in whom the fools of the earth put their trust.

I am living here, with my wife and one son, in one of the prettiest parsonages in England. I am at my ease in point of income, tolerably well for an old man, giving broth and physic to the poor, but no metaphysical dissertations on the Thirty-nine Articles. I have many friends, and always pronounce violent panegyrics on you whenever your name is mentioned.

Sydney Smith.

This letter led to further correspondence, and the remarkable allusion to Peel induced Miss **Martineau** to send her own estimate of that distinguished statesman.

[LX.]   Combe-Florey, 29th Dec., 1842.

DEAR MISS MARTINEAU,—* * * Your character of Peel is striking. I have not studied him enough to verify or dispute it. I doubt if you could have known anything of Francis Horner. I do not think you were invented when he flourished in the world. He was a very remarkable man, and as good as he was wise. The picture you draw of your life is very interesting, as it developes the resources of mental energy, and evinces that empire which a strong mind may obtain over a weak body. Birds and trees, or, as the newspapers would call them, "the vegetable world and the feathered creation," are led into sad mistakes by the weather. The one are beginning to make nests, and the other to put out buds, forgetting the bitterness of March. "You smiled upon me" (says Petrarch), "and I thought it was spring, and my heart put forth the flowers of Hope." Alas! alas! I remain, dear Miss Martineau, with sincere respect and regard, yours always,

SYDNEY SMITH.

His old foe, the gout, attacked him at Christmas, and a few days later he thus moralizes in a third letter to Miss Martineau on the subject.

LXI.]   Combe-Florey, Jan. 4th, 1843.

MY DEAR MISS MARTINEAU,—* * * What an admirable provision of Providence is the gout! What prevents human beings from making the body a larder or a cellar, but the gout? When I feel a pang, I say, ' I know what this is for. I know what you mean. I understand the hint!' and so I endeavour to extract a little wisdom from pain.

SYDNEY SMITH.

The following lines were written more than forty years ago, but the sixth verse is so apt a description of some modern representatives of the same school, that it reads as if it were a criticism on recent events in the Ecclesiastical Courts. Nevertheless, there is a saying that " history repeats itself."

[LXII.]

WHAT IS A PUSEYITE?

" At a recent trial Lord Justice Knight Bruce asked if any of the learned counsel could define a Puseyite, but none of the learned gentlemen attempted a definition."—*vide Morning Herald.*

I.

Pray tell me what's a Puseyite? 'Tis puzzling to de-
    scribe
This ecclesiastic genus of a pious, hybrid tribe.
At Lambeth and the Vatican, he's equally at home,
Altho' 'tis said, he rather gives the preference to
    Rome.

II.

Voracious as a book-worm is his antiquarian maw,
The " Fathers " are his text-book, the " Canons " are
    his law,
He's mighty in the Rubrics, and well up in the Creeds,
But he only quotes the " Articles " just as they suit
    his needs.

III.

The Bible is to him almost a sealèd Book,
Reserve is on his lips and mystery in his look ;
The sacramental system is the torch to illumine his
    night,
He loves the earthly candlestick more than the
    heavenly light.

IV.

He's great in punctilios, where he bows and where he
    stands,
In the cutting of his surplice, and the hemming of his
    bands,
Each saint upon the Calendar he knows by heart at
    least,
He always dates his letters on a " Vigil " or a
    " Feast."

V.

But hark ! With what a nasal twang, betwixt a
    whine and groan,
He doth our noble liturgy most murderously intone ;
Cold are his prayers and praises, his preaching colder
    still,
Inanimate and passionless ; his very look does chill.

VI.

He talketh much of discipline, yet when the shoe doth
    pinch,
This most obedient, duteous son will not give way an
    inch ;
Pliant and obstinate by turns, whate'er may be the
    whim,
He's only for the Bishop, when the Bishop is for him.

VII.

Others as weak, but more sincere, who rather feel than
    think,
Encouraging he leads to Popery's dizzy brink,
And when they take the fatal plunge, he walks back
    quite content
To his snug berth at Mother Church, and wonders
    why they went.

VIII.

Such, and much worse, aye, worse! had I time to
    write,
Is a faint sketch, your worship, of a thorough Puseyite,
Whom even Rome repudiates, as she laughs within her
    sleeve,
At the sacerdotal mimic, the solemn Would-Believe.

IX.

Oh, well it were for England, if her Church were rid
    of those
Half-Protestant, half-Papist, who are less her friends
    than foes.
Give me the open enemy, not the hollow friend ;
With God, and with our Bible, we will the Truth
    defend.

SYDNEY SMITH.

ST. PAUL'S.

CHAPTER XIV.

1843—1845.

Old age—" Honour, love, obedience, troops of friends "—Illness and
death—His place in English literature and life.

A VIVID impression of Sydney Smith still lingers at St.
Paul's, where he is chiefly remembered for the vigilance
with which he watched over the affairs of the Cathedral,
and for the promptitude, tact, and ability he displayed
in connection with the delicate and often complex
business of the Chapter.   At the period when he
became a canon residentiary, there was a considerable degree of laxity in many of the arrangements
connected with the church, and sometimes the services of the minor canons and vicars choral were
performed in anything but a reverent and becoming
manner.   Any irregularity which happened during his
term of residence was certain to attract his notice and
to bring down his censure, for he had the utmost ab-
horrence of the smallest approach to carelessness in the
discharge of duties of so sacred a nature.

The Chapter clerk, the architect, and other officials
connected with the cathedral in his time have borne
witness to his business capacity, and the minuteness
with which he entered into the estimates and accounts
of the Cathedral.   Mr. Hodgson, the then Chapter clerk,

used to declare that Sydney Smith was the first of the canons who for many years had taken the trouble thoroughly to master the affairs of the Chapter; he would investigate the accounts, correct abuses with respect to the appropriation of funds if such were detected, and by every means in his power promote the efficient working of every branch of the business of the Chapter.

It became, indeed, a matter of universal observation that the most brilliant of the canons was likewise the best man of business amongst them. He allowed nothing to be done without obtaining estimates of the expense, and he usually insisted on two or three, in order that he might be able the better to judge of the reasonableness of each. Through his exertions, additional seats were provided in the choir, a better light for the organist was secured, and more appropriate fittings placed in the morning chapel. On one occasion, some necessary work had to be done in the south aisle, and he was informed that the cost in former years had always been 28l. He protested against this as an exorbitant sum for what was required, and taking the matter in hand, found that he could get it done quite as satisfactorily for 14l.; and that was only one illustration amongst many of the way in which he shielded the expenditure from abuse.

He was—especially towards the close of his life when he was constantly in a state of more or less physical pain—a little intolerant of the views of others, and inclined to brush aside proposals of other men in a somewhat abrupt and dictatorial way. He would not believe, for instance, that the cathedral could be warmed, and he declared the idea to be "romantic," and added, "You might as well try and warm the county of

Middlesex;" but, nevertheless, the plan proposed
succeeded, and he was convinced by experience.

There is a tradition at St. Paul's about his musical
predilections, which is not without interest. It appears that music in the minor key always had a most
depressing effect upon him; he felt unnerved by it, and
was compelled to forbid its introduction into the
services, whenever he was in residence.

The last two or three years of his life were unmarked
by special incident, and they naturally witnessed his
gradual withdrawal into comparative privacy. The
breakfast parties which he was accustomed during the
closing years of his life to give at Green Street were
delightful gatherings, and the " feast of reason and the
flow of soul" which marked them, frequently rendered
them memorable occasions in the social experiences of
the guests. His invitations to these assemblies were
models of terse and clear composition, and he usually
contrived in two or three words not only to issue his
mandates, but also to describe the nature of the party
to which he summoned his friends :—

[LXIII.]   56, Green Street, May 10th, 1842.

MY DEAR GEORGIANA—Will you and Egerton breakfast here on Saturday morning, precisely at ten? Real
philosophers, no assertion admitted without reasoning
and strict proof.

                                    Yours affectionately,
                                        SYDNEY SMITH.

Miss G. Harcourt.

Fortunately for himself, his gay spirits remained
with him to the last, his mental vigour was unim-

paired, and though his energy was unabated, his physical powers no longer responded with the same alacrity to the demands made upon them. The railroad was undoubtedly one of the consolations of his old age, and he declared that when he thought of it, and of some other modern changes, he was ashamed that he had not been discontented in his youth with the privations which he then endured! In 1842, he chronicles the fact that the railway had reached a point (where it still remains) only five miles from Combe-Florey. "Bath in two hours, London in six— in short, everywhere in no time!" he gleefully exclaims; and then with a touch of his peculiar humour, he levels a shaft in the old direction—"What we want is an overturn which would kill a bishop, or at least a dean. This mode of conveyance would then become perfect."

In two or three exceedingly witty letters to the *Morning Chronicle*, after admitting that railway travelling is a delightful improvement of human life, and that by it time, distance, and delay are practically abolished, he points out the dangers of the new mode of locomotion, and protests against being locked in the carriages during a journey with the pleasing reflection that he may be "burned alive" ere its conclusion; and he implores "our dear Ripon, or our youthful Gladstone" to come "cheerfully to the rescue" of imperilled and terrified humanity.

The allusion to the "youthful Gladstone" of Sydney Smith's old age, suggests a reminiscence of the Canon of St. Paul's with which the greatest Liberal Premier since Lord Grey has enriched this sketch of his life and times.

[1] Published Correspondence, p. 478.

[LXIV.]   10, Downing Street, Whitehall,
                            Oct. 16th, 1883.

I knew Mr. Sydney Smith for a good many years,
but I was not intimate with him. I remember,
however, one incident that may be told to the credit of
his modesty. I was invited in 1833 to meet him at
dinner in the house of Mr. Hallam, the historian, the
house made famous through *In Memoriam*.

After dinner he spoke to me for some time very
kindly. The conversation at one moment turned on
the improvement which was then becoming visible
in the character and conduct of the clergy. He dwelt
upon the rapid advance and wide scope of this improvement, and good-humouredly added in illustration
of what he had said, ' Whenever you meet a man of
my age, you may be sure he is a bad clergyman.'

                                W. E. GLADSTONE.

It would be unfair to deny that the High Church
Party, whatever—from Sydney Smith's point of view
—may be their theological errors, are entitled to no
small share of credit for the improvement in the zeal
and devotion of the clergy, to which he thus directed
the attention of Mr. Gladstone.

The number of those who met Sydney Smith in
society forty or fifty years ago, is naturally now very
limited, nevertheless Mr. Gladstone is happily not the
only distinguished man in England who is able to
recall with pleasure social hours spent in the witty
canon's company. At a banquet in 1843, at Sir Robert
Peel's, in honour of the King of Saxony, Sir Richard
Owen made the acquaintance of Sydney Smith, and he
has also kindly transcribed for these pages his recollections of the circumstances :—

[LXV.]   Richmond Park, October 15th, 1883.

On the occasion of the visit to London in 1843 of the King of Saxony, attended by Professor Carus, the noted comparative anatomist, Sir Robert Peel, then Prime Minister, was honoured by his Majesty's acceptance of an invitation to dinner in Whitehall Gardens to meet a select party of representatives of administrative, literary, scientific, and artistic notability.

As a literary celebrity, the Rev. Canon Sydney Smith received an invitation; but his relations to the Premier were such, or so slender, as led him to decline the invitation. Sir Robert quite understood the state of the case, and prevailed on his friend Dr. Buckland to see the canon and explain the nature and representative character of the proposed party; whereupon Sydney Smith wrote a genial note to Sir Robert, praying for a "Locus penitentiæ," and Sir Robert replied in the same good-natured strain.

I was honoured with an invitation, my friendly relations with Professor Carus being known to our host. In the drawing-room before dinner, I was struck by the entry of a remarkable figure and physiognomy whose name I did not catch, and noticed also the *empressement* with which Sir Robert Peel advanced to shake hands with this guest. On asking Dr. Buckland, he told me it was Sydney Smith, and related the circumstances of the double invitation.

At the dinner-table Professor Carus and I sat opposite to Sydney Smith and Dr. Buckland, and through their genial wit the time passed jovially. At the dessert, Buckland narrated to his neighbour the circumstance of his having shortly before received from a missionary clergyman in New Zealand, an Oxford

B b

graduate, a box of bones of the great extinct birds of New Zealand, the former existence of which in that island had been deduced from a fragment of such a bone which I had received a few years before. Buckland kindly brought the box at once to the College of Surgeons, and now expatiated to Sydney upon the rapturous pleasure with which I handled and inspected a specimen. 'Oh,' said Sydney, 'no wonder the Professor was overjoyed; it was his—Magnum Bonum!' and another hearty laugh resounded from our end of the table. Sir Robert and his royal guest had more than once turned their faces our way, and I thought they did so with regret at not being within ear-shot of the sources of our hilarity.

RICHARD OWEN.

Amongst those who knew Sydney Smith intimately during the last decade of his life were Earl Granville and Lord Houghton, both of whom were his guests at Combe-Florey. The testimony of Earl Granville tends to confirm the attractive view of his character, which all who personally knew him appear to share:—

[LXVI.]   Walmer Castle, Deal,
                                       Dec. 3rd, 1883.

I met the Rev. Sydney Smith constantly for some years at Lord Lansdowne's, Lord Holland's, Lord Carlisle's, Miss Berry's, and at his and my own house. In his most joyous moods it was impossible not to be struck with the earnestness with which he attacked everything he thought wrong, and defended what seemed to him to be right.

His kindliness was overflowing, and entirely took

away the sting from the repartees which were perpe-
tually bubbling up in his talk. * * *

GRANVILLE.

Lord Houghton's estimate of the character of
Sydney Smith has already been given to the world in
the pages of " Monographs : Personal and Social;" a
volume which contains a graceful and vivid descriptive
sketch not only of the Canon of St. Paul's, but also of
some of the most eminent and remarkable of his contemporaries.

The interest to an admirer of Sydney Smith of
the engraved portrait at the beginning of this book will
perhaps be enhanced by the fact that so competent a
judge as Lord Houghton has pronounced it to be an
excellent likeness of his friend. The original miniature is the property of Miss Holland, and it dates from
the closing years of his life at Foston. The picture is
regarded by the family as a faithful portrait.

A great deal has been said and written at various
times about the irreverence of Sydney Smith, and his
levity on subjects which are usually supposed to lie
beyond the province of the jester. A distinction,
however, must of course be drawn between jokes on
ecclesiastical topics and those which can even re-
motely be termed profane. Some of the most brilliant and caustic witticisms of Sydney Smith were
levelled against members of his own profession, and
his humour seemed to run riot whenever it approached clerical affairs, especially if a bishop hovered
in the distance. It has been truthfully said, however,
that if he sported with the tassel of his pulpit-cushion,
he refrained from playing with the leaves of his Bible,

and as a rule to which it would be difficult to prove exceptions, it can also be confidently asserted that his humour rarely trespassed beyond the harmless limits prescribed by ecclesiastical questions and institutions.

Scarcely anything could well be more misleading or unjust than the persistent assertions, which have been freely made from time to time in certain quarters, concerning that licence of speech which Sydney Smith is supposed to have allowed himself in regard to themes which no right-minded man can ever handle without the deepest reverence. It is satisfactory therefore to be able to declare that if there is one point more than another which has been brought into prominence in the course of the investigations which have led to this book, it is the remarkable unanimity with which those who knew him best declare that there was little or nothing—even in his most unguarded hours—to countenance such a view of his character.

It is admitted by those who are competent to give an opinion on the subject, that no person now living was better acquainted with Sydney Smith or stood higher in his regard, than his attached and valued friend Mrs. Malcolm, who, as Miss Georgiana Harcourt, had constant opportunities during a long term of years of arriving at a correct impression concerning him. The accompanying estimate of the nature of Sydney Smith's wit will therefore be read with pleasure, especially by those who are aware how singularly entitled Mrs. Malcolm is to speak on such a subject :—

[LXVII.]   67, Sloane Street, London, W.
                                    May 19th, 1884.

I have been asked, as an old and intimate friend of

dear Sydney Smith, to give my impressions of his character on some points on which the world in general is much mistaken. It is too commonly imagined that he was merely a wit and humorist, clever in every way, but with little serious thought or feeling. This, however, was very far from the truth. His sense of fun was so great that he could not help sometimes making a joke on *ecclesiastical* subjects, but never on religious topics.

Indeed, charming as his wit and humour were, we used to think him still more agreeable in his serious moods, when his conversation was most interesting and instructive. All his friends will be very thankful to see this phase of his character brought forward.

GEORGIANA MALCOLM.

It is gratifying in this connection to be able to support such a statement with the authority of so keen and competent an observer as Lord Houghton, who assured the writer that he " never knew, except once, Sydney Smith to make a jest on any religious subject, and then he immediately withdrew his words and seemed ashamed that he had uttered them." His wit appeared to play naturally around his own profession, and its flow was not only spontaneous but perpetual; and it is therefore a matter for congratulation that it so seldom led him astray or was of a nature to merit legitimate censure. It is at least certain that no other humorist can be named whose wit and satire were more conspicuously under the sway of a pure and generous heart.

The following tribute to the memory of Sydney Smith will be read with interest by every Englishman who can appreciate the genius and self-denial, the simplicity and strength, which meet in the character of John Ruskin :—

[LXVIII.]   Oxford, Nov. 15th, 1883.

MY DEAR SIR,—I wanted to tell you what deep respect I had for Sydney Smith, but my time has been cut to pieces ever since your note reached me. He was the first in the literary circles of London to assert the value of 'Modern Painters,' and he has always seemed to me equally keen-sighted and generous in his estimate of literary efforts. His 'Moral Philosophy' is the only book on the subject which I care that my pupils should read, and there is no man (whom I have not personally known) whose image is so vivid in my constant affection.

Ever your faithful servant,
JOHN RUSKIN.

Stuart J. Reid, Esq.

The letters which Sydney Smith wrote during the course of 1843, whilst full of mirth and good-humour, reveal in their passing allusions, how much bodily pain he was now called upon to endure ; but if his physical powers were enfeebled, there was no symptom of a decline either in the interest or the ability with which he turned to the affairs of life. At seventy-three he was learning to sing some of Moore's Irish melodies, and at seventy-four, that vivacious little poet himself discovered the grey-haired canon manfully redeeming the enforced seclusion of the gout by copying out the conjugations and tenses of a regiment of French verbs.

His brief notes to absent friends moreover retained their old characteristics, and were distinguished by the quality of lucidity to a degree which would have satisfied Mr. Matthew Arnold himself.

[LXIX.]   56, Green Street, Grosvenor Square, W.,
                                        July 4th, 1843.

MY DEAR GEORGIANA,—We propose to be at Nuneham on Tuesday, the 11th, to dinner, and to stay with you till Friday after breakfast, which statement does not mean " Ask us to stay longer," but is our real ultimatum honestly placed before you ; and I do so because it is of some consequence to know when guests go away as well as when they come. You will be glad to hear that I can walk better, and that Mrs. Sydney is at last really recovered.

Ever, dear Georgiana,
Yours affectionately,
SYDNEY SMITH.

Miss G. Harcourt.

[LXX.]   Combe-Florey, Sept. 16th, 1843.

DEAR LORD LANSDOWNE,—I received the haunch of venison, but as there was no intimation on the package from whence it came, I could not thank my benefactor as I now do. It struck me at the time that to send venison to the clergy without saying from whence it came was an act of profound and high-principled piety.

Ever sincerely yours,
SYDNEY SMITH.

A visit which Moore paid to Combe-Florey in the course of the summer, and which is referred to in the following letter to Miss Harcourt, was a source of unmixed pleasure both to poet and parson :—

[LXXI.]   Combe-Florey, September, 1843.

My DEAR GEORGIANA,—I am retiring from business as a diner-out, but I recommend to attention as a rising wit, Mr. Milnes,[2] whose misfortune I believe it is not to be known to you. * * * Little Tommy Moore sent me some verses after leaving Combe-Florey, which I send to you even though they are laudatory of me, trusting in your constant goodness and kindness to the subject of his panegyric.[3] Moore has one or two notes, and looks when he is singing like a superannuated cherub.

You and I are both inn-keepers, and are occupied from one end of the week to the other in looking after company. I think we ought to have soldiers billeted upon us. My sign is the " Rector's Head," yours the " Mitre." My Devonshire curate and his wife are just come, and are drinking in the tap. Mrs. Sydney and I are tolerably well; I have quite got rid of my gouty knee, but the hot weather makes me very languid.

I suppose you will soon be at Bishopthorpe, sur-

---

[2] Lord Houghton.

[3] In Lady Holland's " Memoir " of her father there is a genial letter from Moore written from Bowood at the end of August, 1843, and with it is the poetical tribute referred to, which concludes in the following strain :—

" Rare Sydney ! thrice honour'd the stall where he sits,
And be his every honour he deigneth to climb at !
Had England a hierarchy formed all of wits,
Whom, but Sydney, would England proclaim as its Primate ?
And long may he flourish, frank, merry, and brave,
A Horace to feast with, a Pascal to read !
While he *laughs* all is safe ; but when Sydney grows grave,
We shall then think the Church is in danger indeed."

" Memoir of the Rev. Sydney Smith," by his daughter, Lady Holland, chapter x. page 191.

rounded by the sons of the prophets. What a charming existence to live in the midst of holy people, to know that nothing profane can approach you, to be certain that a dissenter can no more be found in the Palace than a snake can exist in Ireland, or ripe fruit in Scotland. To have your society strong and undiluted by the laity, to bid adieu to human learning, to feast on the Canons, and revel in the Thirty-Nine Articles. Happy Georgiana!

My curate's name is Tin Lin. I must go and do the honours. God bless you, dear Georgiana. Look at the map where those dwell who have a regard and affection for you, and make a strong mark in the neighbourhood of Taunton.

SYDNEY SMITH.

Writing in October to Lady Holland, he gives his impressions of Mr. and Mrs. Grote, and his verdict on public affairs :—

[LXXII.] Combe-Florey, Oct. 9th, 1843.

MY DEAR LADY HOLLAND,— * * * I have been making a tour to Ilfracombe and Lynton. The moral of my journey is, I am too old to make journeys, and had better stay at home. Mr. and Mrs. Grote have been staying here some days. She is very clever and very odd.[4] Grote is a reasonable and reasoning Radical, with manners a little formal but very polished. The Lansdownes were here for a night. Dr. Holland

---

[4] "I remember at a party being seated by Sydney Smith, when Mrs. Grote entered with a rose-coloured turban on her head, at which he suddenly exclaimed, 'Now I know the meaning of the word grotesque!'—Kemble's "Records of Later Life," vol. ii. p. 65.

has not been to Jerusalem, but to Africa, and is now
supposed to be in Brook Street. His wife and family
are here. Mrs. Sydney and I are tolerably well, but I
feel weak, and want a more bracing air.

My prediction is that Peel will be driven out by the
concessions to be made to Ireland, and that it will fall
to Lord John to destroy the absurd Protestant Church
in that kingdom. It will hardly do to pay the priests;
the thing is beyond that now. You *must* remove the
flockless pastors. I have heard nothing of Samuel
Rogers. I want very much to show him Combe-Florey,
but he holds us cheap. Moore came and wrote verses
upon us; he was so much pleased. I hope to see you
soon, dear Lady Holland, and in vigorous health.
Till then, believe me, your affectionate friend,

SYDNEY SMITH.

One of his last literary efforts was a petition to
the House of Congress at Washington, to "institute
some measures for the restoration of American
credit, and for the repayment of debts incurred and
repudiated by several of the States." The petition,
which was caustic and vigorous, was followed by one
or two letters to the *Morning Chronicle*, explaining the
matter to the English public. His own loss was insignificant, but he was incensed by the cool audacity with
which the State of Pennsylvania—at that time the rich-
est in the Union—repudiated the interest on its bonds,
and he felt it a public duty to expose an act of bad
faith, which he declared to be—taking all the circumstances into consideration—without parallel, and
without excuse. Some of the American newspapers
hurled abuse upon him for the open charge of dis-

honesty which he fearlessly made and maintained; but the sympathy of the best people in the States was with him in his endeavour to restore the nation, in one direction at least, to moral health.

In a letter from Pennsylvania, when the excitement was at its height, Fanny Kemble says: " You ask me what is said to Sydney Smith's petition? Why the honest men of the country say, ' 'Tis true, 'tis pity; pity 'tis, 'tis true.' It is thought that Pennsylvania will ultimately pay and not repudiate, but it will be some time first." [5] Letters from America, many full of gratitude, and some full of abuse, reached him by almost every post; and people in this country, smarting under the burden of the income-tax, or some other grievance of a real or imaginary nature, kept appealing to him to champion their cause. Sometimes moreover peace-offerings from American admirers arrived, as well as letters :—

[LXXIII.]   56, Green Street, Grosvenor Square,
                                    December 7th, 1843.

SIR,—I am much obliged for your present of apples, which I consider as apples of concord, not discord. I have no longer any pecuniary interest that your countrymen should pay these debts, but as a sincere friend to America, I earnestly hope they may do so.

                    I am, sir, yours,
                                    SYDNEY SMITH.

Mr. Morgan.

Sydney Smith was what he here describes himself —a sincere friend of America, too sincere a friend,

[5] " Records of Later Life," vol. iii. p. 19.

indeed, to indulge in flattery. He recognized more clearly than most of his contemporaries, the vast and ever-increasing resources of the great Republic of the West, and his criticisms were meant to quicken and conserve a fine sense of honour amongst those in whose veins ran English blood. It was because he was jealous for the reputation of the American name that he pounced like a hawk on the public repudiation of debt, and every honest man in the United States has reason to be grateful to him for the part which he took at a grave crisis in the national history. Several distinguished Americans were personal friends of the canon's, and the American people to-day are amongst his greatest admirers.

There was one matter connected with the Americans, however, which he resented deeply, and which he never forgave, even when his grievance against the Pennsylvanians was both forgiven and forgotten, and that was the habit of expectoration. Concerning this very disagreeable subject, it may perhaps be enough to quote his own words: "All claims to civilization are suspended in America till this secretion is otherwise disposed of. No English gentleman has spat upon the floor—since the Heptarchy."

One of the most intimate of Sydney Smith's clerical friends was his colleague at the cathedral, the Rev. R. H. Barham, known wherever English literature is appreciated as the author of the inimitable *Ingoldsby Legends*. Mr. Barham (who was a Minor Canon of St. Paul's and Rector of St. Augustine and St. Faith's, London) was a genial, unassuming, and delightful companion, and was respected and admired by all who knew him. He died in June, 1845,—four months after

Sydney Smith, and his " Life "—which was written a number of years ago by his son, the Rev. R. H. D. Barham—contains several amusing reminiscences of his distinguished friend, who was a frequent visitor at his house.

Barham relates a very droll story which he heard Sydney Smith tell at the house of Charles Dickens in December, 1843, when the company included, amongst others, Rogers, Talfourd, Albany Fonblanque, Maclise, and Forster.   A well-known publisher called one day, it appears, on the Canon, and after a respectful and sympathetic allusion to his recent losses in American Bonds, threw out the hint that he might make good the ravages in his fortune by writing a novel to appear in the orthodox three volumes, for which the gentleman to whom he was indebted for the hint would be glad to make a liberal offer on the spot. " Well, sir," said Mr. Smith, after some seeming consideration, " if I do so, I can't travel out of my own line—*ne sutor ultra crepidam*, you know ; I must have an archdeacon for my hero, to fall in love with the pew-opener, with the clerk for a confidant, tyrannical interference of the churchwardens, clandestine correspondence concealed under the hassocks, appeal to the parishioners, &c., &c." " With that, sir, I would not presume to interfere ; I would leave it all entirely to your inventive genius."   " Well, sir," replied the Canon with urbanity, " I am not prepared to come to terms at present ; but if ever I *do undertake* such a work, you shall certainly have the refusal." [6]

His high spirits, as he moved to and fro amongst

[6] "Life of R. H. Barham," by his son, vol. ii. pp. 167-8.

his friends in town, never seemed to desert him, and the most ordinary topic of conversation was enough to call his wit into play.   At the Athenæum one day, talking with the Bishop of London, the conversation glided towards two members of the club, one of whom was preternaturally taciturn and the other not less loquacious.   " I never shall feel satisfied," said Sydney Smith, " till a marriage is brought about between a son of L—— and a daughter of D——.   The progeny would be quite perfect.   I would not undertake the marriage though, for D—— never could keep silence so long, and would infalliably interrupt the ceremony."

" Many thanks," he writes at the beginning of 1844 to Charles Dickens, " for the ' Christmas Carol,' which I shall immediately proceed upon in preference to six American pamphlets I found upon my arrival, all promising immediate payment ! " [1]

In a letter to his daughter he states that, whilst he looks as strong as a cart-horse, he is so deficient in nervous energy that he is unable to get round the garden without resting once or twice.   In the spring he was in residence at St. Paul's for the last time, and living, as he himself describes it, " among the best society in the metropolis, at ease in my circumstances ; in tolerable health, a mild Whig, a tolerating Churchman, and much given to talking, laughing, and noise."[1]

To an invitation from Mr. Greville, he despatched the following amusing reply :—

[LXXIV.]   Green Street, May 13th, 1844.

MY DEAR SIR,—On the 23rd (if you will allow me to bring thirteen people to dinner) I shall be most happy

---

[1] Published Correspondence, p. 614.

to dine with you, but as I can hardly calculate on such expanded hospitality, I must, I fear, decline your kind invitation, and try to entertain my thirteen in Green Street.

I remain, my dear sir,

Very truly yours,

SYDNEY SMITH.

Old acquaintances who met him in what proved to be the last summer of his life were filled with unspoken apprehensions as they witnessed the rapid failure of his bodily health, and it was only too obvious even to a casual observer, in spite of the buoyant attitude of the man, that his bright and useful career was approaching its close.

In July, on the last Sunday of his term of residence, he uttered his final words from the pulpit of St. Paul's, and he seems even then to have realized himself that the end was not distant. His text was Exodus xx. 8 :—" Remember the Sabbath day, to keep it holy," and the sermon that followed was a solemn and vigorous plea for the righteous observance of the Fourth Commandment. He lays stress on the fact that the spiritual life can only prosper when due attention is given to the means of grace, and that self-examination is the peculiar duty which the Sabbath brings round to every Christian man. " Can a man be religious," he asks, " who assigns no time for thinking of religion? Can the most perfect state of the human heart be obtained by absolute neglect and inattention? Is godliness the only great good upon this earth which can be had for nothing, and does the piety which fits a man for heaven grow up spontaneously in

the mind of him who neither asks it of God, nor strives
to gain it by the exertion of his reason, and the subju-
gation of his passions? The man who has no rules, no
place, no day for that which requires the strictest rules
for its guidance, the noblest places for its exercise, and
the most solemn day for its recurrence?

It is in the absence of our usual occupations and at
the season of leisure, that conscience regains her empire over us, and that man is compelled to hear the re-
proaches of his own heart; the mind turned inwardly
on itself beholds the melancholy ravages of passion,
the treacherous power of pleasure, and the sad waste
of life. Every recurring Sabbath properly spent is a
fresh chance of salvation.

I must suspect the virtue and religion of that man
who imagines he can attain the quality or the excellence
without submitting to the rules and practices by which
the excellence and the quality are to be attained; who
believes he can be a good Christian without Sabbaths
and without prayer, and reach the end without submitting to the means."

Contrary to his usual custom, the sermon did not
end without a personal reference, and the simple
words of farewell which were then spoken must
afterwards have flashed with strange pathos upon
the memory of some who perhaps heard them un-
moved that day:—"I never take leave of any one,
for any length of time, without a deep impression
upon my mind of the uncertainty of human life, and
the probability that we may meet no more in this
world." When Sydney Smith quitted the pulpit of
St. Paul's that day, he had made his last appeal to the
great congregation which assembled within its walls.

At the end of July he was back at Combe-Florey, and one who visited him about this time found him completely at home with the villagers, and most attentive to their needs—old age, it was obvious, made no difference in his devotion to the sick and the poor. "After breakfast his laboratory was full of poor people where they not only had their griefs listened to, but where they also received at the hand of the rector medicines calculated to meet their manifold sicknesses." His generosity led him to bring down to Somerset a poor family living in London; they needed a change of air, which they were not able to obtain, so he took them home, and kept them for three weeks, and they went back to town "extremely corpulent, and with no other wish than to be transported after this life to the paradise of Combe-Florey." [*] In a letter to Miss Harcourt he gives a somewhat startling account of his own character and appearance, and manages in a passing allusion to extract a graceful compliment to that lady out of the incident of the visit of his musical friends :—

[LXXV.]   Combe-Florey, July, 1844.

MY DEAR GEORGIANA,—Nothing can exceed the beauty of the country; I am forced to admit that. Mrs. Sydney also revives. I see the Westmorelands are come to England. Lady Westmoreland produced a great impression upon me. Pray recall me to her recollection, mentioning my leading attributes of mind and body. Slender, grave, silent, and modest, but don't overdo me in this last quality. I thought her a very interesting woman.

I have treated that poor musical family, the K——s,

* Published Correspondence, p. 616.

C C

with three weeks of fresh air, as they were all sick and
fading away. They came here on Monday, so that you
will find me when we meet, much improved in my
singing—not in singing your praises, for in that
exercise I have long been perfect.

Believe me always,

Your affectionate friend,

SYDNEY SMITH.

Miss G. Harcourt.

During the sultry weather in August, he spent a
few weeks at Sidmouth, and in a letter to Lady Grey,
he states that he has nothing to do but to look out of
a window. "The events which have turned up are
a dog and a monkey for a show, and a morning con-
cert. I say to every one who sits near me on the
marine benches, that it is a fine day, and that the prospect is beautiful; but we get no further—I can get no
water out of a dry rock." [9] In the same letter he states
that he has just received intelligence that "a Sydney
Smith" had arrived in New York, and that society
there had been divided between two proposals, one
of which was to give him a public dinner, and the
other to tar and feather him! The question, however,
was set at rest by the surprised traveller's declaration
that he was a journeyman cooper.

September found him at Combe-Florey, in a state
of extreme lassitude; without strength, indeed, as he
ruefully declared, even to "stick a dissenter," and
early in October alarming symptoms appeared. Dr.
Holland was immediately summoned, and as the patient
revived somewhat under his care, it was determined

[9] Published Correspondence, p. 619.

that he should proceed at once to his house in Green Street, in order that he might have the advantage of his son-in-law's medical skill. The journey to town was accomplished with tolerable ease, and once there, surrounded by the love of his family and the sympathy of a wide and attentive circle of friends, his strength again revived for a few weeks, and he was able almost to the close of the year to take carriage exercise, and to enjoy in his own home the intercourse of many old and attached friends.

It was in this brief " Indian summer" of his life that he penned the accompanying letter,—almost the last he ever wrote,—to his friend Miss Harcourt. It was written two or three weeks after the note to Lady Grey with which his published correspondence ends, and it reveals the same kindly thought for others which ran like a golden thread through all his intercourse with those around him.

[LXXVI.] 56, Green Street, Grosvenor Square,
November 27th, 1844.

MY DEAR GEORGIANA,—I received great pleasure from your agreeable letter. It was full of pleasant details pleasantly told, and convinced me (of which I was thoroughly convinced before) that I was not forgotten. Such a collection of conspicuous men are seldom assembled under one roof. The one amongst them I can the least digest is S——, who is anything but a polished corner of the Temple ; he seems to me to have hardly courtesy enough for the common purposes of life, but this opinion may possibly proceed from my knowing him so little.

I had a severe attack at the beginning of October

of giddiness, which, with faintness and breathlessness,
remained upon me for many days, and left me, as I
have since remained, in a state of great weakness. I
believe I am getting better.

Many thanks to the Archbishop for his kind message. I had not heard of any fall he had met with till
you mentioned his recovery. May I always hear of
his misfortunes (if any are to happen to him) in the
same way. Poor Lord Grey is pining away in great
pain. * * * I grieved sadly for poor Lætitia Mildmay.
I suppose her anxiety for her brother was the real
cause of her death.

Give, if you please, dear Georgiana, my kindest regards to each member of the family, and a double
portion to the Archbishop, and believe me always,

Your sincere friend,
SYDNEY SMITH.

Lady Holland has given a touching picture of her
father's last days, and of his gentle and loving
thought for those around him, and of the cheery
patience with which he endured his increasing infirmities. He was greatly touched by the incessant inquiries which friends and strangers alike made at the
door concerning his health, and he remarked that it
gave him pleasure to be the object of such attentions,
because " it shows that I have not misused the powers
intrusted to me." [1] The words are significant, and
are in keeping with the fact that through life he was
impressed with the responsibility which his gifts imposed upon him, and eager to direct even his wit to
the common advantage.

[1] " Memoir of Sydney Smith," chap. xii., p. 259.

Many a visitor who at other times had left that well-known house in Green Street in merry mood and with heightened respect for its master, now went slowly up to its hospitable door with an anxious and heavy heart. During his illness those about him saw how completely he acted on his own maxim, " Take

LAST LONDON HOME—56, GREEN STREET, GROSVENOR SQUARE.

short views, hope for the best, and put your trust in God." His thoughtfulness for others revealed itself in a variety of beautiful ways, and it was manifest that he anticipated the end with the humble confidence of a thorough Christian. Years before he had declared that he was persuaded that the real pang of death

was the remembrance of an ill-spent life, and now he
had not that to trouble him.

One of the last acts of his life was to present the
living of Edmonton, a piece of patronage which fell
to him as Canon of St. Paul's, to the son of the former
vicar, and the stay of his old and sorrowing mother.
The family had no claim whatever upon him, beyond
the common ones of worth and need, and that act of
patronage, so delicately bestowed, was in keeping with
the generous spirit of his life, and disposes effectually
of the charges of interested motive which were sometimes made against him when he opposed the
Ecclesiastical Commission.

Lord Grey, who was seven years his senior, was
lying ill at Howick when his old friend was dying in
Green Street, and tender messages were continually
passing between the two sick-rooms in Northumberland and London. His brother Bobus, who only
survived Sydney Smith a couple of weeks, crept to his
bedside, and did all that brotherly love could do
to cheer the sufferer.

As death approached, the thought of his long
lost and much loved son Douglas, appeared frequently
to be present to his mind, and sometimes in the
gathering gloom he even called him to his side. The
end came quietly, and it found him in the firm possession of that Faith, Hope, and Charity, of which
he had so often preached to others. On Saturday
evening, February 22nd, 1845, life's work honourably
accomplished, he entered into rest, in his seventy-fifth
year. He was buried at Kensal Green Cemetery, on
Friday the 28th; the funeral was strictly private, and
only a few of his nearest relatives and friends were

present; but in spirit at least, there was no section of the nation which was not represented by the sorrow round that grave.

There is an official handbook to the vast and silent city of the dead in which he sleeps, and yet so late as the summer of 1883, the name of one of the truest benefactors of the English people who rests within its gates, was not judged of sufficient importance to be included in the pages of that manual. Those who wish to make a pilgrimage to the grave of Sydney Smith, will therefore be glad to know that they can easily find it, by following the north walk until they are opposite the entrance to the catacombs. Turning to the left at that point, they will discover in the fifth row from the walk a raised tomb of Portland stone, which bears on a weather-beaten marble slab the following half-obliterated inscription :—

TO PERPETUATE,

WHILE LANGUAGE AND MARBLE STILL REMAIN,

THE NAME AND CHARACTER OF

THE REV. SYDNEY SMITH,

ONE OF THE BEST OF MEN.

HIS TALENTS, THOUGH ADMITTED BY HIS CONTEMPORARIES TO BE GREAT,

WERE SURPASSED BY HIS UNOSTENTATIOUS BENEVOLENCE,

HIS FEARLESS LOVE OF TRUTH, AND HIS ENDEAVOUR TO PROMOTE THE HAPPINESS OF MANKIND

BY RELIGIOUS TOLERATION AND RATIONAL FREEDOM.

HE WAS BORN THE 3RD OF JUNE, 1771.

HE BECAME CANON RESIDENTIARY OF ST. PAUL'S CATHEDRAL, 1831.

HE DIED FEBRUARY 22ND, 1845.

With the solitary exception of a small painted window (erected through the efforts of his successor, Mr. Sanford) in the church at Combe-Florey, the grave in Kensal Green is the only memorial to Sydney Smith which England has to show. At Foston, where he spent the best years of his life, there is not so much as a line upon the walls to commemorate his presence, and the church, which will ever be associated with the magic of his name, is rapidly falling into decay. Even in St. Paul's to this hour, the astonished visitor inquires in vain for the monument of Sydney Smith, and there is no trace whatever in the great metropolitan cathedral of its world-renowned canon.

He himself, it is evident, anticipated no such neglect. In a letter in his published correspondence, written in the last decade of his life to a friend who held a prominent government appointment in the far East, he intimates that he hopes that he shall live to see him again, but that he is going slowly down the hill of life, and that if he delays his return to England much longer, he will find him "at St. Paul's, against the wall."

It is reported that Dean Milman on his death-bed urged that a memorial to Sydney Smith should be placed in the cathedral, but nearly forty years have rolled away since that quiet funeral at Kensal Green, and the matter is still in abeyance. Strangers from distant shores occasionally still wander from aisle to aisle of that vast and stately church searching for some memorial of Sydney Smith, only at last to learn with chagrin that, amid all the monuments which there silently appeal to the living on behalf of the dead, no place has yet been found " at St. Paul's, against the wall," for even so much as a line on marble or brass to the memory of a man whom Macaulay admired as a great reasoner, and whom he termed the greatest master of ridicule who has appeared in England since Swift.

Sydney Smith will, however, remain in English Literature—though widely different to both men—as welcome and as irrepressible a figure as Samuel Johnson or Thomas Carlyle, and his words—no less than theirs—by virtue of their commanding common sense, will still leap to men's lips to replenish and enliven the dull controversies of the passing hour. Even though he thus requires no monument to perpetuate his fame, the reputation of the English nation for gratitude will be permanently diminished, if the century is allowed to slip on without some appropriate recognition within the walls of St. Paul's of one who was not only a man of genius, but a courageous friend of the people, who was always ready, in spite of obloquy and reproach, to employ his dreaded and dazzling gifts in the interests of the neglected, the desolate, and the oppressed.

It was not given to Sydney Smith to sound the depths or soar into the heights of religious experience, and he had but little sympathy with the fervour and enthusiasm which marked the evangelical revival of the Eighteenth century, or the missionary zeal which glowed in the Nonconformist Churches with so much warmth at the beginning of the Nineteenth. His sweeping charges against the Methodists at home, and the Missionaries abroad, are indeed as unsatisfactory, and more unjust than anything else he ever wrote, and Robert Hall was right in maintaining that such attacks "stabbed Religion itself through the sides of Fanaticism." But in the main, with a courage and consistency which are beyond challenge, he devoted his genius to the public good, and used the trenchant weapons with which nature had endowed him in the cause of liberty, progress, and reform.

Nevertheless he was not a perfect man, and would have scorned to pose as such; indeed Lord Murray, who knew him intimately through a long term of years, and saw him under a great variety of circumstances, declared that he was more severe towards himself than he was towards any other person. He loathed all pretence; and, through his passionate desire not to seem better than he was, he frequently failed to do himself justice.

The world has long recognized the wit of Sydney Smith, and has travelled more slowly to the recognition of his wisdom, but those who knew him best and tested his heart in life's common experiences of joy and sorrow, place foremost to-day in their tender reminiscences of the man—his worth.

THE GRAVE OF SYDNEY SMITH.

INDEX.

ADDINGTON, The, Cabinet, p. 97.
Addison, Joseph, *note* 29, 118.
Advice, A little moral, 112.
Advice concerning low spirits, **222**.
Aitkin, Miss, 232.
Alderley Church, **Cheshire, Sermon at**, 196.
Alison, Rev. Archibald, 46, **95**.
Allen, Dr. John, physician and librarian at Holland House, 121; early life, 122; literary pursuits of, 123; social influence with **the** Whigs, 124; Lord **Byron's** opinion of, 124; elected **Warden and** afterwards Master **of Dulwich** College, 125; his **room at Holland** House, 125; **the violence of** his language **towards** all oppressors, 125; **the goodness of** his heart, 125; report to, about Foston, 172; arguments with, 277.
America, Repudiation of State Bonds by, 378; Sydney Smith **a** sincere friend of, 379.
Amesbury, Town of, 22.
Ampthill, Living of, 203.
Aristotle, The philosophy **of, 135**, 136.
Ashburton, **Lady,** *note* **164**.
Athenæum **Club, Membership of**, 348, 382.
Austin, Mrs., Letter **to, 343**.

BACON, Lord, Sydney Smith's view of his philosophy, 135.
Ball, Mr. Edward A.: reminiscences of Sydney Smith at Taunton, 321, *note* 323.
Ballot, Pamphlet on the, 337-340.
Banks, Sir Joseph, Royal Institution founded at house of, 133.

Barham, **The Rev. R. H., friendship** with, 380.
————, The Rev. R. **H. D.,** **381**.
Baring, Sir Francis, 13.
Bennett, Lady Mary, 196.
Bentham, Jeremy, 120.
Berkeley Chapel, Mayfair, Morning preacher at, 132; popularity in pulpit of, 132; residence near, 319.
Bernard, Sir Thomas, assists Sydney Smith to obtain preachership at the Foundling Hospital, 129; friendship with, 130; philanthropic devotion to the London poor of, 130, 131; Sydney Smith invited through his influence to **lecture at** the Royal Institution, 133.
Berrys, The Miss, 341, 370.
Beverley, Meeting of clergy at, **244**.
Bishopthorpe, 164, 181, 376.
Bishopric, Sydney Smith **and a**, 294.
Blake, **Admiral, 300**.
Boileau, **84**.
Bonds, **American**, Repudiation of, 378, **380**.
Boswell, James, 344.
Bowood, 13, 163, 273.
Bristol, Sydney Smith presented to a stall at, 262; preacher in the cathedral, 265; excitement occasioned by his sermon to the Mayor and Corporation of, on the "Rules of Christian Charity," 267.
Brougham, Henry, Lord, **Commencement of** Sydney Smith's acquaintance with, 41, 45; one of the first group of *Edinburgh Reviewers*, 55, 56; statement by,

concerning the origin of the *Review*, 57, 58 ; his contributions to the first four numbers, 61 ; his rapidity as a writer, 73 ; a provoking contributor, 73 ; Maclise's pen-and-ink sketch of, 73 ; energy and versatility of, 74 ; the lights and shadows of his character, 74, 75 ; a member of the Friday Club, 95 ; an audacious criticism by, 98 ; a visitor at Holland House, 125 ; a grumble by Jeffrey at, 154 ; a guest at Heslington, 159 ; a visitor at Foston, 192 ; an advocate of Catholic Emancipation, 254, 264 ; and of Parliamentary Reform, 287.

Brown, Dr Thomas, 57, 95.

Buckland, Dr., 369.

Buller, Charles, M.P., Death of, 71.

" Bunch," 190, 191.

Buonaparte (Napoleon), 86, 138.

Burke, Edmund, M.P., 6, 29, 118, 314.

Byron, Lord, 119, 124, 314.

CAITHNESS, Countess of, 238.

Campbell, Lord, 71.

———, Thomas, 41.

Camperdown, Countess of, Reminiscences of, 237

Canning, Right Hon. George, M.P. Eton school-days, 10 ; friendship with Bobus Smith, 10 ; writer in the *Microcosm*, 11 ; remark on, on Bobus's choice of language, 14 ; attitude towards Catholic claims, 240, 257 ; death of, 258.

Canova, 120.

Canterbury, Archbishop of, 265.

Carew, Lady, 238.

Carlisle, (fifth) Earl of, neighbour and friend to Sydney Smith at Foston, 173 ; gives the new rector free access to the library at Castle Howard, 174 ; a remark to, by Sydney Smith on Castle Howard, 174 ; congratulation from, on an unexpected accession of fortune, 221.

———, (sixth) Earl of, school-fellow at Eton with Bobus Smith,

10 ; friendship with Sydney Smith of, 173, 174, 352, 370.

Carlisle, (seventh) Earl of : Sydney Smith's opinion of him as a boy, 211 ; his character and career, 211, 212.

Carlyle, Thomas, 66, 76, 341, 393.

Castle Howard, 163, 173, 174, 221.

Castlereagh, Viscount, 142.

Cemetery, Kensal Green, 268, 390 ; inscription on the grave of Sydney Smith at, 391.

Chambers, Dr. Robert, 56, 58.

Chronicle, Morning, Letters to, 367, 378.

Clarence, H.R.H. the Duke of, 120.

Clergy Residence Bill, 150.

Cliffords, The noble family of, 246.

Club, Athenæum, 348, 382.

———, The Friday, 95, 96.

Cockburn, Henry, Lord, 95, 227.

Coffee, Abstinence from, 115.

Coleridge, Samuel Taylor, 62, 68.

Combe-Florey, Exchanges Foston for the living of, 269 ; removal to, 269-271 ; the rectory of, 272 ; the parish clerk of, 273 ; visit of Jeffrey to, 275 ; Sydney Smith in his study at, 277 ; kindliness to the poor of, 278 ; the " foreign deer " in the rectory grounds of, 279 ; anxiety to encourage habits of thrift amongst the villagers, 279, 280 ; visit of Lord John Russell to, 304 ; attention to his parishioners at, 305 ; his journeys to and fro between London and, 317, 319 ; neighbourly intercourse at, 320, 321 ; reminiscences of his visits to Taunton, 321-323 ; a candid criticism by the parish clerk of, 334 ; Mrs. Grote at Combe-Florey, 345 ; the " poor man's loaf " at, 347 ; in church at, 354 ; a child's remembrance of the rector's sermon, 354 ; the parish school of, 356 ; life-long devotion to the sick and poor evinced at, 385 ; last days at, 386 ; memorial window in church of, 392.

Commandment, The Fourth, 383.

Commission, Ecclesiastical, 103 ; Letters to Archdeacon Singleton on the, 326-332.

Constable, Archibald, 60, 61, 213.
Conversation, Some snatches of Sydney Smith's, 349.
Corner, Exclamation, 174.
Corse, Gloucestershire, Proposal of Sydney Smith to exchange Foston for living of, 268.
Croker, J. W., 317.
Crowe, Mrs., 352.

DAVENPORTS, The, of Capesthorne, 195, 237.
Davenport, Dennis, Esq., M.P., Letter to, 245.
——— —, Edward, Esq., Letters to, 202, 225.
———, W. Bromley, Esq., M.P. See Preface.
Davy, Sir Humphrey, 119, 133.
—— Lady, Letters to, 308, 325.
Devon, North, Scenery of, 304.
Derwentwater, 39.
Dickens, Charles, 108, 109, 341, 382.
Dundas, The party of, in Scotland, 70.
Durham, (first) Earl of, a visitor at Holland House, 119; proposal to visit Foston, 223; friendship with Sydney Smith, 228; an uncompromising champion of Reform, 284; an advocate in the Grey Cabinet of the ballot, 337.
———, Letters to, 204, 224, 228, 340.
Duty, Sydney Smith's deep sense of, 155, 305, 388.

EDINBURGH, Arrival of Sydney Smith at, 39, note 39; acquaintances at, 40; chief citizens of, 41; social life of, 41; lodgings at, 43; house to which he brought his bride, 44; Episcopalians of, 46, 100; description of Charlotte Chapel at, 46.
——— Review. See Review, Edinburgh.
Edmonton, Living of, 390.
Eighteenth century, Evangelical revival of, 393.

Eldon, Lord, 241, 261.
Electors, Letter to, on the Catholic question, 254.
Epitaph on Sydney Smith at Kensal Green Cemetery, 391.
Erskine, Lord Chancellor, appoints Sydney Smith to the living of Foston, 144.
———, Letter from, 144.
———, Henry, 41, 227.
Everett, Mr. Edward, on the table-talk of Sydney Smith, 351.
"Excursion," The, Wordsworth's, 69.

FALSTAFF, 257.
Ferguson, Adam, 41.
Ferrier, Miss: her saying about visits to country-houses, 195.
Fielding, Henry, Remark upon Aristotle by, 136; at Taunton, 300.
Fitzroy Chapel, Sydney Smith, morning preacher at, 132; note, now St. Saviour's Church, St. Pancras, 132.
Fitzwilliam, Earl, 219.
Flaxton, Village of, 175.
Foston, Sydney Smith presented to the Chancery living of, by Lord Erskine, 144; letter from Lord Erskine on the subject, 144; nature of the new appointment, 145; condition of the parsonage-house at, 151; a rash valuation of, by the village carpenter, 151; an unexpected problem — resign or build? 151; Lady Holland's account of her father's first interview with the parish clerk of, 152; the new rector's report to Jeffrey of the place, 153; his reluctance to leave London, 155; Mrs. Sydney Smith's first impressions of York, 156; the children's hour at, 163; restlessness of his early years in Yorkshire, 167; resolves to build, 168; Mrs. Sydney Smith's account of the building of Foston Rectory, 168-170; the arrival at the new rectory, 171; life at, 172; neighbourhood of, to Castle

Howard, 173; kindness of Lord Carlisle to the new rector of, 173; Sydney Smith's directions for reaching, by road, 174; description of a journey to, by rail, 175; antiquity of Foston Church, 176; a reminiscence of the services at, sixty years ago, 176; condition of the edifice, 176; pulpit in, 177; desolate aspect of the church and burying-ground, 178; the "Screeching Gate" at the rectory, 179; position and appearance of the rectory, 179, 180; Mr. E. V. Harcourt's recollections of visits to, 181, 182; Sydney Smith's practical benevolence to the villagers of, 182, 183, 184; his farming operations at, 184; a strict master, 185; fondness for children, and employment of, at, 185, 186; occasional severity towards, 186; an anecdote concerning the "Immortal," 188; his manner of life at Foston, 189; Bible-class at, 189; his consideration for his servants, 190; the household at, 190; "Bunch" and her successor, 191; Lord Brougham's reminiscences of a visit to, 192; the village carpenter—Jack Robinson, 192; a specimen of his handicraft, 193; Kilvington, the coachman, 193, note 194; the first break in the family circle at, 194; Sydney Smith's visits from, to the country-houses of his friends, 194, 195; isolation at, 199; versatility of his pursuits at, 199; his own statement concerning his outlay upon the rectory of, 201; strict economy of his household, 202; his difficulties as a farmer with Scotch sheep, 213; moral courage, as a country clergyman, 217; an accession of fortune, 221; his love of his home at, 229; popularity with his parishioners, 230; an amusing adventure on the road near, 233; guests at the rectory, 236; Miss Leycester's recollections of a visit there, 237;

friendship with Lord and Lady Wenlock at, 250; statement concerning intercourse with, by their daughter, the Hon. Mrs. J. Stuart Wortley, 251; Lord Macaulay's impressions of Foston, 255; Jeffrey's visit to, 256; marriage of Emily Smith to Mr. Hibbert at church of, 262; nomination of rector of, to a stall at Bristol, 262; proposal to exchange Foston for the living of Corse, Gloucestershire, 268; removal to Combe-Florey, 269; sorrow of the villagers at Foston on his departure, 270; servants from, at Combe-Florey, 271; wanted—the bracing air of, in Somerset, 272.

Foundling Hospital, Sydney Smith appointed preacher at, 129; stipend, 129; connection with, terminated by removal to Yorkshire, 129.

Fox, Right Hon. Charles James, M.P., 118, 123, 140; death of, 141, 258.

——, General Charles, 122.

——, Henry (fourth Lord Holland), as a boy, 211.

French, Opinion of, 256.

Frere, J. H., at Eaton with Bobus, 10; a contributor to the *Microcosm*, 11.

Fry, Elizabeth, 205.

GAME LAWS, 214-218.

Gate, Screeching, at Foston, 179.

"Gazette Extraordinary"—a Reform squib, 286.

George III., 239.

—— IV., 240, 260, 282.

Girdlestone, Rev. Canon, successor to Sydney Smith at Halberton, 281.

Gladstone, Right Hon. W. E., M.P., 338; acquaintance with Sydney Smith, 367.

—————————————, Letter from, 368.

Goderich, Lord, 261.

Goethe, 37.

Goldsmith, Oliver, 6.

Gordon, Mr. Alexander, pupil of Sydney Smith, 92.
——, Dr. John, 227.
Gout, Sydney Smith on the, 310, 360.
Granville, Earl, K.G., friendship with Sydney Smith, 370.
——————, Letter from, 370.
Grattan, Right Hon. Henry, M.P., 240.
Grenville, Lord, 240.
——, Mr.: impressions of Sydney Smith at St. Paul's, 313.
Greville, Mr., Letter to, 382.
Grey, (second) Earl, K.G.: friendship with Lord Holland, 118; Sydney Smith a visitor to, at Howick, 160; life-long friendship with, 161; fondness for the clergy, 204; appoints Sydney Smith a Canon Residentiary of St. Paul's, 293; passes the Reform Bill, 302; retirement from public life, 312; last messages to, 390.
——————, Letter from, 293.
——, Countess, 224.
——————, Letter to, 311.
——, (third) Earl, K.G., 161.
——, Lady Elizabeth, 181.
——————, Georgiana, 161.
"Griffin, Gregory," 11; Queen Charlotte's remark upon, 12.
Grote, George, 337.
——, Mrs., 347, 377, note 377.
Guillemard, Mr., Letter to, 309.
Guizot, M., 74.

HALBERTON, Obtains living of, with stall at Bristol, 269; connection with, 280; controversy about vicar's rights, 281; traditions of, at, 282.
——————, Letter to the Vestry of, 281.
Hall, Rev. Robert, 303.
Hallam, Henry, 344, 368.
Harcourt, The late Egerton Vernon, Esq., J.P.: recollections of Sydney Smith at Foston, 181.
——————, Miss Georgiana: life-long friendship with Sydney Smith, 316, 351, 372, 385, 387. See also Malcolm, Mrs.

Harcourt, Miss Georgiana, Letters to, 316, 325, 333, 352, 375, 385, 387.
——————, Miss G. (Mrs. Malcolm), Letter from, 372.
——————, Rev. William Vernon, 244, 249; lines on the marriage of, 250.
——————, Right Hon. Sir William Vernon, M.P., 181. See also Preface.
——————, Dr. Vernon, Archbishop of York, 164; anecdotes of, 165-166; gets Windham Smith to the Charterhouse, 235; visits Foston to marry Miss Emily Smith to Mr. Hibbert, 263; a remark concerning, 265; a final message to, 388.
Hayward, Mr. Abraham, Q.C., 306.
Heptarchy, The, and English habits, 380.
Herder, 37.
Heslington, Village of, 129; hires a house at, 157; description of, 157; guests at, 159; quietude of, 159; acquaintance with the squire of, 160; the children's hour at, 163; birth of Windham at, 168; removal from, to Foston, 170.
Hibbert, Mr. Nathaniel, of Munden, Herts, son-in-law of Sydney Smith, 263, 318.
——————, Mrs. N., Emily, younger daughter of Sydney Smith, 15; marriage of, 263; subsequent life of, 263; accompanies her father to Paris, 318; Sydney Smith at Munden, 354.
Highlands, Tour in, 80.
Holland House, Dinner parties at, 83; Sydney Smith becomes a visitor at, 117; historical and literary associations of, 117; Sydney Smith's description of, 126; society at, 314.
——————, Vassall, Lord, at Eton with Bobus Smith, 10; criticism of Jeffrey's English, 64; on Brougham's versatility, 74; friendship with Sydney Smith, 117; unique associations of Holland House, 117; his hospitality, 118 "nephew of Fox, and friend of

'Grey," 118; his guests, 119; Sydney Smith's estimate of his character, 120; John Allen's relationships with, 121; exerts his political influence on behalf of Sydney Smith, 144; offers the living of Ampthill, 203; meets Sydney Smith in Paris, 256; George IV.'s attitude towards, 261; death of, 346.

Holland, Lady, Friendship with, 121; her imperious nature, 121; her treatment of Macaulay, 121; and of Sydney Smith, 121; *note*, health of, 310.

——————, Letters to, 203, 264, 377.

——————, (fourth) Lord : Sydney Smith's opinion of, as a boy, 211; succeeds to the peerage, 211; British Minister at Florence, 211; death at Naples, 211; his character, 211.

——————, Sir Henry, M.D., Anecdote of Bobus Smith and, 15; marriage to Saba, eldest daughter of Sydney Smith, 310; wanted, a prescription from, 318; African travels of, 377; attends Sydney Smith in last illness, 386.

——————, Saba (wife of Sir Henry): birth in Edinburgh, 93; origin of Christian name of, 94; married to Dr. Henry Holland at Foston, 94; death, 94; authoress of the "Memoir of the Rev. Sydney Smith," 95; childish recollection of a visit to Sonning, 145; her account of her father's first interview with the parish clerk of Foston, 152; remark as a child when her father was from home, 163; on her father's treatment of servants, 190; illustrations of his wit in the pages of her "Memoir," 197; statement by, concerning her father's visit to Newgate with Mrs. Fry, 206; her account of her father's last illness, 388. See also Preface.

——————, Miss (daughter of Sir Henry Holland), 168, 345, 371. See also Preface.

Honeymoon, Lines on Mr. and Mrs. Wm. Harcourt passing their, at the Lakes, 250.

Horner, Francis, Friendship with, 41, 45; a founder of the *Edinburgh Review*, 56; his special subject as a reviewer, 57; his early contributions, 61; removal to London, 61; Jeffrey writes to place before him the *pros* and *cons* about the *Review*, 62; son of an Edinburgh merchant, 69; his education, 69, 70; his pronounced Liberal views, 70; called to the English Bar, 70; his mastery of finance, 70; enters Parliament through the influence of Lord Henry Petty, 70; his remarkable speeches on the question of the Currency, 71; Lord Campbell's remark concerning him, 71; early death, 71; monument in Westminster Abbey, 71; last interview with, 72; Sydney Smith's estimate of his character, 72; the character of his work in the *Edinburgh Review*, 72; a member of the Friday Club, 95; kindness to Sydney Smith in London, 107; "Knight of the Shaggy Eyebrows," 107; described by Sydney Smith as a "Literary Tiger," 108; introduces Sydney Smith to his London circle of friends, 110; a visitor at Holland House, 125; verdict of, on Sydney Smith's qualifications as a lecturer on moral philosophy, 134; writes the political epitaph of the Ministry of "All the Talents," 142; Jeffrey's complaints to Horner about his flagging interest in the *Review*, 153; a visitor at Foston, 159; death of, 227; remark of Sydney Smith to Miss Martineau upon character of, 360.

Hospital, Foundling. See "Foundling Hospital."

Houghton, Lord, 138, 345, 370, 371, 376.

Howard, Mr. Geo., M.P. See Preface.

Howard, John, 205.
————, Philip, Letter to, 272.
————, Hon. Mrs., Lines entitled the " Poetical Medicine Chest" presented to, by Sydney Smith, 323.
Howley, Archbishop, 7.
Humboldt, Alex. von, 119.
Hume, David, 41.
————, Joseph, M.P., **14.**
Hunt, Leigh, 342.

" IMMORTAL," The, Sydney Smith's Foston carriage, **188,** 193, 200, 321.
" Ingoldsby Legends," 380.
Institution, Royal, Sydney Smith a lecturer at, 133 ; his immediate success, 133 ; his own estimate to Jeffrey and Whewell of the Lectures, 134, 135 ; Horner's account of them, 134 ; Lord Jeffrey's criticism on, when published, 137 ; a remark by Sydney Smith on the subject to Lord Houghton, 138.
Ireland, 86, 377
Irishmen, Society of United, 87.
Irreverence, Alleged, of Sydney Smith, 82, 371, 372, 373.
Irving, Rev. Edward, 308.
————, Washington, 119.

JEFFREY, Francis, Lord, a contemporary of Sydney Smith at Oxford, 19 ; opinion of the University, 19 ; position in Edinburgh, 41 ; guest of Sydney Smith, 45 ; *Edinburgh Review* projected at his house, 55 ; his statement to Dr. Robert Chambers on the subject, 56 ; Brougham's description of Jeffrey's "doubts and fears," 57 ; the house in Buccleuch **Place,** 59 ; Jeffrey's contributions to the early numbers of the *Review,* 61 ; his reluctance to become a journalist, 62 ; his early years, 64 ; at Queen's College, Oxford, 64 ; Lord Holland's verdict on his stay at Oxford, 64 ; called to the Bar, 64 ; marriage, 65 ; poverty, 65 ; death of Mrs. Jeffrey, 65 ; his second wife, grandniece of John Wilkes, 65 ; Jeffrey as a critic, 66 ; his knowledge of men, 66 ; his treatment of Wordsworth, 67 ; Southey's indignation, 69 ; connection with the Friday Club, 95 ; a visitor at Holland House, 125 ; criticism on Sydney Smith's lectures at the Royal Institution, 137 ; difficulties with the *Review,* 153 ; Sydney Smith's account of Jeffrey's position in Edinburgh, 155 ; a visitor at Heslington, 159 ; a return visit from Sydney Smith, 226 ; Jeffrey and the "Pantheon Meeting" on Reform, 228 ; Lord Rector of Glasgow University, 228 ; visits Foston, 256 ; friendship with Mrs. Hibbert, 263 ; a guest at Combe-Florey, 275 ; appointed Lord Advocate of Scotland, 276 ; a remark of Sydney Smith upon, 276 ; the services of, to the nation, 335 ; a demand note to, 344.
————, Lord, Letters to, 98, 137, 154.
Jeffreys, Judge, 300.
Johnson, Dr. Samuel, 6 ; at Oxford, 18 ; opinion of the Scotch, 42, 168, 314, 348, 393.
————, Thomas, village tailor at Foston, An altercation with, 188.
Jones, Sir William, 95.
Journalism, Former position of, 95.
Jury, Trial by, Difficulties in the way of introducing, in Australia, 315.

KAYE, Annie, 170, 191, 271.
Kemble, Fanny, *note* 377, 379.
Kilvington, Wm., coachman to Sydney Smith, 193 ; chair in his possession, 193 ; death of, *note* 194.
Kinglake, Mr. Robert Arthur, J.P., Reminiscences by, of Sydney Smith's "Dame Partington speech" at Taunton, 299-302. See also Preface.

D d
..

Kingsley, Rev. Charles, 217.
Kirkham, Village of, in Yorkshire,
- 175; a roadside encounter near,
233.
Kindness of Sydney Smith to
children, at Nether Avon, 23,
34, 35; at Howick, 161; at Heslington, 163; at Foston, 185, 189;
at Weston House, 237; at
Combe-Florey, 347, 354, 356,
385.
Kindness of Sydney Smith to the
poor and aged, at Nether Avon,
35; at Foston, 182, 183, 184,
270; at Combe-Florey, 278, 347.

LAMB, Charles, 62.
Lambton, John George, M.P. See
Durham, Earl of,
Lambton Castle, 204, 226; Syd-
uey Smith's admiration of, 229.
Law, Poor, Amendment Act, 311;
Law, Reform of Criminal, 206-209.
Lansdowne, Marquis of, 13, 119,
206, 257, 261, 370, 377.
——————————, Letters to,
207, 209, 273, 317, 325, 332, 375.
Lauderdale, Earl of, 122, 226, 229.
Leef, David, 271.
Lennox, Lady Sarah, 118.
Lethbridges, The, of Sandhill Park,
Taunton, 300, 322.
Leycester, Miss, Reminiscences of
Sydney Smith by, 196, 237.
Leycesters, The, of Toft, 195, 237.
Leyden, John, 96.
Liddon, Dr., of Taunton, 278.
——————, Rev. Canon, note 278.
Lindsay, Theophilus, 224.
Lisle, Alice, 300.
Liverpool, Earl of, 142, 241, 257,
261.
Loaf, The poor man's, 347.
Londesborough, Temporary gift of
living of, to Sydney Smith, 246;
description of village, 246; his-
torical and literary associations
of, 247; anecdotes of Sydney
Smith at, 247, 248.
London, Bishop of, 382.
——————, Sydney Smith's love of,
348.
Longman, Mr., 324.

Lovelace, Thomas, parish clerk at
Combe-Florey, 273; 356.
Luttrell, Henry, 120, 307, 314.
Lyndhurst, Lord, 258, 262, 269.
Lynton, 304.
Lyttleton, Lord, on the writings of
Sydney Smith, 78.
Lyveden, (first) Lord, nephew of
Sydney Smith, 15.

MACAULAY, Lord, contributor
to the Edinburgh Review, 76, 119,
121; visits Foston, 255, 341, 342.
Mackenzie, Henry, 96.
Mackintosh, Sir James, 13, 62, 70,
100, 120, 159, 161; death of, 309,
318.
Maclise's sketch of Brougham, 73.
Malcolm, Mrs., A statement by, con-
cerning Sydney Smith and Ma-
caulay, 342; letter from, on the
alleged irreverence of Sydney
Smith, 372. See also Harcourt,
Miss G.
Marcet, Dr., 110.
Markham, Archbishop, 145, 151.
Martineau, Miss H., Letters to,
358, 360.
Matlock, Opinion of, 38.
"Medicine Chest, The Poetical,"
323.
Melbourne, Lord, 326.
Methodists, Sydney Smith's unjust
strictures upon the, 80, 393.
Metternich, Prince, 120.
Microcosm, 10; republished by
Charles Knight, 11; Queen
Charlotte a reader of, 12.
Mildmay, Mrs. H., 317.
Mills, Molly, 190.
Milman, Dean, 392.
Missions, Foreign, misrepresented
by Sydney Smith, 81, 393.
More, Hannah, 24, 33.
Moore, Thomas, 98, 119, 235, 275,
375, note 376.
——————————, Letter to, 347.
Morgan, Mr., Letter to, 379.
Morley, Earl of, 306.
——————, Countess of, 273; Sydney
Smith a frequent guest at Sal-
tram, 305; witty letters to, 305;
Mr. Hayward's estimate of, 306;
her appreciation of Sydney

Smith, 306 ; visits Combe-Florey, 208 ; remark to, 344.

Morley, Countess of, Letters to, 306, 308, 310.

Morpeth, Lady Georgiana, 212, 219, 222.

———— ————, Letters to, 212, 220, 230.

Munden House, Watford, Herts, the home of Mrs. Hibbert, 263, 354.

Murchison, Sir R., 346.

Murray, Lindley, 157.

————, John, A., Lord Advocate, 41, 56, 57, 159, 318, 394.

Music, Effect of, in the minor key, upon Sydney Smith, 366.

NABURN, Village of : a tardy arrival at church, 248.

Nelson, Lord, 139.

Nervousness, Remedies against, 115.

Nether Avon, Village of, 22 ; curate at, 22 ; seclusion of new position, 23 ; establishes Sunday and day-schools, 23 ; Yew-Tree Walk at, 25 ; church and parsonage of, 29 ; description of village, 30 ; notes, 30, 31 ; apathy of villagers, 32 ; beneficial results of the schools at, 35.

" Newmania," 357. See also Puseyite Movement.

Newton, Sir Isaac, 85.

Nick, Poor, epitaph upon Mrs. Pybus's dog, 52.

Nonconformists, missionary zeal of, caricatured by Sydney Smith, 80, 393.

OBSERVANCE, Sunday, 383.

O'Connell, Daniel, 240, 260, 294.

Olier, Maria, mother of Sydney Smith, 4. See Smith, Maria.

" Orchards," Sydney's, at Foston, 184.

Ossory, Earl of, 203.

Owen, Sir Richard, Letter from, 369.

Oxford, Sydney Smith student at, 16 ; obtains a fellowship at New College, 17 ; dreary life at the University, 18 ; Jeffrey's impressions of the University, 19.

PAINTERS, Modern, Ruskin's Sydney Smith's appreciation of, 374.

Panic, The financial, of 1826, 253.

" Pantheon Meeting," The Edinburgh, 227.

Paris, Visits to, 255, 319.

Parties, Breakfast, at Green Street, 366.

————, Supper, at Doughty Street, 127.

Partington, Dame, 295, 298-302.

Paul's, St., Cathedral, Appointed Canon of, 293 ; description of the atmosphere of, in winter, 309 ; popularity as a preacher at, 312 ; appearances in the pulpit of, 313 ; characteristics of his sermons at, 357 ; attention to the business of the Chapter of, 364 ; music at, 366 ; last words at, 383 ; a strange omission in the monuments of, 392-3.

Peel, Right Hon. Sir Robert, M.P., 257, 289, 326, 368, 378.

Perceval, Right Hon. S., M.P., 142, 147, 150.

Peterloo Massacre, 219, 223.

Petrarch, 360.

Petty, Lord Henry, M.P., 40, 70, 206. See also Lansdowne, Marquis of.

Philips, Sir George, of Manchester, 194, 224, 237, 241.

Pisa, Horner's journey to, 72.

Pitt, Right Hon. William, M.P., Death of, 140, 258, 300.

Playfair, Professor, 40, 57, 95 ; death of, 227.

Plunket, Lord, 240.

Plymley, Peter, Letters on the subject of the Catholics by, 146 ; sensation they created, 146 ; Peter's reverend brother, a representative man, 147 ; characteristics of the letters of, 148, 295.

Poor, Kindness towards. See Kindness.

Prestwich Church near Manchester, 196.

Prisons, Proposed rules for, 207, 209.

Prisoners, Treatment of, note 215.

Pulpit in Foston Church, 177.

Puseyite, The, movement, 352 ; antagonism towards, 357 ; his own account of his reasons against, 358-359; "What is a Puseyite?" 361.

Pybus, Miss Amelia, Marriage to Sydney Smith of, 51; her father, 51; epitaph by Sydney Smith on Mrs. Pybus's dog at Cheam, 52; married at Cheam Church, 52; conduct of brother of, 53; her mother's kindness to, 53; prospects of, as bride, 53-54; sale of her mother's pearls, 109. See also Smith, Mrs. Sydney.

QUEBEC, 156.
Queen Victoria, Marriage of, 344.

RAIKES, Robert, 24.
Railway, The, 352, 367.
Reading, Love of, 113, 200, 277.
Reform, Parliamentary, Interest in, 282; Lord Grey's proposals for, 284; second reading of Reform Bill, 286; "Gazette Extraordinary," 286; the struggle in Parliament, 291; Bill thrown out by the Lords, 292; indignation in the country, 292; Reform meeting at Taunton, 297; the Dame Partington speech, 298-302; the Reform Bill becomes law, 303.
Regent, The Prince, 120.
Reid, Dr. Thomas, 41.
Review, Edinburgh, 51; Sydney Smith's account of its projection, 55; Lord Jeffrey's statement concerning it, 56; Lord Brougham's reminiscences of its origin, 57; the first contributors to, 57; comparison of the various accounts of, 57-68; Jeffrey's house, Buccleuch Place, at which the scheme was mooted, 59; Sydney Smith revises the first articles, 60; published by Constable, 60; the secrecy observed by the literary conspirators, 60; their agreement with Constable, 61; immediate success of, 61; Jeffrey appointed editor, 63; the ability with which he conducted it, 65; Francis Horner, Brougham, and Sydney Smith as contributors,

72-78; an anecdote of Brougham and Sydney Smith, 98; the opinion in London on its opening numbers, 108; Allen as a contributor, 123; growing influence of, 133; Jeffrey's indignation at the apathy of his colleagues, 153-154; Sydney Smith's motives for writing reviews, 154; his remark on the editor's payment, 155; work for, at Heslington, 159; exposes the Game Laws in the pages of, 214-217; champions the climbing-boys in, 218; declines to revise a manuscript for, 231; advocates the Catholic claims in, 242; last contribution to, 259; Jeffrey's resignation of the editorial chair of, 276; the contributions of Sydney Smith to, collected and republished, 334; services in the pages of, 335-336; the payment of his articles to, 344; strictures in the pages of, upon the Methodists, and on Foreign Missions, 80-81, 393.
Revival, Wesleyan, misunderstood by Sydney Smith, 80, 393.
Rivers, Sir Thomas, on Weimar, 37.
Robertson, Dr. William, 41.
Robinson, Henry Crabb, 344.
———, Jack, village carpenter at Foston, 190, 192.
Rogers, Samuel, 119, 198, 235, 307, 314, 342.
Romilly, Sir Samuel, M.P., 70, 73; friendship with Sydney Smith, 110; a visitor at Holland House, 120; a guest at Heslington, 159.
Rumford, Count, 119, 133.
Ruskin, John, Letter from, 374.
Russell, Lord John, M.P., 40, 66, 119, 284, 304, 326, 332, 378.

SALISBURY, City of, 22; Bishop of, 24.
Salisbury Plain, 23, 30.
Sanford, Rev. Edward A., 355, 392.
Satire, characteristics of Sydney Smith's, 82, 136, 248.
Scarlett, James (Lord Abinger), 110.
Schiller, Frederick, 37.

Schools, Day and Sunday, established at Nether Avon, 23.

Scotch, Character of, 42.

Scotland, Definition of, 42; travel in, 42.

Scots Greys, Remark upon a young officer of, 321

Scott, Sir Walter, 41, 95, 97, 210.

Sermons, Publishes first volume of, 48; dedication to Lord Webb Seymour, 49; practical character of, 49-50 early sermons in London, 111; benevolence of their tone, 128; characteristics of, 128; at St. Paul's, 312; a criticism of, by Mr. Grenville, 313.

Sewell, Dr., Warden of New College, Oxford, on Sydney Smith's connection with the University, 16.

Seymour, Lord Webb, 40; friendship with, 48; dedicates first book to, 49, 70; death of, 227.

Sharp, Mr. Richard, M.P., 314.

Sheep, Scotch, 213.

Sheil, Richard Lalor, M.P., 241.

Short, Dr. Vowler, 252.

Shute, Dr., Bishop of Salisbury, an advocate of Sunday-schools, 24.

Sidmouth, Viscount: family motto, 14, 142.

Simpson, Rev. F., 176.

Singleton, Archdeacon, Letters to, 103; letters to, on the Ecclesiastical Commission, 326-332.

Skiddaw, 39.

Slavery, Abolition of, colonial, 311.

Smith, Adam, 41.

———, Cecil, Birth of, 4; character as a lad, 5; educated with eldest brother at Eton, 6: Accountant-General of Madras, 15; death at the Cape, 15.

———, Courtenay, Birth of, 4; sent to Winchester under Sydney Smith's care, 6; runs away from school, 8; subsequent school triumphs, 9; follows Bobus to India, 15; rises to the rank of a Supreme Judge, 16; sudden death, 16; his Winchester debts, 18; death of, 340.

———, Douglas, 94, 138, 168, 172,

182, 194, 196, 199, 203, 204, 205, 235, 251, 252; death of, 268; inscription on grave of, 269, 390.

Smith, Emily, birth of, 138. See Hibbert, Mrs.

———, Maria, mother of Sydney Smith, daughter of a Languedoc emigrant, 4; her resemblance to Mrs. Siddons, 4; her character and influence on her children, 4; Sydney's indebtedness to her, 4; early death of, 5.

———, Robert, of Devonshire extraction, 2; abandons a business career in youth, 2; restlessness and eccentricity, 2; marriage, 3; character, 3; death, 3; Sydney's description of his father's old age, 3; his opposition to his son's desire to follow the Law, 20; fondness for uncommon Christian names, 93; visited by Sydney, 205; last years at Bishop's Lydiard, 222.

———, Robert Percy, M.P. (Bobus), Birth of, 4; educated at Eton, 6; his classical attainments, 10; early friendships, 10; starts the *Microcosm*, with his schoolfellows Canning and Frere, 10; interview with Queen Charlotte, 12; his career at King's College, Cambridge, 13; called to the Bar, 13; married at Bowood by Sydney to Miss Vernon, 13; Advocate-General at Calcutta, 13; enters Parliament, 14; his wit, 14; anecdotes of, 14-15; death, 15; life-long friendship of the two brothers, 353; devotion of, to Sydney at the last, 390.

——— ———, Letter to his brother Sydney in old age, 353.

———, Saba. See Holland, Lady.

———, Sydney: birth at Woodford, Essex, 1; armorial bearings, 2; his father, 2; character, 3; his mother, 3; her influence, 4; his brothers and sister, 4, 5; his first school, 6; admitted scholar at Winchester, 6; his experiences at Winchester school,

7, 8, 9; proceeds to New College, Oxford, 16; obtains a fellowship, 16; his poverty at Oxford, 17; generosity to youngest brother, 18; choice of a profession, 19; desire for the Bar, 19; his father's attitude, 20; resolve to enter the Church, 20; ordination, 22; Curate of Nether Avon, 22; solitude of his new position, 22; traditions of his curacy, 23; establishes schools on Sundays and week-days, 23, 24; the squire of Nether Avon, 25; condition of the poor, and his comments upon it, 26, 27, 28; the church and parsonage, 29, 30; visits Williamstrip Park, 31, 32; life at Nether Avon, 35; appointed travelling tutor to Michael Beach, 36; new plans, 37, 38; arrival in Edinburgh with his pupil, 39; his criticisms of the Scotch, 42; houses he occupied in Edinburgh, 43, 44, 45; attends University lectures, 46; occasional preacher at Charlotte Chapel, 46, 47; publishes first book, 49; its character and contents, 49, 50, 51; marriage to Miss C. A. Pybus, of Cheam, 51; Epitaph on Mrs. Pybus's dog, 52; prospects, 53; an opportune gift, 54; *Edinburgh Review*,—its projection, 55; his contributions to the early numbers, 61; quits Edinburgh, 61, his characteristics as a reviewer, 77; courage, humour, and common-sense, 78, 79, 80; errors of judgment, 80, 81; his ecclesiastical jokes, 82; unpublished "Treatise on Wit and Humour," 83-86; relations with pupil, 88-93; birth of eldest daughter, 94; origin of name, Saba, 94; death of his mother, 94; intimacy with Dugald Stewart, 94; other Edinburgh friends, 95, 96; Scott and Leyden, 96, 97; Jeffrey and the *Review*, 99; arrival in London, 100, first impressions, 100; his position in the Church, 103-105; first London home, 108; birth of eldest son, 109; Mrs. Smith and the pearls, 109; new acquaintances, 110; "a little moral advice," 112; remedies against nervousness, 115; regarded as a dangerous man, 116; introduction to Holland House, 117; friendship with Lord Holland, 120; attitude of Lady Holland, 121; Sydney Smith and the aristocracy, 126; his poverty, 126; portrait at Holland House, 127; home in Doughty Street, 127; position in the Church, 128; evening preacher at the Foundling Hospital, 129; friendship with Sir Thomas Bernard, 130; morning preacher at Berkeley Chapel, 132; lecturer at the Royal Institution, 133; sudden popularity, 134; his own account of the Lectures, 135; Lord Jeffrey's verdict upon them, 137; removes to Orchard Street, 138; birth of Douglas, 138; presentation to Foston, 144; the "Peter Plymley" letters, 146; the sensation they created, 146; the parsonage-house at Foston, 151; the parish clerk's verdict on the new rector, 152; Sydney Smith's clerical prospects, 155; publishes two volumes of sermons, 156; removal to Yorkshire, 157; his house at Heslington, 157; acquaintance with the village squire, 160; friendship with Earl Grey, 160; Sydney Smith at his own fireside, 162; kindness to children, 163; Dr. Harcourt and Sydney Smith, 164; the Archbishop's guest at Bishopthorpe, 164; birth of Windham, 168; builds Foston Rectory, 168; settles at Foston, 170; life at Foston, 173; friendship with the Earl of Carlisle, 173; Castle Howard, 174; in church at Foston, 176; the rectory and grounds, 178; Mr. E. V. Harcourt's recollections, 181; village doctor, 183; kindness to the villagers, 183; "Sydney's Orchards," 184;

Sydney Smith as a farmer, 184; an anecdote of the "Immortal," 188; the rector's Bible-class, 189; kindness to servants, 190; the furniture at the rectory, 193; visits Manchester, 194; preaches at Alderley, 196; Miss Leycester's recollections of him at Prestwich Church, Manchester, 196; impromptu sayings, 197; Douglas at Westminster School, 199; isolation at Foston, 200; love of reading, 200; his own account of his Living, 201; illness of Douglas, 204; visits Newgate with Mrs. Fry, 206; correspondence with the Marquis of Lansdowne on the reform of the Criminal Laws, 206-210; opinion upon the "heirs-apparent" at Holland House and Castle Howard, 211; his troubles with Scotch sheep, 213; the Game Laws, 214; Sydney Smith as a magistrate, 218; sudden accession of fortune, 221; death of his father, 222; advice concerning low spirits, 222; visit to Edinburgh, 226; guest of Mr. Lambton, M.P., 228; Lambton Castle and the introduction of gas, 228; advice to a literary aspirant, 231; an awkward episode on the Malton Road, 233; sends Windham to the Charterhouse, 235; treatment of dumb animals, 237; sermons in York Minster, 237; Lady Camperdown's recollections of Sydney Smith at Weston House, 238; first appearance on a political platform, 243; speech at Beverley on the Catholic claims, 244; temporary gift of the living of Londesborough, 246; his visits there, 247; his absent-mindedness, 248; lines on Mr. and Mrs. Harcourt passing their honeymoon at the Lakes, 250; friendship with Lord and Lady Wenlock, 250; reminiscences by their daughter, the Hon. Mrs. Stuart Wortley, 251; "Letter to the Electors," 254; Macaulay at Foston, 255; Sydney Smith in Paris, 256; of the family of Falstaff, 256; last contribution to *Edinburgh Review*, 259; advice to foes of Catholic emancipation, 259; view of political affairs in 1827, 261; appointed Canon of Bristol, 262; friendship with Lord Lyndhurst, 262; marriage of youngest daughter Emily to Mr. Hibbert, 262; first impressions of Bristol, 264; popularity as a preacher at the cathedral, 265; sermon on the treatment of the Catholics, 266; mortification of the civic authorities, 267; a newspaper war, 267; proposal to settle at Corse, 268; serious illness of Douglas, 268; death of Douglas, 268; triumph of the Catholic Emancipation Bill, 268; epitaph on the grave of Douglas, 269; receives the living of Halberton, 269; exchanges Foston for Combe-Florey, 269; distress of his Yorkshire parishioners, 270; first impressions of Combe-Florey, 272; the *amen-ity* of the parish clerk, 273; Combe-Florey Rectory, 273; visit of Lord Jeffrey, 275; Sydney Smith in his study at, 277; kindliness to the poor of, 278; attention to the sick, 278; pedestrian exploits, 279; the "foreign deer" at, 279; connection with Halberton, 280; controversy with the vestry of, 281; traditions of, at, 282; takes part in the agitation for reform, 285; "Gazette Extraordinary—Glorious Victory!" 286; appointed by Earl Grey a Canon Residentiary of St. Paul's, 293; the question of a bishopric for, 295; "Dame Partington speech" at Taunton, 297-302; a succession of visitors at Combe-Florey, 304; friendship with Lord and Lady Morley, 305; popularity at St. Paul's, 312; his appearances in the pulpit of, 313; his wit in society, 314, 315; takes Mrs. Smith to Paris, 318;

new house in Charles Street, Berkeley Square, 319; adventures on the Bath Road, 319; neighbourly intercourse at Taunton, 320; some reminiscences of his visits there, 321; the "Poetical Medicine Chest," 323; characteristics of his brief notes, 324: "Letters to Archdeacon Singleton on the Ecclesiastical Commission, 326-332; republishes his contributions to the *Edinburgh Review*, 334; variety of subject and versatility of treatment, 334; his endeavour to put things right, 336; pamphlet on the "Ballot," 337-340; unexpected accession of fortune, 340; friendship with Dickens, 341; curiosity about Carlyle, 341; encounters with Macaulay, 341, 342; his last London home — 56, Green Street, Grosvenor Square, 343; a political and literary resort, 343; Mrs. Grote at Combe-Florey, 345; the poor man's loaf, 347; a member of the Athenæum Club, 348; fondness for London, 348; some snatches of his conversation, 349, 350; in church at Combe-Florey, 354; characteristics of his sermons at St. Paul's, 356; attitude towards the Puseyite movement, 356, 357; correspondence with Miss Martineau, 358-360; "What is a Puseyite?" 361; his attention at St. Paul's to the business of the Chapter, 364-365; occasional intolerance, 365; effect of music in the minor key upon, 366; gradual withdrawal into comparative privacy, 366: letters to the *Morning Chronicle* about the railway, 367; Mr. Gladstone's reminiscences of Sydney Smith, 368; Sir Richard Owen's ditto, 368-370; Earl Granville's ditto, 370; alleged irreverence of, testimony of Lord Houghton and Mrs. Malcolm, 371-373; John Ruskin and Sydney Smith, 374; vivacity of last letters of, 374;

Thomas Moore at Combe-Florey, 375; petition to Congress against the public repudiation of American Bonds, 378, 379; a sincere friend to America, 380; his friendship with the Rev. R. H. Barham, 380, 381; high spirits, 381; increasing physical infirmity, 382; final words at St. Paul's, 383, 384; unabated interest in the poor of Combe-Florey, 385; last glimpse of the sea, 386; the beginning of the end, 386; a brief "Indian summer," 387; last letter to Miss Georgiana Harcourt, 387; gratitude for the attentions of his friends, 388; a touching act of patronage, 390; last messages to Earl Grey, 390; the brotherly sympathy of Bobus, 390; his humble confidence as a Christian, 389-390; death of, 390; funeral at Kensal Green, 390; inscription on the grave at, 391; strange lack of memorials of, at Foston, and at St. Paul's, 392; his character and public services, 393, 394.

Smith, Mrs. Sydney, 1; parentage, 51; marriage, 52; her own account of her mother's attitude in reference to her marriage, 53; prospects as a bride, 53; the first home of her married life—46, George Street, Edinburgh, 45; the sale of her mother's pearls, 109; early London home of, 127; an entreaty from, to her husband, 131; her description of the removal to Yorkshire, 156; her account of the building of Foston Rectory, 168-170; her kindness to the young at Foston, 189; accompanies her husband to Paris, 318; her health, 343, 346; her interest in the village children of Combe-Florey, 356.

——, Windham, 94, 168, 170, 172, 190, 194, 235.

Southey, Robert, 69.

Spirits, animal, On the cultivation of, 112; remedies for nervousness of, 115.

Staël, Madame de, 14.

Stanleys, The, of Alderley, 195, 237.

Stewart, Dugald, Professor, 40, 41, 46, 48, 57, 95, 159.

Stonehenge, 23.

Storey, Jack, a Yorkshire peasant, Encounter with, 233.

Stowell, Lord, 145, 148.

Sunday observance, 283.

Sydenham, Lord, 309.

TALENTS, Ministry of all the, 142.

Talleyrand, Prince de, 120, 256.

Tankerville, Earl of, 196, 202, 326.

Taunton, 269, 285.

Tea, Abstinence from, 115.

Thirsk, Meeting of clergy at, 243.

Thomson, Dr. John, 56.

Thornton-le-Clay, 180, 183, 270.

Ticknor, Mr. George, Sydney Smith's remark on the aristocracy to, 126, 344.

Tierney, Right Hon. George, M.P., 257.

Tinling, Rev. Canon, curate to Sydney Smith, 282.

Tug, Lug, Hawl, Crawl, 169.

ULLESWATER, 39.

VERNON, Miss (half-sister to Lord Henry Petty): marriage to Bobus Smith, 38.

Verrey, Mr. (steward to Mr. Hicks-Beach): "List of Nether-Avon Poor, 1793," 26, 27.

Victoria, Queen, Marriage of, 344.

Virgil, 8.

Voltaire, Retort of, 84.

WAR, Peninsular, 183.

Warton, Dr. Joseph, 6, 9.

Wellington, Duke of, 257, 261, 283, 288.

Wenlock, Lord, 250.

Whewell, Dr., 134.

Whigs, The, and Sydney Smith, 294.

Wieland, Christopher Martin, 37.

Wilbrahams, The, of Delamere, 195.

Wilkes, John, M.P., 212.

Wilkie, Sir David, 120.

William IV., 283, 286.

Willison, Printing office of, at Edinburgh, 56.

Winchester College, Sydney Smith's connection with, 6.

Windermere, 39.

Wishaw, 256.

Wit and Humour, An essay on, 83.

Wit, Characteristics of Sydney Smith's, 78, 81, 136, 148, 164, 197, 252, 256, 336, 342, 351, 371, 373.

Woodford, Essex, birthplace of Sydney Smith, 1.

Wordsworth, William, Jeffrey's treatment of, 67.

Wortley, The Hon. Mrs. Stuart, Reminiscences by, of Sydney Smith, 251.

Wrangham, Archdeacon, 244.

YARBURGH, Major, of Heslington, 159.

York, 175, 178, 180.

York, H.R.H. the Duke of, 242.

York Minster, 180, 237, 246.

ZENITH, The English, 213.

LONDON:
PRINTED BY GILBERT AND RIVINGTON, LIMITED,
ST. JOHN'S SQUARE.

A Catalogue of American and Foreign Books Published or Imported by MESSRS. SAMPSON LOW & CO. can be had on application.

Crown Buildings, 188, Fleet Street, London, October, 1884.

A Selection from the List of Books

PUBLISHED BY

SAMPSON LOW, MARSTON, SEARLE, & RIVINGTON.

ALPHABETICAL LIST.

ABOUT Some Fellows. By an ETON BOY, Author of "A Day of my Life." Cloth limp, square 16mo, 2s. 6d.

Adams (C. K.) Manual of Historical Literature. Crown 8vo, 12s. 6d.

Alcott (Louisa M.) Jack and Jill. 16mo, 5s.

—— *Old-Fashioned Thanksgiving Day.* 3s. 6d.

—— *Proverb Stories.* 16mo, 3s. 6d.

—— *Spinning-Wheel Stories.*

—— See also "Low's Standard Novels" and "Rose Library."

Aldrich (T. B.) Friar Jerome's Beautiful Book, &c. Very choicely printed on hand-made paper, parchment cover, 3s. 6d.

—— *Poetical Works.* Édition de Luxe. 8vo, 21s.

Alford (Lady Marian) Needlework as Art. With over 100 Woodcuts, Photogravures, &c. Royal 8vo.

Allen (E. A.) Rock me to Sleep, Mother. Illust. Fcap. 4to, 5s

Amateur Angler's Days in Dove Dale : Three Weeks' Holiday in July and August, 1884. By E. M. Printed by Whittingham, at the Chiswick Press. Fancy boards, 1s.; also on large hand-made paper (100 only printed), 5s.

American Men of Letters. Lives of Thoreau, Irving, Webster. Small post 8vo, cloth, 2s. 6d. each.

Andersen (Hans Christian) Fairy Tales. With 10 full-page Illustrations in Colours by E. V. B. Cheap Edition, 5s.

Anderson (W.) Pictorial Arts of Japan. With 150 Plates, 16 of them in Colours and Gold. Large imp. 4to, gilt binding, gilt edges.

Angler's Strange Experiences (An). By COTSWOLD ISYS. With numerous Illustrations, 4to, 5s.

Angling. See "British Fisheries Directory," "Cutcliffe," "Lambert," "Martin," and "Theakston."

Archer (William) English Dramatists of To-day. Crown 8vo, 8s. 6d.

A

Art Education. See "Biographies of Great Artists," "Illustrated Text Books," "Mollett's Dictionary."

Artists at Home. Photographed by J. P. MAYALL, and reproduced in Facsimile. Letterpress by F. G. STEPHENS. Imp. folio, 42s.

Audsley (G. A.) Ornamental Arts of Japan. 90 Plates, 74 in Colours and Gold, with General and Descriptive Text. 2 vols., folio, £15 15s. On the issue of Part III. the price will be further advanced.

—— *The Art of Chromo-Lithography.* Coloured Plates and Text. Folio, 63s.

Audsley (W. and G. A.) Outlines of Ornament. Small folio, very numerous Illustrations, 31s. 6d.

Auerbach (B.) Brigitta. Illustrated. 2s.

—— *On the Heights.* 3 vols., 6s.

—— *Spinoza.* Translated. 2 vols., 18mo, 4s.

BALDWIN (J.) Story of Siegfried. 6s.

Barlow (Alfred) Weaving by Hand and by Power. With several hundred Illustrations. Third Edition, royal 8vo, 1l. 5s.

Bathgate (Alexander) Waitaruna: A Story. Crown 8vo, 5s.

Batley (A. W.) Etched Studies for Interior Decoration. Imperial folio, 52s. 6d.

Baxter (C. E.) Talofa: Letters from Foreign Parts. Crown 8vo, 4s.

THE BAYARD SERIES.

Edited by the late J. HAIN FRISWELL.

Comprising Pleasure Books of Literature produced in the Choicest Style as Companionable Volumes at Home and Abroad.

"We can hardly imagine better books for boys to read or for men to ponder over."—*Times.*

Price 2s. 6d. each Volume, complete in itself, flexible cloth extra, gilt edges, with silk Headbands and Registers.

The Story of the Chevalier Bayard. By M. De Berville.

De Joinville's St. Louis, King of France.

The Essays of Abraham Cowley, including all his Prose Works.

Abdallah; or, The Four Leaves. By Edouard Laboullaye.

Table-Talk and Opinions of Napoleon Buonaparte.

Vathek: An Oriental Romance. By William Beckford.

Words of Wellington : Maxims and Opinions of the Great Duke.

Dr. Johnson's Rasselas, Prince of Abyssinia. With Notes.

Hazlitt's Round Table. With Biographical Introduction.

The Religio Medici, Hydriotaphia, and the Letter to a Friend. By Sir Thomas Browne, Knt.

Ballad Poetry of the Affections. By Robert Buchanan.

Bayard Series (continued) :—

Coleridge's Christabel, and other Imaginative Poems. With Preface by Algernon C. Swinburne.

Lord Chesterfield's Letters, Sentences, and Maxims. With Introduction by the Editor, and Essay on Chesterfield by M. de Ste.-Beuve, of the French Academy.

The King and the Commons. A Selection of Cavalier and Puritan Songs. Edited by Professor Morley.

Essays in Mosaic. By Thos. Ballantyne.

My Uncle Toby ; his Story and his Friends. Edited by P. Fitzgerald.

Reflections ; or, Moral Sentences and Maxims of the Duke de la Rochefoucauld.

Socrates : Memoirs for English Readers from Xenophon's Memorabilia. By Edw. Levien.

Prince Albert's Golden Precepts.

A Case containing 12 Volumes, price 31s. 6d.; or the Case separately, price 3s. 6d.

Bell (Major): Rambla—Spain. Irun to Cerbere. Cr. 8vo, 8s. 6d.

Beumers' German Copybooks. In six gradations at 4d. each.

Bickersteth's Hymnal Companion to Book of Common Prayer may be had in various styles and bindings from 1d. to 31s. 6d. Price List and Prospectus will be forwarded on application.

Bickersteth (Rev. E. H., M.A.) The Clergyman in his Home. Small post 8vo, 1s.

———— *Evangelical Churchmanship and Evangelical Eclecticism.* 8vo, 1s.

———— *From Year to Year: a Collection of Original Poetical* Pieces. Small post 8vo, 3s. 6d.; roan, 6s. and 5s.; calf or morocco, 10s. 6d.

———— *The Master's Home-Call; or, Brief Memorials of Alice* Frances Bickersteth. 20th Thousand. 32mo, cloth gilt, 1s.

———— *The Master's Will.* A Funeral Sermon preached on the Death of Mrs. S. Gurney Buxton. Sewn, 6d. ; cloth gilt, 1s.

———— *The Shadow of the Rock.* A Selection of Religious Poetry. 18mo, cloth extra, 2s. 6d.

———— *The Shadowed Home and the Light Beyond.* New Edition, crown 8vo, cloth extra, 5s.

Bilbrough (E. J.) " Twixt France and Spain." Crown 8vo, 7s. 6d.

Biographies of the Great Artists (Illustrated). Crown 8vo, emblematical binding, 3s. 6d. per volume, except where the price is given.

Claude Lorrain.*
Correggio, by M. E. Heaton, 2s. 6d.
Della Robbia and Cellini, 2s. 6d.
Albrecht Dürer, by R. F. Heath.
Figure Painters of Holland.

Fra Angelico, Masaccio, and Botticelli.
Fra Bartolommeo, Albertinelli, and Andrea del Sarto.
Gainsborough and Constable.
Ghiberti and Donatello, 2s. 6d.

* *Not yet published.*

A 2

Biographies of the Great Artists (*continued*) :—

Giotto, by Harry Quilter.

Hans Holbein, by Joseph Cundall.

Hogarth, by Austin Dobson.

Landseer, by F. G. Stevens.

Lawrence and Romney, by Lord Ronald Gower, 2s. 6d.

Leonardo da Vinci.

Little Masters of Germany, by W. B. Scott.

Mantegna and Francia.

Meissonier, by J. W. Mollett, 2s. 6d.

Michelangelo Buonarotti, by Clément.

Murillo, by Ellen E. Minor, 2s. 6d.

Overbeck, by J. B. Atkinson.

Raphael, by N. D'Anvers.

Rembrandt, by J. W. Mollett.

Reynolds, by F. S. Pulling.

Rubens, by C. W. Kett.

Tintoretto, by W. R. Osler.

Titian, by R. F. Heath.

Turner, by Cosmo Monkhouse.

Vandyck and Hals, by P. R. Head.

Velasquez, by E. Stowe.

Vernet and Delaroche, by J. Rees.

Watteau, by J. W. Mollett, 2s. 6d.

Wilkie, by J. W. Mollett.

Bird (*F. J.*) *American Practical Dyer's Companion.* 8vo, 42s.

Bird (*H. E.*) *Chess Practice.* 8vo, 2s. 6d.

Black (*Wm.*) *Novels.* See "Low's Standard Library."

Blackburn (*Charles F.*) *Hints on Catalogue Titles and Index* Entries, with a Vocabulary of Terms and Abbreviations, chiefly from Foreign Catalogues. Royal 8vo, 14s.

Blackburn (*Henry*) *Breton Folk.* With 171 Illust. by RANDOLPH CALDECOTT. Imperial 8vo, gilt edges, 21s.; plainer binding, 10s. 6d.

——— *Pyrenees* (*The*). With 100 Illustrations by GUSTAVE DORÉ, corrected to 1881. Crown 8vo, 7s. 6d.

Blackmore (*R. D.*) *Lorna Doone. Édition de luxe.* Crown 4to, very numerous Illustrations, cloth, gilt edges, 31s. 6d.; parchment uncut, top gilt, 35s. Cheap Edition, small post 8vo, 6s.

——— *Novels.* See "Low's Standard Library."

——— *Remarkable History of Sir T. Upmore.* New Edition, 2 vols., crown 8vo, 21s.

Blaikie (*William*) *How to get Strong and how to Stay so.* Rational, Physical, Gymnastic, &c., Exercises. Illust., sm. post 8vo, 5s.

——— *Sound Bodies for our Boys and Girls.* 16mo, 2s. 6d.

Boats of the World, Depicted and Described by one of the Craft. With Coloured Plates, showing every kind of rig, 4to, 3s. 6d.

Bock (*Carl*). *The Head Hunters of Borneo: Up the Mahak-kam,* and Down the Barita; also Journeyings in Sumatra. 1 vol., super-royal 8vo, 32 Coloured Plates, cloth extra, 36s.

——— *Temples and Elephants.* A Narrative of a Journey through Upper Siam and Lao. Coloured, &c., Illustrations, 8vo, 21s.

Bonwick (*J.*) *First Twenty Years of Australia.* Crown 8vo, 5s.

——— *Lost Tasmanian Race.* Small 8vo, 4s.

Bonwick (J.) **Port Philip Settlement.** 8vo, numerous Illustrations, 21*s.*

Bosanquet (Rev. C.) Blossoms from the King's Garden : Sermons for Children. 2nd Edition, small post 8vo, cloth extra, 6*s.*

Bourke (J. G.) Snake Dance of the Moquis of Arizona. **A** Journey from Santa Fé. With 16 page Chromolithographs and other Illustrations. 8vo, **21***s.*

Boussenard (L.) Crusoes of Guiana ; or, the White Tiger. Illustrated by J. FERAT. 7*s.* 6*d.*

—— *Gold-seekers, a Sequel.* Illustrated. 16mo, 7*s.* 6*d.*

Boy's Froissart. King Arthur. *Mabinogion.* **Percy.** See LANIER.

Bracken (T.) Lays of the Land of the Maori and Moa. 16mo, 5*s.*

Bradshaw (J.) New Zealand as it is. 8vo, 12*s.* 6*d.*

Brassey (Lady) Tahiti. With **31** Autotype **Illustrations** after Photos. by Colonel STUART-WORTLEY. Fcap. 4to, 21*s.*

Braune (W.) Gothic Grammar. Translated by G. H. BULG. 3*s.* 6*d.*

Brisse (Baron) Ménus (366, one for each day of the year). Each Ménu is given in French and English, with recipes. Translated by Mrs. MATTHEW CLARKE. 2nd Edition. Crown 8vo, 5*s.*

British Fisheries Directory, 1883-84. **Small 8vo, 2***s.* **6***d.*

Brittany. See BLACKBURN.

Broglie's Frederick II. and **Maria** *Theresa.* 2 vols., 8vo, 30*s.*

Browne (G. Lathom) Narratives of Nineteenth Century State Trials. Period I.: 1801—1830. 2nd Edition, 2 vols., cr. 8vo, cloth, 26*s.*

Browne (Lennox) **and** *Behnke (Emil) Voice, Song, and Speech.* Illustrated, 3rd Edition, medium 8vo, 15*s.*

Bryant (W. C.) and Gay (S. H.) History of the **United States.** 4 vols., royal 8vo, profusely Illustrated, 60*s.*

*Bryce (***Rev.** *Professor) Manitoba.* With **Illustrations** and Maps. Crown 8vo, 7*s.* 6*d.*

Bull (J. W.) Early Experiences of Life in Australia. Crown 8vo, 7*s.* 6*d.*

Bunyan's Pilgrim's Progress. With **138** original **Woodcuts.** Small post 8vo, cloth gilt, 3*s.* 6*d.*; gilt edges, 4*s.*

*Burnaby (***Capt.***) On Horseback through Asia Minor.* 2 vols., 8vo, 38*s.* **Cheaper Edition,** 1 vol., crown 8vo, 10*s.* 6*d.*

Burnaby (Mrs. F.) High Alps in Winter; or, Mountaineering in Search of Health. By Mrs. FRED BURNABY. With Portrait of the Authoress, Map, and other Illustrations. Handsomely bound in cloth, **14***s.*

Butler (W. F.) The Great Lone Land; an Account of the Red River Expedition, 1869-70. New Edition, cr. 8vo, cloth extra, 7s. 6d.

———— *Invasion of England, told twenty years after, by an Old Soldier.* Crown 8vo, 2s. 6d.

———— *Red Cloud; or, the Solitary Sioux.* Imperial 16mo, numerous illustrations, gilt edges, 5s.

———— *The Wild North Land; the Story of a Winter Journey* with Dogs across Northern North America. 8vo, 18s. Cr. 8vo, 7s. 6d.

Buxton (H. J. W.) Painting, English and American. Crown 8vo, 5s.

CADOGAN *(Lady A.) Illustrated Games of Patience.* Twenty-four Diagrams in Colours, with Text. Fcap. 4to, 12s. 6d.

California. See " Nordhoff."

Cambridge Staircase (A). By the Author of " A Day of my Life at Eton." Small crown 8vo, cloth, 2s. 6d.

Cambridge Trifles; or, Splutterings from an Undergraduate Pen. By the Author of " A Day of my Life at Eton," &c. 16mo, cloth extra, 2s. 6d.

Carleton (Will) Farm Ballads, Farm Festivals, and Farm Legends. 1 vol., small post 8vo, 3s. 6d.

———— See " Rose Library."

Carlyle (T.) Reminiscences of my Irish Journey in 1849. Crown 8vo, 7s. 6d.

Carnegie (A.) American Four-in-Hand in Britain. Small 4to, Illustrated, 10s. 6d. Popular Edition, 1s.

———— *Round the World.* 8vo, 10s. 6d.

Carr (Mrs. Comyns) La Fortunina. 3 vols., cr. 8vo, 31s. 6d.

Chairman's Handbook (The). By R. F. D. PALGRAVE, Clerk of the Table of the House of Commons. 5th Edition, enlarged and re-written, 2s.

Challamel (M. A.) History of Fashion in France. With 21 Plates, coloured by hand, imperial 8vo, satin-wood binding, 28s.

Changed Cross (The), and other Religious Poems. 16mo, 2s. 6d.

Charities of London. See Low's.

Chattock (R. S.) Practical Notes on Etching. Sec. Ed., 8vo, 7s. 6d

Chess. See BIRD (H. E.).

China. See COLQUHOUN.

Choice Editions of Choice Books. 2s. 6d. each. Illustrated by
C. W. COPE, R.A., T. CRESWICK, R.A., E. DUNCAN, BIRKET
FOSTER, J. C. HORSLEY, A.R.A., G. HICKS, R. REDGRAVE, R.A.,
C. STONEHOUSE, F. TAYLER, G. THOMAS, H. J. TOWNSHEND,
E. H. WEHNERT, HARRISON WEIR, &c.

Bloomfield's Farmer's Boy.	Milton's L'Allegro.
Campbell's Pleasures of Hope.	Poetry of Nature. Harrison Weir.
Coleridge's Ancient Mariner.	Rogers' (Sam.) Pleasures of Memory.
Goldsmith's Deserted Village.	Shakespeare's Songs and Sonnets.
Goldsmith's Vicar of Wakefield.	Tennyson's May Queen.
Gray's Elegy in a Churchyard.	Elizabethan Poets.
Keat's Eve of St. Agnes.	Wordsworth's Pastoral Poems.

" Such works are a glorious beatification for a poet."—*Athenæum,*

Christ in Song. By PHILIP SCHAFF. New Ed., gilt edges, 6s.

Chromo-Lithography. See "Audsley."

Cid (Ballads of the). By the Rev. GERRARD LEWIS. Fcap.
8vo, parchment, 2s. 6d.

Clay (Charles M.) Modern Hagar. 2 vols., crown 8vo, 21s.
See also " Rose Library."

Collingwood (Harry) Under the Meteor Flag. The Log of a
Midshipman during the French Revolutionary War. Illustrated,
small post 8vo, gilt, 6s.; plainer, 5s.

Colquhoun (A. R.) Across Chrysê; From Canton to Mandalay.
With Maps and very numerous Illustrations, 2 vols., 8vo, 42s.

Colvile (H. E.) Accursed Land.

Composers. See "Great Musicians."

Confessions of a Frivolous Girl. Cr. 8vo, 6s. Paper boards, 1s.

Cook (Dutton) Book of the Play. New Edition. 1 vol., 3s. 6d.

—— *On the Stage: Studies of Theatrical History and the
Actor's Art.* 2 vols., 8vo, cloth, 24s.

Coote (W.) Wanderings South by East. Illustrated, 8vo, 21s.
New and Cheaper Edition, 10s. 6d.

—— *Western Pacific.* Illustrated, crown 8vo, 2s. 6d.

Costume. See SMITH (J. MOYR).

Cruise of the Walnut Shell (The). In Rhyme for Children
With 32 Coloured Plates. Square fancy boards, 5s.

Curtis (C. B.) Velazquez and Murillo. With Etchings, &c.
Royal 8vo, 31s. 6d.; large paper, 63s.

Curzon (G.) Violinist of the Quartier Latin. 3 vols., crown
8vo, 31s. 6d.

Cutcliffe (H. C.) Trout Fishing in Rapid Streams. Cr. 8vo, 3s. 6d.

D'ANVERS (N.) An Elementary History of Art. Crown
8vo, 10*s.* 6*d.*
——— *Elementary History of Music.* Crown 8vo, 2*s.* 6*d.*
——— *Handbooks of Elementary Art—Architecture; Sculpture ; Old Masters ; Modern Painting.* Crown 8vo, 3*s.* 6*d.* each.

Davis (C. T.) Manufacture of Bricks, Tiles, Terra-Cotta, &c.
Illustrated. 8vo, 25*s.*

Dawidowsky (F.) Glue, Gelatine, Isinglass, Cements, &c. 8vo,
12*s.* 6*d.*

Day of My Life (A) ; or, Every-Day Experiences at Eton.
By an ETON BOY. 16mo, cloth extra, 2*s.* 6*d.*

Day's Collacon : an Encyclopædia of Prose Quotations. Imperial 8vo, cloth, 31*s.* 6*d.*

Decoration. Vols. II., III., IV., V., VI., VII., VIII. New
Series, folio, 7*s.* 6*d.* each.
——— See also BATLEY.

De Leon (E.) Egypt under its Khedives. Illust. Cr. 8vo, 4*s.*

Deverill (F. H.) All Round Spain, by Road or Rail. Visit to
Andorra, &c. Crown 8vo, 10*s.* 6*d.*

Donnelly (Ignatius) Atlantis ; or, the Antediluvian World.
7th Edition, crown 8vo, 12*s.* 6*d.*
——— *Ragnarok : The Age of Fire and Gravel.* Illustrated,
Crown 8vo, 12*s.* 6*d.*

Dos Passos, Law of Stockbrokers and Stock Exchanges. 8vo, 35*s.*

Dougall (James Dalziel) Shooting: its Appliances, Practice,
and Purpose. New Edition, revised with additions. Crown 8vo, 7*s.* 6*d.*
"The book is admirable in every way. . . . . We wish it every success."—*Globe.*
"A very complete treatise. . . . . Likely to take high rank as an authority on
shooting."—*Daily News.*

Drama. See ARCHER, COOK (DUTTON), WILLIAMS (M.).

Durnford (Col. A. W.) A Soldier's Life and Work in South
Africa, 1872-9. 8vo, 14*s.*

Dyeing. See BIRD (F. J.).

EDUCATIONAL Works published in Great Britain. A
Classified Catalogue. Second Edition, 8vo, cloth extra, 5*s.*

Egypt. See "De Leon," "Foreign Countries," "Senior."

Eidlitz, Nature and Functions of Art and Architecture. 8vo, 21*s.*

Electricity. See GORDON.

Emerson Birthday Book. Extracts from the Writings of R. W.
Emerson. Square 16mo, illust., very choice binding, 3*s.* 6*d.*

Emerson (R. W.) Life. By G. W. COOKE. Crown 8vo, 8*s.* 6*d.*

English Catalogue of Books. Vol. III., 1872—1880. Royal 8vo, half-morocco, 42s. See also "Index."

English Philosophers. Edited by E. B. IVAN MÜLLER, M.A.

A series intended to give a concise view of the works and lives of English thinkers. Crown 8vo volumes of 180 or 200 pp., price 3s. 6d. each.

Francis Bacon, by Thomas Fowler. | *John Stuart Mill, by Miss Helen
Hamilton, by W. H. S. Monck. | Taylor.
Hartley and James Mill, by G. S. | Shaftesbury and Hutcheson, by
Bower. | Professor Fowler.
  | Adam Smith, by J. A. Farrer.

* Not yet published.

Esmarch (Dr. Friedrich) Treatment of the Wounded in War Numerous Coloured Plates and Illust., 8vo, strongly bound, 1l. 8s.

Etcher (The). Containing 36 Examples of the Original Etched-work of Celebrated Artists, amongst others: BIRKET FOSTER, J. E. HODGSON, R.A., COLIN HUNTER, J. P. HESELTINE, ROBERT W. MACBETH, R. S. CHATTOCK, &c. Vols. for 1881 and 1882, imperial 4to, cloth extra, gilt edges, 2l. 12s. 6d. each.

Etching. See BATLEY, CHATTOCK.

Etchings (Modern) of Celebrated Paintings. 4to, 31s. 6d.

FARM Ballads, Festivals, and Legends. See "Rose Library."

Fashion (History of). See "Challamel."

Fawcett (Edgar) A Gentleman of Leisure. 1s.

Feilden (H. St. C.) Some Public Schools, their Cost and Scholarships. Crown 8vo, 2s. 6d.

Felkin (R. W.) and Wilson (Rev. C. T.) Uganda and the Egyptian Soudan. With Map, Illust., and Notes. 2 vols., cr. 8vo, 28s.

Fenn (G. Manville) Off to the Wilds: A Story for Boys. Profusely Illustrated. Crown 8vo, 5s.

——— *The Silver Cañon: a Tale of the Western Plains.* Illustrated, small post 8vo, gilt, 6s.; plainer, 5s.

Fennell (Greville) Book of the Roach. New Edition, 12mo, 2s.

Ferguson (John) Ceylon in 1883. With numerous Illustrations. Crown 8vo, 7s. 6d. "Ceylon in 1884," 7s. 6d.

Ferns. See HEATH.

Fields (J. T.) Yesterdays with Authors. New Ed., 8vo, 10s. 6d.

Fleming (Sandford) England and Canada: a Summer Tour. Crown 8vo, 6s.

Florence. See "Yriarte."

Flowers of Shakespeare. 32 beautifully Coloured Plates, with the passages which refer to the flowers. Small 4to, 5*s.*

Folkard (R., Jun.) Plant Lore, Legends, and Lyrics. Illustrated, 8vo, 16*s.*

Foreign Countries and British Colonies. A series of Descriptive Handbooks. Crown 8vo, 3*s.* 6*d.* each.

Australia, by J. F. Vesey Fitzgerald.	Peru, by Clements R. Markham, C B.
Austria, by D. Kay, F.R.G.S.	
*Canada, by W. Fraser Rae.	Russia, by W. R. Morfill, M.A.
Denmark and Iceland, by E. C. Otté.	Spain, by Rev. Wentworth Webster.
Egypt, by S. Lane Poole, B.A.	Sweden and Norway, by F. H. Woods.
France, by Miss M. Roberts.	
Germany, by S. Baring-Gould.	*Switzerland, by W. A. P. Coolidge, M.A.
Greece, by L. Sergeant, B.A.	
*Holland, by R. L. Poole.	*Turkey-in-Asia, by J. C. McCoan, M.P.
Japan, by S. Mossman.	
*New Zealand.	West Indies, by C. H. Eden, F.R.G.S.
*Persia, by Major-Gen. Sir F. Goldsmid.	

* *Not ready yet.*

Fortunes made in Business. 2 vols., demy 8vo, cloth, 32*s.*

Franc (Maud Jeanne). The following form one Series, small post 8vo, in uniform cloth bindings, with gilt edges :—

Emily's Choice. 5*s.*	Vermont Vale. 5*s.*
Hall's Vineyard. 4*s.*	Minnie's Mission. 4*s.*
John's Wife: A Story of Life in South Australia. 4*s.*	Little Mercy. 4*s.*
	Beatrice Melton's Discipline. 4*s.*
Marian; or, The Light of Some One's Home. 5*s.*	No Longer a Child. 4*s.*
	Golden Gifts. 4*s.*
Silken Cords and Iron Fetters. 4*s.*	Two Sides to Every Question. 4*s.*

Francis (F.) War, Waves, and Wanderings, including a Cruise in the "Lancashire Witch." 2 vols., crown 8vo, cloth extra, 24*s.*

Frederick the Great. See "Broglie."

French. See "Julien."

Froissart. See "Lanier."

GENTLE Life (Queen Edition). 2 vols. in 1, small 4to, 6*s.*

THE GENTLE LIFE SERIES.

Price 6*s.* each ; or in calf extra, price 10*s.* 6*d.* ; Smaller Edition, cloth extra, 2*s.* 6*d.*, except where price is named.

The Gentle Life. Essays in aid of the Formation of Character of Gentlemen and Gentlewomen.

About in the World. Essays by Author of "The Gentle Life."

Like unto Christ. A New Translation of Thomas à Kempis' " De Imitatione Christi."

Familiar Words. An Index Verborum, or Quotation Hand- book. 6s.

Essays by Montaigne. Edited and Annotated by the Author of "The Gentle Life."

The Gentle Life. 2nd Series.

The Silent Hour: Essays, Original and Selected. By the Author of "The Gentle Life."

Half-Length Portraits. Short Studies of Notable Persons. By J. HAIN FRISWELL.

Essays on English Writers, for the Self-improvement of Students in English Literature.

Other People's Windows. By J. HAIN FRISWELL. 6s.

A Man's Thoughts. By J. HAIN FRISWELL.

The Countess of Pembroke's Arcadia. By Sir PHILIP SIDNEY. New Edition, 6s.

George Eliot: a Critical Study of her Life. By G. W. COOKE. Crown 8vo, 10s. 6d.

German. See BEUMER.

Germany. By S. BARING-GOULD. Crown 8vo, 3s. 6d.

Gibbs (J. R.) British Honduras. Crown 8vo, 7s. 6d.

Gilder (W. H.) Ice-Pack and Tundra. An Account of the Search for the "Jeannette." 8vo, 18s.

———— *Schwatka's Search.* Sledging in quest of the Franklin Records. Illustrated, 8vo, 12s. 6d.

Gilpin's Forest Scenery. Edited by F. G. HEATH. **Post 8vo,** 7s. 6d.

Glas (John) The Lord's Supper. Crown 8vo, 4s. 6d.

Gordon (J. E. H., B.A. Cantab.) Four Lectures on Electric Induction at the Royal Institution, 1878-9. Illust., square 16mo, 3s.

———— *Electric Lighting.* Illustrated, 8vo, 18s.

———— *Physical Treatise on Electricity and Magnetism.* **2nd** Edition, enlarged, with coloured, full-page, &c., Illust. 2 vols., 8vo, 42s.

Gouffé. The Royal Cookery Book. By JULES GOUFFÉ; trans- lated and adapted for English use by ALPHONSE GOUFFÉ, Head Pastrycook to Her Majesty the Queen. New Ed., with large plates printed in colours. 161 Woodcuts, 8vo, cloth extra, gilt edges, 42s.

———— Domestic Edition, half-bound, 10s. 6d.

Great Artists. See "Biographies."

Great Historic Galleries of England (The). Edited by LORD RONALD GOWER, Trustee of the National Portrait Gallery. *Permanent* Photographs of celebrated Pictures. Vol. I., imperial 4to, gilt edges, 36s. Vol. II., 2l. 12s. 6d.; III., 2l. 12s. 6d.; IV., 2l. 12s. 6d.

Great Musicians. Edited by F. HUEFFER. A Series of Biographies, crown 8vo, 3s. each :—

Bach.	Handel.	Purcell.
*Beethoven.	Haydn.	Rossini.
*Berlioz.	*Marcello.	Schubert.
English Church Composers. By BARETT.	Mendelssohn.	Schumann.
	Mozart.	Richard Wagner.
*Glück.	*Palestrina.	Weber.

* *In preparation.*

Grohmann (W. A. B.) Camps in the Rockies. 8vo, 12s. 6d.

Groves (J. Percy) Charmouth Grange : a Tale of the Seven- teenth Century. Illustrated, small post 8vo, gilt, 6s.; plainer 5s.

Guizot's History of France. Translated by ROBERT BLACK. Super-royal 8vo, very numerous Full-page and other Illustrations. In 8 vols., cloth extra, gilt, each 24s. This work is re-issued in cheaper binding, 8 vols., at 10s. 6d. each.

"It supplies a want which has long been felt, and ought to be in the hands of all students of history."—*Times.*

—————— **Masson's School Edition.** The History of France from the Earliest Times to the Outbreak of the Revolution ; abridged from the Translation by Robert Black, M.A., with Chronological Index, Historical and Genealogical Tables, &c. By Professor GUSTAVE MASSON, B.A., Assistant Master at Harrow School. With 24 full-page Portraits, and many other Illustrations. I vol., demy 8vo, 600 pp., cloth extra, 10s. 6d.

Guizot's History of England. In 3 vols. of about 500 pp. each, containing 60 to 70 full-page and other Illustrations, cloth extra, gilt, 24s. each ; re-issue in cheaper binding, 10s. 6d. each.

"For luxury of typography, plainness of print, and beauty of illustration, these volumes, of which but one has as yet appeared in English, will hold their own against any production of an age so luxurious as our own in everything, typography not excepted."—*Times.*

Guyon (Mde.) Life. By UPHAM. 6th Edition, crown 8vo, 6s.

HALL (W. W.) *How to Live Long; or,* 1408 *Health Maxims,* Physical, Mental, and Moral. 2nd Edition, small post 8vo, 2s.

Hamilton (E.) Recollections of Fly-fishing for Salmon, Trout, and Grayling. With Notes on their Habits, Haunts, and History. Illustrated, small post 8vo, 6s.; large paper (100 numbered copies), 10s. 6d.

Hands (T.) Numerical Exercises in Chemistry. Cr. 8vo, 2s. 6d. and 2s.; Answers separately, 6d.

Hargreaves (Capt.) Voyage round Great Britain. Illustrated. Crown 8vo, 5*s*.

Harland (Marian) Home Kitchen: a Collection of Practical and Inexpensive Receipts. Crown 8vo, 5*s*.

Harper's Monthly Magazine. Published Monthly. 160 pages, fully Illustrated. 1*s*.

> Vol. I. December, 1880, to May, 1881.
> ,, II. June to November, 1881.
> ,, III. December, 1881, to May, 1882.
> ,, IV. June to November, 1882.
> ,, V. December, 1882, to May, 1883.
> ,, VI. June to November, 1883.
> ,, VII. December, 1883, to May, 1884.
> ,, VIII. June to November, 1884.

Super-royal 8vo, 8*s*. 6*d*. each.

> "'Harper's Magazine' is so thickly sown with excellent illustrations that to count them would be a work of time ; not that it is a picture magazine, for the engravings illustrate the text after the manner seen in some of our choicest *éditions de luxe*."— *St. James's Gazette.*
> "It is so pretty, so big, and so cheap. . . An extraordinary shillingsworth— 160 large octavo pages, with over a score of articles, and more than three times as many illustrations."—*Edinburgh Daily Review.*
> "An amazing shillingsworth . . . combining choice literature of both nations."— *Nonconformist.*

Harrison (Mary) Skilful Cook: a Practical Manual of Modern Experience. Crown 8vo, 5*s*.

Harrison (Mrs. Burton) The Old-fashioned Fairy Book. Illustrated by ROSINA EMMETT. 16mo, 5*s*.

Hatton (Joseph) Journalistic London: with Engravings and Portraits of Distinguished Writers of the Day. Fcap. 4to, 12*s*. 6*d*.

——— *Three Recruits, and the Girls they left behind them.* Small post 8vo, 6*s*.

> "It hurries us along in unflagging excitement."—*Times.*

——— See also " Low's Standard Novels."

Heath (Francis George) Autumnal Leaves. New Edition, with Coloured Plates in Facsimile from Nature. Crown 8vo, 14*s*.

——— *Fern Paradise.* New Edition, with Plates and Photos., crown 8vo, 12*s*. 6*d*.

——— *Fern Portfolio.* Section I. Coloured Plates. Folio, 5*s*.

——— *Fern World.* With Nature-printed Coloured Plates. New Edition, crown 8vo, 12*s*. 6*d*.

——— *Gilpin's Forest Scenery.* Illustrated, 8vo, 12*s*. 6*d*. ; New Edition, 7*s*. 6*d*.

——— *Our Woodland Trees.* With Coloured Plates and Engravings. Small 8vo, 12*s*. 6*d*.

Heath (Francis George) Peasant Life in the West of England. New Edition, crown 8vo, 10s. 6d.

————— *Sylvan Spring.* With Coloured, &c., Illustrations. 12s. 6d.

————— *Trees and Ferns.* Illustrated, crown 8vo, 3s. 6d.

————— *Where to Find Ferns.* Crown 8vo, 2s.

Heber (Bishop) Hymns. Illustrated Edition. With upwards of 100 beautiful Engravings. Small 4to, handsomely bound, 7s. 6d. Morocco, 18s. 6d. and 21s. New and Cheaper Edition, cloth, 3s. 6d.

Heldmann (Bernard) Mutiny on Board the Ship "Leander." Small post 8vo, gilt edges, numerous Illustrations, 5s.

Henty (G. A.) Winning his Spurs. Illustrations. Cr. 8vo, 5s

————— *Cornet of Horse : A Story for Boys.* Illust., cr. 8vo, 5s.

————— *Jack Archer : Tale of the Crimea.* Illust., crown 8vo, 6s.

Herrick (Robert) Poetry. Preface by AUSTIN DOBSON. With numerous Illustrations by E. A. ABBEY. 4to, gilt edges, 42s.

Hill (Staveley, Q.C., M.P.) From Home to Home : Two Long Vacations at the Foot of the Rocky Mountains. With Wood Engravings and Photogravures. 8vo.

Hitchman, Public Life of the Right Hon. Benjamin Disraeli, Earl of Beaconsfield. 3rd Edition, with Portrait. Crown 8vo, 3s. 6d.

Hodson (J. S.) Art Illustration for Books, Periodicals, &c. 8vo, 15s.

Hole (Rev. Canon) Nice and her Neighbours. Small 4to, with numerous choice Illustrations, 12s. 6d.

Holmes (O. Wendell) Poetical Works. 2 vols., 18mo, exquisitely printed, and chastely bound in limp cloth, gilt tops, 10s. 6d.

Hoppus (J. D.) Riverside Papers. 2 vols., 12s.

Hugo (Victor) "Ninety-Three." Illustrated. Crown 8vo, 6s.

————— *Toilers of the Sea.* Crown 8vo, fancy boards, 2s.

————— *History of a Crime. Story of the Coup d'État.* Cr. 8vo, 6s.

Hundred Greatest Men (The). 8 portfolios, 21s. each, or 4 vols., half-morocco, gilt edges, 10 guineas. New Ed., 1 vol., royal 8vo, 21s.

Hurrell (H.) and Hyde. Law of Directors and Officials of Joint Stock Companies. 8vo, 3s. 6d.

Hutchinson (Thos.) Diary and Letters. Demy 8vo, cloth, 16s.

Hutchisson (W. H.) Pen and Pencil Sketches : Eighteen Years in Bengal. 8vo, 18s.

Hygiene and Public Health. Edited by A. H. BUCK, M.D. Illustrated. 2 vols., royal 8vo, 42s.

Hymnal Companion of Common Prayer. See BICKERSTETH.

ILLUSTRATED Text-Books of Art-Education. Edited by
EDWARD J. POYNTER, R.A. Each Volume contains numerous Illustrations, and is strongly bound for Students, price 5*s*. Now ready :—

PAINTING.

Classic and Italian. By PERCY | French and Spanish.
R. HEAD. | English and American.
German, Flemish, and Dutch. |

ARCHITECTURE.

Classic and Early Christian.
Gothic and Renaissance. By T. ROGER SMITH.

SCULPTURE.

Antique: Egyptian and Greek.

Index to the English Catalogue, Jan., 1874, *to Dec.,* 1880.
Royal 8vo, half-morocco, 18*s*.

Irish Birthday Book; from Speeches and Writings of Irish
Men and Women, Catholic and Protestant. Selected by MELUSINE.
Small 8vo, 5*s*.

Irving (Henry) Impressions of America. By J. HATTON. 2
vols., 21*s*.; New Edition, 1 vol., 6*s*

Irving (Washington). Complete Library Edition of his Works
in 27 Vols., Copyright, Unabridged, and with the Author's Latest
Revisions, called the "Geoffrey Crayon" Edition, handsomely printed
in large square 8vo, on superfine laid paper. Each volume, of about
500 pages, fully Illustrated. 12*s*. 6*d*. per vol. *See also* "Little Britain."

————————————— ("American Men of Letters.") 2*s*. 6*d*.

JAMES (C.) Curiosities of Law and Lawyers. 8vo, 7*s*. 6*d*.

Japan. See AUDSLEY.

Jarves (J. J.) Italian Rambles. Square 16mo, 5*s*.

Johnson, W. Lloyd Garrison and his Times. Cr. 8vo, 12*s*. 6*d*.

Johnston (H. H.) River Congo, from its Mouth to Bolobo.
New Edition, 8vo, 21*s*.

Johnston (R. M.) Old Mark Langston: a Tale of Duke's Creek.
Crown 8vo, 5*s*.

Jones (Major) The Emigrants' Friend. A Complete Guide to
the United States. New Edition. 2*s*. 6*d*.

Jones (Mrs. Herbert) Sandringham: Past and Present. Illustrated, crown 8vo, 8*s*. 6*d*.

Joyful Lays. Sunday School Song Book. By LOWRY and
DOANE. Boards, 2*s*.

Julien (F.) English Student's French Examiner. 16mo, 2s.
—— *First Lessons in Conversational French Grammar.*
Crown 8vo, 1s.
—— *French at Home and at School.* Book I., Accidence,
&c. Square crown 8vo, 2s.
—— *Conversational French Reader.* 16mo, cloth, 2s. 6d.
—— *Petites Leçons de Conversation et de Grammaire.* New
Edition, 3s.
—— *Phrases of Daily Use.* Limp cloth, 6d.
Jung (Sir Salar) Life of.   [*In the press.*

KELSEY *(C. B.) Diseases of the Rectum and Anus.*
Illustrated. 8vo, 18s.
Kempis (Thomas à) Daily Text-Book. Square 16mo, 2s. 6d. ;
interleaved as a Birthday Book, 3s. 6d.
Khedives and Pashas. Sketches of Contemporary Egyptian
Rulers and Statesmen. Crown 8vo, 7s. 6d.
Kingston (W. H. G.) Dick Cheveley. Illustrated, 16mo, gilt
edges, 7s. 6d.; plainer binding, plain edges, 5s.
—— *Heir of Kilfinnan.* Uniform, 7s. 6d. ; also 5s.
—— *Snow-Shoes and Canoes.* Uniform, 7s. 6d. ; also 5s.
—— *Two Supercargoes.* Uniform, 7s. 6d. ; also 5s.
—— *With Axe and Rifle.* Uniform, 7s. 6d. ; also 5s.
Knight (E. F.) Albania and Montenegro. Illust. 8vo, 12s. 6d.
Knight (E. J.) The Cruise of the "Falcon." A Voyage round
the World in a 30-Ton Yacht. Illust. New Ed. 2 vols., crown 8vo,
24s.

LANGSTAFF-HAVILAND *(R. J.) Enslaved.* 3 vols.,
31s. 6d.
Lanier (Sidney) The Boy's Froissart, selected from the Chronicles
of England, France, and Spain. Illustrated, cr. 8vo, gilt edges, 7s. 6d.
—— *Boy's King Arthur.* Uniform, 7s. 6d.
—— *Boy's Mabinogion ; Original Welsh Legends of King*
Arthur. Uniform, 7s. 6d.
—— *Boy's Percy : Ballads of Love and Adventure, selected*
from the "Reliques." Uniform, 7s. 6d.
Lansdell (H.) Through Siberia. 2 vols., demy 8vo, 30s. ; New
Edition, unabridged, very numerous illustrations, 8vo, 10s. 6d.
Larden (W.) School Course on Heat. Second Edition, Illus-
trated, crown 8vo, 5s.
Lathrop (G. P.) Newport. Crown 8vo, 5s.
Legal Profession : Romantic Stories. 7s. 6d.

Lennard (T. B.) To Married Women and Women about to be Married, &c. 6*d.*

Lenormant (F.) Beginnings of History. Crown 8vo, 12*s.* 6*d.*

Leonardo da Vinci's Literary Works. Edited by Dr. JEAN' PAUL RICHTER. Containing his Writings on Painting, Sculpture, and Architecture, his Philosophical Maxims, Humorous Writings, and Miscellaneous Notes on Personal Events, on his Contemporaries, on Literature, &c.; for the first time published from Autograph Manuscripts. By J. P. RICHTER, Ph.Dr., Hon. Member of the Royal and Imperial Academy of Rome, &c. 2 vols., imperial 8vo, containing about 200 Drawings in Autotype Reproductions, and numerous other Illustrations. Twelve Guineas.

Lewald (Fanny) Stella. Translated. 2 vols., 18mo, 4*s.*

Library of Religious Poetry. The Best Poems of all Ages. Edited by PHILIP SCHAFF and ARTHUR GILMAN. Royal 8vo, 1036 pp., cloth extra, gilt edges, 21*s.*; re-issue in cheaper binding, 10*s.* 6*d.*

Lindsay (W. S.) History of Merchant Shipping and Ancient Commerce. Over 150 Illustrations, Maps, and Charts. In 4 vols., demy 8vo, cloth extra. Vols. 1 and 2, 11*s.* each; vols. 3 and 4, 14*s.* each. 4 vols. complete, 50*s.*

Lillie (Lucy E.) Prudence : a Story of Æsthetic London. 5*s.*

Little Britain; together with *The Spectre Bridegroom,* and *A* Legend of Sleepy Hollow. By WASHINGTON IRVING. An entirely New *Edition de luxe.* Illustrated by 120 very fine Engravings on Wood, by Mr. J. D. COOPER. Designed by Mr. CHARLES O. MURRAY. Re-issue, square crown 8vo, cloth, 6*s.*

Logan (Sir Wm. E.) Life. By B. J. HARRINGTON. 8vo, 12*s.* 6*d.*

Long (Mrs. W. H. C.) Peace and War in the Transvaal. 12mo, 3*s.* 6*d.*

Lorne (Marquis of) Memories of Canada and Scotland. Speeches and Verses. Crown 8vo, 7*s.* 6*d.*

Low's Standard Library of Travel and Adventure. Crown 8vo uniform in cloth extra, 7*s.* 6*d.*, except where price is given.
1. The Great Lone Land. By Major W. F. BUTLER, C.B.
2. The Wild North Land. By Major W. F. BUTLER, C.B.
3. How I found Livingstone. By H. M. STANLEY.
4. Through the Dark Continent. By H. M. STANLEY. 12*s.* 6*d.*
5. The Threshold of the Unknown Region. By C. R. MARKHAM. (4th Edition, with Additional Chapters, 10*s.* 6*d.*)
6. Cruise of the Challenger. By W. J. J. SPRY, R.N.
7. Burnaby's On Horseback through Asia Minor. 10*s.* 6*d.*
8. Schweinfurth's Heart of Africa. 2 vols., 15*s.*
9. Marshall's Through America.
10. Lansdell's Through Siberia. Illust. and unabridged, 10*s.* 6*d.*

Low's Standard Novels. Small post 8vo, cloth extra, 6s. each,
unless otherwise stated.

A Daughter of Heth. By W. BLACK.
In Silk Attire. By W BLACK.
Kilmeny. A Novel. By W. BLACK.
Lady Silverdale's Sweetheart. By W. BLACK.
Sunrise. By W. BLACK.
Three Feathers. By WILLIAM BLACK.
Alice Lorraine. By R. D. BLACKMORE.
Christowell, a Dartmoor Tale. By R. D. BLACKMORE.
Clara Vaughan. By R. D. BLACKMORE.
Cradock Nowell. By R. D. BLACKMORE.
Cripps the Carrier. By R. D. BLACKMORE.
Erema; or, My Father's Sin. By R. D. BLACKMORE.
Lorna Doone. By R. D. BLACKMORE.
Mary Anerley. By R. D. BLACKMORE.
An English Squire. By Miss COLERIDGE.
A Story of the Dragonnades, or, Asylum Christi. By the Rev.
    E. GILLIAT, M.A.
A Laodicean. By THOMAS HARDY.
Far from the Madding Crowd. By THOMAS HARDY.
Pair of Blue Eyes. By THOMAS HARDY.
Return of the Native. By THOMAS HARDY.
The Hand of Ethelberta. By THOMAS HARDY.
The Trumpet Major. By THOMAS HARDY.
Two on a Tower. By THOMAS HARDY.
Three Recruits. By JOSEPH HATTON.
A Golden Sorrow. By Mrs. CASHEL HOEY. New Edition.
Out of Court. By Mrs. CASHEL HOEY.
History of a Crime: Story of the Coup d'État. VICTOR HUGO.
Ninety-Three. By VICTOR HUGO. Illustrated.
Adela Cathcart. By GEORGE MAC DONALD.
Guild Court. By GEORGE MAC DONALD.
Mary Marston. By GEORGE MAC DONALD.
Stephen Archer. New Ed. of "Gifts." By GEORGE MAC DONALD.
The Vicar's Daughter. By GEORGE MAC DONALD.
Weighed and Wanting. By GEORGE MAC DONALD.
Diane. By Mrs. MACQUOID.
Elinor Dryden. By Mrs. MACQUOID.
My Lady Greensleeves. By HELEN MATHERS.
Alaric Spenceley. By Mrs. J. H. RIDDELL.
Struggle for Fame. By Mrs. J. H. RIDDELL.
Daisies and Buttercups. By Mrs. J. H. RIDDELL.
The Senior Partner. By Mrs. J. H. RIDDELL.
John Holdsworth. By W. CLARK RUSSELL.
A Sailor's Sweetheart. By W. CLARK RUSSELL.
Sea Queen. By W. CLARK RUSSELL.
Wreck of the Grosvenor. By W. CLARK RUSSELL.
The Lady Maud. By W. CLARK RUSSELL.

Low's Standard Novels—continued.

Little Loo. By W. CLARK RUSSELL.
My Wife and I. By Mrs. BEECHER STOWE.
Poganuc People, their Loves and Lives. By Mrs. B. STOWE.
Ben Hur: a Tale of the Christ. By LEW. WALLACE.
Anne. By CONSTANCE FENIMORE WOOLSON.
For the Major. By CONSTANCE FENIMORE WOOLSON. 5*s.*
French Heiress in her own Chateau.

Low's Handbook to the Charities of London. **Edited and revised** to date by C. MACKESON, F.S.S., Editor of "A Guide to the Churches of London and its Suburbs," &c. Yearly, 1*s.* 6*d.*; Paper, 1*s.*

M*cCORMICK* (*R., R.N.*). *Voyages of Discovery in the* Arctic and Antarctic Seas in the "Erebus" and "Terror," in Search of Sir John Franklin, &c., with Autobiographical Notice by R. MCCORMICK, R.N., who was Medical Officer to each Expedition. With Maps and very numerous Lithographic and other Illustrations. 2 vols., royal 8vo, 52*s.* 6*d.*

Macdonald (*A.*) "*Our Sceptred Isle*" *and its World-wide* Empire. Small post 8vo, cloth, 4*s.*

MacDonald (*G.*) *Orts.* Small post 8vo, 6*s.*

——— **See also** "Low's Standard Novels."

Macgregor (*John*) "*Rob Roy*" *on the Baltic.* 3rd Edition, small post 8vo, 2*s.* 6*d.*; cloth, gilt edges, 3*s.* 6*d.*

——— *A Thousand Miles in the* "*Rob Roy*" *Canoe.* 11th Edition, small post 8vo, 2*s.* 6*d.*; cloth, gilt edges, 3*s.* 6*d.*

——— *Voyage Alone in the Yawl* "*Rob Roy.*" New Edition, thoroughly revised, with additions, small post 8vo, 5*s.*; 3*s.* 6*d.* and 2*s.* 6*d.*

Macquoid (*Mrs.*). See LOW'S STANDARD NOVELS.

Magazine. See DECORATION, ETCHER, HARPER.

Magyarland. Travels through the Snowy Carpathians, and Great Alföld of the Magyar. By a Fellow of the Carpathian Society (Diploma of 1881), and Author of "The Indian Alps." With about 120 Woodcuts from the Author's sketches and drawings. 2 vols., 8vo, 38*s.*

Manitoba. See BRYCE and RAE.

Maria Theresa. See BROGLIE.

Marked "*In Haste.*" A Story of To-day. Crown 8vo, 8*s.* 6*d.*

Markham (*Adm.*) *Naval Career during the Old War.* 8vo, 14*s.*

Markham (*C. R.*) *The Threshold of the Unknown Region.* Crown 8vo, with Four Maps, 4th Edition. Cloth extra, 10*s.* 6*d.*

——— *War between Peru and Chili,* 1879-1881. Third Ed. Crown 8vo, with Maps, 10*s.* 6*d.* See also "Foreign Countries."

Marshall (W. G.) Through America. New Edition, crown 8vo, with about 100 Illustrations, 7s. 6d.

Martin (F. W.) Float Fishing and Spinning in the Nottingham Style. Crown 8vo, 2s. 6d.

Marvin (Charles) Russian Advance towards India. 8vo, 16s.

Maury (Commander) Physical Geography of the Sea, and its Meteorology. New Edition, with Charts and Diagrams, cr. 8vo, 6s.

Men of Mark: a Gallery of Contemporary Portraits of the most Eminent Men of the Day, specially taken from Life. Complete in Seven Vols., 4to, handsomely bound, cloth, gilt edges, 25s. each.

Mendelssohn Family (The), 1729—1847. From Letters and Journals. By SEBASTIAN HENSEL. Translated. New Edition, 2 vols., 8vo, 30s.

Mendelssohn. See also " Great Musicians."

Mesney (W.) Tungking. Crown 8vo, 3s 6d.

Millard (H. B.) Bright's Disease of the Kidneys. Illustrated. 8vo, 12s. 6d.

Mitchell (D. G.; Ik. Marvel) Works. Uniform Edition, small 8vo, 5s. each.

Bound together.
Doctor Johns.
Dream Life.
Out-of-Town Places.

Reveries of a Bachelor.
Seven Stories, Basement and Attic.
Wet Days at Edgewood.

Mitford (Mary Russell) Our Village. Illustrated with Frontispiece Steel Engraving, and 12 full-page and 157 smaller Cuts. Crown 4to, cloth, gilt edges, 21s.; cheaper binding, 10s. 6d.

Mollett (J W.) Illustrated Dictionary of Words used in Art and Archæology. Terms in Architecture, Arms, Bronzes, Christian Art, Colour, Costume, Decoration, Devices, Emblems, Heraldry, Lace, Personal Ornaments, Pottery, Painting, Sculpture, &c., with their Derivations. With 600 Wood Engravings. Small 4to, 15s.

Morley (H.) English Literature in the Reign of Victoria. 2000th volume of the Tauchnitz Collection of Authors. 18mo, 2s. 6d.

Muller (E.) Noble Words and Noble Deeds. Containing many full-page Illustrations by PHILIPPOTEAUX. Square imperial 16mo, cloth extra, 7s. 6d.; plainer binding, plain edges, 5s.

Music. See "Great Musicians."

NEW Child's Play (A). Sixteen Drawings by E. V. B. Beautifully printed in colours, 4to, cloth extra, 12s. 6d.

New Zealand. See BRADSHAW.

Newbiggin's Sketches and Tales. 18mo, 4s.

Newfoundland. See RAE.

Nicholls (J. H. Kerry) The King Country: Explorations in New Zealand. Many Illustrations and Map. New Edition, 8vo, **21s.**

Nicholson (C.) Work and Workers of the British Association. 12mo, 1s.

Nordhoff (C.) California, for Health, Pleasure, and Residence New Edition, 8vo, with Maps and Illustrations, 12s. 6d.

Nothing to Wear; and Two Millions. By **W. A. BUTLER.** **New Edition.** Small post 8vo, in stiff coloured wrapper, 1s.

Nursery Playmates (Prince of). **217** Coloured Pictures for Children by eminent Artists. **Folio,** in coloured boards, **6s.**

O'*BRIEN (P. B.) Fifty Years of Concessions to Ireland.* Vol. I., 8vo, 16s.

—————— *Irish Land Question, and English Question.* **New** Edition, fcap. 8vo, 2s.

Orvis (C. F.) Fishing with the Fly. Illustrated. 8vo, 12s. 6d.

Our Little Ones in Heaven. **Edited by** the Rev. H. ROBBINS. With Frontispiece after Sir JOSHUA REYNOLDS. Fcap., cloth extra, New Edition—the 3rd, with Illustrations, 5s.

Outlines of Ornament in all Styles. A Work of Reference for the Architect, Art Manufacturer, Decorative Artist, and Practical Painter. By W. and G. A. AUDSLEY, Fellows of the Royal Institute of British Architects. Only a limited number have been printed and the stones destroyed. Small folio, **60 plates, with** introductory text, cloth gilt, 31s. 6d.

Owen (Douglas) Marine Insurance Notes and Clauses. 10s. 6d.

P*ALGRAVE (R. F. D.).* See " Chairman's Handbook."

Palliser (Mrs.) A History of Lace, from the Earliest Period. **A** New and Revised Edition, with additional cuts and text. 8vo, 1l. 1s.

—————— *The China Collector's Pocket Companion.* With **up-wards** of 1000 Illustrations of Marks and Monograms. Small 8vo, **5s.**

Perseus, the Gorgon Slayer. With Coloured Plates, square 8vo, 5s.

Pharmacopœia of the United States of America. 8vo, 21s.

Philpot (H. J.) Diabetes Mellitus. Crown 8vo, 5s.

—— *Diet System.* Three Tables, in cases, 1s. each.

Photography (History and Handbook of). See TISSANDIER.

Pinto (Major Serpa) How I Crossed Africa : from the Atlantic to the Indian Ocean, Through Unknown Countries ; Discovery of the Great Zambesi Affluents, &c.—Vol. I., The King's Rifle. Vol. II., The Coillard Family. With 24 full-page and 118 half-page and smaller Illustrations, 13 small Maps, and 1 large one. 2 vols., 8vo, 42s.

Poe (E. A.) The Raven. Illustrated by GUSTAVE DORÉ. Imperial folio, cloth, 63s.

Poems of the Inner Life. Chiefly from Modern Authors. Small 8vo, 5s.

Polar Expeditions. See KOLDEWEY, MARKHAM, MACGAHAN, NARES, NORDENSKIÖLD, GILDER, MCCORMICK.

Politics and Life in Mars. 12mo, 2s. 6d.

Powell (W.) Wanderings in a Wild Country; or, Three Years among the Cannibals of New Britain. 8vo, Map and Illustrations, 18s.; new Edition, crown 8vo, 5s.

Prisons, Her Majesty's, their Effects and Defects. New and cheaper Edition, 6s.

Poynter (Edward J., R.A.). See "Illustrated Text-books."

Publishers' Circular (The), and General Record of British and Foreign Literature. Published on the 1st and 15th of every Month, 3d.

*R*AE *(W. Fraser) From Newfoundland to Manitoba ; a* Guide through Canada's Maritime, Mining, and Prairie Provinces. With Maps. Crown 8vo, 6s.

Rambaud (A.) History of Russia. 2 vols., 8vo, 36s.

Reade (A.) Tea and Tea-Drinking. Illustrated. Crown 8vo, 1s.

Reber (F.) History of Ancient Art. 8vo, 18s.

Redford (G.) Ancient Sculpture. Crown 8vo, 5s.

Richer than Wealth. 3 vols., crown 8vo, 31s. 6d.

Richter (*Dr. Jean Paul*) *Italian Art in the National Gallery.* 4to. Illustrated. Cloth gilt, 2*l.* 2*s.*; half-morocco, uncut, 2*l.* 12*s.* 6*d.*

—— See also LEONARDO DA VINCI.

Robin Hood; Merry Adventures of. **Written and** illustrated by HOWARD PYLE. Imperial 8vo, 15*s.*

Robinson (*Phil*) *In my Indian Garden.* With a Preface by EDWIN ARNOLD. Crown 8vo, limp cloth, 4th Edition, 3*s.* 6*d.*

—— *Noah's Ark. A Contribution to the Study of Unnatural* History. Small post 8vo, 12*s.* 6*d.*

—— *Sinners and Saints : a Tour across the United States of* America, and Round them. Crown 8vo, 10*s.* 6*d.*

—— *Under the Punkah.* Crown 8vo, limp cloth, 5*s.*

Robinson (*Serjeant*) *Wealth and its Sources. Stray Thoughts.* 5*s.*

Rockstro (*W. S.*) *History of* **Music.** 8vo, 14*s.*

Roland ; the Story of. Crown 8vo, illustrated, 6*s.*

Romantic *Stories of the Legal Profession.* Crown 8vo, 7*s.* 6*d.*

Roosevelt (*Blanche*) *Stage-struck ; or, She would be an Opera* Singer. **2 vols.,** crown 8vo, 21*s.*

Rose (*F.*) *Complete Practical Machinist.* New Ed., 12mo, 12*s.* 6*d.*

—— *Mechanical Drawing.* Illustrated, small 4to, 16*s.*

Rose Library (*The*). Popular Literature of all Countries. Each volume, 1*s.*; cloth, 2*s.* 6*d.* Many of the Volumes are Illustrated —

Little Women. By LOUISA M. ALCOTT.

Little Women Wedded. Forming a Sequel to "Little Women."

Little Women and Little Women Wedded. 1 vol., cloth gilt, 3*s.* 6*d.*

Little Men. By L. M. ALCOTT. 2*s.*; cloth gilt, 3*s.* 6*d.*

An Old-Fashioned Girl. By LOUISA M. ALCOTT. 2*s.*; cloth, 3*s.* 6*d.*

Work. A Story of Experience. By L. M. ALCOTT. 3*s.* 6*d.* ; 2 vols., 1*s.* each.

Stowe (Mrs. H. B.) The Pearl of Orr's Island.

—— **The Minister's Wooing.**

—— **We and our Neighbours.** 2*s.*; cloth gilt, 6*s.*

—— **My Wife and I.** 2*s.*; cloth gilt, 6*s.*

Hans Brinker ; or, the Silver Skates. By Mrs. DODGE.

My Study Windows. By J. R. LOWELL.

The Guardian Angel. By OLIVER WENDELL HOLMES.

My Summer in a Garden. By C. D. WARNER.

Dred. By Mrs. BEECHER STOWE. 2*s.*; cloth gilt, 3*s.* 6*d.*

Farm Ballads. By WILL CARLETON.

Farm Festivals. By WILL CARLETON.

Farm Legends. By WILL CARLETON.

The Clients of Dr. Bernagius. 3*s.* 6*d.*; 2 parts, 1*s.* each.

The Undiscovered Country. By W. D. HOWELLS. 3*s.* 6*d.* and 1*s.*

Baby Rue. By C. M. CLAY. 3*s.* 6*d.* and 1*s.*

The Rose in Bloom. By L. M. ALCOTT. 2*s.*; cloth gilt, 3*s.* 6*d.*

Eight Cousins. By L. M. ALCOTT. 2*s.*; cloth gilt, 3*s.* 6*d.*

Under the Lilacs. By L. M. ALCOTT. 2*s.*; also 3*s.* 6*d.*

Silver Pitchers. By LOUISA M. ALCOTT. 3*s.* 6*d.* and 1*s.*

Jimmy's Cruise in the "Pinafore," and other Tales. By
LOUISA M. ALCOTT. 2*s.*; cloth gilt, 3*s.* 6*d.*

Jack and Jill. By LOUISA M. ALCOTT. 5*s.*; 2*s.*

Hitherto. By the Author of the "Gayworthys." 2 vols., 1*s.* each;
1 vol., cloth gilt, 3*s.* 6*d.*

Friends: a Duet. By E. STUART PHELPS. 3*s.* 6*d.*

A Gentleman of Leisure. A Novel. By EDGAR FAWCETT.
3*s.* 6*d.*; 1*s.*

The Story of Helen Troy. 3*s.* 6*d.*; also 1*s.*

Round the Yule Log: Norwegian Folk and Fairy Tales.
Translated from the Norwegian of P. CHR. ASBJÖRNSEN. With 100
Illustrations after drawings by Norwegian Artists, and an Introduction
by E. W. Gosse. Imperial 16mo, cloth extra, gilt edges, 7*s.* 6*d.*

Rousselet (Louis) Son of the **Constable of France.** Small post
8vo, numerous Illustrations, 5*s.*

———— *King of the Tigers: a Story of Central India.* Illus
trated. Small post 8vo, gilt, 6*s.*; plainer, 5*s.*

———— *The Drummer Boy: a Story of the Days of Washington.*
Small post 8vo, numerous Illustrations, 5*s.*

Russell (W. Clark) English Channel Ports and the Estate
of the East and West India Dock Company. Crown 8vo, 1*s.*

———— *Jack's Courtship.* 3 vols., crown 8vo, 31*s.* 6*d.*

———— *The Lady Maud.* 3 vols., crown 8vo, 31*s.* 6*d.* New
Edition, small post 8vo, 6*s.*

———— *Little Loo.* New Edition, 6*s.*

———— *My Watch Below; or, Yarns Spun when off Duty.*
2nd Edition, crown 8vo, 2*s.* 6*d.*

———— *Sailor's Language.* Illustrated. Crown 8vo, 3*s.* 6*d.*

Russell (W. Clark) Sea Queen. 3 vols., crown 8vo, 31s. 6d.

———— *Wreck of the Grosvenor.* 4to, sewed, 6d.

———— See also Low's STANDARD NOVELS.

Russell (W. H., LL.D.) Hesperothen: Notes from the Western World. A Ramble through part of the United States, Canada, and the Far West, in 1881. By W. H. RUSSELL, LL.D. 2 vols., crown 8vo, 24s.

———— *The Tour of the Prince of Wales in India.* By W. H. RUSSELL, LL.D. Fully Illustrated by SYDNEY P. HALL, M.A. Super-royal 8vo, gilt edges, 52s. 6d.; large paper, 84s.

*S*AINTS *and their Symbols: A Companion in the Churches* and Picture Galleries of Europe. Illustrated. Royal 16mo, 3s. 6d.

Saunders (A.) Our Domestic Birds: Poultry in England and New Zealand. Crown 8vo, 6s.

Scherr (Prof. J.) History of English Literature. Cr. 8vo, 8s. 6d.

Schuyler (Eugène). The Life of Peter the Great. By EUGÈNE SCHUYLER, Author of "Turkestan." 2 vols., 8vo, 32s.

Schweinfurth (Georg) Heart of Africa. Three Years' Travels and Adventures in the Unexplored Regions of Central Africa, from 1868 to 1871. Illustrations and large Map. 2 vols., crown 8vo, 15s.

Scott (Leader) Renaissance of Art in Italy. 4to, 31s. 6d.

Sea, River, and Creek. By GARBOARD STREYKE. *The Eastern* Coast. 12mo, 1s.

Sedgwick (Major W.) Light the Dominant Force of the Universe. 7s. 6d.

Senior (Nassau W.) Conversations and Journals in Egypt and Malta. 2 vols., 8vo, 24s.

Shadbolt and Mackinnon's South African Campaign, 1879. Containing a portrait and biography of every officer who lost his life. 4to, handsomely bound, 2l. 10s.

———— *The Afghan Campaigns of* 1878—1880. By SYDNEY SHADBOLT. 2 vols., royal quarto, cloth extra, 3l.

Shakespeare. Edited by R. GRANT WHITE. 3 vols., crown 8vo, gilt top, 36s.; *édition de luxe,* 6 vols., 8vo, cloth extra, 63s.

Shakespeare. See also " Flowers of Shakespeare."

Sidney (Sir Philip) Arcadia. New Edition, 6s.

Siegfried : The Story of. Illustrated, crown 8vo, cloth, 6s.

Sikes (Wirt). Rambles and Studies in Old South Wales. With numerous Illustrations. 8vo, 18s.

———— *British Goblins, Welsh Folk Lore.* New Ed., 8vo, 18s.

———— *Studies of Assassination.* 16mo, 3s. 6d.

Sir Roger de Coverley. Re-imprinted from the " Spectator." With 125 Woodcuts and special steel Frontispiece. Small fcap. 4to, 6s.

Smith (G.) Assyrian Explorations and Discoveries. Illustrated by Photographs and Woodcuts. New Edition, demy 8vo, 18s.

———— *The Chaldean Account of Genesis.* By the late G. SMITH, of the Department of Oriental Antiquities, British Museum. With many Illustrations. 16s. New Edition, revised and re-written by PROFESSOR SAYCE, Queen's College, Oxford. 8vo, 18s.

Smith (J Moyr) Ancient Greek Female Costume. 112 full-page Plates and other Illustrations. Crown 8vo, 7s. 6d.

———— *Hades of Ardenne: a Visit to the Caves of Han.* Crown 8vo, Illustrated, 5s.

Smith (Sydney) Life and Times. By STUART J. REID. Illustrated. 8vo, 21s.

Smith (T. Roger) Architecture, Gothic and Renaissance. Illustrated, crown 8vo, 5s.

———————————— *Classic and Early Christian.* Illustrated. Crown 8vo, 5s

Smith (W. Robert) Laws concerning Public Health. 8vo, 31s. 6d.

Somerset (Lady H.) Our Village Life. Words and Illustrations. Thirty Coloured Plates, royal 4to, fancy covers, 5s.

Spanish and French Artists. By GERARD SMITH. (Poynter's Art Text-books.) 5s.

Spiers' French Dictionary. 29th Edition, remodelled. 2 vols., 8vo, 18s.; half bound, 21s.

Spry (W. J. J., R.N.) The Cruise of H.M.S. "Challenger." With Route Map and many Illustrations. 6th Edition, demy 8vo, cloth, **18s.** Cheap Edition, crown 8vo, with some of the Illustrations, 7s. 6d.

Spyri (Johanna) Heidi's Early Experiences : a Story for Children and those who love Children. Illustrated, **small post 8vo,** 4s. 6d.

—— *Heidi's Further. Experiences.* Illustrated, **small post** 8vo, 4s. 6d.

Stack (E.) Six Months in Persia. 2 vols., crown 8vo, 24s.

Stanley (H. M.) How I Found Livingstone. 8vo, **10s. 6d. ;** crown 8vo, 7s. 6d.

—— *"My Kalulu," Prince, King, and Slave.* With numerous graphic Illustrations after Original Designs by the Author. Crown 8vo, 7s. 6d.

—— *Coomassie and Magdala.* A Story of **Two British** Campaigns in Africa. Demy 8vo, with Maps and Illustrations, 16s.

—— *Through the Dark Continent.* Crown 8vo, 12s. 6d.

Stanton (T.) Woman Question in Europe. A Series of Original Essays. Introd. by FRANCES POWER COBBE. 8vo, 12s. 6d.

Stenhouse (Mrs.) An Englishwoman in Utah. Crown 8vo, 2s. 6d.

Stevens. Old Boston : a Romance of the War of Independence. 3 vols., crown 8vo, 31s. 6d.

Stirling (A. W.) Never Never Land : a Ride in North Queensland. Crown 8vo, 8s. 6d.

Stockton (Frank R.) The Story of Viteau. With 16 page Illustrations. Crown 8vo, 5s.

Stoker (Bram) Under the Sunset. Crown 8vo, 6s.

Story without an End. From the German of Carové, by the late Mrs. SARAH T. AUSTIN. Crown 4to, with 15 Exquisite Drawings by E. V. B., printed in Colours in Fac-simile of the original Water Colours ; and numerous other Illustrations. New Edition, 7s. 6d.

—— with Illustrations by HARVEY. Square 4to, 2s. 6d.

Stowe (Mrs. Beecher) Dred. Cloth, gilt edges, 3s. 6d.; boards, 2s.

—— *Little Foxes.* **Cheap Ed., 1s. ;** Library Edition, 4s. 6d.

Stowe (*Mrs. Beecher*) *My Wife and I; or, Harry Henderson's History.* Small post 8vo, cloth extra, 6s.*

———— *Minister's Wooing.*

———— *Old Town Folk.* 6s.; Cheap Edition, 2s. 6d.

———— *Old Town Fireside Stories.* Cloth extra, 3s. 6d.

———— *Our Folks at Poganuc.* 6s.

———— *We and our Neighbours.* 1 vol., small post 8vo, 6s. Sequel to "My Wife and I."*

———— *Poganuc People: their Loves and Lives.* Crown 8vo, 6s.

———— *Chimney Corner.* 1s.; cloth, 1s. 6d.

———— *The Pearl of Orr's Island.* Crown 8vo, 5s.*

———— *Woman in Sacred History.* Illustrated with 15 Chromo-lithographs and about 200 pages of Letterpress. 4to, 25s.

Sullivan (*A. M., late M.P.*) *Nutshell History of Ireland.* From the Earliest Ages to the Present Time. Paper boards, 6d.

Sutton (*A. K.*) *A B C Digest of the Bankruptcy Law.* 8vo, 3s. and 2s. 6d.

TAINE (*H. A.*) "*Les Origines de la France Contemporaine.*" Translated by JOHN DURAND.

> Vol. 1.   The Ancient Regime. Demy 8vo, cloth, 16s.
> Vol. 2.   The French Revolution. Vol. 1.   do.
> Vol. 3.   Do.   do.   Vol. 2.   do.

Talbot (*Hon. E.*) *A Letter on Emigration.* 1s.

Tangye (*R.*) *Reminiscences of Australia, America, and Egypt.* 2nd Edition, crown 8vo, 6s.

Tauchnitz's *English Editions of German Authors.* Each volume, cloth flexible, 2s.; or sewed, 1s. 6d. (Catalogues post free.)

Tauchnitz (*B.*) *German and English Dictionary.* Paper, 1s. 6d.; cloth, 2s.; roan. 2s. 6d.

———— *French and English Dictionary.* Paper, 1s. 6d.; cloth, 2s.; roan, 2s. 6d.

* *See also* Rose Library.

Tauchnitz (B.) Italian and English Dictionary. Paper, 1s. 6d.; cloth, 2s.; roan, 2s. 6d.

———— *Spanish and English.* Paper, 1s. 6d.; cloth, 2s.; roan, 2s. 6d.

———— *Spanish and French.* Paper, 1s. 6d.; cloth, 2s.; roan, 2s. 6d.

Taylor (W. M.) Paul the Missionary. Crown 8vo, 7s. 6d.

———— *Moses the Lawgiver.* Crown 8vo, 7s. 6d.

Thausing (Prof.) Preparation of Malt and the Fabrication of Beer. 8vo, 45s.

Theakston (M.) British Angling Flies. Illustrated. Cr. 8vo, 5s.

Thoreau. By SANBORN. (American Men of Letters.) Crown 8vo, 2s. 6d.

Tolhausen (Alexandre) Grand Supplément du Dictionnaire Technologique. 3s. 6d.

Tolmer (Alexander) Reminiscences of an Adventurous and Chequered Career. 2 vols., 21s.

Tourist Idyll, and other Stories. 2 vols., crown 8vo, 21s.

Tracks in Norway of Four Pairs of Feet, delineated by Four Hands. Fcap. 8vo, 2s.

Treloar (W. P.) The Prince of Palms. With Coloured Frontispiece of the Cocoa-Nut Palm, also Engravings. Royal 8vo, cloth extra, 1s. 6d.

Trials. See BROWNE.

Tristram (Rev. Canon) Pathways of Palestine: A Descriptive Tour through the Holy Land. First Series. Illustrated by 44 Permanent Photographs. 2 vols., folio, cloth extra, gilt edges, 31s. 6d. each.

Tunis. See REID.

Turner (Edward) Studies in Russian Literature. Cr. 8vo, 8s. 6d.

UNION Jack (The). Every Boy's Paper. Edited by G. A. HENTY. Profusely Illustrated with Coloured and other Plates. Vol. I., 6s. Vols. II., III., IV., 7s. 6d. each.

Up Stream: A Journey from the Present to the Past. Pictures and Words by R. ANDRÉ. Coloured Plates, 4to, 5s.

BOOKS BY JULES VERNE.

CELEBRATED TRAVELS and TRAVELLERS. 3 Vols., Demy
8vo, 600 pp., upwards of 100 full-page Illustrations, 12s. 6d.;
gilt edges, 14s. each :—

I. The Exploration of the World.

II. The Great Navigators of the Eighteenth Century.

III. The Great Explorers of the Nineteenth Century.

☞ The letters appended to each book refer to the various Editions and Prices
given at the foot of the page.

a e TWENTY THOUSAND LEAGUES UNDER THE SEA.

a e HECTOR SERVADAC.

a e THE FUR COUNTRY.

a f FROM THE EARTH TO THE MOON, AND A TRIP
ROUND IT.

a e MICHAEL STROGOFF, THE COURIER OF THE CZAR.

a e DICK SANDS, THE BOY CAPTAIN.

b c d FIVE WEEKS IN A BALLOON.

b c d ADVENTURES OF 3 ENGLISHMEN AND 3 RUSSIANS.

b c d AROUND THE WORLD IN EIGHTY DAYS.

b c { *d* A FLOATING CITY.
{ *d* THE BLOCKADE RUNNERS.

b c { *d* { DR. OX'S EXPERIMENT.
{ { MASTER ZACHARIUS.
{ *d* { A DRAMA IN THE AIR.
{ { A WINTER AMID THE ICE.

b c { *d e* THE SURVIVORS OF THE "CHANCELLOR."
{ *d* MARTIN PAZ.

b c d THE CHILD OF THE CAVERN.

THE MYSTERIOUS ISLAND, 3 Vols. :—

b c d I. DROPPED FROM THE CLOUDS.

b c d II. ABANDONED.

b c d III. SECRET OF THE ISLAND.

b c { *d* THE BEGUM'S FORTUNE.
{ THE MUTINEERS OF THE "BOUNTY."

b c d THE TRIBULATIONS OF A CHINAMAN.

THE STEAM HOUSE, 2 Vols. :—

b c d I. DEMON OF CAWNPORE.

b c d II. TIGERS AND TRAITORS.

THE GIANT RAFT, 2 Vols. :—

b I. EIGHT HUNDRED LEAGUES ON THE AMAZON.

b II. THE CRYPTOGRAM.

b GODFREY MORGAN.

d THE GREEN RAY. Cloth, gilt edges, 6s.; plain edges, 5s.

KERABAN THE INFLEXIBLE, 2 Vols. :—

b I. THE CAPTAIN OF THE GUIDARA.

b II. *In the press.*

a Small 8vo, very numerous Illustrations, handsomely bound in cloth, with gilt
edges, 10s. 6d.; ditto, plainer binding, 5s.

b Large imperial 16mo, very numerous Illustrations, handsomely bound in cloth,
with gilt edges, 7s. 6d.

c Ditto, plainer binding, 3s. 6d.

d Cheaper Edition, 1 Vol., paper boards, with some of the Illustrations, 1s.; bound
in cloth, gilt edges, 2s.

e Cheaper Edition as (*d*), in 2 Vols., 1s. each; bound in cloth, gilt edges, 1 Vol.,
3s. 6d.

f Same as (*e*), except in cloth, 2 Vols., gilt edges, 2s. each.

VELAZQUEZ and Murillo. By C. B. CURTIS. With Original Etchings. Royal 8vo, 31*s.* 6*d.*; large paper, 63*s.*

Verne (Jules) Keraban the Inflexible. Illustrated. Small post 8vo, cloth extra, gilt, 7*s.* 6*d.*

Victoria (Queen) Life of. By GRACE GREENWOOD. With numerous Illustrations. Small post 8vo, 6*s.*

Vincent (F.) Norsk, Lapp, and Finn. By FRANK VINCENT, Jun., Author of "The Land of the White Elephant," "Through and Through the Tropics," &c. With Frontispiece and Map, 8vo, 12*s.*

Viollet-le-Duc (E.) Lectures on Architecture. Translated by BENJAMIN BUCKNALL, Architect. With 33 Steel Plates and 200 Wood Engravings. Super-royal 8vo, leather back, gilt top, 2 vols., 3*l.* 3*s.*

Vivian (A. P.) Wanderings in the Western Land. 3rd Ed., 10*s.* 6*d.*

Voyages. See McCORMICK.

WAHL (W. H.) Galvanoplastic Manipulation for the Electro-Plater. 8vo, 35*s.*

Wallace (L.) Ben Hur: A Tale of the Christ. Crown 8vo, 6*s.*

Waller (Rev. C. H.) The Names on the Gates of Pearl, and other Studies. By the Rev. C. H. WALLER, M.A. New Edition. Crown 8vo, cloth extra, 3*s.* 6*d.*

———— *A Grammar and Analytical Vocabulary of the Words in* the Greek Testament. Compiled from Brüder's Concordance. For the use of Divinity Students and Greek Testament Classes. Part I. Grammar. Small post 8vo, cloth, 2*s.* 6*d.* Part II. Vocabulary, 2*s.* 6*d.*

———— *Adoption and the Covenant.* Some Thoughts on Confirmation. Super-royal 16mo, cloth limp, 2*s.* 6*d.*

———— *Silver Sockets; and other Shadows of Redemption.* Sermons at Christ Church, Hampstead. Small post 8vo, 6*s.*

Warner (C. D.) Back-log Studies. Boards, 1*s.* 6*d.*; cloth, 2*s.*

Washington Irving's Little Britain. Square crown 8vo, 6*s.*

Watson (P. B.) Marcus Aurelius Antoninus. Portr. 8vo, 15*s.*

Webster. (American Men of Letters.) 18mo, 2*s.* 6*d.*

Weismann (A.) Studies in the Theory of Descent. With a Preface by the late CHARLES DARWIN, and numerous Coloured Plates. 2 vols., 8vo, 40*s.*

Wheatley (H. B.) and Delamotte (P. H.) Art Work in Porce- lain. Large 8vo, 2*s.* 6*d.*

———— *Art Work in Gold and Silver.* Modern. Large 8vo, 2*s.* 6*d.*

———— *Handbook of Decorative Art.* 10*s.* 6*d.*

White (R. G.) England Without and Within. New Edition, crown 8vo, 10*s.* 6*d.*

———— *Every-day English,* crown 8vo, 10*s.* 6*d.*

White (R. G.) Fate of Mansfield Humphreys, with the Episode of Mr. Washington Adams in England, and an Apology. Crown 8vo, 6s.

———— *Words and their uses.* New Edit., crown 8vo, 10s. 6d.

Whittier (J. G.) The King's Missive, and later Poems. 18mo, choice parchment cover, 3s. 6d.

———— *The Whittier Birthday Book.* Extracts from the Author's writings, with Portrait and Illustrations. Uniform with the " Emerson Birthday Book." Square 16mo, very choice binding. 3s. 6d.

———— *Life of.* By R. A. UNDERWOOD. Cr. 8vo, cloth, 10s. 6d.

Wild Flowers of Switzerland. With Coloured Plates, life-size, from living Plants, and Botanical Descriptions of each Example. Imperial 4to, 63s. nett.

Williams (C. F.) Tariff Laws of the United States. 8vo, 10s. 6d.

Williams (H. W.) Diseases of the Eye. 8vo, 21s.

Williams (M.) Some London Theatres: Past and Present. Crown 8vo, 7s. 6d.

Wills, A Few Hints on Proving, without Professional Assistance. By a PROBATE COURT OFFICIAL. 7th Edition, revised, with Forms of Wills, Residuary Accounts, &c. Fcap. 8vo, cloth limp, 1s.

Winckelmann (John) History of Ancient Art. Translated by JOHN LODGE, M.D. Many Plates and Illustrations. 2 vols., 8vo, 36s.

Winks (W. E.) Lives of Illustrious Shoemakers. With eight Portraits. Crown 8vo, 7s. 6d.

Witthaus (R. A.) Medical Student's Manual of Chemistry. 8vo, 16s.

Woodbury (Geo. E.) History of Wood Engraving. Illustrated, 8vo, 18s.

Woolsey (C. D., LL.D.) Introduction to the Study of International Law; designed as an Aid in Teaching and in Historical Studies. 5th Edition, demy 8vo, 18s.

Woolson (Constance F.) See " Low's Standard Novels."

Wright (Rev. H.) Friendship of God. With Biographical Preface by the Rev. E. H. BICKERSTETH, Portrait, &c. Crown 8vo, 6s.

YRIARTE (Charles) Florence: its History. Translated by C. B. PITMAN. Illustrated with 500 Engravings. Large imperial 4to, extra binding, gilt edges, 63s.; or 12 Parts, 5s. each.
History; the Medici; the Humanists; letters; arts; the Renaissance; illustrious Florentines; Etruscan art; monuments; sculpture; painting.

London:
SAMPSON LOW, MARSTON, SEARLE, & RIVINGTON,
CROWN BUILDINGS, 188, FLEET STREET, E.C.

www.ingramcontent.com/pod-product-compliance
Lightning Source LLC
Chambersburg PA
CBHW022015110726
47901CB00006B/1530